I0664124

WORN BY POWER

Book 1: Wraithburn

BY Zach Hickok

Copyright © 2025 by Zach Hickok

All rights reserved.

The characters and events portrayed in this book are fictitious. Any similarity to real persons, living or dead, is coincidental and not intended by the author.

No part of this book may be reproduced, or stored in a retrieval system, or transmitted in any form or by any means, electronic, mechanical, photocopying, recording, or otherwise, without express written permission of the publisher.

ISBN-13: 979-8-9930202-0-4

Cover design by: Ksaeoren & ZPM Designs

Layout by: NH Arafat & Zach Hickok

Printed in the United States of America

Published by: Crimson Realms Publishing

Graham, Washington

PUBLISHING

For those carrying the weight of their past and still choosing to fight for tomorrow.

For my Wife, who guided me here.

For my children, who showed me the stars.

And for Tom, who didn't have to be, but chose to be.

"We are not worn down by power.
We are worn into it—scar by scar, choice by choice."
—The Pilgrim Archives, Fragment 27.

CONTENTS

CHAPTER 1

WRAITHBURN

The Wraithburn drifted alone through the endless black, her scarred hull a whisper in the void. Space wrapped around her like a shroud, stars distant and cold. Her thrusters pulsed faintly, more flicker than fire, and every panel groaned with the wear of too many fights and not enough rest.

In the engine compartment, Eryx Thorne was elbow-deep in misery. Sweat clung to his skin in sticky layers. His mechanic's overalls were half-unzipped and tied around his waist, revealing a sleeveless shirt soaked in coolant. The tools scattered around him looked like they'd lost a fight, and so did he. The drive core's casing flickered again.

"Come on, just hold together.." Ryx muttered, jamming a fusionspanner into a warped panel. Sparks snapped at his fingers. He swore and yanked his hand back, flexing numb fingers. "Damn it."

He sat back on his heels and wiped his forehead with a grease stained rag. At 27, Ryx felt every year like a scar. He wasn't old by any standard, but war had a way of aging you from the inside out. Dregan IV had taught him that. So had the Varrix Prime military. So had the nine years of running jobs across the galaxy just to stay ahead of poverty, and his own past.

The old man's gonna kill me

He thought to himself. Kaelen would take one look at the ship and start swearing in six languages. And Tess? She might actually try to throw him out the nearest air lock. Again.

He allowed himself a faint smile at the thought, then leaned forward to check the last patch. The repair looked rough but functional. Good enough to limp them home. Maybe. He patted the drive core.

"Sorry, old girl. You deserve better than this."

The Wraithburn groaned like she was offended. Once a Vandrix YSX-9 scout-class used by Varrix Prime special forces, built for infiltration and recon. She was now a mismatched beast of salvaged parts and brilliant upgrades.

Kaelen Rhoen had saved him once, rescued his drifting, broken ship from the black, stripped every military tag, and re-engineered her. Tuned her into a sleeper-class predator, all thanks to the genius of the only man Ryx trusted.

Kaelen Rhoen hadn't only given Ryx a ship that felt like his alone, unique in almost everyway. No one else flew a YSX-9 like this. No one eles flew any ship like the Wraith. No one else survived what they had. The old man had also given him something far more important: a place to return to.

Ryx scrubbed the thoughts from his mind and began cleaning up his tools. *If Kaelen doesn't kill me, Tess definitely will.* He chuckled under his breath and headed toward the Wraithburn's living quarters.

The scout-class vessel had been retrofitted to fit Ryx's needs. Originally designed for a max crew of six, the interior now housed only two living spaces: the captain's quarters and a four-bunk barracks for passengers or captured bounties. The rest had been repurposed into two multi-person holding cells, practical additions for a working hunter.

Ryx made his way into his cabin, stepping into the compact bathroom. He caught his reflection in the mirror and stared for a long moment. His shaggy hair hung just below the base of his skull in uneven waves, a mess that somehow still worked for him. His face, young but hardened, was marked by a single long scar running from beneath his left eye to the edge of his jaw, a permanent reminder of the day he fled Varrix Prime for good. A cold reminder of his defiance, of the crime he almost commited in their name.

He looked away. His shirt and mechanic's overalls were soaked in coolant and sweat. He stripped and tossed them into the ship's cleaning module. The automated unit would have them scrubbed and dry by the time he was done.

He stepped into the sonic shower. The hot water hit his skin like a wave of relief. He leaned into it, trying to wash away the tension of another near-death job and the bitter memories clawing at the back of his mind. All he could think about now was getting back to Vorrthani Station alive.

Six more hours until the warp drive finished charging, six hours of waiting and hoping the hull held together.

He raised his right hand to slick back his hair and paused. There it was.

The bracelet.

Slim, gold, and ancient-looking. It clung to his wrist like it had always belonged there. He'd nearly forgotten it in the chaos of repairs. It was the source of all his current problems, and maybe something far more dangerous.

What was it? How did it work? Who had made it, and why had someone been willing to kill for it?

The questions churned in his mind as the shower steamed around him. He shook them off, for now. One thing at a time.

He finished rinsing off, activated the drying system, and stepped out into his quarters. His clothes were clean, folded, and waiting. He dressed in a loose shirt and comfortable pants, stashing the overalls and tools away for later. Sleep tugged at the corners of his mind.

The bracelet glinted in the dim light, a silent weight on his wrist. He'd deal with it, just not tonight.

Ryx laid back on his bunk, eyes heavy, heart restless.

First things first, he thought, staring at the ceiling.

Get home alive.

ΔΔΔ

He woke to the alert chime.

WARP DRIVE ONLINE.

He rubbed his eyes, groaning, and swung his legs off the bed. The ache in his shoulders flared as he stretched, and the bracelet shifted against his skin, a whisper of metal that never stopped reminding him it was there.

His eyes darted to it.

Still there. Still strange. Slim, gold, and impossibly smooth, like it had never been made by human hands. Part of him wondered if it would activate on its own again... or if he could even trigger it deliberately. He hadn't tried. Not really.

Too many unknowns.

He shook off the unease and moved to the closet.

Time to suit up.

The dark grey flight suit he slid into was worn, familiar, and reinforced at the joints, enough to survive light combat and stay mobile. If life had taught him anything, it was this: never trust a quiet trip home.

He stepped to the back of the closet and pressed his palm to a blank wall panel. Faint blue light pulsed at the edges, and with a low hiss, the panel folded outward, revealing a hidden armory shelf.

He began with the white neoplate armor, securing the leg and hip pieces first. The plates were light, an alloy of synthetic polymers and lightweight metals, but sturdy enough to stop low-caliber rounds or weak laser fire. They wouldn't hold up in a full firefight, but for quick jobs or station walk-throughs, they did the trick.

His chest and back plate still bore scorch marks from his last mission. Ryx ran his fingers along one of the burns with a scowl.

Gonna need a visit to Rexa Vorn after this, he thought. If I survive Kaelen yelling at me, I'll have to beg her for a refurb.

Rexa Vorn had been his first bounty fixer. She ran a weapons shop on Vorrthani Station, sharp-eyed, no-nonsense, and the only person on the station who could out-talk Tessa when she was angry.

Ryx strapped on his arm guards, slid into his plate-lined gloves, and clipped the rounded shoulder plates into place. Then came his weapons belt, brown synthetic fiber with multiple compartments for ammo, tools, and stims. He was running low on everything. Rexa was going to drain him dry next time he came by, and she'd enjoy every second of it.

From the rack, he grabbed his TalonX-5 sidearm. Old tech, sure, but it had outlived plenty of shinier toys. The semi-auto pistol fired laser charged ballistic rounds, fast, precise, and effective against flesh based targets. Less damage to interior structures, too. That made it ideal for fighting in ships or stations.

High-powered lasers might do better against synthetics or armored aliens, but the TalonX had always gotten the job done, and Ryx trusted it.

He left the BR-77 "Ironhowl" on its rack. Heavy-caliber, ex-military, with switchable energy and ballistic modes, too much firepower for a station drop. If the warp failed, he wouldn't need it. And if it worked? The TalonX would be enough for whatever came next.

Last came the mask.

White neoplate like the rest of the suit, with a single green visor-line at eye level, sleek, minimalist, functional. It wasn't a full helmet, but it didn't need to be. It had optical enhancement, a built-in air filter, and a comm unit he could link to local transponders. More importantly, it let him move and turn his head freely in tight quarters.

He clipped the mask to his belt, sealed the armory, and headed for the cockpit.

The cockpit was dim, lit only by the soft glow of control panels. A single blinking icon pulsed on his display, a message.

Ryx slid into the pilot's chair, tapped the notification, and watched as the message opened in plain text.

Tessa:

"Yo! Haven't heard from you in a few days, little brother. Pop's worried, even if he'll never admit it. Hope the job went alright. Send us a message when you're close so we know when to expect you.

P.S. If you damaged my baby again, I'm pushing you out an airlock.

– Love, Tess

Ryx smirked. Classic Tess.

The long-range messaging system worked on distance-delay, meaning she'd probably sent this a few days ago. It must've come through while he was asleep.

He sighed and opened the voice message function. If he was going to reply, he'd rather speak. Just in case.

"Hey Tess," he started, his voice a little raw from sleep. "I'm alive." He chuckled quietly. It sounded weak, even to him.

"But you better get that airlock ready… the job went sideways. Took a hit to the propulsion systems."

He paused, then added more softly, "Luckily, you and Kaelen taught me enough to patch it. I did my best. Warp drive's charged. I'm about to jump."

Another breath. Another hesitation.

"If this doesn't work… I'm sorry. For everything. And thank you, for everything…"

He let the silence linger for a moment, then forced a smile into his voice.

"But don't get sentimental yet. I'll be home soon, because you two geniuses beat enough engine repair into my skull to make even me competent. So, save the scolding for when I get there."

A beat. "Looking forward to it."

He ended the message, slumped back in the chair, and stared at the ceiling.

The ship was quiet. It was time to jump.

He entered the coordinates for Vorrthani Station. His hand hovered over the warp key.

He took one long breath.

Ryx closed his eyes and slammed his palm onto the warp trigger.

For a few agonizing seconds, nothing happened, then Wraithburn shuddered beneath him, groaning like a dying beast. Sweat beaded on his forehead and rolled down the side of his face. Somewhere beneath his seat, deep in the engine core, a high-pitched squeal rang out.

Not good.

He gripped the armrests so tightly his knuckles turned white. Then the ship lurched forward with a violent jolt, and for a split second, Ryx was sure he was going to die.

His eyes flew open just in time to see the jump drive engage. The stars outside blurred into brilliant streaks, light stretching into infinity.

He let out a shaky laugh, half-relief, half-hysteria, and exhaled the breath he hadn't realized he'd been holding.

They were jumping. They'd actually made it.

Ryx stood up and fist-pumped the air, his grin wide even though no one was around to see it. He jogged around the cockpit, patting and hugging different parts of the console like a madman.

"You are far too good to me, baby!" he said to the ship. "When we get home, I'm gonna beg Tess and Kaelen to pamper you like it's your birthday."

He whooped again, energized, and sprinted toward the engine room.

The Wraithburn coasted into subspace. Back in engineering, he checked the diagnostics readouts with the urgency of a medic watching a patient's vitals. The systems weren't great, but they were holding. Just barely.

"Close enough," he muttered and made his way to the living quarters. His stomach growled.

He hadn't eaten in what felt like days, and if Tess was going to beat him senseless for wrecking her beloved ship, he'd rather face it on a full stomach.

He opened the refrigeration unit and winced.

Empty. Mostly.

He rummaged around and found a half-eaten sandwich from a station diner he'd visited two days ago. It smelled... edible. He took a cautious bite. Cold and rubbery but not spoiled.

Good enough.

He chewed thoughtfully, washing it down with lukewarm water from the purifier. As he ate, his thoughts drifted to the costs piling up: ammo, fuel, food, repairs, armor patches, and whatever mystery tech had embedded itself onto his arm.

The job had gone sideways. No bounty. No payout. Nothing but damage and questions.

He had a small personal fund stashed, what little was left after constant ship repairs and resupply runs. Most of his money went back into the Wraithburn, and what didn't, he tried to give to Kaelen in thanks for everything the man had done for him.

Of course, Kaelen always refused. Said Ryx didn't owe him anything.

So Ryx gave the credits to Tess, who would sneak them into her father's account when he wasn't looking. It wasn't much, but it felt better than doing nothing.

They weren't poor, just out of fashion. A father-daughter team of independent mechanics didn't draw much business in a galaxy ruled by mega corps and mass-produced ships. Kaelen could be gruff, but he had a soft spot for strays. He helped people who couldn't afford corporate rates and sometimes couldn't afford to pay at all.

It made for lean times now and then. But they got by. They always had.

Ryx cleaned up his mess just as Wraithburn's systems chimed.

Exiting jump in T-minus one minute.

He ran back to the cockpit and strapped in, just in case. The streaking stars outside compressed in an instant, snapping back into pinpoints of light. Ahead, a dense asteroid belt loomed, its jagged bodies drifting slowly across the dark.

He recognized it immediately.

"The Dratheos Belt," he muttered. "We made it!"

He let out a short, victorious laugh and engaged what little thrust he had left, steering toward the largest asteroid, home.

As he approached, he drank in the view.

Built directly into the heart of the biggest asteroid in the belt, Vorrthani Station looked like a glittering hive. Dozens of lights blinked from open docking bays and hollowed-out entry points. Ships came and went, everything from luxury liners to barely-held together pirate rigs.

Vorrthani was self-governed, which meant it was lawless, chaotic, and dangerous. Murder and slavery were still frowned upon, but just about everything else could be bought, sold, or ignored... for the right price.

It wasn't the worst place in the galaxy, but it definitely wasn't safe either.

A crackle from Wraithburn's comms broke through his thoughts. "Inbound ship, this is Vorrthani Station control. State your business." The voice was bored, flat, just another day in the belt.

Ryx smirked and keyed the mic.

"Vorrthani Station, this is Eryx Thorne. Requesting permission to dock at Rhoen's Maintenance." There was a pause.

He could almost hear the traffic controller checking bay availability and scanning his ship's ID.

"Wraithburn, you are cleared to dock at Rhoen's Maintenance. Please observe all bylaws during your stay. Welcome back." The comm cut off.

15

Ryx plotted an auto-course through the field and let the ship guide itself the rest of the way.

Five minutes later, just as the docking bay came into view, another comm request flashed on his console.

This one was from the shop.

He opened it immediately.

"Eryx? That you?" came a familiar, gravel-lined voice.

A flood of relief washed over him. "It's me, Kaelen. Though… Wraith's seen better days." He scratched the back of his head, sheepish. "Sorry about that." A long pause.

Then: "Just glad you're home, kid. Things have been quiet. Too quiet. Tess is getting lazy."

Ryx chuckled and could just make out muffled yelling in the background.

"Copy that, Kaelen. I'll be docked in a few."

"Just watch your back when you get in," Kaelen warned, tone wry. "Tess got your message an hour ago. She's furious. Said something about introducing a wrench to a very personal part of your anatomy."

Ryx groaned. "Yeah… sounds about right. See you soon, pops." The comm beeped as Kaelen ended the transmission.

Ryx went to close the channel and paused.

The bracelet caught the light again, gleaming like it had always been there.

His smile faded.

He had no idea how he was going to explain this to Kaelen and Tess. And worse… he wasn't sure he even understood what it was yet.

Several minutes later, The Wraithburn silently breached the light screen, an energy barrier that separated the vacuum of space from the pressurized interior of Rhoen's Maintenance Hangar and glided smoothly into the dock. Her landing gear deployed with a quiet thunk, and to Ryx's surprise, she touched down with grace.

"You're still too good to me old girl."

He waited for the hangar systems to confirm the docking sequence had completed, then stood and made his way to the main exit hatch, just a few paces from the cockpit. He paused, took a breath, and thumbed the release.

The door hissed, gears rotating as the twin outer panels parted to reveal the hangar bay.

Ryx stepped out into a place that felt more like home than anywhere else in the galaxy.

Rhoen's Maintenance was a single-vessel hangar, modest and unassuming. The Wraithburn fit neatly inside, but anything larger would've been a tight squeeze. The space was old, scorched walls, rusted seams, pockmarked flooring from decades of welding sparks and engine burns. But despite its age, it was meticulously maintained.

Every power tool was cleaned, parked, and labeled with military precision. Through a wall of armored glass, Ryx could see the machine shop, neat as a soldier's locker. Tools hung in perfect symmetry. Surfaces gleamed. Everything had its place.

He took in a deep breath. The familiar scent of grease, oil, and hot metal filled his lungs and relaxed his muscles.

Home.

Ryx descended the Wraithburn's ramp and headed for the inner door that connected the hangar to the shop and residence. As he approached the keypad, the door hissed open before he could touch it.

And a giant steel wrench came swinging at his head.

Ryx instinctively threw himself backward. The wrench whooshed past his face and smashed into the floor, denting the reinforced metal with a clang that echoed through the hangar. Ryx caught his balance, rolled back, and came up in a ready stance.

Standing in the doorway, breathing hard, was Tessa Rhoen.

She was short, barely five and a half feet tall, but she burned with unmistakable fury. Her curly brown hair was tied back messily, and her tan skin was smudged with grease and soot. Dressed in stained coveralls and wielding a wrench like a battle axe, she looked like a grease-smeared goddess of vengeance.

"YOU!" she roared, charging again.

"Tessa, wait!" Ryx dodged a backhand swing.

"DON'T," Wham! Another overhead strike missed him by inches and dented the floor again.

"GET," She lunged, wrench raised.

"TO CALL ME THAT AFTER WHAT YOU DID!"

Ryx waited until she committed to the next swing, stepped inside her guard, looped his arm under hers, and hip-checked her into a controlled throw.

She hit the ground with a heavy thud, air leaving her lungs in a pained oomph as the wrench skidded across the floor.

Ryx stood over her, and smirked. "Sorry, Tess. Forgot you hate when we use your full name." He offered her a hand.

She glared up at him, then took it, only to sock him in the chest plate as soon as she was on her feet.

"Asshole," she muttered.

Ryx winced with a grin. "Deserved."

Tess's expression cracked. Her bright green eyes filled with moisture. "Do you know how worried we were? Before your message even got here. We didn't know if you were dead, Ryx." His smirk faded. He pulled her into a hug.

"I know," he said quietly. "I'm sorry. The job went… bad. Worse than I expected."

She hit him again, lighter this time, more like punctuation than anger.

Ryx stepped back and tried to smile. "Honestly, if I wasn't such a crack pilot, I would be dead. But me and Wraith, we're the best team in the galaxy. We're not going down to a bunch of second-rate mercs."

Tess's eyes narrowed. "Mercenaries? Who the hell sent mercs after you?"

Ryx frowned. The black-armored attackers flashed through his mind.

"No idea," he said. "Could've been another corp. The job was through Black Sable Dynamics."

Tess scowled. "They're that nano-tech company, right? I told you not to take jobs directly from shady corps. You need to run them through fixers."

"Fixers can't predict which mega Corp is gonna crash the party, Tess."

She crossed her arms. "How do you know it wasn't Black Sable themselves that sent the hit squad?"

Ryx hesitated, then shook his head. "Doesn't track. They hired me to recover a stolen tech prototype. Wouldn't make much sense to gun me down before finding out if I got it." *Unless… they already knew I had it.*

The thought unsettled him. Too many pieces weren't lining up: the absurdly high payout, being contacted directly by name, the fact that he knew the thief personally, and now... this bracelet fused to his wrist.

"Come on," Tess muttered, picking up her wrench. "Old man'll want to see you. And hear all the juicy details before I kill you for real."

Ryx laughed and fell in step beside her. "Kaelen said things were slow. Doesn't look like you've been slacking off."

She glanced at him with a smirk. "I've got a side project, little bro."

"Of course you do," Ryx said. "What is it?"

Tess had always been the brains behind most of Ryx's gear, his mask, the Wraithburn's holding cells, all the gadgets he used on hunts. Where Kaelen was a master at repairing and upgrading, Tess could invent. Engineer. Innovate.

She responded without missing a step, by flipping him off over her shoulder.

"None of your business."

Ryx rolled his eyes, smiling as he followed her into the workshop, and back into whatever madness came next.

CHAPTER 2

THE BRACELET

Ryx followed Tess into the small kitchen. Like the rest of Kaelen Rhoen's home, it was spotless and meticulously organized. Nothing was new, of course, but everything was in perfect working order. It paid to be a mechanical genius, it seemed.

The scent of metal polish, faint grease, and some kind of herbal cleaner filled the air. Ryx took a moment to absorb it. No smoke. No blood. No recycled coolant. Just home. Just peace. And after the week he'd had, that peace felt almost alien.

Kaelen sat at the kitchen table, a half-full glass of what Ryx assumed was his favorite, Teyvari rum, resting near his hand. When he caught sight of them, he stood immediately, arms outstretched.

Kaelen Rhoen was an inch or two shorter than Ryx's six-foot frame, with tan skin lined by light scars, veins of hardship earned through years of working starships. His close-cropped beard and hair were bone white, and his emerald eyes, so like Tess's, shone with quiet intensity and age-earned wisdom.

He pulled Ryx into a powerful embrace, and Ryx was reminded that Kaelen's strength came from a lifetime of labor. It felt like hugging a wall made of stone. There was warmth in it, too, rough, weathered warmth. Like a forge that still burned, no matter the ash.

For a second, Ryx allowed himself to sink into the moment. It was the kind of hug he'd never gotten as a child, the kind that didn't come with conditions or regrets. Just safety. Gods, how long had it been since something felt safe?

"Still alive." Kaelen said under his breath. It wasn't a question. More a quiet prayer answered.

Kaelen stepped back and gave him a critical once-over.

"No new scars, all limbs attached... The way your message sounded, I thought you'd be limping back in pieces," Kaelen grunted, voice gravelly with sarcasm.

"You should see the ship," Tess muttered from the counter, her annoyance unmistakable.

Kaelen's expression turned serious. "What happened?"

Ryx sank into a chair across from him. Tess tossed a chilled canister of blue liquid from the fridge, sunburst Cider, a sweet, carbonated juice from the Aetherian Groves. One of Tess's favorites. He cracked it open, grateful for anything besides water.

The first sip hit cold and sweet. A strange comfort.

"I was attacked," he said after a long drink. "Some heavily armored mercs, no markings, no IDs. One minute I'm in a shootout with my mark, the next I'm trying to stop him from bleeding out. Then six guys storm in and light me up like I'm the only target in the system." Kaelen leaned forward, brows knit. "Start from the beginning."

Ryx stared down at the floor, cider can resting in his hands, and let the memories flood back.

ΔΔΔ

The interview room in Black Sable Dynamics's tower had smelled like artificial lilacs and high-tension power conduits. Ryx had never liked that combination. It was too clean, too sterile. Like they were trying to scrub away the blood that funded their skyscrapers.

"Eryx Thorne," the executive said crisply.

He sat in a plush, high-rise office across from a meticulously dressed woman whose tight ponytail was the only softness in her demeanor. Her expression made it clear she'd rather be doing anything else than interviewing a bounty hunter, especially one from the gutters.

"Born on Dregan IV. No known blood relatives. Orphaned by war and raised in an orphanage until the age of fourteen. Correct?"

Ryx nodded. "Yeah, you nailed the highlights."

She didn't smile. "What did you do before enlisting with the Varrix Prime military?"

"Conscripted," Ryx corrected her, matching her tone.

"The Varrix Prime Military conscripts fourteen-year-olds to fight their wars."

He stiffened. Realizing he was jeopardizing the job by rising to her bait. *Don't let her get under your skin.*

"I worked in a factory at ten. Assembly lines. Four years. Barely paid. When the military showed up, I didn't need convincing."

She raised an eyebrow but returned her gaze to the datapad in her hands.

"Impressive military record. Top recruit in sidearms. Best fighter pilot in your class. Top five in hand-to-hand combat. Top twenty IQ score."

She rattled it off like it bored her.

"After two years at the academy, you were selected for the Elite Scouting Regiment. Special ops, covert missions, classified files, all marked successful. Correct?"

Ryx clenched his jaw. Memories surged, missions, losses, friends left behind, innocents caught in the crossfire. How many ghosts had he collected before he was even old enough to drink?

"My superiors were satisfied with the results," he said evenly.

"And then you defected. During a full-scale planetary conflict. Another classified mission." Her tone sharpened.

"I had a disagreement with my superiors," Ryx said carefully.

"Yet here you are, a free man. Why hasn't the Varrix Prime military hunted you down?"

Ryx met her eyes. "They have bigger fish to fry than one AWOL scout. Nine years is a long time for giants to chase ants." The executive tilted her head, finally intrigued.

"Well," she said, "your success rate with bounties is quite… consistent."

That's an understatement, Ryx thought. He'd only failed three captures, and the ones he failed to bring in alive were all marked as "dead or alive." He still got paid, just less. You learn to stop asking questions when the credits clear.

Then her tone changed. "Your military record shows you served alongside a recruit: Kolen Vess." Ryx blinked. That name hit like a punch to the gut.

Kolen. A young Draenari. One of the first Ryx had ever met. With scaled crests, elongated skulls, and skin like smooth, blue tinted glass, the Draenari were as strange as they were brilliant. Draenari, he found out, had low level telepathic ability to communicate.

Kolen.

He hadn't heard that name in a long time, and hearing it now felt like peeling back a scar that hadn't fully healed.

A young Draenari. Quiet. Brilliant. Too good for the war they'd been thrown into. Kolen had been the kind of friend you never expected to make in the military, a quiet loyalty, a brain that never stopped turning, and a rare, fragile idealism. Ryx remembered late nights talking tech, ethics, and alien philosophy in the bunk barracks. He remembered Kolen's laugh. Low and watery. Sincere.

"I remember him," Ryx said cautiously.

The woman stood and moved to the window, arms clasped behind her back, gazing out at the neon skies of Delva Minor. The HQ of Black Sable Dynamics towered above the endless sprawl of megacities and corporate power.

"We believe Kolen Vess has absconded with a valuable prototype," she said. "Nano-tech. Top secret."

24

Ryx's stomach dropped. *Why you, Kolen? You weren't built for this kind of war.*

"We're hoping your familiarity with him will make him easier to retrieve." She turned. "Alive, ideally. But if you can get us the prototype or its exact location, his condition becomes… secondary."

Ice pooled in Ryx's gut. That kind of phrasing meant they were desperate. And desperate corps didn't leave witnesses.

"We're prepared to offer 500,000 U-Credits for Kolen or the prototype. Bring both, we'll pay one million."

He blinked. "Did you say… a million?"

She smirked. "Indeed. A hefty bounty, wouldn't you agree?"

He was stunned. 500,000 was more than triple the value of every bounty he'd ever done, combined. With a million he could buy a space station for the Rhoens. Set them up for life.

Which made him deeply suspicious.

"And if I refuse?"

She scoffed. "Then we send someone else. The Guild won't care. But ask yourself, would you rather someone else hunt your old friend?"

The threat was unspoken but clear. Plenty of bounty hunters would take the job and not hesitate to shoot first. Hell, some would go after Kolen just for fun.

Ryx sighed. At least if I go, I can bring him in alive.

"I'll take the job," he said.

"Good," she nodded. "Last sighting was a passenger liner to Tarrin Station in the Trivar System. Here." She handed him a datapad. "His dossier. Daily habits, routine, contacts. We're thorough."

Ryx scanned through it and realized just how thoroughly they had tracked his old comrade. *These people mean business.*

After a few more formalities, Ryx was out the door, and on the hunt for Kolen Vess.

ΔΔΔ

Back at the table, Ryx blinked back to the present. Kaelen hadn't spoken once during the retelling.

Now he did.

"And this prototype, what exactly did it do?"

Ryx hesitated. His fingers closed around the chilled can again. The metal felt suddenly heavier in his hand. Like it knew what was coming.

"I don't think it was a prototype."

Kaelen and Tess both looked at him.

"I think it was… something older. Xeno maybe, before the known races. Kolen said it was a relic. From a dig site Black Sable funded under fake survey orders."

Kaelen's jaw tightened. "And you have it?" Ryx didn't answer right away.

He pulled up the sleeve of his shirt. The bracelet glinted in the overhead light.

Tess stepped closer. Her breath caught.

"What the hell is that?"

"That," Ryx said, "is why we're probably screwed."

ΔΔΔ

After a few days in warp, Ryx found himself staring at Tarrin Station.

A compact trade port orbiting in the shadows of larger planets in the system. Despite its size, it held close to a hundred thousand permanent residents and served as a commerce hub between star systems.

It was ugly in that charming, rust-patched kind of way. Practical over pristine. Honest, in the way only places run by desperate people could be. Ryx had always preferred ports like this. They didn't lie to you.

26

He started with the basics. Using his Hunter's Guild ID, he traced the passenger ship Kolen had boarded and requested docking records and footage from the port's archives. To his surprise, and mild dismay, it was almost too easy to find what he needed.

There he was: Kolen, hurrying off the passenger liner the moment the doors opened. A hood concealed most of his face, and he clutched a loosely wrapped bundle in his arms. He was also the only Draenari on board.

Kolen... what are you doing?

Ryx remembered him as brilliant, level-headed, the last person he'd expect to make a reckless break from a mega Corp. Either Kolen had a plan he hadn't put into motion yet... or he was scared out of his mind. That idea scared Ryx more than he'd like to admit.

Later that day, Ryx checked in with station security to pull surveillance from the rest of Tarrin. Within hours, he had tracked Kolen's movements. He had a temporary apartment and had been attempting to book travel, anywhere far from Delva Minor and Black Sable Dynamics.

More interestingly, Kolen had developed a routine. Every morning and evening, he ate at a small diner near the apartment. It was a pattern Ryx could exploit.

That evening, Ryx scouted the diner. He chose a corner booth with a clear line of sight to the entrance and ordered an old favorite, a Ratcha Wrap: a greasy, protein-packed sandwich stuffed with spiced meat substitute and tangy saurian sauce. He only ate half of it,

along with the side salad, while scanning every patron who came and went.

Each bite tasted like cardboard. Not because the food was bad, but because he couldn't stop watching the door. He hated this part, the waiting. The second-guessing. The weight of everything unsaid between him and a man who used to be like a brother.

Hours passed. Kolen never showed.

Hopefully this isn't a bad sign. I'll try again in the morning before pulling more footage.

Ryx returned to the Wraithburn and slept restlessly, a knot of uncertainty in his chest.

At dawn, Ryx took his seat in the corner booth again. Fifteen minutes passed, nerves gnawing at his gut. Then, finally, the door opened.

A tall, hooded figure entered the diner, moving with hesitant familiarity. Kolen.

Ryx let a few minutes pass, allowing his mark to get comfortable. Then he stood and casually walked past the table, just close enough.

"Kolen?" he said softly, stopping as if in sudden recognition. "Kolen Vess? From Varrix Prime Military Academy?"

The Draenari froze. Ryx wasn't an expert in Draenari physiology, but even he could tell Kolen had paled. His large black eyes widened.

"Eryx Thorne?" Kolen's voice was low and watery, like someone speaking through a filter underwater.

"Holy stars, it is you!" Ryx grinned. "Do you mind if I sit for a second? I already ate, but I'd love to catch up."

Kolen hesitated, glancing around the diner. The tension was thick enough to chew.

"Everything okay, Kolen?" Ryx asked, lacing his concern with genuine undertones, not for the moment, but for what it meant.

"Uh… yeah," Kolen said at last. "I have a little time for an old friend." His smile was thin. Forced.

Ryx slid into the seat across from him.

"How've you been?"

"I've been well, Eryx. Just traveling. Trying to find my place in the universe."

You already had a place, Ryx wanted to say. *They just didn't let you keep it.*

"It's just Ryx, old friend. 'Eryx' makes my skin crawl."

Kolen chuckled, a soft, guttural sound, and seemed to relax slightly. But it didn't last.

"So," Ryx continued, "you're traveling. Where to next?" Kolen looked down, distracted. A moment passed.

"Kolen?"

"Sorry," the Draenari said. "Just a lot on my mind. I don't know where I'm going next. Just... moving for now." That told Ryx everything he needed to know.

Running. Not drifting. Not exploring. Fleeing.

Ryx nodded sympathetically. "Well, before you vanish again, we should grab a drink. Unless you're leaving immediately?" The probing question asked innocently enough.

"I haven't booked anything yet," Kolen said. He smiled, then it faltered. "What are you doing on Tarrin Station, Ryx?"

There it was. The pivot. Ryx could feel the shift. Caution had returned to Kolen's voice.

"The last I heard of Eryx Thorne," Kolen added, "he was an elite scout gone rogue."

Ryx groaned and rubbed his face. "I'd rather not talk about my... defection."

He knew the act was wearing thin. Kolen had every reason to be suspicious. He'd seen Ryx's armor, his poise, his questions. There weren't many career paths for someone with Ryx's particular talents, and even fewer that required this much discretion.

"I'm just taking odd jobs," Ryx said smoothly. "I'm a soldier at heart. You know me."

Beneath the table, he slipped his left hand into a pouch and palmed a thin metal disc.

Then he stood slowly. Kolen tensed.

Ryx reached his right hand into another pouch and pulled out a small, rectangular card. He held it out casually.

"You seem tense, brother. I'll leave you be. Here, my ship's transponder code. I'll be around for a few days. Message me if you want to get that drink."

Kolen accepted the card cautiously.

Ryx patted him on the back as he turned to go, pressing a little harder with his left hand than necessary.

"Catch you later, Kolen. Stay safe, friend."

He could feel Kolen's eyes burning into his back as he exited the diner.

Down the walkway a few minuets later, Ryx ducked into a side corridor and leaned against the wall. He pulled a small screen from his coat pocket; a tiny light blinked steadily in the center.

I need to remember to thank Tess for the new micro tracking beacons.

The amber dot began to move, fast.

Damn. He knows.

Ryx pulled on his Neoplate mask. The familiar click as it sealed sent a little comfort down his spine. Green HUD data flickered across his vision, ambient temps, life signs, structural layouts. He raised the tracker and activated beacon overlay. Kolen's signal streaked through walls and corners like a glowing pulse.

Kolen was on the move, fast, headed back to his apartment. But something in his pathing was off. No hesitation. No pauses. No zigzags. Kolen wasn't just going home, he was bolting for something.

Probably an escape route, Ryx thought grimly. *Or a data cache. Or, the prototype.*

He broke into a jog, weaving through the morning crowds. His boots barely made a sound, movements fluid, muscle memory honed by years of urban ops. He followed the trail past the apartment block and down a narrow maintenance lane. Then he spotted it, Kolen's silhouette, just before he ducked into a squat, windowless warehouse at the fringe of the docks.

Of course. Old industrial zone. No cameras. No interference. *Perfect place to die,* Ryx thought, only half-joking.

The main doors of the warehouse were sealed. Ryx didn't even bother trying them. He slid into the shadows, followed the perimeter, and found a side door, rusted and patched with industrial sealant. Locked.

Naturally.

He pulled Tess's ice pick from a thigh pouch. The thing looked like a glorified pen, but it could crack half the galaxy's smart locks in under ten seconds. It would also get him arrested in any system, no matter his guild ties. He pressed it to the panel. It beeped softly, lights flickering.

Five seconds later, the lock clicked. Ryx drew his pistol carefully and stepped inside.

The warehouse was cavernous, silent save for the distant hum of a still-powered grid. Rows of metal crates towered over him, casting long shadows in the dim light. A dry, metallic scent hung in the air. Dust. Ozone. The faint smell of fear.

Kolen's beacon blinked from somewhere deep in the maze of containers.

Ryx moved like a ghost, one careful step at a time. He kept the TalonX-5 low and ready.

Then,

A sharp crack split the air. Orange laser fire lanced past his head, close enough to singe hair.

He dove behind a crate. Another bolt hit the metal with a sizzling shriek.

"Why are you following me, Eryx Thorne?!" Kolen's voice echoed, ragged, panicked.

Because I had to, Ryx wanted to say. But words didn't matter now.

"Do you work for them? Have you come to kill me, and take the artifact?" *Artifact?* That word chilled Ryx more than the gunfire.

"I just want to talk, Kolen!" he shouted, ducking behind a second crate. The Talon was steady in his hand, but his heartbeat thundered in his ears.

Another shot. Closer.

"Kolen, listen to me!"

"Talk? To my corpse, maybe. These people don't negotiate."

I'm not them, Ryx wanted to yell. *I'm not the monster you think I am.*

"Look," Ryx called out again. "I was told to bring you back or retrieve the prototype. Just give it to me, and I'll let you go."

Silence. Then,

"I think you've been deceived, Eryx Thorne." Ryx's eyes narrowed behind the mask.

"This isn't some prototype," Kolen said. "It's ancient. Pre-society.

Found it during a corporate dig. We weren't even told what we were looking for."

Ryx pressed tighter against cover. "What does it do?"

"I don't know," Kolen admitted. "It's… it reacts to touch. Light. Thought maybe. It woke up when we opened the chamber were we found it."

A beat passed. Then another shot cracked past Ryx's position, this one low and wide.

"Okay," Ryx replied cautiously. "Maybe I don't have the whole story. But I was given explicit orders: retrieve the object. That's it. I can let you go."

A hollow laugh echoed through the warehouse.

"Strangely enough, I believe you," Kolen said. "You always were an honest man, Eryx Thorne. But they won't let me go. Not after this. Whether it's today or five years from now, someone will come. And they will not get the artifact." Kolen was getting desperate.

Ryx could feel it now, pressure in his skull. A pulsing throb behind his eyes. Not physical. Not quite.

Telepathy. Kolen was pushing, lightly, but enough to hurt. His old friend was trying to read him. Or scramble him.

"Don't do this," Ryx yelled, voice drowned by the hum of dying systems.

He rolled, fired a warning shot into the air.

Then Kolen fired again, and Ryx saw the angle. The shimmer of movement near the catwalks.

Kolen was advancing.

He's going to kill me, Ryx realized. Another shot. Too close.

Kolen Vess wasn't an elite scout, but he was still ex-military. And every shot was a chance to kill.

Ryx didn't think, just reacted. He popped up from cover, leveled the Talon, and fired.

Three shots. Tight grouping. Chest-level.

The pressure in his skull vanished almost instantly.

Ryx heard Kolen's weapon drop.

Then he saw the Draenari collapse backward, cloak folding beneath him like a shroud.

Ryx sprinted forward, boots scraping steel. The mask retracted into its frame as he dropped to his knees.

Kolen's breath hitched once. Then again. Then stopped.

"No… no, no, no." Ryx grabbed his shoulders. "I didn't want this. I didn't want,"

Kolen blinked once. The faintest flicker of understanding.

"Can't… have… it," he rasped.

Then he was gone. No warning, no pretense.

Ryx's hands trembled.

"I'm sorry," he whispered. "Stars forgive me." But the stars didn't answer.

Only the tracker did, still blinking from Kolen's pocket.

Ryx stared for a long moment. Not sure what else to do, what else to feel. He knew he needed to keep moving, or he'd stay rooted here forever.

Then, quietly to himself: "I need to inform station authorities about the body... file the Guild paperwork..." He sighed.

The artifact.

Ryx rose. His legs felt leaden. He moved to a crate near the back where the first shots had come from. There he found the cloth bundle from the videos. Ryx pulled aside the cloth from the tightly wrapped bundle. And there it sat. A small black box.

It was covered in intricate, circular carvings, flowing designs that looped and spiraled across every surface. Unlike anything Ryx had seen before.

Definitely not new nanotech, he thought wryly, reaching out to secure it.

As his hand touched the surface, the carvings lit up, a brilliant blue, almost blinding.

Ryx jerked his hand away instinctively. The box didn't explode to his surprise... it dissolved. The glowing lines intensified, and then the entire object began to dematerialize, erasing itself in cascading light.

"Oh shit," Ryx whispered. "What's happening?"

As the box vanished, something shimmered within the glow. He leaned closer, transfixed.

When the light faded, only one thing remained.

A gold band.

A bracelet.

But he didn't have time to think about it.

An explosion rocked the side of the warehouse.

Ryx flew backward, hit a crate hard as his mask reformed around his face. Lights flickered. His HUD screamed warnings.

The front-loading door was obliterated.

He rolled behind a crate, coughing, and instinctively snatched the bracelet off the ground.

Peeking around the edge of the crate, his mask's optics highlighted six figures entering through the wreckage, black-clad, heavily armored, heavily armed.

Not station security.

"Fuck," Ryx muttered under his breath. "What the hell is going on?" The mercenaries advanced toward Kolen's body.

Ryx crouched lower. His TalonX-5 wouldn't pierce that kind of armor. He thought of his Ironhowl rifle, left in his weapons cache.

Station security never would've let me carry that in. How the hell did they get armed?

He checked the station's public feed through his mask.

Status: ALERT. Entire station on lockdown.

Figures. These assholes probably triggered it.

No way out. No way to fight. He needed to run. Fast.

He glanced at the bracelet.

Can't carry it… but I can't leave it.

"Fuck it," Ryx muttered.

He ripped off his armored glove and slid the bracelet over his hand, intending to tuck it beneath his armor.

The moment the metal touched his skin, it constricted.

Ryx gasped. Pain seared into his wrist like molten steel. His whole body tensed. It was like being branded by fire, and lightning.

WHAT THE FUCK!?

Then, just as quickly, it stopped.

The bracelet loosened slightly, now resting against his skin like it had always been there.

He barely had time to whisper, "What the," before a static-laced voice echoed through the warehouse:

35

"Come out. We know you're in here." A helmeted voice. One of the mercs.

Ryx slid his glove back on, hiding the band.

He could worry about the bracelet later.

Right now, it was time to run.

CHAPTER 3

ESCAPE

T he back of the warehouse had no exit, just a wall of thick alloy panels and rusted loading gears. If he wanted out, he'd have to go through the mercs, or past them. And judging by the synchronized way they moved, they knew he was still in here.

Hunting him. Closing in.

He crouched behind a massive crate and ran trembling hands over the pouches and compartments on his belt, mentally cataloging his gear.

Not much left.

A few spare ammo clips. Two tracking beacons. His ice pick. Neoplate combat knife...

Then,

Tessa's flare disks!

His eyes widened as he yanked three thin, circular disks from his thigh pouch. They gleamed faintly in the dark, the etchings along their rims reflecting HUD data.

"I owe you, Tess," he muttered with a crooked smirk.

He reached up to his mask and activated Solar Light Mode. His visor dimmed instantly, rendering the warehouse a dark silhouette landscape of boxes and shadowed outlines. A ghost world.

I hope this works.

He tossed the first disk straight up and squeezed his eyes shut. The moment before he could trigger it, Crack!

A pinpoint shot from one of the mercs shredded the disk midair. The device still went off.

A supernova of blinding light erupted, turning darkness into daylight. Even through his solar-filtered visor, Ryx flinched.

He heard the groans. Armor scraping concrete. Shouted curses. A few of them were caught off guard.

Good. Blind rage is better than coordinated death.

Ryx exploded from behind the crate, sprinting full speed across the warehouse floor. He tried to shoot the gap between two stunned mercs, his footsteps thudding hard as adrenaline surged.

Then,

Wham!

A laser bolt smashed into his left chest plate, spinning him sideways mid-run. He tumbled, hit the ground hard, and rolled behind another crate.

"Gahh, shit!"

His breath hitched. The armor took the brunt, but pain flared hot across his ribs. Bruised for sure. Maybe burned.

Still breathing. Still moving. Keep going.

He peered around the crate, just in time to see it, a drone.

A sleek, humming combat drone hovered behind the mercs, barrel glowing faintly orange.

Precision fire. Military-grade tactics. These aren't freelancers.

His mind raced. He was outgunned, outnumbered, and now injured. Not good. Not good at all.

I need to run, not fight. His mind spun, desperatley seeking his options.

His eyes scanned upward. High windows. Reinforced. No chance.

Then he looked down at his hand, two flare disks left.

Time to get risky.

He slapped one disk against the crate, sticking it in place, and then rolled into a crouch, moving down the line of canisters.

A shot rang out. One of the mercs took a preemptive shot, blasting the crate he'd just left. A scare tactic.

Ryx waited for a minute. He knew they would advance to his last known location. He counted out their pacing, and with a thought, Ryx activated the second disk.

Another flash. More screams. He counted at least two.

They'd fanned out, some would still be unaffected. But it was enough.

Ryx fired off two rounds toward where the drone had hovered. First shot wide. Second clipped a wing. It jerked.

The drone fired back, its shot going wide, sparking off a beam near Ryx's head.

He took the chance, broke into a sprint again, and fired six more shots while moving. The first few missed. But then, four rapid hits, charged rounds,

The drone sparked and dropped like a dying bird.

"Hell yes," Ryx hissed under his breath.

He dashed toward the next row of crates, and nearly slammed into a figure in black armor.

The merc had been waiting.

His rifle lifted.

Blam!

Another shot hit Ryx in the chest. He flew backward, hit hard.

No, no no no, His mind screamed at him through the pain.

His vision swam. The soldier advanced, rifle lowering toward Ryx's head.

Not like this.

He was going to die.

Out of instinct, out of fear, he threw his right arm up to shield his head in vain.

He watched the mercenary take aim and the world slowed. He watched the man's finger start to squeeze the trigger.

Then; Pain.

Fire & lightning shot through his blood.

His wrist ignited in blinding blue light.

Ryx gasped. Half in pain, half in awe. A high-tech gauntlet materialized over his arm in a burst of shimmering energy, metal dark grey, laced with glowing red lines, and pulsing blue light at every joint.

No time.

The shot came.

Ryx flinched. Waited for death.

Then, nothing.

He opened his eyes.

A glowing shield of blue energy covered the gauntlet. The merc stumbled, his shoulder smoking.

"What the hell?" Ryx whispered.

The shield looked like nothing he'd ever seen. Not hardlight. Not standard tech. It pulsed with an alien kind of power, somewhere between solid and intangible. And it beat in time with his heart.

What are you?

He didnt have time to dwell on it. The merc recovered fast. Raised his weapon again.

Ryx surged up, shield first. More shots. He flinched, but they deflected off the shield.

With a roar, Ryx body-checked the merc with the shield. The man staggered, but not enough. He caught his balance and began to bring his gun around. He was strong, trained.

Ryx pushed with his arm in desperation, and the gauntlet's blue lights flared. Lightning flared up his entire arm.

And then, his arm snapped out wide as if nothing was there, as if he just back-handed empty space.

The merc flew. Launched like a ragdoll, he crashed through crates and canisters, smashing into the far wall.

He didn't get up.

Ryx stood, chest heaving, eyes wide.

What the fuck...

A cold thrill ran down his spine. Not fear. Not excitement.

Awe.

Two more mercs rounded the aisle.

Ryx didn't wait.

He charged them. Blue light pulsed again.

This time, as he cocked his arm back to strike, hoping for a similar result.

But this time, no burning filled his blood or muscles.

Instead, a blade of light shot out from a joint above the wrist of the gauntlet, bright blue, at least twelve inches long, shaped like it only had one purpose.

Kill.

It stabbed clean through the first merc's chest plate.

The man choked and stumbled into the soldier behind him. Ryx stepped back, opened his hand, and the blade vanished. Both mercs dropped. One dead. The other stunned.

Ryx reformed the blade by closing his fist again. The blade came to him as if he had called it. He took aim at the second merc struggling to his feet and finished it.

Quick. Clean.

This thing... is it.. learning me? Responding to my thoughts?

Laser fire barked behind him.

Ryx spun, arm up defensively. He wasn't sure how, but the shield was raised. The last three mercs had regrouped.

Shots bounced off his arm.

He sprinted forward, drew his combat knife with his left hand.

Close quarters it is.

He ducked a blast, drove his knife into a soldier's neck seam.

Another flare disk found its way into his now empty hand. *Last one.*

He hurled it like a frisbee, eyes shut, then he triggered it.

Screams. Chaos.

Solar mode on, Ryx tore through the final two soldiers with the gauntlet's blade, clean and quick. Killing with muscle memory built from years of spec ops missions.

Then, it was quiet.

Ryx stood alone, breath ragged, the buzzing of adrenaline still thick in his ears. He raised his hand slowly, staring.

"What," he panted, "the fuck... is going on?" The gauntlet pulsed. A heartbeat.

Then, light flared at the joints, and it began to fade. Dematerialize, just as the box had.

A moment later, only the gold band remained on his wrist.

It glowed faintly. Waiting.

What is this thing?

He looked down at it, chest rising and falling in sharp bursts. A deep ache started to creep in, under his ribs, in his legs, behind his eyes.

Adrenaline was fading. And with it came the real weight of what had just happened.

And somehow, Ryx knew, this was only the beginning.

Quickly he surveyed the scene before him. Smoke hung in the air like ghosts, curling through the shafts of dying sunlight from the destroyed warehouse roof. The scent of scorched steel clung to everything, the aftermath of a battlefield masquerading as a back-alley raid.

He still didn't know who these mercs were, who had sent them, or if this was all of them. The unanswered questions gnawed at him, each one like a tick burrowed beneath his thoughts.

His breathing slowed as he stepped over scorched armor and crumpled limbs. Carefully, he bent down and searched the three nearest bodies. His fingers worked automatically, movements rehearsed from a dozen missions just like this.

No markings. No IDs. No transponders. Not even comms. Not a single clue.

"Clean," he muttered.

Too clean. Too professional.

On each of the men, he found incendiary grenades. Not for defense, these were for erasure. Burn the scene, torch the witnesses, leave nothing behind.

This wasn't just a grab-and-go. This was scorched earth. Full spectrum black ops.

Was this military? Corporate? Something else entirely?

He reached for one of the mercs' laser rifles, then paused.

Security will arrest me for carrying this around in the station, he thought. *Even if these aren't all of them, no one's seen my face.*

Everyone who did... didn't live to report it.

A pulse of guilt shivered under his ribs. He didn't have time to feel it.

His stomach twisted.

The drone.

The thought struck like ice water. Combat drones almost always recorded. Tactical archives, squad logs, facial recognition overlays.

Shit. They could have footage.

Paranoia surged. But paranoia had kept him alive more than once. Sometimes survival meant assuming the worst, especially when the worst was hunting you.

He grabbed the nearest rifle, walked over to the drone's shattered frame. The black orb-like chassis looked like a floating eye, an eye that might have seen too much. A lidless, silent witness.

Without hesitation, he raised the weapon and unloaded the remaining clip into the drone. Sparks burst. Metal buckled. Circuits screamed.

No one's pulling footage from that scrap heap.

He tossed the rifle and jogged to the warped doorway. One peek outside, and his visor lit up with movement, panicked civilians sprinting, ducking for cover.

The station's alarm klaxons blared. The sound sent a chill down his spine. High-pitched and shrill, it felt like a scream of the whole station.

I can use the crowd. File a report, lay low, wait out the lockdown.

He saw an opening and darted into the road, slipping into a current of people surging toward the shelter corridors. His boots echoed off the alloy street, masked by hundreds of pounding footsteps.

He barely made it twenty feet.

A red flare blinked on his HUD, left side.

Reflex took over. Ryx threw himself into a forward roll, colliding with two civilians. They all went down in a tangle of limbs and cursing.

The wall behind them exploded.

A blast from a laser cannon ripped through the space they'd just occupied. Shrapnel screamed through the air like metal hornets.

Ryx didn't stop to think.

"Well, that explains the door," he growled as he untangled himself, his voice low and edged with disbelief.

"They had external eyes."

Another blast. It struck the street just behind him, launching him forward. He skidded across the alloy surface, armor scraping sparks into the ground.

"Gah, shit!" he shouted, rolling hard. Pain flared along his side where plating had thinned.

They had a scout watching. Of course they did.

His training barked in his skull. *Support teams. Scanners. Cannon overwatch. I've done this before.*

"FUCK," he spat, staggering upright. Fury surged alongside the adrenaline now.

He knew better. This was textbook, suppress, sweep, erase. He'd run these missions himself back in the war.

Laser cannons, three shots per cell. Scout's reloading now if it's standard issue.

Ryx's visor picked up the scout just as he dropped to one knee to reload the shoulder-mounted cannon.

The man moved with sharp economy, no wasted motion. Trained. Fast. But predictable.

Not fast enough.

Ryx broke into a dead sprint. No hesitation. No fear. Just violence waiting to be unleashed.

The merc finished reloading, but didn't expect Ryx to charge down the barrel.

TalonX-5 drawn, Ryx closed the gap in seconds, slammed into the merc, and drove the pistol into the neck joint of his armor.

He meant to hold him. Ask questions. Get something.

But the merc was fast. Hands snapped up, grappling, shifting for leverage. A fighter. Not a pawn.

Shit.

Ryx pulled the trigger.

No exit wound. No blood.

Then, red seeped from the joint.

The merc slumped.

"Dammit," Ryx muttered, letting the body fall. "There goes a good lead."

He scanned the area again. No new signals. No unexpected movement.

A long minute passed.

Only the sound of sirens and distant gunfire. Then he moved.

The main hallway was chaos.

Flashing red lights bathed the corridors in a stuttered glow, casting long, jagged shadows against the polished steel walls. Sirens wailed above, piercing and dissonant, as Security barked frantic orders to the crowds of terrified civilians.

"Move! Shelter to the south corridor, now!"

"Black-armored hostiles confirmed on Level Five!"

Ryx ducked into the press of the crowd, slipping between a pair of shouting dockhands and a mother dragging two crying children. The mass of bodies surged like a wave, all crashing toward the docking bays. Fear was a current in the air, thick, sharp. People shoved, screamed, clawed their way past each other with wild eyes and flailing limbs. Someone fell. Someone else screamed. No one looked twice.

Ryx kept low, hood up, eyes scanning. His heartbeat thundered in his ears, syncing with the station's shrieking alarms.

He reached the corridor that would take him to his ship, but just as his boots hit the threshold, chaos erupted again.

Gunfire. Screams. The sound of automatic plasma bursts tore through the air like a storm of electric needles. A wave of people crashed backward down the hallway, panic igniting like fire in dry grass.

Ryx braced against the surge, slamming his shoulder into a wall to keep upright.

Then he saw them.

Twelve. Maybe more.

Black-armored mercenaries, methodical and precise. They moved like machines, firing short bursts, executing security with clean, practiced shots, and turning their weapons on anyone who dared to run. Blood painted the durasteel floors. The mercs weren't herding anymore. They were cleansing.

They're not letting anyone leave until they get it.

Ryx gritted his teeth and dove behind a stack of cargo crates, breath ragged. He could feel the heat from a recent blast still radiating off the metal. Smoke drifted through the hallway like phantoms.

Every instinct screamed at him to move, to run, but he waited.

Watched.

The gunfire stopped.

A heavy silence followed, broken only by the crackle of static from mercenary comms and the whimpering of wounded civilians still hidden in the corridors.

The mercs converged at the port's center, regrouping. Recalculating.

Now.

Ryx moved.

He crept low through the smoke and debris, his boots whispering against the deck. Crates. Wall supports. Abandoned luggage, he used it all for cover, inching toward his docking tube.

He was almost there when a command rang out.

"Check every ship. No one leaves."

Ryx froze. Mercs fanned out. One peeled away, heading directly for the Wraithburn's hatch.

Fuck.

He didn't wait.

He slipped behind the merc like a phantom, each step precise, deadly. The man stepped into the docking tube, and Ryx followed. Quick.

A hand clamped over the merc's mouth. The other drove his knife deep between the armor's weak point at the neck. The merc twitched once. Ryx caught him before he hit the floor, dragging the body back into the shadows. No sound. No hesitation.

He stepped onto the Wraithburn, sealing the hatch behind him.

The air inside felt cooler, familiar. Safer.

He bolted for the cockpit, slid into the pilot's seat, and began the start-up sequence. Power systems surged online, filling the cabin with a rising hum that felt like a heartbeat coming alive. Engines primed. Shields warming. Weapons ready.

Course plotted, an empty system, one jump out. He wasnt about to lead these mercs back home.

He hovered his hand over the emergency dock release. A deep breath. Fingers tight. Then, He hit it.

The Wraith shuddered as it broke free from the station. The view ahead lit with alarm strobes and flashing proximity alerts. Ryx slammed the throttle. The ship roared from the docking tube, rotating sharply into open space.

But he wasn't alone.

"Shit," he growled.

Three enemy fighters lit up his display. Black and fast and already firing.

Plasma scorched the void. Ryx dove, slammed the yoke left, flipping the Wraithburn into a downward spiral that pulled the ship beneath the firing arc. He yanked back, boosted thrusters, and came up behind the nearest fighter.

Trigger squeeze.

Green energy javelins lanced through space.

The first fighter exploded in a burst of fire and debris.

The others tightened formation. They were trained. Relentless.

Ryx rolled the ship hard, shields flaring from repeated impacts. Warning lights flashed. He pulled a hairpin turn and fired again, tagging the second fighter. A missile lock followed. The target spun, trying to evade, but he wasn't fast enough.

The missile struck home. Another burst of light.

The third fighter held position. Smarter. More cautious. It stayed behind him. They danced, two ships in a deadly ballet. Pulse fire lit the stars, turning vacuum into war.

Minutes bled like hours.

Sweat trickled down Ryx's temple. The fighter gained ground, locked on. "Shit." Missiles inbound.

Ryx ejected two probe decoys, twisting the ship through a sharp banking maneuver. The missiles veered, slamming into empty space.

But the fighter stayed with him. Ryx snarled and flipped the cover on a red switch.

"Time to improvise." He hit it.

A blinking orb shot from the belly of the Wraith, one of his few proton mines. Too heavy for dog fights. Too dangerous for proximity.

But Ryx and the Wraith had never been conventional.

The fighter couldn't correct its course in time.

Impact.

Fire.

"Gotcha, asshole."

He didn't have time to celebrate. Alarms screamed. Every warning light on his console lit up red. "What the fuck?!"

The dying pilot had emptied his entire payload, one last barrage.

Ryx hit the jump controls.

Too late.

A brutal impact slammed into the Wraithburn's aft. Shields cracked. Panels burst with sparks. The ship jolted, systems flickering.

Then,

Stars stretched.

And they were gone.

CHAPTER 4
HUNTER VS PREY

Ryx came back to himself from his memories to find Kaelen and Tess staring at him, speculation written plainly across their faces.

"There's no way," Tess said quietly. Her voice was barely above a whisper, as if saying it too loudly might make it more real. "There's no tech like that. Not anywhere in the galaxy."

Her face hardened as she crossed her arms. "You said that little metal bracelet turned into a full, heavily armored gauntlet?" She shook her head. "Where is all that mass stored now? Nothing, nothing, can create or remove mass at will. That's insane." She stared at the floor, jaw tight, lost in calculation.

"I know, Tess," Ryx said, his voice strained. "Nothing about this makes sense. But I'm telling you, it happened."

Kaelen leaned forward, elbows on the table, voice lower but no less intense. "Did it interface with your brain at all? You mentioned the pain racing through you when it activated. Did it ever reach your head?"

Ryx blinked. Thought back.

"No," he said finally, slowly. "Not my head."

Kaelen didn't pull back. "But you claim it responded to your thoughts?"

Ryx slumped back in his chair, hands lifting. "I know it doesn't make any sense. I know I sound crazy. But I'm only alive because of

51

this weird thing." He held up his wrist and shook it a little, the golden band glinting in the light Kaelen leaned back, folding his arms across his chest. Thoughtful. Quiet. The kind of silence that made Ryx's skin itch. A long minute passed.

"Have you tried to activate it again?" Kaelen finally asked, his voice low, deliberate.

Ryx hesitated, his fingers instinctively brushing the smooth golden band still fused to his wrist. "No," he admitted. "I was too busy trying to survive. And…" He trailed off, glancing away. "Honestly? I was scared to."

Tessa, leaning on the counter, looked up sharply at that. Kaelen didn't flinch.

"Try," he said simply. But the word carried weight, a challenge, a request, and a warning all at once. "I've never known you to be a liar, Eryx. I don't want to start doubting you now. But this is…" He shook his head. "This is a lot."

Ryx nodded, jaw tight. He could feel it now, the subtle shift in the air. Not anger, not mistrust, but doubt. Heavy and unspoken, like a storm about to break.

I get it, he thought bitterly. *I'd doubt me too.*

His hand hovered over the table. His fingers trembled. He stared down at the band on his wrist. Cool. Silent. Innocent looking. Nothing about it suggested the impossible thing it had once become, no hum, no glow, not even warmth. Just a lifeless cuff of strange metal.

What if it doesn't work? What if it only activates under threat? What if I'm broken now? What if they think I made it all up?

The knot in his stomach twisted tighter. His breath came shallow.

What if I really am crazy?

But Kaelen was still watching. Tessa too, her eyes narrowed in that curious, analytical way of hers, always searching for the trick behind the curtain. Ryx could almost feel the wedge forming between them, the moment stretching into something dangerous and irreversible.

Here goes… everything.

He raised his hand slowly, palm out, fingers splayed. His eyes locked on the gold band. He tried to remember how it had felt the last time, the pulse of instinct, the pressure of danger, the way the world had narrowed down to now.

He focused.

For a breath, nothing happened.

His heart stuttered.

Then, FWAM.

A flash of cerulean light erupted from his wrist, cascading down his forearm like liquid lightning. The gauntlet snapped into existence with a violent hum, blue energy coalescing into armored plates that wrapped his arm in less than a second.

The force of it jolted him back, literally.

Ryx yelped as the chair kicked out from under him. He hit the ground hard, landing on his back with a grunt, his arm still thrust upward in reflex. The gauntlet blazed, crackling with low, radiant power. He stared at it, half in awe, half in shock, breath coming in ragged gasps..

Kaelen jumped, clutching his chest, while Tess let out a strangled gasp and spat her cider across the kitchen.

"WHAT THE FUCK!" Tess shouted, scrambling to her feet.

She bolted to Ryx's side, eyes wide and glowing with manic curiosity. Kaelen followed, crouching beside Ryx and jabbing at the gauntlet with a pen pulled from his shirt.

Once he was sure it wasn't about to explode, he reached out and pressed a weathered palm to it.

"No way," he whispered.

"What!?" Tess and Ryx said in unison.

Kaelen's voice was low. Reverent.

"It's solid matter. Real metal. A legit alloy of some kind. I don't know what… but it's definitely not a projection."

He turned Ryx's arm gently, inspecting every angle. "Where's the bracelet?"

"I think… I think the gauntlet is the bracelet," Ryx said, eyes wide with awe. "I don't know how to explain it. But I can feel it. Like it's aware of me. Whether it's a bracelet or this… it's the same presence."

Tess started pacing. Fast. Her cider forgotten.

"Nope. Nope. NOPE," she said, voice climbing. She stopped and pressed both palms to her head. "I'm insane. This is insane. It breaks every natural law I know."

Kaelen helped Ryx to his feet. His touch was firm. Grounding.

"You said it could do more," he said, half-question, half-command.

Ryx nodded, feeling his pulse rise. He hadn't expected it to work, but now that it had, a flicker of excitement burned in his gut.

He drew his arm in tight, clenched his fist.

A circular blue shield of light erupted from the gauntlet.

Kaelen's breath hitched. "Holy… shit."

Tess lunged back over, grabbed the pen from her father, and jabbed the shield with the pen.

The metal hissed. She recoiled.

"That's not laser tech or hardlight," she breathed.

"What do you mean?" Ryx asked.

Kaelen answered, voice sharp. "Laser tech flickers. It's unstable, scattered. It would've melted that pen."

Ryx's brows furrowed. "So… hardlight, then? Right?"

Tess shook her head. "No. Hardlight is layered, a projection of condensed photons stacked millions of times. There's no projection here. No emitter. That-" she pointed, "-is one seamless sheet of light."

Ryx stepped back, suddenly overwhelmed. "Then what the hell is it!?"

Tess didn't answer.

54

"We don't know," Kaelen said. "It's impossible. That's what it is." Ryx looked between them. Then down at his arm.

"There's more," he said quietly.

"What?" Tess and Kaelen said together.

"Come with me."

He led them to the garage, then into the machine shop. He moved quickly, his excitement mounting, and dug through the piles of scrap.

He pulled out a long titanium rod. Held it up with his left hand.

"What are you doing?" Tess asked, her voice wary.

Ryx just smiled. He clenched his gauntleted fist and focused. He willed the blade to appear.

It appeared instantly, blue, bright, and humming.

The Rhoens jumped as Ryx swung his fist sideways and sliced cleanly through the rod. Metal parted with a whisper.

"HOLY SHIT!" Tess shrieked.

She snatched up the severed piece of rod, running her fingers along the cut.

"It's too clean," she muttered. "No scorch marks. No resistance. It's like it just… gave way." Kaelen stared. Silently.

"Is that all?" he asked. Ryx met his eyes and slowly shook his head.

He gripped the remaining half of the rod. The gauntlet flared, and lightning shot up his arm. Ryx winced but held on. The titanium screamed. Then it crumpled in his fist like paper.

He dropped the twisted scrap onto the bench.

Kaelen sat hard on a crate.

"What in the stars…" he whispered.

Deep grooves marked where Ryx's fingers had crushed through the alloy.

"It augments my strength," Ryx said. "I wasn't exaggerating when I said I threw that merc through a warehouse." Silence.

Then, Tess laughed. Both men looked at her.

Between fits of laughter, she gasped, "You're finally gonna be useful in the garage. You're a living, breathing piece of equipment now." Ryx grinned. But Kaelen didn't. "What are you going to do with it?" The question hit like a fist.

"What do you mean?" Ryx asked.

"Isn't Black Sable Dynamics, and whatever mercenary group that attacked you, looking for this?"

Ryx hesitated. Willed the gauntlet to retract. The glow faded, and the bracelet returned.

"I'm not sure they even know what this is. Kolen was the one who found it, and even he didn't seem to know. He called it a box."

Tess folded her arms. "He could've been hiding something. Out of fear."

Ryx shook his head. "If he knew, he would've worn it. He wouldn't have left it behind."

Kaelen stood. Silent for a long minute before he spoke. "Maybe. But we need to be careful. Powerful people are involved, whether they understand this thing or not." He met Ryx's eyes.

"Black Sable is going to want a mission report. What are you going to tell them?"

Ryx took a breath. He had been debating this same question for days. "I don't know yet. But when I checked the feeds, there was nothing about Tarrin Station. No reports. No news. So, I might have a few days before they start asking."

Kaelen nodded slowly. "Be smart, Ryx. You might have to hand it over."

Ryx grimaced. Kalen's' face grew stern, knowing.

Tess looked between them. "What?"

Ryx rubbed the back of his neck. "I kind of… can't."

Kaelen's face darkened. "This isn't a joke. That thing is dangerous."

Ryx grabbed the bracelet and tugged. It didn't budge. He yanked harder. Nothing.

"I can't take it off," he said, voice tight. "I tried. First day in the Wraith. Tried everything. It doesn't move." He let both of them try.

Every time the bracelet constricted and fused to his skin.

Kaelen pressed a hand to his face.

"Shit. This just keeps getting worse."

Ryx exhaled, long and low. "I'll figure something out. I'll keep it quiet."

Kaelen stepped close. His voice dropped to a growl.

"You better do more than try. Word gets out that a bounty hunter's running around with unknown tech? You'll go from the hunter to the hunted faster than the Wraith can jump systems."

ΔΔΔ

That night, Ryx had dinner with the Rhoens in the house and caught up with their lives while he'd been away. The food was simple, warm, and grounding, just the way he remembered. A comfort he didn't know he'd missed until he sat at the table.

Kaelen hadn't lied. Business had been slower than usual. He'd started taking small, local jobs, repairing household machinery, optimizing aging climate units, even rebuilding a couple of obsolete kitchen bots. They were scraping by but managing.

Tess, predictably, wouldn't budge on the details of her secret project. All she offered was a smug smile and a vague hint: something involving hardlight projection.

That was enough to get Ryx's curiosity blazing. He peppered her with guesses and theories, half to annoy her, half because he genuinely couldn't help himself. She deflected every question with snarky remarks, exaggerated eye-rolls, or rude gestures over the table.

Eventually, Ryx gave up. He let the warmth of home settle around him like a cloak. He bid his foster family goodnight and returned to the Wraithburn to do a quick inventory before his resupply run in the morning.

The ship was silent when he entered, still damaged, her systems in a semi-sleep state. But she felt alive. Waiting.

He began with medical and food supplies, anything for general living. His list grew fast. The Wraith would be grounded for at least a few days while Kaelen and Tess worked her back to health, so he planned to stay busy restocking and helping however he could.

Kaelen seemed genuinely excited to work on the Wraithburn again. The man lit up when ships were involved. He even agreed to let Ryx pay him for labor, not just parts, which surprised Ryx and made him deeply grateful.

They had poured uncounted hours, sweat, and sacrifice into this ship. The Wraith wasn't just a vessel; it was a shared legacy. Ryx would never repay that debt, not truly, but he could try.

After finishing his general inventory, he moved to the back of the closet and pulled out the small munitions and tools locker. Time for the important count: ammo, armor refurb, gadgets.

Between ship repairs, armor restoration, and the restock from Tess, it was going to gut his nest egg. Not getting paid for the last job stung more than just his pride, it was a financial hit.

This would be his first official failure as a hunter.

He hated it.

He knew it wouldn't ruin his rep; even top-ranked bounty hunters had a few botched jobs. But Ryx had prided himself on a near flawless record. Years clean. Just a few hiccups. Now it had a dent.

He packed his Neoplate armor into a compact case for delivery to Rexa Vorn the next morning, leaving his mask behind in the hidden compartment of the Wraith's armory wall. He closed it with a soft hiss, locking it out of sight.

A quick shower followed. Then brushing his teeth. Then bed.

The Wraith's morning alarm woke him hours later with a soft chime. Familiar. Comfortable.

He rose from bed feeling more rested than he had in weeks.

At the closet, he threw on a dark grey shirt and a pair of well-worn jeans. Socks. Work boots. He layered it with a brown nanoleather jacket, scuffed, but reliable.

Then he moved to the hidden armory. The panel hissed open.

He selected a plain belt with a simple holster. His armored rig was getting refurbished today. He slotted his TalonX-5 into place with practiced ease.

Vorrthani might've been home, but it was still a station full of criminals. He didn't expect trouble, but he was always ready for it. And having the blaster on his hip just felt... right.

He ran a hand through his thick brown hair, pulling it back into its usual shaggy sweep, and noticed the bracelet again.

This time, he smiled.

I should be scared of this thing he thought. It hijacked my body, and I can't even take it off.

But the fear was fading.

Instead, he felt something strange.

Gratitude.

It kept me alive.

He didn't know if the bracelet could hear thoughts. But he felt its faint hum against his skin like it acknowledged him. Ryx couldn't explain it, but he was glad it was still there.

He grabbed the armor case and exited into the garage. But instead of heading straight into the house, he veered into the machine shop.

He knelt beside the far-right workbench and pulled it away from the wall. Beneath it, a loose floor panel.

Tess had shown him this hiding spot years ago. Not even Kaelen knew about it.

He peeled it back, revealing a narrow compartment filled with credit chips.

Banks were unreliable. Accountants were worse. Ryx didn't trust either, especially on a place like Vorrthani.

He scanned each card with a pocket reader. Most were in the 1K to 15K range. One had just 80 credits left.

He tallied the total: roughly 90K Universal Credits.

Not bad.

He pulled two 15K chips for Tess and Kaelen, payment for parts and labor. He knew Kaelen would push back, but this was nonnegotiable. They'd charge that to even a close friend, and Ryx refused to shortchange them.

Then came the rest: a 1K card for general resupply. A 500 for the armor refurb. It was double the cost, he knew Rexa would cut him a deal, and he planned to buy information too. Staying in her good graces was always worth it.

Lastly, he pocketed the 80-credit chip. Lunch money. Maybe a few hours of peace while the Rhoens bring the Wraith back to life.

He closed the cache, replaced the floor panel, and slid the workbench back.

When he entered the house, Kaelen was already up.

Always early. Ryx remembered the old man's mantra: "Daylight's just wasted starlight."

Kaelen didn't look back. "Morning," he said, voice low but warm, as he worked at the stove.

"Mornin', Pops," Ryx replied. He moved to the coffee machine and started a fresh brew.

"Hungry?" Kaelen asked.

"Could eat," Ryx said, pouring two mugs.

They sat together at the small table. Kaelen slid him a plate, two fried eggs and toast. The same sat in front of him. They ate in silence. Not uncomfortable. Peaceful. When they finished, both men leaned back, mirroring each other without meaning to.

"Headed into the station today?" Kaelen asked.

"Yeah. Gotta restock and figure out how I'm going to deal with Black Sable Dynamics."

Kaelen raised a brow. "Any idea what you'll say?"

Ryx shrugged. "Mostly the truth. Found Kolen. He forced me to defend myself.." Ryx paused for a minuet remembering Kolen, and the brief few seconds that ended their relationship. Before he continued. "Then I was attacked. Escaped. I'll let them check the timelines to back it all up."

Kaelen leaned forward, eyes serious. "And the prototype?"

"I'll say I didn't have time to hunt it down with mercs crawling all over me. I wiped the drone footage. Station cams wouldn't have seen the bracelet, it didn't activate again until last night." Ryx looked at the bracelet. He was betting everything on Black Sable Dynamics not knowing what it really was.

Kaelen grunted in reluctant agreement. "Risky."

"Yeah, well, best I've got. I'm going to try and squeeze some info out of Rexa Vorn today, see what I can dig up about B.S.D. or Kolen's expedition."

Kaelen nodded. They drank their coffee in silence for a minute.

"You working on the Wraith today?"

Kaelen grinned. "You couldn't keep me off that ship even if it was mint-condition. I've been going stir-crazy waiting on a real job. And now I've got my baby back."

Ryx smiled. Kaelen's joy was contagious.

As he stood, Ryx cleared their plates and placed them in the cleaner. On his way back, past the table, he dropped the two 15K chips in front of Kaelen.

The older man scowled. "This better not be too much." "It's less than you deserve," Ryx said simply.

Kaelen tried to push one chip back. Ryx blocked it with a hand.

"You'll take my money, old man, or you're not touching my ship."

Kaelen's eyes narrowed in mock challenge. "Careful, boy. Even with that bracelet and all that fancy training, you'd have a hard time keeping me off that ship."

Ryx barked a laugh as Kaelen scooped up the chips and tucked them into his coveralls.

"I'll be back tonight," Ryx said, heading for the door. "I'll bring dinner."

He stepped into the corridors of Vorrthani Station, leaving the scent of breakfast and solder behind.

Ryx stepped out into a dirty street. The overhead lighting buzzed above, casting its cold, sterile glow to simulate daytime aboard Vorrthani Station. The illusion of daylight did little to hide the grime caked into every crevice of the industrial port sector.

Vorrthani wasn't the worst dump Ryx had ever been on, but it definitely had character. Pipes and conduits snaked along every wall and ceiling, some hissing faintly, others dripping from unseen leaks.

Most streets down here had at least a few puddles where the water lines bled out into the walkways. But not outside the Rhoens' place.

Pays to have two mechanical geniuses in your sector, Ryx thought, smirking as he stepped over clean pavement.

The Rhoens' garage sat tucked into the port edge of Vorrthani's lowest tier. The station itself was divided into three stacked sections, each multi-level. The bottom tier, where Ryx stood, was almost entirely industrial. Maintenance. Freight. Mechanics. Everyone who kept the lights on and the hull sealed.

Level Two housed most of the general population, along with the entertainment district. Bars. Casinos. Bazaars. The lifeblood of any station.

Level Three? That was where the upper crust lived. Corporate execs. Station officials. Private security firms. Not Ryx's crowd.

He glanced up at the faded sign bolted to the side of the Rhoens' garage. By night, the old neon lettering cast the street in a wash of magenta light, turning the alley into something almost beautiful. But now, in daylight mode, it looked tired. Flickering. Like it hadn't slept in years.

He adjusted the weight of the armor case on his shoulder and headed down the street toward the lower markets.

Ten minutes later, Ryx passed through the heavy double doors that marked the sector's boundary. Stamped above them in dull yellow paint were the words: MARKET SECTOR.

Inside, the chaos of morning commerce was already taking shape.

Pop-up stalls lined the open floor, packed in like cargo pallets. Some were sleek kiosks with flashing signage. Others were half-collapsed canopies manned by shifty vendors.

Walk-in stores lined the perimeter, their roll-up windows thrown open to hawk wares directly into the flow of foot traffic.

The scent of fried synth-meat, machine oil, and cheap perfume hung thick in the air.

Ryx moved through the crowd, eyes scanning out of habit. Purveyors sold everything from firearms to fungi. He passed at least three seedy-looking bars and a half-dozen stalls offering bootleg holovids or counterfeit tech.

Then he saw it. WAR VORN WEAPONS.

He couldn't help but chuckle at the sign, the kind of name only an old woman like Rexa would find clever. He stepped inside.

The shop was dim but orderly. Rows of reinforced nano-glass displays lined the walls, showcasing weapons and armor behind protective barriers. The back wall held a thick, barred counter like a fortress gate.

"Eryx!"

The voice cracked through the room with unexpected warmth.

Rexa Vorn.

The old woman stood behind the counter, her silver hair tied up in the same bun she'd worn for as long as Ryx could remember.

Her face bore the lines of a life spent smiling and surviving, and her eyes twinkled with fierce intelligence.

Ryx smiled. "Morning, Rexa."

"Finally come to replace that bolt thrower you call a blaster?" she cackled.

He patted the TalonX-5 on his hip. "Not yet. This one's saved my ass more times than I can count."

She waved a dismissive hand. "Bah! That thing couldn't kill a drallbat."

Ryx snorted. Drallbats were the flying rats of mountainous worlds, big eyes, twitchy wings, and more bark than bite.

"You need one of these."

She reached under the counter and produced a heavy matte-gray pistol. It looked like it could down a dropship.

Ryx let out a low whistle. "Is that a Fury?"

"RZ7, newest model. Switches between hardlight mag rounds and dense laser cell rounds. Seamlessly."

He took the gun carefully, testing its weight. He turned it in his hands until he found the dual cell ports. "Two power cells?"

Rexa leaned forward and pointed to a discreet toggle switch near the trigger guard. "Flick that with your middle finger. Switches modes in an instant."

"That's so clean." Ryx took aim in mock fashion. "I'd cut my favorite hunter a deal on my last one," Rexa said with a wink.

Ryx smiled, tempted. "I can't. This thing's overkill for most of my work. I'm not usually hired to vaporize people."

She barked a laugh and slid the pistol back under the counter. "Never hurts to try."

She folded her arms. "So, what brings Eryx Thorne to my shop today?"

He set the carrying case on the counter and slid her the 500-credit chip. "Armor took a beating. Needs a full refurb."

She opened the case, eyeing the scorched Neoplate with a frown. "A beating? Looks more like someone tried to air condition your chest the hard way."

He gave her a sheepish grin. "Nothing gets past you."

She scanned the chip. "This is too much. You'll have change."

He held up a hand. "I also need a little info."

Her smile faded. "Ryx. You in trouble?"

"Not sure," he admitted. "But I need you to keep this quiet. I need anything you can dig up on Black Sable Dynamics' xenoarchaeology division. Especially a scientist named Kolen Vess."

Her expression turned wary. "That's the corp that hired you directly, isn't it?"

Ryx nodded. "Yeah. Something doesn't add up. I don't want you taking any risks. Just... see what you can find. Quietly."

He smiled again. "Do that, and maybe I'll save up for that cannon you tried to sell me."

"For you?" Rexa smirked. "Only thirty thousand." Ryx scoffed.

"I could upgrade every piece of gear I own for that."

Rexa leaned on the counter and peered at him over her glasses.

"None of your gear can punch through a hardlight shield," she countered.

Ryx raised an eyebrow. "There's no way."

She grinned like a kid with a secret. "Wanna test it?"

He returned the smile. A pulse of wild excitement coursing through him. "Why not?"

They stepped into the back of the shop, into a modest but high-end firing range.

She handed him the Fury. "You get the honors."

The pistol felt heavier than he expected, solid, purposeful. The matte finish drank in the light like it had something to hide. Ryx held it with both hands, familiarizing himself with the balance and grip. The handle was molded perfectly to a gloved hand, textured in all the right places. It felt like a weapon that was meant to be used, not displayed.

The firing range was simple but well-constructed. Each stall was segmented by carbon-composite dividers, sturdy enough to absorb minor ricochets. The ceiling was lined with smart lights that dimmed the moment a target was engaged, and the soundproofing kicked in with a quiet hum as soon as they stepped inside.

He stepped into the lane, boots crunching softly on the padded metal floor. It smelled faintly of oil and carbon scoring, evidence of countless test shots from more exotic weapons than he dared guess.

His eyebrows lifted. "You're letting me shoot it?" "After you try, you might buy," she teased.

She keyed in a target. A holo dummy materialized downrange.

"These are high-density laser rounds," she said, handing him a smaller energy cell. "Try it on the unshielded target."

He loaded the cell with practiced ease, sighted down the barrel, and fired.

The moment his finger depressed the trigger, a slight vibration buzzed through the grip, like the gun was charging its breath. The green charge indicator pulsed once as the weapon responded.

A sharp beam of emerald light lanced forward with a muted hiss. The instant the shot connected, the dummy's shoulder erupted into a puff of simulated debris. The beam cut so cleanly it was almost surgical, no lingering glow, no delayed effect. Just instant disintegration.

The dummy twitched as its onboard servos tried to compensate for the lost limb before resetting.

"Whoa," Ryx breathed.

"Ready for the real fun?" Rexa asked, handing him a larger, darker cell.

She keyed in a command, and a shimmering purple hardlight shield appeared in front of the next dummy.

"I still don't believe you," Ryx muttered, eyeing the shield.

"Shoot first. Doubt later."

He toggled the weapon's mode, sighted in, and pulled the trigger.

The charge light near the new cell glowed a deep, ominous blue. A low hum built in the chamber, rising in pitch until the weapon practically vibrated in his hands.

There was a moment's delay. Then, CRACK.

The sound was thunderous, reverberating through the stall like a shockwave. The weapon kicked with force, the kind of power that demanded respect. Ryx's shoulder jolted slightly from the impact, his stance absorbing the recoil with practiced reflex.

The blazing blue slug screamed forward like a comet, its trail crackling in the air. As it struck the purple hardlight shield, there was a sharp flash, the shield flared once, then shattered like glass, shards of glowing purple evaporating midair.

The slug didn't even slow down. It tore through the dummy's head with terrifying efficiency, the projection flickering violently as it collapsed backward in a tangle of pixels and smoke.

"NO WAY!" Ryx shouted, bouncing on his heels. "Rexa, this thing is a cannon!"

She just beamed.

He handed the pistol back reverently.

"Glad you liked it." She turned and led the way back to the front of the shop.

As Ryx trailed behind, still riding the high from firing the Fury, he noticed the subtle shift in Rexa's body language. Her steps were slower now, heavier, something ahead of her distracting. The moment they crossed through the range's bulkhead door into the main storefront, he saw the tension in her shoulders. She didn't speak right away.

Ryx slowed his own pace as she approached the counter. The light from her terminal cast a pale glow on her lined face, highlighting the crease forming between her brows.

Something was wrong.

The cheer from a few moments ago had completely drained away, replaced by something colder. Focused. Her fingers tapped the screen rapidly, then paused as she read. The soft hum of the shop displays filled the silence.

Ryx felt the weight return to his gut.

"Rexa?" he asked.

She didn't answer immediately. Her eyes were locked on the terminal as if what it showed would change if she stared long enough.

A second later, she slowly turned toward him, her voice quieter now, measured.

"Eryx," she said softly, eyes meeting his with a gravity he hadn't seen in her since the last time she'd pulled a blaster on someone.

"When's the last time you checked your guild terminal?"

"Last night. Why?"

"I just got a priority ping from the guild for you. Black Sable Dynamics wants an urgent in-person debrief."

CHAPTER 5

BELLY OF THE BEAST

Ryx stood quietly inside Rexa Vorn's weapons shop, arms heavy at his sides, every muscle in his neck and shoulders wound tight. Thoughts and worries spun through his head in a manic, chaotic loop.

Every angle was a dead end. Every what-if felt like a countdown ticking faster. His fingers twitched, as if looking for something to grip, a weapon, a lifeline, anything to anchor him. The moment felt suspended in static, the weight of what he'd seen, and what he hadn't, crashing against his mind like waves on fractured metal.

He'd made it out alive, but survival didn't mean safety. It didn't mean clarity.

He was still in the eye of the storm, and the wind was shifting.

"Eryx?" Rexa's soft, concerned voice pulled him back to the present.

He blinked. Twice. Her lined face came back into focus across the counter. "Oh. Yeah. Thanks for telling me, Rexa. Respond and let them know you delivered the message. I'll get back to my terminal shortly and follow up with the Guild and the client." She didn't move.

"Eryx, you seem… flustered."

He tried to give her a reassuring shrug, but the gesture fell flat. She knew him too well. He didn't have the energy to lie, and his gut was a tangle of adrenaline and dread.

"I'll be alright, Rexa. Just…" he hesitated, then offered her a half-truth. "My last job was my first real failure. It's eating at me."

Her eyes narrowed, not in suspicion, but with the kind of deep concern only age and experience could cultivate. He didn't lie. But he also didn't tell her everything. Rexa had earned his trust ten times over, but the fewer people involved, the better.

Hell, maybe he shouldn't have even told Kaelen and Tess.

"Be careful, Eryx," she said at last, lowering her voice. "The Guild will back you as long as you followed the bylaws, but mega corporations? They don't play fair. If you're in deep, let the Guild help you."

Ryx gave a shallow nod, but inside, the words cut.

The Guild would turn me in.

His stomach twisted again. The cold truth of it wrapped around his spine. He could already see the sterile conference rooms, the cold bureaucratic language, the handshake from some BSD executive as the Guild handed him over like an invoice. Not out of malice.

Out of procedure.

He'd read the bylaws himself a hundred times. He knew what they said about unauthorized xeno tech. What they demanded from hunters who encountered it. And what they required if the hunter refused to comply.

"Thanks, Rexa. I also need an ammo resupply," he said, reaching for another credit chip.

She waved him off instantly. "You've given me enough money, Eryx. Your cheap power cells and standard flash and concussion grenades are covered."

He opened his mouth to argue, but she cut him off.

"Get home. Get this sorted out. I'm serious."

"I've got a few more errands to run in the market," he relented, lifting a hand in mock surrender. "Then I swear I'll head back." She sighed, but didn't push further. As he turned toward the door, her voice followed him.

70

"Be careful, Ryx. If you need help, any help, you ask. No pride. No delay. Just ask."

He paused, hovering over the door panel.

"I will," he said quietly. "Thanks, Rexa." Then he stepped back into the fray.

The market air hit him like a wall, spice, oil, and the buzz of a hundred overlapping conversations. Ryx moved quickly through the remaining stalls, weaving past merchants and shoppers with the kind of practiced grace only someone born to busy streets could manage. But his mind was elsewhere, wound tight with the urgency he kept locked behind calm eyes.

Ryx spent the next two hours visiting his normal shops ordering resupply deliveries: Grocery, medical, personal items. He placed delivery orders for all his missing items. All the while his mind never stopped racing. Once he was done placing orders he turned to head home.

Just as he reached the edge of the sector, he stopped short.

I was supposed to pick up dinner.

He pivoted sharply and doubled back toward the noodle shop near the market entrance, footsteps quick and purposeful. As he neared the familiar storefront, the scent of simmering broth and grilled synth proteins wrapped around him like a warm cloak. His stomach growled, reminding him he hadn't eaten since morning.

The restaurant was dim and inviting. Holographic paper lanterns floated near the ceiling, casting soft golden light across the narrow row of tables that lined the left wall. On the right stood the counter and open kitchen, where the sizzle of boiling pots echoed off metal surfaces.

Behind the counter stood Lyn, the owner's daughter, no older than twenty, with long dark hair pulled back into a neat ponytail. The moment she saw him; she nearly dropped her data pad.

"He, hey, Ryx!" she stammered, cheeks blooming red.

He gave a friendly wave. "Hey, Lyn. Sorry to rush, but I need to place a dinner order for delivery to Rhoen's Maintenance later tonight."

Her fingers fumbled over the tablet as she pulled up the order form. "O-of course! I didn't know you were back from your last job."

Ryx scratched his chin. "Yeah, got in kinda late last night." Lyn nodded quickly, eyes darting to the screen. "Okay! What can I get for you?"

"One spicy synth noodle bowl for me. Tess will want her Vorrth soup and dumplings, extra broth if you can swing it. And Kaelen gets noodles too. Add extra veggies to his."

She arched an eyebrow at him, a smirk tugging at the corner of her mouth. "Kaelen hates veggies." Ryx chuckled. "Doctor's orders. Plus, if I don't, Tess'll brain me with a wrench."

Lyn laughed, then typed in the order. "When do you want it delivered?"

"Three hours should be perfect."

He handed her the 80-credit chip. She scanned it, handed him the tablet for confirmation. Ryx left a fifteen-credit tip and handed back the tablet. Lyn took it and then blinked when she saw the total. "Ryx, the meal's only fifteen creds, this is way too much."

He smirked as he signed off on the transaction. "It's for our favorite spot. That's five creds for each of you."

Lyn flushed again, holding back a smile. "You're too much."

"See you soon, Lyn," Ryx said as he turned and headed out.

Back on the industrial street, Ryx picked up his pace, boots clanging faintly against metal panels as he moved with purpose. His thoughts had barely settled by the time he reached the Rhoens' garage. He ducked inside, triggering the front bell.

"Just me, guys!" he called up toward the security cam. "I'll be out in a second!"

He moved to the main terminal and accepted the incoming delivery requests tied to his earlier market runs, syncing them to the garage's auto-receive protocols. Then he passed through the kitchen and out into the garage proper.

Kaelen was half-buried under the Wraithburn's rear hull, the clink of tools echoing beneath the ship. The machine shop buzzed in the background, Tess, no doubt, elbows deep in something explosive.

"Hey, Pops. I'm back."

Kaelen slid out from beneath the ramp, wiping sweat from his brow. "Back early. What happened?"

Ryx's face tightened. "BSD's already contacted the Guild. They want an in-person."

Kaelen's expression darkened. "Shit."

"Still need to file my report first," Ryx added. "If the Guild accepts it, maybe it'll buy me a buffer."

Kaelen sighed, tossing the rag onto a bench. "Wraith's not going anywhere for a few days. If you need to jump systems, you'll need another ride."

"Yeah. I don't want to bring her anywhere near this until I know how BSD's gonna play it."

Kaelen looked him dead in the eyes. "Your life's worth more than that ship, Ryx. I don't like the idea of you walking into this without her, either."

Ryx raised his hands. "I know, I know. I'm not thrilled about it either. But if I dodge BSD now, both a mega corp and the Guild come hunting. And let's not forget the merc team that came for the artifact."

Kaelen pinched the bridge of his nose. "Tess thinks they worked for BSD. Me? I'm not sure she's wrong."

"Yeah," Ryx muttered. "It's crossed my mind too. BSD wouldn't want to piss off the Guild, at least not openly. But if they thought they could contain the fallout…"

Kaelen gave a grim nod. "Speaking of containment, you heard the news from Tarrin Station?"

Ryx's brow furrowed. "No?"

"They're saying a ship exploded in the dock. That's what killed those people. That's what damaged the systems."

Ryx froze. "No way. There were too many witnesses. How could anyone buy that?"

"With enough credits, you don't need to buy the truth. Just the headlines."

Ryx pressed a hand to his temple. "This is so fucked."

Kaelen clapped a hand on his shoulder. "You're smart. Your story holds up. No one's seen that bracelet but us. You never found the artifact."

Ryx nodded slowly, tension bleeding into his breath. "If I don't go to them, I'm the one under fire. I feel like I'm stuck between an asteroid and a proton missile."

Kaelen offered a tired smile. "You're a damn good pilot, Ryx. That missile wouldn't touch you. And you know it."

Ryx smiled faintly, the corners of his mouth tugging upward even as his chest stayed tight. He gave Kaelen a pat on the back, fingers lingering for a second longer than normal before he turned toward the Wraithburn.

He stepped inside. The familiar hiss of the boarding ramp closing behind him echoed through the ship's hull. It was quieter inside than he remembered, like the Wraith was holding its breath.

Ryx moved through the corridor, each footfall resonating softly beneath him as he reached the cockpit. He paused at the entrance, letting his fingers trace the edge of the bulkhead. Everything was in its place. Every switch and dial exactly how he left it.

This was his sanctuary. His fortress.

And right now, it felt like a war room.

He sank into the pilot's seat, letting out a breath he didn't realize he'd been holding. The leather creaked under him.

Time to write that report.

Ryx stared at the Wraith's main console for a long minute. The display was quiet, diagnostic screens flickering in standby. She was still in maintenance mode. A small yellow alert blinked in the corner, four unread messages.

He toggled open the inbox. As expected: one request for a mission update from the Guild and another from BSD.

But the other two... those weren't expected. Encrypted. Unknown senders.

"What..." Ryx whispered, sitting up straighter as his heart tapped faster in his chest.

He opened the first encrypted message. It was short. Cryptic. But Ryx smiled with immediate recognition.

Kid,

I already started looking into your request and hit a wall. A big thick wall with flashing warning signs. Every contact I reached out to told me no. I've received zero information and I'm sure I've lost the willingness of several of my contacts with my questions in only a few short hours. Cowards. Don't feel bad, I needed to refresh my network anyway. Sorry I couldn't help more immediately. I'll keep digging.

– Cannoneer

"Rexa," Ryx breathed with a small smile. Only someone who knew her well, and the context of their last meeting, would recognize the tone or the signature. She was protecting him, even now.

"You did help, Rexa," he murmured aloud. "Now I know how far they'll go to bury this."

He leaned back and steepled his fingers beneath his chin. The reality chilled him. Black Sable Dynamics didn't just want to retrieve the artifact; they wanted it erased from history. And anyone who sniffed too close? Gone.

I need to be careful how I talk to BSD. I can't call it an artifact. Can't act like I understand anything. If they think I know too much...they'll bury me.

He exhaled slowly and tapped into the second encrypted message.

This time, the words hit him like a shot to the chest.

Eryx Thorne, my friend,

I know that you hunt me. I know not when you will receive this message, but I hope it reaches you before you do anything foolish. The people who hired you are not to be trusted in any sense. I worked with Black Sable Dynamics for seven years, and in that time, more colleagues of mine disappeared than I cared to count.

I cannot tell you what I did in earnest or what they want from me. But I can tell you it is dangerous. I do not yet understand it fully, but I know it is tied to something violent and vast.

I know your heart, Eryx Thorne. I touched your mind more than once in the Academy. You do not wish to hurt me. Part of you believes you can let me go. I saw it in your thoughts.

Please know I have most likely left the station by the time you read this. Even I do not know where I will end up. I plan to board the first ship willing to take me.

Stay far from this, my friend. It will only bring you pain. Stay well,

-Kolen Vess

Ryx's mouth hung open, his heart thundering in his chest. His lungs seized as if the very air had turned to iron. He blinked hard, once, twice, trying to steady the wave crashing over him. Kolen. His friend. His classmate. A man he once trusted with his life. A man who saw him, not the bounty hunter, not the ex-scout, but him.

And Ryx had killed him. He sent this at that diner. He must've written it while I was already on his tail.

Ryx ran both hands through his hair, gripping tight.

"I'm sorry, Kolen," he whispered. "I didn't want this."

But it didn't matter. Kolen was dead. Gunned down in a warehouse by someone he once called brother.

Not because of the artifact, Ryx thought bitterly. Because of BSD.

Because they fed me a lie and hung a target around Kolen's neck. He let the pain stew for a moment longer, then forced himself to open the third message.

BSD's message was as cold and formal as he expected.

Eryx Thorne,

We formally request a status update on the bounty job you accepted. We have also reached out to your Guild handlers for formality's sake. We ask that you meet us in person within 24 hours of receiving this message.

– Darna Kent, BSD Executive of Internal Affairs

"Twenty-four hours?" Ryx muttered. Dread churned in his gut.

That's not protocol. That's pressure.

He toggled to the Guild terminal and filed his mission report. Every keystroke felt like dragging a blade across his nerves. He had to breathe evenly, focus on the rhythm, enter, tab, and describe. He kept it clinical. Who he met. Where he tracked Kolen. The plan to apprehend alive. The confrontation. The self-defense kill. (That part required an additional form.)

He described the attack by unknown mercenaries, non-descript black armor, no insignias, military precision. He mentioned the bazooka-wielding assailant on the street, the narrow escape, the damage to local infrastructure. Filed a claim for that kill, attaching the coordinate log and timestamp as evidence.

But everything about the warehouse? Fabricated. He said he slipped out during the chaos, left through a back access tunnel when the mercs turned on each other in confusion. No visuals, no confirmation of casualties. Didn't see what happened inside. No mention of the gauntlet. No mention of the blue light. No mention of throwing a man through metal crates like he weighed nothing. No mention of power that scared him as much as it saved him.

Let them think someone else cleaned up. He submitted the report and waited.

The system flagged an error.

No bodies reported during report time frame on Tarrin Station. File report anyway?

Ryx's blood went cold. *They cleaned the scene. Covered everything. This is a test.* If he withdrew his claim, BSD would know he was scared. They would know he knew. If he submitted, he risked exposure.

He submitted.

Better to look like an honest idiot than a loose thread.

The confirmation came through.

He flipped back to BSD's message and replied:

Understood.

Here is the report confirmation I have submitted to the Guild. I will make my way back to Black Sable Dynamics HQ by tomorrow afternoon.

Look forward to meeting with you again.

– Eryx Thorne

He hit send.

And nearly vomited.

This was spiraling. His guts told him BSD wanted more than answers. They wanted silence. They wanted control.

The Guild knows. Tess and Kaelen know. BSD killing me now would raise too many flags. But intimidation? Blackmail? Discrediting me? All still on the table.

He closed the console. He'd have to leave tonight. Book a ride to Delva Minor and be at BSD's tower by afternoon.

"Dinner's going to be fun," he muttered, pushing up from the chair and heading for the garage.

Ryx found Tess and Kaelen in the machine shop, huddled over a blueprint they had made of the Wraithburn after her last major upgrade. The smell of soldered alloy and starship grease clung to the air.

"Hey, you two starship nerds hungry? Dinner should be here soon."

Both of them turned and, in perfect mirrored unison, gave him the bird.

Ryx doubled over with laughter, the moment of levity cutting through the haze of dread like a clean blade.

A few minutes later, the Rhoens were getting cleaned up for dinner, and Ryx busied himself organizing the recent deliveries in the front room. No sign of dinner yet. He stacked the crates in orderly rows near the front desk of the garage, every click of metal on metal oddly comforting in the silence.

Tess emerged from her room wearing clean clothes, a towel wrapped around her damp hair.

"Hey Tess, can I ask you a favor?"

She eyed him warily. "Need a new gadget?" There was excitement in her voice, like she was halfway hoping he'd say yes.

Ryx chuckled. "No, you're not gonna like this favor. Not at all." Her smile faded. "You're leaving."

Ryx smirked over his shoulder. "Your dad ever tell you you're too damn smart?" Tess struck a pose like royalty. "He doesn't need to." Ryx grinned, but it quickly faded. "I've got to meet the client on Delva Minor tomorrow afternoon. Booking a shuttle tonight."

Tess's face fell, replaced with concern. "Can't you wait until we're done with the Wraith? Or at least until you get your gear back?" Ryx shook his head grimly. "What's that gonna do? You expect me to fight a whole mega Corp with just my armor and a ship? It won't mean squat once I'm inside a BSD tower surrounded by corpo thugs."

Tess exhaled, defeated. "I just want you to be safer. Anything helps. I don't like this, Ryx, and neither does Dad."

"He told me. I know. I hate it too. But dodging this makes it worse. You know that."

She nodded reluctantly. "Can your bots move these crates into the Wraith for me tonight? I don't think I'll have time after dinner."

Tess nodded and blinked rapidly, as if forcing herself not to cry. "Thanks, sis." Ryx gave her a rare hug, and she stiffened in surprise before squeezing him tightly back.

Together, they returned to the kitchen to find Kaelen brewing iced tea in a clear pitcher.

"I hope whatever you ordered goes well with Drellberry tea," Kaelen muttered. Tess sat down just as the front door chime rang.

"I ordered from our favorite spot," Ryx said, retrieving the food from the delivery bot at the front door.

The moment he returned with the containers, the smell filled the small space, savory broth, sizzling spice, steamed dumplings. Tess inhaled deeply.

"YES. I haven't had takeout in weeks."

Ryx handed her a rounded container and the dumplings. She took both like precious cargo.

Kaelen received his box with a grunt of appreciation, and Ryx sat beside Tess, setting his own box on the table.

She noticed the flowing "S" drawn on the lid of Ryx's container.

"Oooo," she teased, elbowing him. "Someone gave your box extra special attention, little bro."

Ryx rolled his eyes but smiled as he opened the box. His mouth instantly watered.

They ate in peace for a few minutes, savoring the food and shared silence. The kind only real family could manage. For Ryx, the warmth of the meal and the easy rhythm of clinking utensils felt like a fragile dream, a moment stolen from the chaos that waited for him just beyond the walls of the garage. He watched Kaelen chew with focus, and Tess dunk her dumpling with ritualistic precision, and part of him wanted to bottle this stillness, take it with him. Even the aroma of the soup felt grounding, nostalgic.

Eventually, the conversation picked back up, first Ryx asked about repairs on the Wraithburn, with Kaelen animatedly describing a new thermal coupler setup Tess was experimenting with. Ryx nodded along, inserting a few questions here and there, grateful for the reprieve. But soon, inevitably, the subject shifted, like a gravity well pulling their words inward, to Ryx's imminent departure.

"I don't like this, Eryx," Kaelen said, his tone edged with tension.

"None of us do, Pops. But I filed the report with the Guild. They know about the meeting. That buys me at least a sliver of protection."

Kaelen grunted. "Better than nothing. But you can't buy safety from a corp like Black Sable."

Ryx shrugged, forcing himself to keep calm.

The table fell quiet. Heavy.

"I should go," Ryx said finally, standing and gathering the used containers. Tess joined him in the kitchen to help clean, then pulled him into a tight hug.

"Be safe," she whispered.

He nodded, not trusting his voice, and stepped into the entryway. Kaelen followed.

"Do me a favor," the old man said, voice gruff with buried emotion.

Ryx turned. "Yeah?"

"After you get back, no more direct mega Corp jobs."

The words settled like a balm over Ryx's nerves. The confidence that Ryx would be back in a few days like any other job. Kaelen smiled, the rare, genuine kind that made Ryx feel like the young teen Kaelen had taken in again.

"Also," Kaelen added, squaring his shoulders, "when I get the Wraith fixed again... I get to fly her."

The words confused him for a second. Ryx blinked. Then, slowly, a grin spread across his face.

"You got it, old man."

Ryx's grin deepened as he took in Kaelen's words. For as long as he could remember, Kaelen had poured his soul into the

Wraithburn, upgrading her, tuning every system, repairing damage like a surgeon stitching up a patient. The ship wasn't just a vessel; it was family. And Kaelen, despite all his love for the craft, had never once accepted Ryx's offer to fly her.

To hear him ask now, to ask meant everything. It was an unspoken trust, a dream Ryx thought Kaelen would always keep in the shadows of his quiet pride. The idea of Kaelen in the pilot's seat, hands on the controls of the ship they built together... it lit something warm and grateful in Ryx's chest.

"I'll even polish the seat for you," Ryx added, his voice thick with fondness.

They gripped each other's forearms tightly, a shared promise in their eyes.

Then Kaelen pulled him into a tight, powerful embrace. "See you soon, kid."

And just like that, Ryx was gone.

ΔΔΔ

Two hours later Ryx was on a passenger shuttle staring into a screen that projected them traversing through space. It wasn't real, of course, the vessel was mid-jump, and real space would look like little more than an unbroken blur if he could actually see it. Still, he stared at the simulation, eyes unfocused.

He had credits left after restocking. Plenty enough to book the first outbound shuttle off Vorrthani Station. Delva Minor was the second stop on the route, and he wouldn't arrive until sometime tomorrow morning. Until then, all he could do was sit and think.

And thinking was the problem. His thoughts spiraled, latching onto one paranoia after another. *I'm marching into my own execution,* he thought. *No armor. No ship. Just my Talon, a few credits, and whatever luck hasn't run out yet.*

Dwelling wasn't helping. He stood, pushing away from the seat with more force than necessary, and made his way toward the back of the shuttle. Communal bathrooms and shower stalls lined the corridor. He palmed a cred chip and slotted it into the terminal.

"I'm not gonna die stinking and in dirty clothes," he muttered grimly.

He stripped, setting his gun belt and credit chips carefully on the metal counter. His clothes went into the sonic washer. He stepped into the shower stall, hot water and steam cloaking him like a temporary armor.

Twenty minutes later, Ryx lay on his back on a lower bunk in the mostly empty common room. The hum of the jump drive pulsed in the walls. He stared at the ceiling, thoughts like razors behind his eyes.

He lifted his right hand, holding it over his face.

The bracelet caught the dim light. Silent. Dormant.

What do they want with you?

He didn't know if they were even looking for a bracelet. Maybe they still thought it was a box. Maybe they had no idea what it had become.

I'm betting everything on that.

The thought chilled him more than the shuttle's recycled air. If things went sideways, the artifact, this thing, was all he had. All that stood between him and a one-way trip to a corporate grave.

He didn't remember falling asleep. But the shuttle's announcement woke him like a gunshot.

"Now arriving at Delva Minor."

Ryx exited the shuttle into a towering, sterile business center, polished alloy and nanoglass towering stories above him. It was a place of suits and speed, of silence masquerading as power. He hated it on instinct.

He found a terminal to hail a hover car. Local time: just past ten in the morning. His meeting wasn't for two more hours.

But waiting?

Waiting was poison.

Daylight is just wasted starlight; Kaelen's voice echoed in his mind.

He took a breath, straightened his jacket, and summoned the car immediately.

ΔΔΔ

The hovercar sliced through the vertical layers of the megacity. Every building was a shimmering fortress of wealth, mirrored and gleaming, suffocatingly pristine. Ryx sat with his arms crossed, his fingers twitching against the fabric of his coat.

He trusted alleys and blaster scars more than this. Streets bled truth. Towers whispered lies.

Fifteen minutes later, he was stepping out onto a high landing pad one hundred stories above the ground, staring at the façade of Black Sable Dynamics Headquarters.

A mousy man in a pressed grey suit greeted him.

"G-good morning, Mr. Thorne, was it?" The man's voice trembled.

Ryx nodded and shook the offered hand. "Yeah."

"I'm Darna Kent's assistant. She said to bring you straight in."

"Lead the way."

The man practically scurried, and Ryx followed.

Every inch of the BSD office floor was extravagant. Not in a showy way, no gold, no marble. Just… exactness. Every plant pot the same black-silver alloy. Every desk a reflection of quiet power. Even the styluses were high-end alloy, probably costing more than a month's rent in the slums of Vorrthani.

They reached a desk just outside a familiar office.

The assistant pressed a button. "Ms. Kent, Eryx Thorne is here." No reply.

The office door hissed open.

Darna Kent stood there, every inch of her as taut and composed as Ryx remembered, a woman made of razor edges and sleepless nights. Her posture was perfect, her dark suit immaculate, and her expression unreadable.

"Follow me, Mr. Thorne." she said, already turning down a sterile white corridor.

Ryx followed in silence. The floor beneath him absorbed sound with corporate efficiency, the kind of place designed to make people forget they ever had a voice. They passed rows of identical doors, no labels, no noise, just the faint hum of machines behind seamless walls.

Eventually, she ushered him into a sleek, windowless conference room. The air was too cold. The lights were too bright. The ceiling too high. The room was engineered for one thing: psychological pressure. It reeked of synthetic polish and recycled air, like the inside of a coffin polished for display.

Ryx's eyes flicked around the room. Subtle surveillance nodes blinked softly in the corners of the ceiling, concealed behind matte plastic ridges, standard BSD overkill. The chairs were modern and unsympathetic. The table gleamed like the hull of a warship.

Darna gestured toward one of the chairs. "Please sit."

Ryx didn't. "Why are we here? Expecting company?"

She gave him a level, cold look, then moved to sit across the table, legs crossed, movements precise. "No. This is temporary."

She reached into her coat and placed a slim rectangular recorder onto the center of the table, matte black, embossed with the BSD insignia like a signature on a death warrant. No frills. No blinking lights. Just purpose.

She pressed a button. The recorder clicked softly, like a chambered round.

"Tell me about the job, Mr. Thorne. Your report was enlightening, but I can't help but feel something is missing."

Ryx arched a brow. He didn't move from where he stood. "My report is time-stamped and corroborated by local feeds. It's airtight."

Her fingers folded together in a deliberate clasp, but her shoulders betrayed her. They were tight, not from anxiety, but from restraint.

"Except for the part where our prototype disappeared." There it was.

She leaned in slightly, the lighting catching the faint shine in her eyes, not warmth, not humanity. A predator's focus. She wasn't here to interrogate him. She was here to evaluate him.

"Kolen Vess brought something into that warehouse. We confirmed it from surveillance footage. What happened to it?"

Ryx's heart thumped once, hard. They don't know about the bracelet. That was something. But how long would that last?

He schooled his expression. Locked his voice into neutral gear. "I was fighting for my life," he said evenly. "Your merc problem became my merc problem. Between dodging plasma fire and a street-level bazooka, I wasn't exactly logging inventory."

He finally stepped forward, slow and calm, and pulled the chair back to sit. Every movement a show of confidence he didn't entirely feel.

"I wasn't taking notes between volleys of blaster fire, Ms. Kent. If something slipped through the cracks, it was because I was too busy not dying."

She stared at him, unblinking.

"Am I being accused of theft?" Ryx asked, his voice growing sharper. "Do the feeds show me leaving with the prototype? Or are we just playing corporate charades?"

Darna's jaw tightened, just enough to tell him he'd scored a point.

"No," she admitted. "But I didn't take you for a coward, Mr. Thorne. You went in after a prototype. And you left without it."

There it was. The knife between the ribs, not suspicion, but disappointment. The kind that cut deeper.

"I'm not a coward," Ryx said flatly. "I'm a survivalist. It's why you hired me."

He leaned forward, voice lowering, fingers curled just tight enough on the edge of the table to betray the heat behind his words.

"I also went in after a friend. And I left without him too." A long pause.

"Anything else became irrelevant the moment your security was compromised. The second those mercs hit the station, it became a war zone. You want neat closure? Next time send an army."

Darna stood abruptly. She didn't raise her voice. Didn't show anger. But her movements were sharper now, clipped, her mouth a thin blade.

She picked up the recorder and clicked it off.

"If you'll follow me back to my office," she said crisply, "we'll make the contract voiding official." Ryx blinked once.

She's letting me walk?

He gave her a long, considering look, then slowly stood. "Then let's finalize the paperwork."

He didn't trust it, not for a second.

But if BSD was letting him go, it was either because they believed him...

Or because they'd already decided how they were going to keep him quiet.

Ryx stood outside the office door, pulse quickening. The walls around him were too pristine, the air too still. The mousy assistant had long since retreated behind his terminal, pretending not to eavesdrop. Every second of silence made Ryx's nerves buzz like a live wire.

Darna Kent's door stood open. She'd left it like a silent summons. He stepped through the threshold, and every instinct in his body screamed.

There, in front of the window, framed by the towering skyline of Delva Minor, stood a tall, broad-shouldered man. His dark green military uniform was pressed with surgical precision, each crease sharp enough to cut. The silver "X" insignia gleamed on his chest, unmistakable, undeniable.

Ryx didn't just recognize the uniform.

He recognized the man.

He felt his breath hitch in his chest. His limbs tensed as if expecting a blow. A storm of old memories surged forward, training camps, firelit battles, betrayal sewn into every command barked from that voice.

"General Kennedy Rendyll," Ryx said flatly, voice colder than steel.

The man turned with glacial calm. His goatee was meticulously trimmed. His eyes were the color of storm-lit oceans. And his expression was unreadable.

"Admiral," the man corrected with clipped authority.

Ryx didn't move. Didn't blink. His heart was pounding now, echoing behind his ribs like a war drum.

"What's Varrix Prime's Military doing here?" Ryx asked, his voice laced with sarcasm and defiance. "Last I checked, Delva Minor isn't under your jurisdiction."

A faint smile tugged at the corners of Rendyll's mouth. "Delva Minor's council informed us they were in possession of a missing asset. They invited us to retrieve it."

That was it. The illusion of safety shattered.

They had covered bases Eryx Thorne didnt even think of. This is what dealing with a mega corp was.

Ryx's throat went dry. Every exit in the office felt miles away. A hundred floors up, no armor, no escape plan. He was standing on a glass stage above a pit full of knives.

His fingers curled slightly at his sides, itching toward his hip, toward his bracelet, toward any escape, but he didn't move.

Not yet. He had no escape, even with the bracelet there was no fighting this scenario had never get off the planet alive if he tried.

CHAPTER 6
GHOSTS AT EVERY TURN

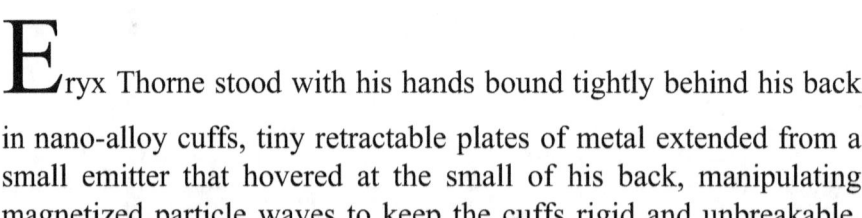

Eryx Thorne stood with his hands bound tightly behind his back in nano-alloy cuffs, tiny retractable plates of metal extended from a small emitter that hovered at the small of his back, manipulating magnetized particle waves to keep the cuffs rigid and unbreakable. He'd studied them in another life. Back when he was the one snapping them on smugglers and defectors.

Now he wore them.

He stood in the brig of a juggernaut-class destroyer, the largest in the Varrix Prime Military's armada. The Empyreon. A vessel that felt like home. Once.

He had received orders on her bridge. Debriefed in her war rooms. Launched more missions than he could count from her cavernous bay, the Wraithburn roaring beneath his boots. Now he stood at the opposite end of that history. A ghost in the bones of his own past.

Ryx stared straight ahead as the brig warden, a square-jawed officer with gray at the temples and no interest in pleasantries, cataloged his belongings.

"These items will be returned to you should you ever be granted your freedom by the glorious Varrix Prime Military," the man droned, reciting the line with the cadence of someone who'd said it too many times.

Ryx didn't recognize him. But that didn't mean much. Nine years gone was a full career for some. And to this man, Ryx was just another file in a system. A traitor with a serial number.

"Your possessions as listed are: 714 U-credits in various chip quantities. Clothes, pants, shirt, socks, underwear, boots, and jacket. One nano-leather belt and holster. One TalonX-5 charge pistol. Can you confirm, prisoner?"

The warden looked up from his datapad with a flat expression.

"Yes," Ryx said flatly.

The man tapped the screen again. "And the gold band embedded in your wrist is?"

The question hung in the air like a live wire.

When Ryx had first been taken into custody back on Delva Minor, he'd feared they would try to remove the bracelet. That it would lash out or expose itself. But it hadn't. Reacting to his panic, it had seamlessly fused tighter against his wrist, taking on the appearance of an implant rather than adornment.

Fancy. Subtle. Dangerous.

"Biotic wrist implant," Ryx said, without hesitation.

The warden didn't press him. Just logged it.

"Which cell am I in?" Ryx asked, eager to end the exchange.

The warden smiled, not kindly. "You don't need to worry about a cell. You're going to see the Admiral for your court martial."

Ryx stiffened. "What? Already? How?"

"Already?" the warden sneered. "It's been nine years in the making, traitor. The Admiral can sentence you himself."

He leaned in over the desk, voice dropping to a conspiratorial murmur. "Between you and me? I think he's been waiting for this."

He straightened with a cackle. Two armed guards stepped forward and roughly spun Ryx around, shoving him toward the elevator.

He didn't resist.

What would be the point? He was unarmed, unarmored, and cuffed.

The bracelet might give him an edge, but not enough to take over a juggernaut-class warship with a complement of nearly two thousand. Some of them had the same training he did. Some had more.

Still, a part of him fantasized about snapping the cuffs, lunging across the table, and ending Admiral Kennedy Rendyll with one strike. He could feel the image burning in his mind, vindication through violence.

Ryx clung to that image. Not as a plan, but as comfort. He wanted Rendyll to see his defiance. To remember the man who spat in the face of authority. The man he failed to break.

Patience, Ryx told himself, teeth clenched. If I'm sentenced to death, I'll resist. If they lock me away, I'll find a way out.

He'd escaped worse.

He just had to survive.

The elevator ride was silent and suffocating. The two guards flanking him didn't speak, didn't twitch, didn't even breathe too loudly. Professionals. Probably special forces.

"You guys, uh… come here often?" Ryx quipped, breaking the tension. Or trying to.

A quiet huff from his left. A smirk? Maybe.

Then, CRACK.

A rifle stock slammed into his ribs from the right. The pain shot through him like liquid fire.

"Mouth closed, prisoner," came the cold reply.

Ryx coughed, biting back a groan. "Got it."

"I said,"

The same guard raised his rifle for another blow.

Ryx didn't wait.

Still doubled over, he pivoted on instinct, planting his heel into the underside of the gunstock. The weapon cracked upward, smashing into the guard's face with a wet crunch.

The man howled.

Momentum carried Ryx into a roll, bound hands giving him just enough leverage. He flipped his feet beneath him and pushed off the floor, delivering a brutal kick to the second guard's sternum. Ribs cracked. The man staggered backward, slamming into the elevator wall.

Ryx got to his feet and spun back to the first guard, now clutching his broken nose. A snap kick to the knee dropped him like a stone. Another kick to the temple silenced him. He turned, just as the other guard regained his footing. And delivered a similar blow. The elevator dinged. Ryx stepped smoothly through the doors.

Into a war room.

Six rifles raised, laser sights painting his chest, face, legs. At the head of the table stood Kennedy Rendyll. Unmoved. Hands clasped behind his back. Eyes like frozen steel. Ryx didn't break stride. Didn't flinch. Instead, he met the Admiral's gaze.

This was the moment.

All the years. All the rage. All the humiliation. He didn't just want to insult the man; he wanted to brand his disdain into Rendyll's mind.

"Sorry I'm late, General. Decided to see how far you've pushed the infantry's training since I left. Gotta say,"

He smirked. Shrugged. Let the mockery drip from every syllable.

"Not impressed."

He savored the flash of irritation that crossed Rendyll's face. Like oxygen to a flame. If all Ryx had left was pain, then let him aim it at the man who made him.

WHAM.

The rifle butt took him across the face. He dropped to the floor, blood pooling in his mouth.

Then they were on him. Six rifles, six sets of fists, six sets of boots.

They didn't stop when he curled. They didn't stop when he bled. They didn't stop until Rendyll raised a hand.

"Enough."

Ryx was dragged upright and shoved into a chair. His body screamed. Something in his side was broken. His fingers wouldn't move. One eye was already swollen shut.

He spat blood onto the floor, aiming for the boot of the nearest soldier.

"There it is," he rasped. "The fighting prowess of the Varrix Prime Military."

He grinned, blood-slicked teeth bared.

"Always six-on-one. Always punching down."

Across the table, Kennedy Rendyll finally sat.

"Eryx Thorne, you have been brought before me, your former commanding officer and Admiral of the Varrix Prime Fleet, to answer for your crimes of desertion."

Ryx straightened, mock solemn.

"I plead not guilty, Your Honor. I just got hungry during that last mission and left to grab everyone some synth-meat pizza. You know how long that takes? Nine years, apparently. But hey, good things come to those who wait." He knew it would earn him another hit. He wanted it to.

A fist cracked against his cheek. Ryx rolled with the punch, using the momentum to rise. He flipped forward in an awkward summersault, catching the soldier with a downward kick to the head. The man crumpled across the table as Ryx landed awkwardly on his own chair, knocking the wind out of himself.

"ENOUGH!" Rendyll bellowed.

The soldiers froze. Eryx let out a pained moan trying to catch his breath. Rendyll stepped forward, towering over Ryx. "Eryx Thorne, I find you guilty of treason and desertion."

Ryx couldn't see his expression, but he could hear the smile in his voice. "So, what's the play, Admiral? You shoot me yourself, or are we going old school with a firing squad?" To Ryx's dismay, Rendyll chuckled. "Oh no. You're not dying yet. First, I'm going to find out who you told about Eleos V. And then,"

His voice dropped to a lethal whisper. "I'm sending you to Varrix Delta." Ryx's heart stopped.

Varrix Delta. A mining colony moon turned prison camp. Isolated. Inescapable. Reserved for political dissidents and buried secrets.

He'd had no plan for this. No contacts. No ship. No way out. And yet, there was something strange about it. Delta wasn't the worst. There were darker places. More violent cells. Why send him there? Why not kill him?

Rendyll leaned closer. "Take him to a cell. Isolate him. I'll be visiting personally." Salutes cracked like gunshots. Ryx felt rough hands under his arms again. He didn't resist.

He let them drag him toward whatever waited next.

But inside, something stirred.

Not dead yet.

Several minutes later, Ryx was shoved roughly into the last cell at the back of the brig. A panel hissed above, and a sheet of transparent nano-glass slid down from the ceiling, sealing him in.

"Place your cuffs into the wall by your bunk, prisoner," said a static laced voice over the intercom.

Ryx noticed a small indentation near the bed, just large enough to accommodate the emitter unit. He backed toward it and felt the cuffs deactivate and pull away, the emitter snapping magnetically into the wall.

He brought his hands forward, rubbing his wrists. They ached, red and tender from the hours of tension. Funny, after everything, his wrists might've been the only part of him not wrecked. The bruises, broken ribs, and swelling across his face reminded him how brutal a uniform could be when worn by the wrong men.

He took stock of the cell. Standard Varrix military. Blank white panel walls. A light overhead behind yet another sheet of nano-glass. A toilet, a sink, and a narrow bunk that looked about as forgiving as a slab of alloy.

"How do I order room service?" Ryx called, his voice hoarse but defiant. "What if I get lonely and need another beating?" No answer.

He smirked bitterly. These men were trained. Soon, every soldier on board would know about his scuffle, how he'd dropped three guards while cuffed. They wouldn't step in here unarmed. Not unless they really wanted a story to tell. Still, none of them knew about the bracelet.

He shifted on the bunk, glancing at his wrist. They think I'm just a defanged mutt. But I've still got fangs. Honestly, he probably didn't even need the bracelet to escape the cell. The thought made him smirk again, his arrogance was a comfort, even if it was masking something deeper.

But he knew the anger still stained his mind like blood on white fabric. He'd picked those fights. Invited the blows. And now, as the adrenaline bled out of him, so did his fire.

Cool off, he told himself. *Think. Survive.*

Escape would come later.

For now, he had to understand his sentence. Varrix Delta. He'd been there once, years ago, during a security drill. Prisoners rotated through mining shifts, some had comm access once a week, and those with "good behavior" could receive approved supply shipments from off-world. Even with a life sentence, there were worse assignments. And if Rendyll had it his way, Ryx expected something much worse.

Which made the whole thing feel... off.

Why send him to Delta?

Why keep him alive?

He leaned back against the cold wall, mind racing through every half-baked escape plan he could concoct, every smuggler contact, every theoretical prison-break scenario he'd once laughed about in mess halls. But his thoughts always circled back to a single, gnawing question: *Why?*

Time passed in silence. No food. No voices. Just the hum of recycled air and the ache in his bones. The waiting was the game. He knew it. Wear him down. Make him desperate. Break the spirit first, then the body. They might not have even left the system yet. He slept. Paced. Waited.

Then, suddenly, the lights cut. Darkness swallowed the cell. Ryx immediately pressed his back to the wall, instinct snapping into place like muscle memory. Defensive posture. Ready for anything.

A soft tsk-tsk-tsk crackled over the intercom.

"Look at my prized catch," Rendyll's voice slithered through the speaker, amused and cold. "Reduced to a cornered rat."

Ryx forced himself to breathe. To relax. He stepped forward, toward the center of the room, and stared at the glass barrier he couldn't see.

"I've been calling for room service for hours," he said. "Can I speak to the manager of this establishment?" The lights snapped back on, blinding. He shielded his eyes with one hand. Through the glare, he made out Rendyll's silhouette beyond the nano-glass.

"I don't remember you being such a smartass under my command," Rendyll said, amusement curling in his voice. "Probably because I kept that part locked up tight. Right until the last time we talked," Ryx shot back.

A pause. Then the Admiral's voice dropped, harder. "I remember. That scar across your cheek, I remember it well." And just like that, the memories hit. Eleos V. His last mission. His betrayal. His survival.

He remembered bursting into the command bay, hurling accusations at Rendyll, genocide, betrayal, war crimes against their own men. Rendyll had drawn first. Ryx barely dodged the shot, It would mark his face forever, diving for cover and returning fire, catching the bastard in the leg. The firefight had been short, brutal, and hopeless.

Ryx had fled. Scrambled for his ship, took off under fire. Shields failing, comms fried, engines screaming. He'd punched the jump at the last second, just as the destroyer's main gun fired.

He escaped by seconds.

He'd drifted in space for days. Systems fried. No nav. No food. No air support. Barely breathing. At one point, delirious and starving, he'd stared at his pistol for hours. A morbid stain on his consciousness.

He didn't remember passing out. He remembered waking.

Kaelen Rhoen's gruff voice was the first thing he'd heard. That old bastard pulling him from the edge like he'd done a hundred times afterward. Fixing what was broken. Giving Ryx something to live for again.

The memory passed like a storm. And Rendyll's voice dragged him back. "And that implant on your wrist... was that my doing as well?" He sounded pleased. Like Ryx's pain was another medal on his chest.

"In a roundabout way, I guess so," Ryx said, glancing down at the bracelet with a wry smile. A flicker of confusion passed over Rendyll's face.

"Before I dump you into your life sentence of hard labor," he said slowly, "I need to know who you told about your last mission on Eleos V."

There it was.

Everything clicked.

He's scared, Ryx realized. Not just Rendyll, the whole damn military. They think I talked. That I have proof. I have mission files from Eleos V. This was his leverage. This was why they hadn't killed him outright. Ryx sat down, right in front of the glass, and stared directly at Rendyll.

"Have there been inquiries? Any system governments come knocking on your door lately?"

Rendyll narrowed his eyes. "No."

"I haven't told anyone, Admiral. I just wanted peace. I thought you wanted the same, that we had an unspoken deal. You leave me alone, I stay quiet."

Rendyll didn't respond, but Ryx could feel the danger coiling in the air. He raised a hand quickly. "But I do have contingencies." The Admiral's jaw clenched. "What kind of contingencies?" he demanded.

Ryx stood again and leaned against the glass, putting their faces inches apart. "You think I'd risk getting caught without leverage? Without a safety net?" The lie rolled easily off his tongue.

Rendyll growled. "What triggers it?"

"My death. Or a little too much silence from my end." He was bluffing. Hard. The files on the Wraithburn were damning, sure, but they weren't rigged to send anywhere. It was just a locked safe. But Rendyll didn't know that.

The Admiral's voice dropped to a lethal growl. "What do you want?" Ryx grinned. If his eye wasn't swollen shut, he would've winked.

"I want to be left alone. Let me go, and you'll never hear from me, or any information I may have, again."

Rendyll slammed a fist into the glass, hard enough that Ryx nearly flinched.

"You're a traitor and a disgrace. I will not let you go." Ryx shrugged, already walking back to the bunk.

"Take it up with your superiors back on Varrix Prime. I'm sure they'll help you come to the right conclusion."

He flopped down, hands behind his head, every inch of him aching. "All I've got is time, Admiral. How much do you have?" solidifying his advantage.

He didn't look back as the intercom clicked off and Rendyll stormed away. But he smiled. Because now, the game had changed.

Ryx tried to force himself to sleep, but his hunger gnawed at him like a parasite as he lay sprawled across the hard bunk. Every few hours, or what felt like hours, the guards flipped the lights on or off without warning.

*Still trying to wear me dow*n. He thought, pressing the back of his hand to his eyes. It was working, in a way. The silence. The hunger. The void of time. But he was used to breaking. That was the difference.

He was just on the edge of drifting when the ship's intercom crackled to life. Even muffled through the brig's soundproofing, the alert tone was unmistakable, they were entering warp.

Ryx sat up fast, adrenaline chasing away fatigue. Something's changed. They'd made a call.

Either they were going to dump him onto Varrix Delta and be done with him… or they had a bargain in mind.

He waited. No sign of Rendyll. No announcements. Just more silence, more stillness, more time.

He pressed his back to the cold wall and stared at the glass, unblinking. Hours passed. The lights no longer flickered. *That's a shift,* he thought. Something in the rhythm had broken.

Movement outside the glass caught his attention.

He stood, expecting to see the hulking silhouette of Admiral Rendyll. But it wasn't him.

A smaller figure stepped forward. The nano-glass cleared, revealing a woman with sharp blonde hair, cold eyes, and the uniform of a high-ranking officer. A tray of synth rations sat in her hands.

Major, Ryx guessed. *Maybe higher.*

She didn't smile. But her voice over the intercom was even. "Please back away from the doorway, Mr. Thorne. I will open the through port and slide in your meal."

He did as he was told, stomach growling loud enough to echo off the walls.

She keyed a panel. A small hatch near the floor opened with a faint hiss. The tray slid through. Ryx waited, barely, until the port sealed again before diving for the food like a starving animal. He didn't care what it was. Flavorless paste. Protein bricks. He'd have eaten gravel if it had calories.

He choked on the first bite and staggered to the sink, slamming the waterspout with his palm. He drank like a dying man, then returned to his meal and finished it slowly, carefully, savoring every bland, nutrient-packed mouthful.

Only when it was gone did he notice the Major was still there, watching.

He wiped his mouth with the back of his hand, then stretched out on the cold floor, letting the relief wash through him.

Not full. But not starving. That was a win.

Eventually, he stood and washed his face as best he could. "Please pass the tray back through, Mr. Thorne," she said again. "Then step back so I may retrieve it." He complied. A moment later, a guard appeared, took the tray, and vanished down the hall.

She remained.

"I am Major Gable," she said finally. "My superiors have instructed me to negotiate with you regarding your incarceration." So that was it. A negotiator. The real game had begun.

Ryx folded his arms, voice sharp. "I want my freedom."

Major Gable didn't flinch. "Your desertion cannot go unpunished, Mr. Thorne. But I can offer you terms."

Ryx exhaled slowly. "Alright. Let's hear the pitch."

"You serve five years on Varrix Delta instead of life," she said. "In return, you surrender all copies of the data you've been holding and permit full system scrubbing."

He laughed, loud and bitter. "You want all my leverage so you can space me once you've wiped the evidence? Yeah, no thanks."

He stepped forward, locking eyes with her. "Those files go out to every contact I've ever made if I miss a single weekly check-in. You're already pushing it, by the way."

She looked at him carefully now. Not with scorn, more like calculation.

"You must serve time," she said. "We cannot establish the precedent that traitors can simply negotiate their freedom."

"The precedent you're worried about," Ryx said calmly, "is the one where your little empire cracks in half when the truth gets out." She bristled.

"Six months," he said, "weekly comms access. And I want better food."

"Two years. One comm check a week. Standard meals."

"One year," Ryx said, pressing harder, "weekly access. No wipe. You leave me the hell alone after. I walk."

She stared at him, jaw clenched. Then turned away, pulled out a secured transponder, and started a rapid, heated exchange with someone on the other end. Her posture said everything, this wasn't easy. She was arguing. Hard.

Finally, she returned to the glass.

"Fine," she said curtly. "One year. Weekly access. Your record will be sealed after. But no special meals."

Ryx smirked. "Deal."

"One more thing," she said coldly. "If those files ever leak, if anything from your stash surfaces, we will bring the full force of the Varrix Prime Military down on your head. And on anyone you've ever known."

Ryx gave her a wide, insufferable grin. "You have my honor as a soldier."

She scowled. "I should space you right now, you arrogant,"

"Knock it off," he cut in. "I stayed quiet for nine years because I just wanted peace. Now I have confirmation that I'll get it. One year's a small price to pay." She said nothing.

"Oh, and Major?" he added. "I'll need terminal access before we hit Varrix Delta. Would hate for your little window to close." Her jaw ticked. "You'll get a mobile unit in a few minutes." He nodded.

"Do you even know what's on those files?" he asked her softly. She didn't respond. "You don't. But if you did…" He met her eyes. "You wouldn't think so poorly of me." She turned and walked away.

Ryx leaned back against the wall, breathing a little easier. *One year,* he thought again.

Then I vanish. For good.

CHAPTER 7

THE LINE

Several minutes later, the sound of armored boots echoed down the corridor. Ryx looked up to see three soldiers approaching his cell, fully armored, visors down, weapons in hand. Two were distinctly human in shape and size. The third was not.

Vlexari, Ryx thought immediately.

Massive. Towering. The Vlexari were a rare but unmistakable sight in the Varrix Prime ranks. Their thick, scaled skin shimmered like polished gemstones, often in vivid tones of green, crimson, or deep cobalt. Their heads were broad and flat like a bull's, with no horns but wide, plate-like cheek ridges. Beneath the translucent scales on their faces, their eyes burned with a bioluminescent yellow glow that seemed to pierce straight through darkness, and people.

Ryx had seen enough of their kind in combat to know what they were capable of. The way the third soldier's armor bulged in unnatural places confirmed his suspicion, this one was Vlexari.

They weren't taking any chances.

Each soldier carried a compact but brutal flechette shotgun. Ryx knew the type: short-barreled, heavy-duty, and designed to fire laser-charged shards of razor-sharp metal. The kind of weapon that turned armor, and bone, into shredded pulp.

They expect me to try something, Ryx thought. *Good. That means they're still scared.*

A deep, guttural voice came over the cell intercom, gravel laced with mechanical distortion. "Move against the far wall, prisoner."

Ryx complied without hesitation, backing up with slow, deliberate steps. He raised his hands slightly, not in surrender, just enough to show he wasn't going to be stupid. Yet.

The nano-glass panel hissed as it slid open. All three soldiers entered with practiced precision. The Vlexari stayed near the door, weapon leveled, its glowing eyes never leaving Ryx. The other two fanned out, one covering his flank, the other stepping forward with a folded mobile comm terminal in hand. It looked like a thin black square until unfolded, when it would bloom into a touch-sensitive screen the size of a small tablet.

Smart formation, Ryx noted silently. *Tight. Minimal angles of exposure. Trained well.*

The lead soldier stepped close enough to hand the terminal through, but his other hand never wavered, shotgun aimed directly at Ryx's heart. His voice crackled through the speaker embedded in his helmet.

"You have ten minutes, prisoner. All communications will be monitored." Ryx smiled. He took the terminal with a casual confidence, unfolded it, and sat down on his bunk.

"No problem, soldier." Ryx said coolly, his voice like ice beneath a torch. The young ensign barely met his eyes as he handed over the compact mobile terminal. The thing was standard-issue, rugged frame, outdated security protocols, and just enough functionality to let a prisoner think he had options. Ryx almost smirked. They think this is a leash. They're handing me a blade.

He waited until the guard had backed out of view, the soft hiss of the nano-glass sealing his cell again with a faint electric whine.

Ryx exhaled slowly. The pain in his body hadn't dulled, ribs still ached, his face felt like someone had stapled it back together blind, but the ache was distant now. Focus.

He sat down on the edge of his bunk and powered on the terminal.

Ryx wasn't a master slicer by any means, he'd worked with experts who could ghost their way into systems mid-warp without tripping a single flag. But Special Ops training had drilled him in message encryption, channel obfuscation, packet bouncing. Tools for getting a distress call out from deep behind enemy lines. Tools to reach allies when no one else could. Tools designed for when you were already as good as dead.

This was one of those times.

They're still bullshitting me at every turn. he thought grimly as the bootup finished. He could practically see Kennedy Rendyll's face, eyes flaring, jaw clenched, when he found out his "ghost traitor" wasn't being buried in a prison mine for the rest of his life. No, Ryx already had a terminal in hand. Already had the chance to reach out.

He opened the comms suite and toggled past the UI. Then, with practiced ease, he held down a combination of keys, thumb, index, pinky, two knuckles. Four fingers, four seconds. The screen flickered.

A buried subroutine activated with a soft beep. Lines of backend code slid into view. This model of terminal was outdated enough that Varrix Prime probably thought no one remembered its vulnerabilities.

But Ryx remembered everything.

Let's see if you're still out there, he thought, scanning the input fields.

He didn't have many options. Messages needed to be short, untraceable, and cryptographically impossible to brute force. He knew they'd get his message.

To: Star/Ship Subject:

Message:

My past finally caught up with me.

I've made a deal. I'll be gone a while, but I'm okay.

DO NOT RESPOND TO THIS MESSAGE.

You'll hear from me again soon.

The message was for Tess and Kaelen. They'd understand the tone, short, careful, measured. It would tell them more than he could safely write.

Hopefully, a year was enough time for Tess to not kill him on sight when he got back. Ryx leaned back, the smallest hint of a smile creeping in. *I'm getting out of this. One way or another.*

Ryx stood, took a few slow steps forward, and carefully set the terminal on the floor before backing away. He knew the drill. These three soldiers could kill him without hesitation and would if ordered. Caution meant survival. That unspoken mantra was the core of Varrix Prime Military life, and Ryx hadn't forgotten it.

The lead soldier stepped forward and retrieved the terminal, flipping it open to scan its contents. The other two kept their weapons trained on Ryx, one of them motioning silently for him to return to his bunk.

Ryx sat casually, elbows on his knees, his face unreadable. "Where's your message?" the helmeted voice asked flatly. Ryx shrugged. "In another system by now. I'm not stupid enough to leave a trail, soldier."

The corporal holding the data pad stiffened, then suddenly lurched forward, an aggressive movement that made the air in the room shift. He didn't make it far.

"Corporal," barked the Vlexari from the doorway, his deep, gravel lined voice cutting through the room like a blade.

The soldier froze mid-step. Ryx smirked, catching his reaction from the corner of his eye. "Major Gable expected this," the Vlexari rumbled. "This one's ex–VPM Elite Scout Regiment."

The lead man hesitated, eyes flicking from the pad to Ryx. "Your friends in med bay?" added the soldier in the center, almost impressed. "They got put there while this guy's hands were cuffed."

Ryx made a mock kiss toward him. Deliberate. Taunting. He was baiting them, needling at their pride, pushing boundaries for the sake of leverage.

The corporal lunged again, angrier this time, but the other soldier caught him, throwing a firm arm across his chest. "Stand down, corporal. He's baiting you. The Major'll toss your ass in the next cell over if you pick a fight with this maggot."

Ryx leaned back on his cot and waved lazily, his voice saturated with sarcasm. "If you boys don't mind, it's my nap time. I'll call if I need anything."

From the doorway, the Vlexari let out a low, guttural growl. "Move out. Any longer in here, and I'll make a decision I regret." They left. Silence reclaimed the cell.

Ryx let out a long breath and slouched into the mattress. He closed his eyes, but rest didn't come easy. His mind was still too alert, too calculating.

Hours passed, he couldn't tell how many. But when the voice came over the intercom, it yanked him violently from sleep.

"Prisoner. Move to the back wall and place your hands behind your back."

Ryx blinked, disoriented. It took him a full minute to remember where he was and why his heart had jumped into his throat.

He rubbed his face, groaning softly, and glanced toward the nanoglass door. It had gone transparent again.

Eight soldiers stood waiting in formation outside. He took them in with a glance, different builds, different gear. The two in front carried the same nasty-looking flechette shotguns he'd seen earlier. Behind them stood two with extended neoplate batons. The rear four leveled standard-issue laser rifles directly at his chest.

"Shit. Am I being evicted?" Ryx muttered with a smirk. Not a single one of them reacted.

He stood slowly, cracking his neck as he turned to face the back wall. *We must be close to Varrix Delta,* he thought grimly.

"Prisoner, back toward the wall and place your palms under the restraining unit."

Ryx rolled his eyes at the rigid protocol but complied, pressing his hands to the familiar indent. The cuffs activated with a metallic click, magnetizing around his wrists. The emitter lifted from the wall and attached to the small of his back.

The first four soldiers moved in.

The shotgun-wielders flanked the door; barrels fixed on him. The baton carriers advanced quickly, roughly seizing him by both arms and dragging him from the cell.

"Geez, guys. You're acting like I'm some kind of dangerous war criminal with spec ops training or something." Ryx chuckled, letting himself be pulled forward. "Relax. I'm housebroken."

In the hallway, he spotted the Vlexari sergeant from the previous visit, impossible to miss. The massive figure stood like a boulder at the formation's head.

"Oh, hello again, sunshine," Ryx quipped, locking eyes with the behemoth.

He saw it coming.

But with two soldiers gripping him tightly, there was no dodging. The Vlexari's rifle came up fast, too fast. The butt of the gun slammed into the side of Ryx's skull.

And everything went black.

△△△

Ryx came to with the sharp scent of moist natural air hitting his senses like a wave. It was damp, earthy, real. Not the sterile, recycled air of the Empyreon.

Two sets of hands held him beneath the arms, dragging his limp body down a loading ramp. His boots scraped uselessly against the metal. He blinked a few times, trying to regain his bearings. Every throb in his skull reminded him of the Vlexari's rifle stock.

How long was I out?

109

He looked around groggily. Tropical forest surrounded the landing zone in thick patches, lush canopies pressing into jagged highlands in the distance. The air was humid, warm, and vaguely metallic. He was on Varrix Delta. No doubt about it.

The semi-fresh atmosphere did help with the throbbing headache.

I wonder how many concussions I've racked up this week, he thought grimly, trying to move his legs in rhythm with the soldiers dragging him.

They both tensed as he shifted his weight.

"Calm down, guys," Ryx muttered. "I just woke up. I can walk."

The soldier on his left gave a grunt but yanked him forward anyway. They marched toward a massive, rust-colored gate, topped with coils of razor wire and reinforced watchtowers. The labor camp.

He'd been here before, once. Not in chains.

The guards dragged him into the intake building and forced him to his knees in front of the reception counter. A clerk, unimpressed and bored, barely looked up.

The clerk was bald on top while the last vestiges of hair hung maticulously trimed around his head. The man had the look of a veteran, healed plasma burns on one cheek and a knowing look in his brown eyes as he scanned Ryx's beaten face.

"Prisoner transfer," one of the soldiers said, sliding over a datapad.

The clerk skimmed it, then stopped mid-scroll. "Eryx Thorne..." he muttered, letting out a low whistle. "This one's a doozy." He leaned forward to get a better look at Ryx's bloodied face. "You look like hell. How'd that happen?"

Ryx gave a crooked smile. "Slipped off my bunk."

The clerk chuckled, with genuine amusement. "Yeah, I can see it now. You've got a mouth on you." Ryx shrugged. "These fine gentlemen and their friends tried to remove it a few times on our scenic route here." The clerk laughed again. "I like you, kid. The other prisoners won't. But it's gonna be a hoot watching you try to survive."

One of the guards huffed impatiently. "Can we move this along? I'm eager to be rid of this space trash." "Just another few buttons, soldier," the clerk replied with a salute, not bothering to hide his sarcasm. "Then he's all ours." He tapped a few keys.

"Eryx Thorne. Charged with desertion. Listed as a Class 1 threat level…" The clerk raised a brow. "We don't get many of those." The guards stayed silent.

"Ex–Varrix Prime Elite Scout," the clerk added, whistling again. "No wonder." He glanced at the guards. "No possessions to document?" Ryx's stomach dropped. "No sir, he didn't have any," the left guard replied quickly. Panic surged through Ryx. He tried to stand but was immediately shoved back to his knees.

"What the fuck, what about my gun?" he growled.

The guard didn't even look at him. "All the paperwork's there. He was detained without possessions." *Kennedy Rendyll,* Ryx thought bitterly. *One last middle finger.*

He lunged again, fury and instinct driving him, only to take a baton straight to the gut. He collapsed, coughing, as pain exploded in his ribs.

"Must've been one hell of a gun," the clerk said, surprisingly sympathetic.

"Alright, gents. We've got the prisoner from here. Go ahead and release his cuffs, my boys'll take him to the Warden."

The guards hesitated.

"What, you think he's gonna pop those cuffs, take down all three of us, bolt out the front gate, hijack a ship, and escape into deep space?" The clerk looked amused.

Ryx let out a chuckle, still wheezing on the floor. "I've thought about it. But I'd rather serve my time and never think about Varrix Prime again."

The clerk gave a snort. "See? Nothing to fear. Let him up." One of the guards pulled out a small device, waved it over the emitter on Ryx's back, and the cuffs disengaged with a soft click. The metal plates slithered back into the unit.

Ryx stood, rolling his wrists and shoulders with a sigh. He turned to the guards. "Thanks, bellhops. Which one of you gets the tip?" Both men moved at once, batons raised.

But Ryx was faster.

In a blink, he ducked under the first guard's swing, grabbed the man's arm, and flipped him onto his back, disarming him midmotion. He twisted, pivoting into the second guard's path and swept his legs out from under him. Another fluid movement, and the baton was in Ryx's other hand.

By the time the guards hit the floor, the clerk had already drawn a sidearm and leveled it at Ryx's spine. Ryx pretended not to notice and casually tossed both batons back to the guards.

"Keep the change."

He looked over his shoulder, smirking. "Good to see you, Dell." The clerk, Dell, smirked right back. "Eryx Thorne. You haven't changed a bit, you smart-mouthed idiot." Dell kept the barrel pressed firmly to Ryx's back.

"What the hell are you doing here?" Ryx asked, glancing around. "How does an elite spec ops soldier end up a desk clerk in a backwater prison?"

"How does an elite spec ops soldier get sentenced to said backwater prison?" Dell shot back. Ryx laughed. "Oh, you shit in Kennedy Rendyll's cereal too?" He smirked. "Close enough. Let's move," Dell said. "I can only cut you so much slack. I still wear the uniform, dumbass."

Ryx raised his hands. "Yeah, yeah. Those two had it coming though, Dell. I won't cause you any more trouble. I meant what I said, I just want to serve my time and get out of this system for good."

Dell snorted. "Forgive me if I don't take your word for it. I've seen what you can do unarmed." Ryx smiled faintly as Dell gave him a gentle shove toward the back door. "Warden'll want to see you." Ryx nodded. "Figured."

As they passed into a long, dim hallway, he glanced back over his shoulder.

"But seriously… Dell Karn. Desk duty?"

Dell sighed. "You didn't corner the market on disobeying orders, you know. A lot of us told Rendyll where he could stick it."

Ryx chuckled, then winced as the motion pulled at his bruised ribs.

"What gun did they take?" Dell asked suddenly, more serious. "My Talon," Ryx said, voice hollow. Dell blinked. "That old piece of junk? Wasn't that your first sidearm? From basic?"

"Yep." Ryx said flatly. "You never upgraded?"

Ryx shrugged. "That old thing's saved my life more times than I can count. Only thing I've trusted since the Wraith." Dell cocked his head. "What the hell is the Wraith?" Ryx waved it off. "Never mind. I've lived a whole other life since I last saw you."

Dell chuckled. Ryx continued dreamily "Last time I saw you Dell Karn, you still had hair."

"And the last time I saw you Eryx Thorne, you were still funny," Dell shoved the barrel of the pistol a little harder into Ryx's back.

They stopped outside a reinforced door at the end of the hall. "Listen to me, Eryx," Dell said suddenly, his voice low and serious. "The Warden's a fair man. A little rigid, but he's why I serve here. He'll respect your record. Probably even cut you some slack." Ryx's brow furrowed. "What's the catch?"

"Respect goes a long way around here. But his favor won't win you any with the other inmates. You'll walk a fine line. Walk it right, and this place won't break you."

Ryx nodded, genuinely grateful. "How'll I know which side of the line I'm on?"

Dell smirked. "You used to be smart. You'll figure it out."

The Warden's office was dimly lit and spotless, not a thing out of place. The walls were bare, save for a mounted feather encased in glass above a minimalist bookshelf, strange, elegant, and a little ominous.

Ryx took in the room quickly before his gaze landed on the tall, thin man in uniform behind the desk. A tidy mustache sat perfectly groomed atop his upper lip. The Warden looked up, removing his glasses as he rose from his chair.

"Is this my new prisoner, Lieutenant?" he asked, voice sharp and precise. "Yes, Warden." Dell answered, stepping forward and offering a datapad with Ryx's file. "The sidearm, Lieutenant?" The Warden's brow arched.

"It was the only way I could convince the escort to release him. He's... apparently dangerous," Dell said, not quite meeting his gaze. The Warden shot him a knowing look, saw right through it, but didn't call him out.

He paced as he read through the file, then settled into his seat and motioned for Ryx to sit across from him. Dell took position by the door, posture straight, eyes forward.

"Eryx Thorne," the Warden said slowly, as if savoring the name. "I remember you, you know." Ryx nodded once.

"I was Warden here the last time you visited. Eleven years ago, give or take." He stroked his mustache. "You made quite the impression." "I remember, sir," Ryx replied evenly.

"Sir?" The Warden raised an amused eyebrow. "That's unexpected. These reports paint you as a wild dog who'd rather spit in my face than speak a civil word."

Ryx caught a flicker of amusement in the man's expression. A twitch at the corner of his mouth. "Those reports were written by people who earned those interactions, sir." That did it, the Warden allowed himself a smile. "Yes, I remember now. You were respectful even then. And your superiors said you were gifted beyond your years. I half expected to be hearing about your rise through the ranks until my retirement." Ryx gave a respectful nod. "Thank you, sir. Sorry to disappoint." No sarcasm. He'd slipped easily back into military rhythm, partly out of instinct, and partly because he remembered Warden Vance. Fair. Firm. A man who treated prisoners like people, even if he never stopped being a soldier.

"I'm not a fan of deserters, Thorne," Vance said, his tone suddenly colder. Ryx's heart ticked faster. "But" the Warden continued, relaxing slightly, "I'm not much of a fan of Kennedy Rendyll either. So, I'm not sure I can blame you."

He waved the thought away like smoke. Ryx stifled a snort. Vance caught it and smiled. "The work here is hard. Mining's no joke. And while some of your fellow inmates are political prisoners, others are… less agreeable. Some won't take kindly to having an ex–VPM soldier in their midst. Especially one with a rep."

Ryx met his eyes evenly. "I've survived worse, sir. You won't have trouble from me." Vance smiled again, wider this time. "Good. Work hard. Keep your nose clean. I can make your life here far more tolerable."

Then his eyes sharpened, voice dropping a register.

"But cause trouble, try to escape, or forget who's in charge, and I'll bury you so deep in the mines they'll need sonar to find your bones."

Ryx nodded without hesitation. "Understood, sir." "Good man." Vance turned to Dell. "Lieutenant Karn." "Yes, Warden," Dell snapped to attention.

"See Mr. Thorne properly outfitted and assigned. He begins work tomorrow."

Ryx stood as Dell gave a nod. "I'll check in on you soon, Eryx Thorne." The Warden said, a strange tone in his voice.

"Thank you, sir," Ryx said to the Warden, then followed Dell out.

Dell led Ryx through the compound in silence for a time. At the supply desk, Ryx received a deep blue prison jumpsuit and a pair of dark gray coveralls. "You'll wear the coveralls every morning on shift," Dell said casually, handing them over. Ryx nodded, accepting the bundle. The two men walked side by side, no cuffs, no tension.

Dell showed him the mess hall, the requisitions terminal he'd be allowed to use once a week, and through a viewport, the sprawling mine complex stretching into the distant ridge lines.

An hour later, they arrived at a single-occupant cell. Like the others, it had a nano-glass door, but Ryx's came with a writing desk and a reading chair in the corner. Ryx gave Dell a curious look. "The Warden likes you," Dell said with a shrug. Ryx smiled faintly and stepped inside.

"Here." Dell handed him a slim datapad. "Access to the prison library. Most inmates don't get this, so don't abuse it, dumbass." Dell said smirking. "No promises." Ryx chuckled.

Dell sealed the door. Over the intercom, his voice came through: "Alarm goes off thirty minutes before shift. Don't piss off the guards." Ryx flipped him off. Dell chuckled and walked away.

△△△

Ryx woke before the alarm the next morning. He tucked the datapad onto the shelf of his desk, dressed in the coveralls, and sat on the edge of his cot waiting.

The guard who arrived held a riot gun lazily and looked bored out of his mind. "Ready, prisoner?" came the voice over the comm. Ryx nodded. The cell opened.

He stepped out and noticed others receiving individual escorts. This block must be for special cases, solitary threats or inmates with unique privileges.

He saw a few humans, a Draenari woman, a Zarneth insectoid, and a dark-skinned woman with bright yellow eyes whose form shimmered slightly, as though she didn't fully occupy this reality.

Miraxa, Ryx thought. Rare shapeshifters. He'd never seen one in person. Or if he had... he hadn't known it. The Miraxa woman grinned mischievously. Ryx nodded in return.

The prisoners were marched into the courtyard, where groups from other cell blocks joined them. Drones hovered above. Guards flanked them on every side.

Ryx noticed a few Vlexari inmates watching him with disdain, and some humans with hungry eyes. Fresh meat.

The head guard barked, "You know the drill. Gear will be issued at the mine. Any funny business, and you're down, solitary and extra shifts. Got it?"

A halfhearted chorus of "Yes, sir," followed.

The march began.

Through multiple checkpoints, fences, and gates, they reached the open pit where the mine plunged deep into the rock.

Prisoners were divided, some sent inside with sonic hammers, others kept on the surface to clear debris.

Ryx was assigned yard work. A low-powered holo-pick was shoved into his hands, and he began quietly splitting rocks into manageable chunks near the outer fence.

The labor was grueling, but meditative. For the first two hours, no one bothered him.

Until break.

He had just sat with his coffee sludge and calorie brick when he heard a voice behind him:

"Well, well... new blood."

Ryx turned. Four men, rough, sneering, strolled toward him. One had prison tattoos all the way to his jawline. Obvious alpha. Obvious problem.

"Your food looks better than ours. Mind sharing?"

Ryx didn't move. He'd expected this. This was the test.

He met the nearest guard's gaze, offered a slight shrug, and mouthed: "Sorry."

Then he turned to the group.

In a blur, he caught the lead man's arm and snapped it with a brutal wrench. The second man took a boot to the groin and folded instantly.

Ryx released the first man and pivoted, unleashing a flurry of strikes into a third's face, dropping him in a heap. He rolled off the back of the hunched-over inmate, kicked the last man in the nose. It cracked, Then he brought his elbow down on the back of the hunched man's neck.

Silence.

For a moment, the entire yard stopped. The only sounds were groans of pain from the ground. Then, expectedly, Ryx was tackled, restrained, and dragged back to the compound. Solitary confinement. No protest.

ΔΔΔ

He lay on the bunk, hands behind his head, waiting for the fallout.

It didn't take long.

The door hissed open. Warden Vance stepped inside, hands behind his back. Ryx stood slowly. "Warden."

Vance studied him for a long moment. Stern. Then slowly he let out a sigh.

"That display in the yard... one-time thing?"

"Yes, sir." Ryx said solemnly.

The Warden shook his head. "It better be. Four men in the medical wing, and now we're behind schedule."

Ryx shrugged, unapologetic. "Hoped it might deter future incidents."

The Warden smirked. "It just might. Not even our Vlexari inmates made that much noise on day one." He stepped closer.

"I'm not revoking your privileges Thorne. I know what this was. But it doesn't go unpunished."

"Understood, sir."

"You'll work extra shifts. Effective tomorrow."

Ryx nodded. "Yes, sir."

"Good man." Vance turned to leave. "Get some rest. You rejoin the yard in the morning." And then he was gone.

ΔΔΔ

Ryx soon settled into a rhythm.

The rest of that first week passed in a blur. He worked multiple shifts each day and crashed hard each night, aching and exhausted. The food was as terrible as he remembered, but he had no further problems from other prisoners. Not that week at least.

He didn't see Warden Vance or Dell again either, which suited him fine.

In what little off-time he had, Ryx developed a tight routine: he showered after second shift when the stalls were less crowded, took last dinner in the mess hall, and late at night he would sit in his cell studying the artifact on his wrist. The bracelet fascinated him. To his surprise, and eventual satisfaction, it shifted forms at his command. Just a thought, and it alternated between its dormant implant state and the elegant band of gold it had first appeared as.

He never dared activate the gauntlet form, not here. But he knew he had to understand it better. What was it? What else could it do?

The datapad Dell had given him quickly became his lifeline. He began checking out texts on xenoarchaeology and ancient galactic history. Most of it was speculative nonsense or focused on known artifacts with little in common with the one fused to his wrist. Still, he picked up a few nuggets about ancient, possibly extinct civilizations that intrigued him. It gave him something to look forward to.

The first weekend, while reading in the rec room, a guard called out his name. "Thorne!" Ryx looked up from his pad to see a guard waving him over toward a terminal booth. "You're up. Twenty minutes."

Ryx stood quickly, excitement building. He'd waited almost two weeks for this. He rushed into the booth and sealed the sound barrier behind him.

He paused, took a breath. If the VPM was still monitoring him, and he knew they were, he had to maintain the illusion that he was still holding his contingency over them. He opened the message terminal first.

To: Cannoneer

I'm safe. My family can fill you in if you ask.

I need information on that Xeno dig I mentioned last time.

Also, I'll need a new gun when I'm out. You know what I like.

-Ryx

The encrypted message fired off. Then he launched the call terminal, punching in the code that would route him through the external relay and to Vorrthani Station, straight to Rhoen's Garage.

A few seconds of silence, then, "Rhoen's Maintenance, Vorrthani's premier, and only, private star garage," came Tess's bright voice through the comm.

Ryx felt a weight lift from his chest. Hearing her voice, clear, sarcastic, familiar, hit him harder than he expected. His jaw clenched with the effort of holding back the wave of relief that surged through him.

"Hey, Tess," he said softly.

There was a beat of silence.

"Ryx…"

Her voice caught on his name like a snag on old fabric. Then the storm hit. "ERYX. FUCKING. THORNE! I SWEAR ON EVERY STAR IN THE BLACK I'M GOING TO PEEL YOUR SKIN OFF WITH A RUSTY FUSION WRENCH THE NEXT TIME I SEE YOU."

She didn't stop for almost two minutes. He let her have it, quietly chuckling between her imaginative curses. It was grounding, in a way, comforting chaos.

"I'm fine, Tess," he said when there was finally a pause. "BSD sold me out to the VPM."

"Shit," she breathed. Her tone shifted instantly. "So, what now? They court-martialed you already? Are you... do you have a shot at getting out of this, or are we prepping your eulogy?"

"Nope, court-martial's done. I made a deal. Twelve months on Varrix Delta."

Silence. Then: "How the hell did you pull that off? You're a high priority deserter, Ryx. That's not supposed to be survivable."

He smiled, though the weight on his shoulders didn't lift. "Let's just say I played my hand right. But the less you know, the better. You know how it is."

Another pause. A breath. "We'll come for you when your time's up. Assuming we haven't gotten used to what peace and quiet sounds like." They laughed together, real laughter. It soothed something raw in him.

After a moment, she asked, "How often can you access the terminal?" "Once a week for now. I'll respond to your messages when I can. Honestly… I'd appreciate them."

"You'll get them," she said firmly. "You're family, Ryx. You always have been." He swallowed thickly. That word meant more than she probably realized.

"Can I talk to Kaelen?"

"Yeah. It'll do him good." He heard her call out, then a shuffle, a pause, "Hello? Who's this?" Kaelen's gravel-rough voice came through, cautious.

Ryx smiled, nerves fluttering in his gut. "Hey, Pops."

"Eryx!?" The old man's voice cracked like a snapped cable line. "You damn knuckle-headed, scrap-for-brains, gear-guzzling idiot!"

Another tirade, this one somehow more colorful than Tess's. Ryx grinned, letting it wash over him. The familiar cadence, the creative swearing, it felt like home.

When Kaelen finally calmed, his voice dropped. "You okay, kid?" Ryx filled him in on what he could, sparing the dangerous details. "Just twelve months, with some luck. Maybe less if I play nice."

Kaelen snorted. "You? Play nice? You'll be lucky not to blow up the mine." They shared a laugh. Then Kaelen's voice softened. "You have no idea how good it is to hear your voice, kid. We've been worried sick." The emotion in his voice hit Ryx harder than he expected. He leaned back in the chair, letting it wash over him like cold water.

"You don't have to worry, Pops. I backed down a whole military with just charm and good looks." Kaelen chuckled. "It's a father's duty to worry about his children. Both of them."

The words landed like a gut punch. Ryx's throat tightened. It had never been said out loud before. Not like that.

"Thanks, Kaelen. I... I'll call soon."

Another knock on the glass. His time was up.

"Take care of my ship 'til I get back, yeah?"

"You got it, kid. Stay safe."

"See you soon, Pops."

And the line went dead.

∆∆∆

Ryx's rhythm continued the following week, steady, uneventful. There was only one scuffle in the showers with three inmates. It ended poorly for them. As expected, it earned Ryx another visit from Warden Vance, this time in his cell.

"Twice in two weeks is not a good look," Vance said, arms folded. "My apologies, Warden. It wasn't my intent to cause trouble."

The Warden smirked. "Lieutenant Karn told me you had a sense of humor."

He chuckled. "We have cameras. I saw what happened. It was self-defense." Ryx nodded, grateful.

"I moved our Vlexari inmates out of gen-pop when they became frequent targets. You're on that path now. Consider your next moves carefully."

"I will. I'd rather not be reassigned unless absolutely necessary."

"Good man," Vance said. "But if I have to move you, I will. I won't let one prisoner jeopardize the fragile peace here."

"No offense taken, sir." And after that, peace returned.

Messages from Tess and Kaelen remained steady, and Ryx even heard again from Rexa Vorn. She hadn't uncovered anything yet on BSD's xenoarchaeology division or Kolen Vess, but she assured him she was still digging.

Then came a more troubling message from Tess.

Ryx,

Some suits came by asking for footage of your last mission. They wouldn't ID themselves, but they were BSD, or mercs. Dad didn't let them push us around, but they're threatening to go to the governing council. They want a search warrant for the Wraith.

We're debating moving her. Don't worry, your stuff's safe.

-Tess

Ryx's stomach turned.

He fired off an encrypted reply:

Tess,

No reason to freak out. They won't find the artifact. Technically, it was never even on the Wraith. If they need to search, let them. Don't let them take anything. And delete your last message, it gave too much away.

Be safe. Don't piss them off.

-Ryx

Weeks passed. No news. No more messages about the suits. The Wraith was operational again. Tess hinted they had surprises for him when he got out.

Ryx's work unit changed unexpectedly in those next few weeks. The Warden had reassigned him without a word. He figured it was for protection, but whose, exactly, he wasn't sure.

The new unit was small. Quiet. Only six inmates. One of them was a massive, dark-hued Vlexari who worked like a quiet machine. Dell told Ryx his name was Shandar Kress, once a general on Eleos V, the very planet Ryx had gone rogue over. Ryx didnt understand why, but the news drew him to the Vlexari.

Every day, Ryx watched Shandar Kress with increasing fascination.

The Vlexari worked with the precision of a man who had long since made peace with monotony. Not a word. Not a gesture wasted. He carried his sonic hammer like an extension of his own massive frame, breaking stone with deliberate, rhythmic efficiency that almost bordered on meditative.

But what truly caught Ryx's attention wasn't the strength. It was the restraint. Shandar never growled at the guards. Never snapped at the other prisoners. He didn't pace or mutter to himself like the rest of them did when the days dragged. He simply worked, ate, and disappeared into his cell without fanfare.

It made Ryx wonder what was going on behind those glowing amber eyes.

He started sitting near the Vlexari in the mess hall, not beside him, not yet, just near. One table over. Always in his eyeline, never in his space. Watching. Studying. Shandar's tray always ended up scraped clean, but he chewed each bite with the slow deliberation of someone trying not to feel hunger. Or anything at all.

Eventually, one night, Ryx crossed the last unspoken line between them and sat directly across from him.

124

"Hope you don't mind," he said casually, managing a disarming smile. No response. Just the scrape of a spoon against a dented metal tray.

Ryx glanced around. Same seat. Same silence. "Always see you here. Made me wonder if this table was special, or if you just liked the view." Still nothing.

But Shandar hadn't told him to leave. Hadn't glared. Hadn't moved. That was something.

When they finished eating, Ryx stood, leaned slightly across the table, and offered his hand toward the empty tray. "May I?"

The Vlexari paused, eyes narrowing slightly. For a second, Ryx thought he'd pushed too far. Then, Shandar gave a small nod and let him take it.

That became their routine.

Every night, Ryx sat across from him. And every night, he carried both trays to the sonic wash. Shandar never acknowledged him. Never spoke. Never changed his posture. But Ryx kept showing up, kept talking in low, meaningless comments. Not pushing, just planting seeds.

He didn't know why he cared so much. Maybe it was the challenge. Maybe it was guilt. Or maybe, in a prison full of noise and bravado, the quietest man in the room was the one Ryx needed to understand the most.

Then one evening, after another silent meal, Shandar rose first. Without a word, he picked up Ryx's tray along with his own and carried them both to the cleaner.

Ryx blinked in surprise. His throat caught around the simple word: "…Thanks."

He got up and followed him out of the mess. "Hey, Shandar," he called gently. The Vlexari stopped, turning slowly, like he'd been expecting this. "I'm Ryx," he said, extending a hand for the second time. This one wasn't about a tray. It was about trust. About something like peace. Shandar looked down at the hand, then back at Ryx's face. His glowing eyes fixed on him, not just at him, but through him.

"I know who you are, Eryx Thorne," he said, voice low and thunderous. The air between them thickened like a closing vice. "I know you well."

He didn't elaborate. Didn't blink. Just stared for one long, heart hammering moment, then turned and walked down the corridor. Ryx stood frozen, hand still half-raised. *What the hell did that mean?*

The next day, he pulled Dell aside after roll call, voice hushed. "What's Shandar's story?" Dell glanced around, clearly wary of being overheard. "You really don't know?" Ryx shook his head slowly. "He said he knows me. Well." Dell exhaled and leaned in.

"Shandar Kress was the High General of the Eleos V navy. During the war. He commanded the fleet that chased your team to the surface." Ryx felt his stomach drop.

"That mission…" he whispered. "He was there?"

"Yeah. It's how he got captured. He's been in this place ever since." Dell's eyes narrowed. "Far as I know, he hasn't spoken a single word to anyone. Not once. Until you." Ryx swallowed hard. "Why hasn't he…?"

"Crushed you like a tin can?" Dell gave a grim smile. "Maybe he sees something in you. Maybe he's tired. Or maybe you're the only other ghost in here who remembers what happened down there."

Dell shrugged after a moment. "Or it could be his vow, or whatever." Ryx looked at him curiously. "What vow?"

Dell took a second to respond. "I don't know that it's a vow exactly, but Shandar never defends himself." This shocked Ryx. "Never?" he asked in disbelief.

Dell shook his head. "He's been attacked multiple times, never once lifted a finger. He's actually the reason Warden Vance created the special work group you're in."

Ryx stared across the yard at Shandar who was getting into line for work. Another mystery.

That night, Ryx waited outside the showers and caught Shandar mid-step. "Hey, can I talk with you for a moment?" The Vlexari turned with that same impassive expression, quiet as carved stone.

"I… I don't know where to start," Ryx admitted. He laughed weakly and rubbed the back of his neck. "Truth is, I've been trying to figure you out since I got here." Shandar was silent for a long time. Long enough that Ryx wondered if the man would just walk away.

Then, "You don't need to fear me, Eryx Thorne."

The voice was deep and resonant. Like it had been echoing in his chest for a decade before finally being released. "You brought pain to my people. You followed orders. You believed in a cause. But in the end, when the future of Eleos V stood on the edge, you turned away."

Ryx's breath caught. He didn't know Shandar had known that. That he remembered. "You betrayed your own," Shandar said. Ryx flinched, but Shandar raised a hand, more like a gesture of peace than condemnation.

"And now, you are here. With me. We were enemies once…" He let the words linger in the air.

"…Now we are brothers in chains."

And with that, he turned and walked past Ryx without another word. Ryx stayed rooted in place, heart pounding, skin hot with shame and something else. Awe, maybe. Or confusion.

Shandar Kress had every reason to hate him. Every reason to crush him, or at the very least, ignore him forever.

But instead, he had offered something rare.

Not forgiveness.

But recognition.

Understanding.

And maybe… the beginning of something that could survive both guilt and war.

INTERLUDE:

BEFORE THE STORM

The sound of the torch was too clean. A perfect hiss, sharp and controlled, slicing through the silence that had settled over the garage like a winter blanket. Kaelen leaned into the angle grinder, metal singing against metal, sparks casting short-lived constellations against the shadowed walls. It was the kind of silence he usually enjoyed, filled with the rhythm of tools and the scent of plasma scorched steel. But now it rang hollow.

Ryx wasn't here. And the garage, though still running, felt like a ship with its engines dead and drifting.

Kaelen shut off the torch. The silence afterward was louder than the hiss had been. He rolled his shoulder slowly, letting out a breath he hadn't realized he was holding. His joints ached from too many hours bent over that stabilizer housing. He could still see the smudges from Ryx's hands on the plating, Ryx always left the panels dirtier than he found them, never quite gentle with anything but fiercely loyal to everything.

Kaelen straightened and turned, letting his gaze sweep the garage floor. Tessa was somewhere in the back, buried in her newest half-built masterpiece. Tools were scattered where Ryx would've scolded her, wires snaked across the floor where he would've tripped and sworn colorfully about "death by clumsy genius."

The Wraithburn loomed in the center of the bay, quiet, dormant. A waiting beast without its handler.

Kaelen sighed and sat on the crate near the ship's rear boarding ramp. From here, he could see the burn marks still left from Ryx's last job. Just a patch of scorched hull and melted coating near the starboard thruster where Ryx had pushed the ship harder than it had ever flown before. Kaelen had always scolded him for being reckless. Ryx always just grinned, that reckless grin that always said, "But I lived, didn't I?"

He rubbed a hand down his face.

Three months. Ryx had been locked up for three months on Varrix Delta. Wrongfully imprisoned, at least Kaelen believed it, deep in his bones. But the law hadn't cared. The VPM claimed every right to imprison Ryx for his defection. And now Eryx Thorne was just another ghost in a concrete tomb.

Kaelen had spent half his life fighting ghosts. He hadn't expected to raise one.

His hand remained on the Wraithburn's hull. The cool metal throbbed faintly with the hum of its idle systems, like a living thing in hibernation. For all its firepower and speed, the ship had always seemed like a second skin for Ryx. Like it was waiting for him every time he was away from it. Kaelen could still remember the day he'd found them, half-dead, missing panels, and held together with little more than spit, desperation, and hope.

"You really think you can fix her?" Ryx had asked. Once he was back on his feet. Still bandaged and limping.

Kaelen chuckled softly at the memory, but it cracked into a sigh halfway through. That was almost a decade ago. Ryx had been... what? Nineteen? Fresh out of the worst hells a young man could face, all brittle edges and wild eyes, a chip on his shoulder big enough to flatten a cruiser.

But underneath all that, Kaelen had seen something.

Something aching to be seen.

He hadn't planned to become a father all over again. Never wanted to. The death of his wife, Tessa's mother, had taken too much of his ability to hope for a future, let alone raise another Kid. But Ryx had just... stuck. No matter how many times Kaelen tried to keep his distance, Ryx had completed the garage like he always belonged there.

And then one day, Kaelen found himself hoping he wouldn't leave.

He remembered one night in particular. A rare quiet evening, Tessa already asleep, the ship cold in dock. Ryx had sat on the floor near the repulsor lift, legs folded, a datapad in his lap.

Kaelen had found him there at 3 a.m., still awake, still tweaking systems on some diagnostic code he hadn't been asked to touch.

"What the hell are you still doing up?" Kaelen had grunted.

Ryx hadn't even looked up. "Didn't feel right going to sleep yet."

Kaelen had started to scold him. Tell him to get rest, that overwork was just as dangerous as neglect. But then Ryx had said something that stopped him cold.

"This is the first place I've ever been where no one's tried to hurt or kill me."

Kaelen hadn't said anything to that.

Instead, he'd walked over, handed Ryx a cup of synthcaff, and sat down next to him on the floor. They didn't speak for the rest of the night. They just sat in companionable silence, the flicker of the datapad the only light between them.

Kaelen had never told him that he considered him a son. He should've. Damn it, he should've.

The pain swelled, sharp and sudden in his chest. It wasn't just the injustice of Ryx being locked away that haunted him, it was the silence. The fear that, down on that prison moon, Ryx might believe he'd been abandoned. That he was facing the dark alone.

He stepped back from the Wraithburn and rubbed his hands down his face, exhaling hard.

130

"I'm sorry, kid," he muttered aloud, voice hoarse. "I should've done more."

But Kaelen had always known how the system worked. BSD had deep pockets and deeper secrets. Their claws ran through the courts, the Guild, the press. Kaelen knew there was nothing he could have done. Ryx knew it too.

His eyes fell to the empty space on the bench beside the ship's tool wall, Ryx's favorite seat, the one he always dropped into after a job, gear still dusty, face split with adrenaline and exhaustion. Kaelen could see him there now; a ghost burned into the steel.

Footsteps approached. The soft, rapid rhythm of boots far too light to be his. Tessa's. "Hey," she said, brushing a dark strand of hair out of her face. Her voice was tired. She always sounded tired now.

Kaelen nodded. "You finish your, uh…" he motioned vaguely toward the back. "I think it's supposed to be a kinetic lens array," she said with a shrug. "Might also be a glorified paperweight. Depends if the capacitor explodes when I test it."

Kaelen cracked a smile despite himself. "Sounds promising." Tessa didn't return it. She looked toward the Wraithburn instead. "Do you think he's okay?" she asked softly.

Kaelen stood and walked to the boarding ramp, resting a hand against the ship's hull. It was still warm from the station's solar lamps.

"I think…" he hesitated, "Ryx is one of the most stubborn bastards I've ever met. If anyone can survive that place, it's him."

Tessa nodded, but she didn't look comforted. "BSD hasn't said anything since the Job. No announcements from Tarrin Station. It's like they're hoping people will just… stop asking."

They stood in silence for a few moments. Then a soft chime echoed through the garage. Kaelen's eyes narrowed. A visitor ping. Tessa checked her wrist pad. "Uh-oh."

"What?"

She turned her datapad screen toward him. "Black Sable Dynamics. Two officials. No appointment." Kaelen's stomach turned to ice.

131

He made his way toward the main doors as the outer locks disengaged, and the heavy doors hissed open.

Two figures entered, both in tailored black coats with BSD's silver chevron subtly gleaming at the collar. They walked with the easy confidence of predators. One was tall and wiry, face unreadable behind a pair of pale-lensed glasses. The other, shorter, broader, smiled with a kind of practiced emptiness.

Kaelen met them halfway across the hangar floor. "Gentlemen," he said coolly. "Can I help you?"

The one with glasses spoke first. "Mr. Rhoen. We're here on behalf of BSD's Internal Asset Division. We'd like to inspect the Eryx Thorne's ship, we believe its docked here." Kaelen didn't blink. "Is that so?"

"It won't take long," the broader one added, already starting to move toward the door. Kaelen stepped into his path. "Do you have a warrant?"

A pause. Then: "We're acting under BSD jurisdiction, Mr. Rhoen. As you know that ship was involved in a case of corporate asset theft." "That case is closed," Kaelen replied, steel threading his voice. "My foster son was found to have not taken your asset."

"We'd still like to verify that nothing proprietary remains aboard. Protocol," the man said with a smile that didn't reach his eyes.

Kaelen smiled back, but his was all teeth.

"Then bring a warrant. Until then, get off my dock." Tessa appeared behind him, arms crossed, eyes blazing. "This is private property," she added. "You can't search the ship without legal cause."

"Miss Thorne, we understand your emotional stake,"

"Don't," Kaelen said sharply. "Don't invoke emotion to gaslight my daughter. You don't have cause. You don't have rights here. You don't even have coffee."

The BSD men stared at him, eyes calculating. Kaelen stared right back, the years of war behind his gaze solid as iron. Finally, the man with glasses adjusted them.

"We'll return," he said.

"I'll be here," Kaelen replied.

They left without another word. The doors hissed closed. Tessa let out a long breath. "Assholes." Kaelen nodded, not looking away from the door. "They'll be back," she said. "I know," he murmured. Then softer, almost to himself: "And we'll be ready."

CHAPTER 8
BROTHERS IN CHAINS

Ryx continued to be haunted by Shandar's words: *Now we are brothers in chains.*

The sentence clung to him like a second skin. Each day they shared the same mess table, the same shift group, the same silence , but everything felt heavier. That brief exchange had cracked something open in Ryx. Now, every time their paths crossed, he saw Shandar not as a fellow prisoner, but as a living remnant of a past he'd spent years trying to bury.

Shandar knew about his last mission. Somehow. He knew what Varrix Prime had done, what Ryx had done. And yet, there he sat, unflinching, unreadable, unafraid.

Their routine didn't change. They worked together, showered late to avoid crowds, and sat across from each other in silence during meals. But Ryx's thoughts never stopped turning.

He wanted to know more. He needed to. Why wasn't Shandar angry? Why hadn't he lashed out? Ryx played his approach carefully, offering gestures, returning trays, waiting in the mess until Shandar left so he could follow and watch his back without being obvious. He didn't want to push. Shandar didn't seem the type to respond well to pressure. But Ryx's curiosity and unease were growing by the day.

And with it came memories.

Old ones.

The kind he hadn't thought about in years.

He would wake up screaming in a cold sweat, convinced he was back on that scarred planet's surface. Dust in the air, the reek of heat-baked refuse, and the distant whine of repulsorlifts echoing off rusted rooftops. The memory always came in pieces, vivid and disjointed, flashes of color, heat, stillness. But it always began the same way:

A civilian settlement nestled in the foothills of a mineral-rich region. Dry wind pushing cracked banners across market stalls. The scent of cooked meat and old oil. People moved slowly through the streets, some human, many not, going about their business beneath a sky that always looked like dusk. The place had life, even in its poverty. Families. Vendors. Laughter. Ryx had watched it all from the shadows, perched in the remains of a bombed-out comm tower on the ridge above.

He spent three days in that tower.

Alone.

Watching. Listening. Waiting for a pattern to emerge.

A convoy passed by twice a day, Military hover transports, clearly repurposed for civilian protection. They circled the compound where the high-value target lived. A former senator, accused of rallying rebel support in the core systems and, more importantly, possessing files that could turn the tide of the looming war.

Ryx was told the mission was a containment measure. Retrieve the files. Prevent escalation. No civilian casualties. No unnecessary force.

He believed that. He wanted to believe that.

The op had been flawless. At 0300, he moved under the cover of darkness, slipping past perimeter sensors using local jammers and a finely tuned pulse-scrambler. He bypassed the door silently, disabling the ancient locking system in under ten seconds. Inside, the target and his family were asleep.

Ryx never saw their faces. He avoided the bedrooms. The data vault was secured by a biometric lock. He bypassed that, too. He swapped the real drive for the decoy and sealed everything behind

135

him, exactly as it had been. No sound. No alarm. No violence. On his way out, he paused briefly to look at a child's drawing on the wall, three smiling faces under a sun drawn in red crayon.

He was proud of the mission. Proud that no one had to get hurt. He'd done it right.

He reported back from low orbit, voice tight with fatigue but full of restrained pride.

"Mission successful, General. I have the files." A hiss of static answered him.

"Did you place the decoy device?"

"Yes, sir. They'll never know." There was a pause.

"You're absolutely right. Good work, Thorne. Proceed to orbit."

He was already there. His ship hovered in geosynchronous position, engines low, sensors quiet. He could still see the settlement out the viewport, tiny clusters of metal and stone clinging to the earth like ants to a sugar cube.

Then, light.

A pulse from orbit.

White-blue. Blinding. Pure.

A proton lance screamed down from high altitude, fired from The Empyreon herself. It hit the center of the settlement like the finger of a god. There was no sound at first, just the flash, and then the shockwave rippling outward, flattening buildings and vaporizing anything within a two-kilometer radius. Heat distortion rippled across his viewport. Static crackled across the comms.

Ryx couldn't move. Couldn't breathe.

He watched as the place he'd infiltrated without firing a shot was erased from the planet's surface in seconds. Hundreds of people. Maybe more.

Gone.

Not a word of warning. Not even a hint.

He stared in horror. The child's drawing swam back into his mind, as if burned onto his retinas.

The next day, he received a secure transmission confirming his success. The files had been retrieved, the strike had "neutralized a developing bioweapon," and the general personally thanked him for his precision. The beacon had worked perfectly, they said.

He'd never spoken a word about it. Never confronted them.

He just nodded.

Saluted.

And began to unravel.

Ryx jolted awake, chest heaving, sweat clinging to his skin like a second layer. The dream, no, the memory, still echoed in his skull, that blinding lance of light splitting the earth, the silence that followed. His heart thudded wildly in his chest.

He lay still for a moment, staring at the dull sheen of the nano-glass ceiling above his bunk. A dim red status light glowed overhead, 3:07 local time.

No chance of sleep now.

He rolled off the cot, his limbs aching more from memory than exertion, and shuffled toward the small metal sink bolted into the corner wall. The water was lukewarm, barely a trickle, but he splashed it on his face anyway, scrubbing at his skin as if he could wash the guilt out of his pores.

The face that stared back from the reflective panel above the sink looked older than it should have. Hollow-eyed. The scar on his cheek ached again, phantom pain. Another gift from Rendyll.

He braced both hands on the edge of the sink and lowered his head, letting the water drip from his hair, listening to the distant hum of the prison's ventilation system.

Keep moving.

That was the only answer he ever had when the past came knocking. Keep moving. Breathe. Push forward.

He pulled on his coveralls, threadbare, itchy, but better than lying awake haunted, and began his morning calisthenics. Stretches. Push-ups. Core work. Not just habit anymore. Discipline was the only thing keeping him from spiraling.

By the time the first chime of the shift alarm blared through the block an hour and a half later, he was already dressed, boots laced, standing at attention at the foot of his cot.

The guard assigned to his block opened the cell without comment, and Ryx filed into line with the others.

He glanced to his right.

Shandar Kress was already there, silent, unmoving, eyes forward. As always.

There was something reassuring about it.

Even after everything, Ryx's doubts, his memories, the weight of the gauntlet hidden beneath his skin, somehow, the sight of Shandar standing there in quiet defiance helped anchor him.

They moved in line toward the outer yard checkpoint, their boots scuffing in rhythm on the smooth floor. As the gates hissed open and the cold morning air hit his face, Ryx let himself believe, if only for a moment, that maybe today would be simple. Just another shift. Just more rock. Just silence and sweat and sore muscles.

But the guards stopped suddenly at the mine gate. Something was off. The work group halted just outside the final security checkpoint to the mines.

Ryx frowned, his breath visible in the chill morning air. The guards around them shifted uneasily. Low murmurs passed between them, too quiet to make out, but enough to set his instincts alight. Next to him, Shandar stood still as stone, but his glowing eyes flicked toward Ryx for the briefest second.

Something was wrong.

A tall, broad-shouldered officer barked out a sudden command. "About face! Return to the yard, shift is canceled!" A ripple of confusion moved through the prisoners. A few muttered curses. One or two cheered. But not Ryx. Not Shandar.

138

They marched back in silence, flanked by more guards than usual. Ryx noticed that the escort wasn't watching for trouble from outside, they were watching them. Eyes locked on the inmates. Fingers near triggers.

Paranoia. They knew something. But what?

As they crossed back into the main compound, the yard gates opened, and Warden Vance stepped out onto the elevated platform overlooking the courtyard. His expression was more severe than usual, his posture tense beneath the crisp lines of his uniform.

"Prisoners," he called, voice sharp and commanding. "You will return to your cells immediately. Your lunch meals will be held in the mess hall. Anyone not in their cell within five minutes will be placed in solitary."

A flurry of protests erupted, why? What was going on?, but Vance raised a single hand and silenced them.

"Would you prefer double shifts in the sulfur fields instead?" he asked, one brow raised.

That shut them up.

Grumbling and cursing, the prisoners dispersed under heavy guard. Ryx walked beside Shandar, lowering his voice as they entered the block corridor.

"I overheard two guards," he said, glancing casually around them. "Two more political prisoners found dead in the mines. This morning."

Shandar's eyes flicked to him again. A slow, subtle nod.

"No signs of a struggle," Ryx continued. "And both were from the war. This isn't some heat-of-the-moment stabbing. These were targeted."

Another nod. No words. But Ryx could see it in Shandar's posture. He understood.

Back in his cell, Ryx sat for a long time on the edge of his bunk, staring at the wall, tension radiating off him in waves. A dozen questions spun in his mind, all orbiting one unshakable fear:

What if Shandar is next?

Or, what if I am?

He couldn't stop thinking about Dell's warning. Shandar never defended himself. Even when attacked. Some kind of vow? A punishment he felt he deserved? Whatever it was, it would get him killed.

That night, after dinner, Shandar left early as always, his tray stacked neatly and made his way toward the showers. Ryx watched him go. Something in his chest tightened.

He waited a few minutes before getting up. Not too quickly. He didn't want to spook anyone. Following Shandar at a stalking pace. He moved through the corridor, senses prickling. Years of infiltration work sharpened every instinct. Footsteps too quiet.

His eyes fell on a someone outside the shower. A guard standing too still. And then he saw it.

The flicker.

The edge of the guard's form wavered, like heat distortion in the air. For a split second, their silhouette blurred, too tall, too narrow, wrong.

Ryx froze. His brain connected the dots before he could stop it.

The Miraxa.

Shapeshifter. Stealth expert. A living ghost. And Ryx had seen her, once, on his first day. That eerie, shifting presence. Yellow eyes. Predatory grin.

And now she was heading into the showers.

Following Shandar.

Ryx's body moved before his brain caught up. He ran.

Not for help, there wasn't time. Not for a weapon, he didn't need one.

He bolted down the corridor and rounded the corner into the shower block, right into the thundercrack of a shotgun blast.

The riot pellets hit him square in the chest. Electricity spiderwebbed through his body. He hit the floor hard, muscles locking up as convulsions took hold. Pain arced down his spine. His vision swam. He couldn't breathe.

Boots approached.

Ryx blinked through the haze. The figure became clearer with every step, yellow eyes, pale skin flickering at the edges, as if barely clinging to form. The Miraxa assassin stood above him, smiling with jagged, predator teeth.

"You're not my target," she whispered, "but I was hoping you'd make this fun."

She crouched beside him, the barrel of the shotgun lowering toward his chest.

"Did Rendyll send you?" Ryx gasped through the pain.

The woman laughed, a dry, sickle-sharp sound.

"No one sent me. I go where the blood flows. I kill who deserves it, and sometimes who doesn't. Either way, I get paid."

She revealed a wicked looking knife tucked in the folds of her uniform. "But tonight's special. Tonight, I get to carve you."

Then, like a comet, A scaled fist the size of a dinner plate smashed into her side.

The assassin slammed into the tile wall with enough force to leave a dent, gasping in pain.

Shandar Kress stood in the doorway.

Ryx, still twitching from the shock, staggered to his knees, eyes wide with disbelief.

"You…" he managed to say, looking at the towering Vlexari. Shandar gave a slow nod.

But it wasn't over.

The Miraxa moved. Ryx could barely believe it, how was she still conscious? She twisted, groaning, and raised the shotgun again.

Ryx reacted on instinct.

His right hand flew up. The golden band on his wrist shimmered, and the artifact gauntlet unfolded in a shimmer of blue light. A shield formed just as the blast struck.

Energy scattered across the shield in a crackling halo.

The Miraxa stared, stunned, but it was too late.

Ryx was on her.

A punch lifted her off her feet. The gauntlet blade extended midstrike, one clean thrust beneath her chin, and the woman slumped to the floor.

Dead.

Ryx collapsed to his knees, chest heaving, blood roaring in his ears. Pain still in full bloom from the riot shot to the chest.

Behind him, Shandar groaned and fell to one knee. Ryx turned.

"You're hit," he said, seeing the dark burns on Shandar's side.

Shandar's glowing eyes met his. "You have a weapon... hidden inside you..." Ryx nodded slowly. "Yeah. It's... complicated."

The Vlexari stared at him for a long moment, then offered a hand. "Thank you," he said.

Ryx hesitated, willed the gauntlet to shift back, then took it. "Right back at you." That's when the guards burst in, weapons raised.

Figures.

ΔΔΔ

Ryx sat in solitary for days. No voices. No footsteps. Just the steady hum of artificial air and the occasional groan of the facility shifting under Varrix Delta's tectonic strain. The silence wasn't peaceful; it was a prison all its own. He knew Shandar was close, somewhere in the adjacent cells. He even thought he could sense the Vlexari's quiet, unshakable presence through the wall.

But even that wasn't enough to keep the weight from pressing down on him. The walls seemed to close in tighter with each passing hour. The same stone-grey surface, the same hum, the same memories, relentless and crawling out of the dark corners of his mind like smoke under a locked door.

He couldn't stop the nightmares now. They came every time his eyes closed. He kept waking with a gasp, sweat-soaked and shaking, convinced for a few terrible moments that he was back on Eleos V, crawling through ash, blood on his hands, his or someone else's, it didn't matter.

Why now? he kept asking himself. Maybe it was everything catching up. Maybe it was the moment Shandar looked him in the eye and said, "We are brothers in chains."

Something about that simple truth had cracked Ryx wide open. He'd spent nine years burying what happened. Now it refused to stay buried.

The hiss of the cell door pulled him from one of those waking nightmares. He stood fast, instinct on edge. Warden Vance stepped in, posture sharp, expression unreadable. "Our investigation is complete, Mr. Thorne." he said evenly. Ryx straightened, trying to look less frayed than he felt. "What did you find?"

"The Miraxa," the Warden said, "killed multiple prisoners, and two of my guards." Ryx exhaled slowly. That alone was a relief. At least they weren't being framed. But Vance didn't leave. His gaze lingered. Something in the way his eyes narrowed made Ryx's nerves spike again.

"Is something the matter, Warden?"

Vance folded his arms, voice calm but deliberate. "There's only one remaining issue. An unanswered question, really."

Ryx felt his heartbeat quicken. "Which is?"

"The wound that killed the assassin. We can't place it."

Shit.

"I'm sorry?" Ryx said, feigning confusion.

Vance took a step closer. Not threatening, just observant. "The kill wound doesn't match anything we recovered from that shower. No weapon. No impact trace we can identify. And certainly not the knife she was carrying."

Ryx swallowed hard. "You recovered her blade?"

"Of course. But it's too thin. Too shallow. The wound is… clean. Deeper than it should've been." Vance's brow furrowed. "Like something more advanced. Something surgical." Ryx held his breath for a heartbeat too long.

"Am I being accused of something, Warden?" he asked, keeping his voice steady. Vance hesitated. "Not directly." He rubbed his jaw, clearly weighing something. "Shandar claims he delivered the killing blow. He says the force of his strike made the wound seem worse." Ryx nodded slowly. "And you don't buy that."

"No," Vance admitted. "But I can't disprove it either."

He turned to pace, as was his habit when deep in thought. "You and Shandar are the most stable inmates in this prison. But if there's a weapon hidden in my facility, or a way to create one, I need to know about it."

He doesn't know about the bracelet.

Ryx breathed easier.

"With all due respect, sir, if there was a hidden weapon in that room, don't you think the Miraxa would've used it?" That made Vance pause. He turned, considering. Then he sighed.

"You're not wrong," he said. "And my guards confirmed you didn't have time to stash anything. No hidden compartments. No tricks." He glanced at Ryx and finally let some of the tension fall from his shoulders. "Unless you and Shandar are hiding an invisible weapon system in my prison,"

"Which would be impressive," Ryx muttered with a dry grin. The Warden chuckled. "Then no. I don't think you caused the problem, Mr. Thorne. I think you helped end it." Ryx's smile faded, seriousness returning. "Any idea who she was working for?"

The Warden's mood darkened immediately. "Not yet. Her communications weren't encrypted, but there are vague phrases, strange phrasing. I think she was trained. Maybe freelance. Maybe a corp. All of her targets were political prisoners. That's the only pattern."

"Except for your guards."

Vance nodded. "Collateral, most likely."

He crossed the room and opened the door. "We're increasing watch around you and Shandar. Just in case." "Do you expect more assassins?" Ryx asked quietly.

"No," the Warden said, his tone hard. "But I didn't expect the last one either."

ΔΔΔ

The next few months passed in quiet rhythm.

Days working in the mines. Nights reading. Meals shared in silence. Occasionally, a conversation sparked between Ryx and Shandar, never about the past. They avoided it like a minefield. Instead, they spoke of simple things: geology, starscapes, food they missed. Ryx found comfort in those quiet, grounded exchanges. Shandar never gave more than he had to, but what he gave felt real.

And then, one afternoon, Ryx was called into Warden Vance's office.

The Warden greeted him with a rare grin. "Have you been enjoying your stay with us, Mr. Thorne?" Ryx raised an eyebrow. "Aside from the beatings, the solitary, and the attempted assassination? Yeah, it's been a dream."

Vance laughed. "Good to hear. I've got news." Ryx sat straighter. "What kind?" Ryx's palms began to sweat.

"We haven't identified who hired the assassin yet," the Warden admitted. "But the political fallout from the murders has forced the Council to act."

He turned, clasping his hands behind his back.

145

"Your sentence has been reduced by three months. Effective immediately. Recommendation came from myself and several of your guards."

Ryx blinked. "Wait,"

"You'll be released at the end of this calendar month."

A breath caught in his throat. *Three weeks. Maybe less.*

He felt the beginnings of a grin stretch across his face. Then it stopped.

Shandar.

"What about Kress?" he asked quietly.

Vance's eyes narrowed. "Shandar Kress is serving a life sentence." Ryx's shoulders sagged, but the Warden wasn't done.

"Don't mistake my tone, Thorne. I've been lobbying for that man's release since I took this position. Reports. Recommendations. Letters the length of novellas. I've pushed every bureaucratic wall I can find."

Ryx stared, a little stunned.

The Warden's expression softened. "This time, it worked." Ryx sat up straighter. "The Council agreed to shorten his sentence. He'll serve two more years. At twelve total, they'll mark it as time served."

Ryx smiled, bitter and grateful all at once. *It's not soon, but it's something.* Does he know yet? Ryx asked with quiet excitement. "I told him before you," Vance said with a smirk. "Seniority counts for something."

"How'd he take it?" Ryx asked not bothering to mask his excitment. The Warden chuckled. "Ever seen a Vlexari cry?"

ΔΔΔ

Warden Vance had a guard escort Ryx to the rec room to use the comms to let his family know the good news.

Ryx and Shandar passed each other in the hall outside the rec room, Shandar flanked by two guards, Ryx headed toward the terminal. Their eyes met.

Nothing was said. But something passed between them all the same. A nod. A shared grin. A silent celebration.

Ryx stepped into the rec room, the low hum of power thrumming through the walls, the same flickering overhead lights bathing everything in dull sterile white.

He could still feel the warmth of Shandar's rare smile as they passed, the weight of everything unspoken between them. Joy. Gratitude. Sadness.

Two more years.

Ryx pushed the thought aside as he approached the terminal booth. A guard nodded him in with practiced indifference, the sound-dampening seal hissing shut behind him.

Just him and the screen. He sat and tapped through the familiar commands, his fingers oddly shaky. A message alert blinked on the top-right corner of the interface. Just one.

From: Tess

Ryx,

It happened.

Suits, definitely BSD.

They damn near kicked in our door, had Vorrthani station security with them, full warrant for the Wraith.

They trashed the ship, Ryx. Tore her apart. Ripped out panels. Scanned every system like they expected her to spit out a confession.

We're fine. The ship's fine. Nothing was taken. But they were pissed.

Call soon.

-Tess

The message gripped his chest like a vice.

He leaned forward, elbows on his knees, knuckles white against the edge of the terminal as he reread it twice more. His mind immediately raced, did they find anything? He forced himself to breathe.

He needed to hear their voices. Now.

Ryx keyed in the encrypted channel and called the only number that mattered. The screen flickered. Once. Twice. The relay satellites clicked into sequence.

Then:

"Rhoen's Maintenance, Vorrthani's premier and only private star garage."

The gravelly voice made him sag with relief.

"Kaelen!?" Ryx practically shouted.

"Calm down, kid, I'm not deaf." Kaelen's voice held its usual gruffness, but there was something behind it. Something Ryx hadn't heard in a while.

Relief.

"You're alright?" Ryx asked breathlessly. "Is Tess okay? Did they hurt either of you?"

Kaelen snorted. "By the stars, we're not the ones in a labor camp. It was just a corporate dick-measuring contest wrapped in legalese. No bruises. Just a lotta mess."

Ryx let out a breath he hadn't realized he'd been holding. He leaned forward and pressed his forehead gently to the screen.

"Stars, I was scared."

"They didn't find a damn thing," Kaelen continued, almost proud. "Just kept tearing things up, shouting about sealed systems and restricted logs. Got even more riled when the Wraith didn't give them anything. Tess told them to eat scrap. Vorrthani security almost laughed."

Ryx allowed himself a smile. "Sounds about right."

"They tried to push their luck," Kaelen added, voice darkening. "Demanded access to the garage itself. Said they had cause to inspect your belongings." He spat the word.

148

"And?" Ryx asked, already feeling his anger rising.

"And I told them they could shove their warrant into a plasma intake until they got one for my shop."

Ryx chuckled, almost tearful. "Damn, I missed you, old man."

Kaelen's voice softened. "Missed you too, kid."

They fell quiet for a beat. Not awkward, just full. Full of everything that didn't need saying.

Then Ryx leaned back and said, "So, how's it been? You and Tess used to surviving without me?"

A pause. Then: "Wait a minute. That tone. That smug little tone of yours, what's going on?"

Ryx tried not to smile too wide. He failed. "Have you enjoyed the peace and quiet, Kaelen? You know… no fires, no impromptu gunfights, no near-death crashes in the middle of a tune-up?" Kaelen went silent.

Then roared, "You're getting out early?!"

"Yeah," Ryx said, practically glowing. "End of the month. About twenty days from now, by local system calendar."

On the other end, he could already hear Tess screaming, "HE'S WHAT!?"

"Tell her to breathe," Ryx chuckled. "You think you two can come pick me up off this oversized rock?"

Tess's voice crashed through the line, even louder now. "YOU BET YOUR ASS WE CAN. I'M BRINGING A WELCOME PARTY AND A CANE TO BEAT YOU WITH FOR MAKING US WORRY THIS MUCH." Kaelen laughed so hard Ryx thought he might choke.

"Gods, it's gonna be good to have you home," Kaelen said finally, voice cracking. Ryx closed his eyes. Let the words sink in.

"Yeah," he said. "I can't wait."

For the next few minutes, they talked about logistics, where to land, what time, what clearance codes the ship would need. Tess kept interjecting with threats and promises in equal measure. Kaelen chimed in with dad jokes and reminders that Ryx would be buying the drinks when he got out.

And Ryx? He soaked in every word. Every curse. Every joke. Every breath.

He had a date. He had a way out.

CHAPTER 9

HOMECOMING

The last few weeks slipped by like half-remembered dreams. One moment Ryx was hauling crates through the mine with Shandar at his side, the next he found himself sitting across from the Vlexari in the mess hall, sharing what would likely be their final meal together.

The room buzzed around them with the usual din of trays clattering, boots stomping, and prisoners muttering in too-loud voices, but at their table, there was only silence.

A familiar silence.

But tonight, it felt heavier. Final.

There was a quiet tension in the air, something unsaid pressing down between them like a weight neither knew how to lift. It reminded Ryx of the first few times they'd sat together, guarded, watchful, uncertain. But it wasn't the same. This was different. This was a silence filled with history. With trust. And with a looming goodbye neither wanted to name.

Over the past eight months, Ryx and Shandar had built something rare. A friendship that had never needed words to exist. They had shared work, pain, space, rhythm. A bond carved from long days and long silences. A kind of wordless understanding that felt more real to Ryx than most of the relationships he'd had in his life.

It was strange, no, impossible, that such a bond could grow in a place like this. And yet...

There was something profound in it. Something honest. There was no pretending here. No masks. No false comfort. Just a Vlexari and a human who should have been enemies, finding peace in the shared stillness of survival.

Ryx stared down at his tray. The last bite of his so-called "meal" stared back at him, a grayish, flavorless nutrient brick that probably had a name, though he doubted it matched the taste. He chewed slowly, trying not to think about what came next.

Across from him, Shandar finished eating, stacked their trays with careful precision, and folded his massive hands in front of him.

Ryx broke the silence.

"I noticed you don't receive packages." It wasn't a question. He didn't even look up. A deep grunt, affirmative. "I doubt the Warden would revoke that privilege from you."

Shandar didn't answer at first. Then, in his gravelly voice: "No one to send them." The words sat between them like stone.

Ryx felt a pang of guilt twist in his gut. He wished he hadn't said anything.

"I'm sorry," he said softly. "Did the war take them?"

Shandar let out a low chuckle, a sound Ryx had heard only a handful of times. It was dry. Hollow. But it was real.

"My mate passed before the war began. I have a daughter... as far as I know."

Ryx looked up, surprised. The Vlexari's glowing eyes were distant now, fixed somewhere far beyond the mess hall walls.

"Is she... upset with you?"

"Likely," Shandar said with a slow nod. "But only because she thinks I am dead."

Ryx froze, his eyes wide. "She doesn't even know you're alive?"

His voice spiked louder than he intended, earning a few side-eyes from nearby tables. He winced and glanced at Shandar, who turned to regard him calmly.

"She was fully grown when I was captured. A physician already. She left Eleos V years ago to provide care in underserved systems. I was… proud. Still am."

There was a softness in Shandar's voice Ryx had never heard before. A kind of reverence.

Ryx leaned in slightly. "You haven't tried to contact her?"

"I don't know where she is," Shandar said simply. "No network. No contacts. And while Warden Vance is a fair man, I would not ask him to hunt across the stars for a ghost of my past."

A moment passed. Then something small and squishy smacked into Shandar's temple with a dull thump.

A napkin.

"You dumbass," Ryx said, grinning. "I'm a bounty hunter, remember? I've got contacts in thirty systems. Fixers, brokers, slicers, hell, half the info-net owes me favors. I could find her in an hour."

Shandar blinked. "You could?"

"Of course I could." Ryx leaned back smugly. "Give me her name, and I'll tell her myself. She'll be pinging this prison with a care package before week's end."

"I can't ask you to do that, Eryx Thorne."

"You're not. I want to. You saved my life. And you're my friend. I've done more for people who meant a hell of a lot less."

Shandar was quiet, his expression unreadable, but something in his posture softened. Then he rose to his feet and followed Ryx to the tray return. They moved together like clockwork, two parts of the same machine.

Outside the mess, they lingered by the corridor. Ryx knew they'd be sent back to their cells soon. He also knew they probably wouldn't see each other again before his release.

"Your daughter's name?" Ryx asked.

"Lanara Kress," Shandar said. "Vlexari. Doctor. Not in the Eleos system."

Ryx nodded as if mentally filing every detail away. "Got it."

"What was that dish you said you missed?" "Elosian Moon Shark," Shandar replied.

Ryx grinned. "Right. Better start hitting rec more often. You're gonna be getting messages. Maybe a few mystery meals." He held out a hand.

Shandar took it with quiet gravity, their palms clasped tight.

"Thank you," the Vlexari said. "Friend." Ryx squeezed his hand once, then let go.

He didn't say anything.

He couldn't.

ΔΔΔ

That night, Ryx couldn't sleep.

He lay on his cot, staring up at the ceiling, arms folded behind his head, eyes wide in the dark. The silence of the cell block had become familiar, almost comforting in its own way, but tonight, it pressed down on him like a weight.

He was supposed to feel relief. Freedom was just hours away. But instead, a strange heaviness sat in his chest. Not dread, not quite sadness, something quieter. Something more complicated.

His boots were polished and placed with care at the foot of his bed.

His coveralls folded neatly beside them. On his desk, the datapad Dell had given him months ago sat wiped and locked, a quiet end to a strange chapter.

He flexed his right hand, turning it palm-up slowly in the dim light.

The golden band on his wrist caught the glow of the overheads, subtle, warm, and alien. It wasn't a bracelet anymore. Not exactly. The metal had fused to his skin. It was part of him now. There was no line, no seam. Just a smooth, ancient ring of something not entirely from this galaxy.

He'd tried everything short of surgery to understand it. In all his obsessive nights of study, Ryx had found nothing. No references in xenoarcheology, no legends, no tech parallels. The thing was a ghost, like it had dropped into existence without history or origin.

That terrified, and fascinated him more than anything he'd ever encountered.

He turned his wrist slowly, studying how the fused metal caught the shadows. When he focused, he could feel it, like a pulse just beneath his skin. Not a hum exactly, but a presence. Waiting. Aware.

It had saved his life.

It had also wrecked it.

His gaze lingered on the band as a thought crept into his mind, one he hadn't let himself say out loud.

You're not done with me, are you?

The artifact didn't respond. It never did. But it was always there, like it knew something he didn't. Something important.

And that was the worst part. Ryx had seen all kinds of tech in his career, military and otherwise. There was always a system, always a user manual, even for things most people never got to touch. But this? This wasn't just alien. It was unknowable.

He flexed his fingers and exhaled through his nose, grounding himself.

Then, like a bad habit, his mind drifted to BSD.

Black Sable Dynamics.

They had sold him out. Lured him back to that mega tower, let the military pick him up like a stray. They wanted him out of the way. They knew they couldn't disappear him quietly. Instead, they tossed him to Varrix Prime's wolves.

And now he was getting out.

They won't like that.

He sat up slowly, the mattress creaking beneath him, a cold ripple spreading across his skin like a warning from some unseen predator.

What happens now? He had made peace with being forgotten. Had learned to live with the idea that no one would come looking. But freedom... it reopened everything. Including risk.

And worse, Tess and Kaelen were still in the crosshairs, whether they knew it or not. BSD might not strike openly, but they'd be watching. Waiting. And if they suspected he still had the artifact, which he did, literally fused to his body, there would be consequences.

He stood and paced to the small sink, splashing cold water over his face, trying to shake off the anxiety curling in his gut. The water ran down his cheeks and neck, dripping onto his collar. He caught sight of himself in the scratched mirror above the sink.

Unshaven. Hollow-eyed. Older than he looked.

But alive.

Still here.

And not finished yet.

He dried his face and leaned forward, resting his palms on the sink. Let the silence stretch. Let the fear settle.

I got through this. I'll get through what comes next.

And with that quiet vow, he stepped back, sat on the edge of his cot, and waited for morning.

∆∆∆

The next morning. The shift alarm buzzed like a thundercrack in the early gloom, echoing down the metal corridors of the cell block.

But no one came to fetch him.

Ryx stayed seated on the edge of his cot, already dressed in his coveralls. Boots laced. Back straight. His heart beat steady, but there was a hum under his skin, like he was standing on the edge of something vast. Something final.

They weren't sending him to the mines today. He knew it. He could feel it. This was it.

The door hissed open fifteen minutes later, quiet and unceremonious, and Dell Karn stood there with his hands on his hips and a cocky grin spread across his face.

"Can't believe they're letting a danger to society like you walk free," Dell said. Ryx stood and returned the grin as they clasped forearms. "Guess they decided to risk it."

"The Warden's orders," Dell said as he stepped aside. "Said I was to walk you out personally."

Ryx raised a brow. "Out of the kindness of his heart?"

Dell snorted. "Please. I volunteered. Figured someone had to make sure you didn't fall face-first down the steps and end up back in solitary."

They started down the corridor, their footsteps soft on the brushed metal floor. Prisoners were already being herded out to the yard. Most didn't notice Ryx. A few did and looked twice.

Eight months ago, they would've tried something.

Now, they just watched him go.

"Feels strange," Ryx murmured as they passed the rec room, the familiar hum of holo-emitters and low prisoner chatter coming through the thick walls.

Dell shrugged. "Freedom always does. You get used to a routine in here, even the shitty ones. Then one day, bam, you're back out there with a whole galaxy staring at you."

Ryx was quiet for a moment. Then: "Not gonna lie, I'm gonna miss some of it." Dell gave him a sideways glance. "You mean the food? The charming decor?"

"No," Ryx said with a small smile. "Just the people who didn't treat me like a monster."

They walked in silence for a few more steps. "I'm serious," Ryx added. "I know you are," Dell said quietly. "You changed here, Thorne. Whether you meant to or not."

Eventually they reached the intake room, though now, it was doubling as release. A plain desk, a terminal, and a pair of unarmed guards who barely acknowledged him.

Dell handed him a datapad and gestured. "Thumbprint here, signature there." Ryx complied. It was surreal, how simple it was. How easy it was to close a chapter that had weighed so heavily on his soul.

"I've got something for you," Dell said as he ducked into a side room. He returned a second later holding a bundle of folded clothes. "Some cutie just handed these off for you. Said she'd be waiting outside."

Ryx laughed as he took them. "Watch your mouth. That's my sister, ass." Dell blinked. "Wait, Tess? That little firecracker is your sister?"

"Not by blood. But close enough."

Dell gave a low whistle. "Well damn, guess the Rhoens really are a family of misfits."

Ryx changed slowly, as if each article of clothing weighed more than it should. The black long-sleeve shirt slid over his head like silk compared to the stiff, scratchy fabric of the prison-issued jumpsuit. The jeans were worn, softened by time and wear, familiar, broken in, not unlike himself. But it was the socks that hit hardest.

Civilian socks. Thick. Clean. Unstained by red dust or sweat or the recycled staleness of a prison laundry unit. He grinned as he pulled them on, rubbing his thumbs across the cotton like they were treasure. He hadn't realized how deeply he'd missed the simple comfort of choice. Of softness. Of being seen as a person again, not a number behind glass.

He stepped into the boots last. Worn leather creaked as he laced them up. They were scuffed and dinged in all the right places; he recognized them from the Wraith's storage compartment. Tess must have gone digging. The thought made his chest tighten.

Ryx stood up and looked down at himself. It wasn't armor. It wasn't tactical gear. But for the first time in a long time, it felt like he was wearing something that belonged to him.

Dell gave a soft whistle. "Well, shit. Look at you, almost like a real person." Ryx chuckled. "Almost?."

But the truth was, something had shifted. The clothes weren't just fabric. They were a signal. A line drawn between the man who had entered Varrix Delta in chains and the man who was leaving. Still scarred. Still uncertain. But lighter.

"Ready?" Dell asked.

Ryx nodded, but there was a flicker of hesitation. He glanced back into the halls of the prison he had spent the last nine months in, damp and cold. And yet it had become familiar. The walls had heard his screams. His nightmares. His confessions to the void. They'd watched him change.

He turned back to Dell. "Let's go before I change my mind." Dell raised an eyebrow. "Second thoughts already, Thorne? Don't tell me you're gonna miss the mess hall meat bricks." Ryx gave a lopsided grin. "They really grew on me."

They laughed, and with that, he followed Dell out of the release room, each step carrying a strange weight, like a ghost of the shackles he no longer wore. The hallway ahead seemed longer than before, the air clearer, the ceiling higher.

Freedom was just beyond the final door. But Ryx could feel the storm waiting behind it, too.

The corridors of Varrix Delta seemed quieter than usual. Not silent, the hum of the lights still echoed faintly, the hiss of pressure seals engaging as doors cycled open, but different. The kind of quiet that came at the end of a long, hard breath.

As Ryx followed Dell down the last stretch of hallway, he counted each step, not because he had to, but because he could. Every stride forward was one he'd earned. One the galaxy hadn't been able to take from him.

When they rounded the final corner and entered the small waiting chamber near the outer access terminal, Ryx's breath hitched.

Tess was already there.

She stood near the far wall talking animatedly with Warden Vance, her arms crossed but her stance relaxed, her foot tapping in time with whatever she was saying. The moment she caught sight of Ryx, everything froze, then she bolted.

"Ryx!" she shouted.

Before he could brace for it, she slammed into him with the force of a meteor strike. Her arms wrapped around him like a vice, and he stumbled back half a step, letting out a quiet grunt of surprise. But he didn't pull away.

He hadn't realized how much he needed this; how much he missed her. Tess smelled like starship grease and the same stubborn defiance she always carried around like a shield.

"Gods above and below," she murmured into his shoulder. "You're thinner." Ryx smirked. "Still devilishly handsome, though." She pulled back just enough to punch him in the arm. "Idiot. Don't make jokes. Not yet."

Ryx winced and rubbed the spot. "You really need to work on your greetings." "You really need to stop getting yourself thrown in war-crime holes."

Dell cleared his throat behind them. "Hate to interrupt this touching reunion, but some of us still have jobs to do." Ryx shot him a grin. "Dell Karn. You look more bureaucratic than usual."

"I moisturized this morning."

The dry response made both siblings laugh, and Ryx felt the tension bleeding from his chest as if someone had finally opened a pressure valve.

Then Warden Vance stepped forward.

"Well, Eryx Thorne," he said, hands clasped neatly behind his back, his expression warm but measured, "you're officially a free man."

Ryx took a breath, deep, steady. "Feels… strange, sir. Like I'm supposed to still have a shovel in my hands."

The Warden smiled. "We offer complimentary trauma with every stay." That earned a chuckle from Tess, but Ryx's smile was more subdued.

"I meant it when I said this place was better than I expected. That's… a low bar, but still."

The Warden gave a small nod. "Other than the beatings, solitary, hard labor, murder attempts…"

"And the coffee," Ryx added dryly. "Don't forget the war crime coffee." The Warden actually laughed. "Fair point."

Tess's eyes widened. "Wait, murder attempts?!" Dell answered before Ryx could. "You think he got out early for charm alone?" Ryx shrugged. "It helped."

Tess started to fume but Ryx gave her a reassuring look. "Later. I'll explain later."

Then Ryx turned back to the Warden, his expression shifting. Something in his posture straightened. Something in his face grew solemn.

Without a word, he stood at attention.

And then, he saluted.

Not out of obligation. Not out of protocol.

But out of genuine respect.

"Thank you, Warden Vance. For your fairness. For treating me like a man, even when the system didn't."

The Warden's brows lifted, visibly taken aback. He returned the salute after a moment's hesitation. "It means more than you know, Eryx Thorne. You didn't just serve your time for your freedom. You earned it."

A beat passed. Then Ryx's smirk returned. "Not that the respect of a scruffy, ex-con bounty hunter carries much weight."

Vance cracked a grin. "It carries more than you think." Ryx lowered his arm. "I'll stay out of trouble... Probably."

161

"That would be ideal," the Warden said. "Though, if you're ever back this way, perhaps consider visiting a certain Vlexari inmate, I'll make sure the coffee's slightly less terrible." That made Tess laugh.

Ryx felt his chest swell again, with a strange mix of pride and sadness. It was over. The worst of it. But something told him, deep down, that this chapter, this place, would never really leave him.

And he wasn't sure he wanted it to.

Tess and Ryx stepped slowly through the front gates of Varrix Delta, walking shoulder to shoulder down the paved path that led toward the landing pads. The sun hung low behind them, casting long shadows across the dusty concrete, and a dry breeze stirred faintly at their backs. Ryx hesitated, glancing over his shoulder.

He hadn't really taken in the building when he first arrived, half-unconscious, bloodied, and defeated. But now, looking at it from the outside, in daylight, as a free man, it struck him how unassuming it looked. Just a cluster of reinforced walls and guard towers nestled against the rising cliffs of the moon.

He'd lived an entire lifetime behind those walls. Part of him wanted to curse the place. But another part, the part that walked beside Tess with his shoulders a little straighter, recognized what he'd gained there, too.

Tess tugged gently on his arm. "Hey. Don't forget the best part of this reunion." She grinned. "Figured you'd push me over to get to your ship."

Ryx blinked. Then his head whipped around so fast it nearly spun off his shoulders.

There she was.

Perched on a visitor's pad just beyond the security checkpoint. Sleek, scarred, and absolutely perfect. The Wraithburn.

Her black and gunmetal hull shimmered under the sun like a storm cloud stretched into the shape of a hunting bird, larger than a standard fighter, smaller than a courier. Agile. Dangerous. Home.

He didn't walk. He bolted.

"Hey,!" Tess barely got the word out before Ryx was sprinting like a madman across the tarmac, arms spread like a kid chasing a dream.

Two guards flinched instinctively as he passed, but Tess waved them off, laughing. "Don't worry, he's just dramatic."

Ryx practically hugged the landing struts, wrapping both arms around one and pressing his forehead to the cool metal. He peppered the hull with exaggerated kisses.

"Oh, I missed you, old girl," he cooed, grinning like an idiot. He played it up for Tess's benefit, half performance, half genuine, but as his hands touched the familiar plates and rivets, something deep in his chest settled. The storm he hadn't realized he'd been carrying quieted. He blinked hard, blinking back tears.

This wasn't just a ship.

It was his ship.

Tess approached, pressing her palm to the biometric scanner. The security light flashed green, and with a hydraulic hiss, the loading ramp began to descend.

"You planning to make out with her all the way home, or do you actually want to fly the damn thing?" she asked, smirking.

Ryx placed a thoughtful hand under his chin, feigning deep consideration. Tess rolled her eyes and turned away with a laugh. "Unbelievable."

He jogged up the ramp after her, running one hand reverently along the interior bulkheads as he stepped into the hold. The hum of the internal power grid buzzed softly underfoot. Every surface was clean, polished. Everything smelled faintly of engine oil, scorched metal, and home.

"Stars, I missed this ship," Ryx murmured.

"You haven't seen the best part yet," Tess said in a sing-song voice, sliding into the co-pilot's seat.

Ryx all but threw himself into the pilot's chair, his hands falling instinctively onto the controls like he'd never left. They fit his palms like old gloves. He began the warm-up sequence automatically, fingers dancing across the console.

The Wraith purred to life beneath them.

Not choked. Not stuttering. But clean, powerful, and responsive. All systems green in under ten seconds. Ryx stared at the readout, mouth slightly agape.

She had never flown like this. Not even fresh out of her last retrofit.

"Whoa," Ryx breathed.

Tess leaned back, arms folded behind her head. "You're welcome."

"You did this?"

"New OS. Custom firmware. Triple-layered encryption. That baby is faster, leaner, and smarter than she's ever been." Tess tapped a few keys to bring up a system schematic on the holo-screen. "The code is mine. Kaelen handled most of the physical work, but the systems? That's all me."

Ryx looked over at her, stunned. "I did not pay you enough for this."

Tess grinned. "Oh, you didn't pay me at all. But I figured, since we didn't know if we'd get you back... I'd keep her flying. Just in case." He looked away for a second, swallowing the lump in his throat.

"You... kept her ready."

"Course I did. She's your ship. You're my brother. And, bonus, she's now basically unhackable." Ryx blinked. "Wait, what?"

"Biometric security," Tess said proudly. "Advanced systems locked to just three people, me, Dad, and you. Anyone else tries to override her AI, they'll fry their link. Or their hand."

Ryx let out a loud whoop and punched the air. "You beautiful genius!"

Then he looked at her seriously. "Tess I did not pay you even close to enough for this, honestly." He was trying to emphasize his point. Tess waved a dismissive hand at him. "This kept me busy for almost a whole year between jobs. Like I said, parts costs were low. No money necessary. Although…" Her voice trailed off, her tone turning playfully suggestive.

"Name it," Ryx said immediately, already bracing himself. "Anything."

She gave him a sly look, clearly enjoying the power. "If you know anyone in your network who's good with neuroscience, I'd love an introduction."

Ryx blinked. "Neuroscience?"

"You said you'd do anything," she reminded him, lifting a brow.

"I did, I did," Ryx said quickly, nodding. "I don't know anyone off the top of my head, but I've worked with research crews before. I can ask Rexa or one of my fixers to dig around."

Tess nodded, satisfied. "Good. Now kick this baby into gear. We've got more to show you."

Ryx's grin widened as he turned back to the controls. He needed no further encouragement. With the ease of a man returning to his own skin, he lifted The Wraithburn smoothly from the landing pad, guiding her into a clean, spiral ascent that cut a perfect arc into the sky. The moment they broke atmosphere and slid into orbit, Tess laughed.

"What?" Ryx asked, glancing sideways.

"Even with all these upgrades, and all the time I've spent crawling around this ship, I can't fly her like that," she said, shaking her head in admiration.

Ryx chuckled. "Practice makes perfect. You build enough muscle memory dodging proton lances and being chased by guns bigger than your ship; it sticks."

Tess leaned back, but her expression sobered slightly. "Speaking of guns, dad got tired of watching you limp home with half your engines blown out. He spent the last few months upgrading your shield systems."

Ryx whooped, but her tone kept him from launching into full celebration. "What's wrong?"

165

"Nothing's wrong," she said carefully. "But what he did… Ryx, I've never seen anything like it. It wasn't just technical; it was like watching someone paint a masterpiece. It was personal."

Ryx stared at her, brow furrowed. "What kind of upgrade are we talking about?"

Tess gave a small, awed smile. "He condensed the shield array of a mid-size battle cruiser into your systems bay." Ryx's hand froze on the controls.

"What!?" he bellowed.

Tess burst out laughing.

"You're not invincible," she clarified between giggles, "but anything smaller than a full cruiser? They're gonna have a real bad time picking on you now. It would take sustained fire from something huge to make you sweat."

Without a word, Ryx jumped up, engaged autopilot, and sprinted down the corridor toward the ship's small engineering section. Tess followed behind, laughing as she caught up.

There it was.

Nestled into the systems bay like it had always belonged there. The shield battery. Its containment unit glowed with a soft golden pulse, casting rhythmic light across the chamber. It looked sleek, dangerously compact, and familiar, in a terrifying way.

Ryx had seen shield cores like this before. On capital ships. On battle cruisers.

Never, never, never on a ship this small.

"How…" he breathed, eyes wide with disbelief.

Tess leaned against the wall, arms crossed, watching him soak it in. "We asked ourselves the same thing. He designed the housing from scratch. Tuned the flow regulators like a concert pianist tuning a grand piano."

Ryx couldn't take his eyes off it. "This tech is worth millions. You could patent this, sell it to any military or private defense corp, and they'd throw fleets and credits at your feet." "We know," Tess said, softly.

He turned to her.

"Pops has the blueprints. Rexa's helping him lawyer up and get it protected before someone else claims it. But he's not taking a dime from you, Ryx. Don't even try. He did this for you. And he's proud of it. Happy you gave him the chance to build it."

Ryx exhaled a stunned breath and gave a shaky laugh. "This is insane."

Tess patted his shoulder. "One more thing."

She led him back up to the cockpit. Once they were seated, she pointed to a new device wired into the Wraith's comms module, a sleek, crystalline box with glowing violet filaments inside.

Ryx stared at it. "What the hell is that?"

"A gift from both of us," Tess said proudly. "We got tired of your cryptic, days-old messages."

Ryx blinked. "Is that a... new communication relay?"

"Bingo." She grinned. "No more laggy messages, no more praying some poor data packet limps its way through three systems. You can bounce messages through public relays now with minimal lag, and even live-call, if you're in-range. Assuming you're not mid-warp."

Ryx stared. "Neither of you are comms engineers... how did you do this?"

"Oh, we didn't build it," Tess said sweetly. "We bought it." Ryx narrowed his eyes. "Tess... those units cost," "About thirty grand," she said, casually. Ryx shot to his feet. "You spent the repair funds on this!?"

She shrugged, utterly unbothered. "We missed you. And, like I said , we were sick of your cryptic bullshit."

Ryx sank into his chair, groaning. "That's not the point, Tess. I paid you both for the work you did on the Wraith and look at this.

167

You've rebuilt my whole damn ship. You've done everything for me. I feel like I gave you nothing in return."

She punched his shoulder, lightly. "We got you back, dumbass. That's what matters."

Her voice was quiet, but steady. It hit Ryx harder than he expected.

A moment passed between them. Then she straightened and motioned to the comms panel. "Call the old man. Let him know we're on schedule. He's already sweeping the landing bay."

Ryx rolled his eyes and keyed in the commands, so familiar now they felt like second nature. Within seconds, the line connected.

"Rhoen's Maintenance," came a gravelly voice.

"Hey old man. Miss me?"

"Well, I'll be damned." Kaelen's voice warmed instantly. "If it isn't my favorite ex-con."

Ryx and Tess both laughed.

"You on your ship?" Kaelen asked.

Ryx hesitated. "Kaelen... I can't accept all of this. Not without,"

"Tess, turn on video," Kaelen interrupted, sounding mildly annoyed. "I wanna see his pouty face while he whines about how good his family is."

Tess reached forward, hit the toggle, and Kaelen's weathered face filled the screen. His backdrop was familiar, his workbench, an array of half-disassembled tech strewn around it.

"There's that tense, moody mug," Kaelen said, smirking. "Tess no doubt told you, we're fancy now. High-def calls and everything. I'm practically royalty."

"I just... I don't even know what to say," Ryx started.

"Don't," Kaelen waved a hand. "And don't think I haven't noticed the credits you and Tess keep sneaking into my account every few months. I'm old, not blind. You think I don't know what my numbers look like?"

Ryx and Tess shared a guilty glance.

"Now it's your turn to deal with our charity," Kaelen continued. "Sucks, doesn't it?"

"I just got out of jail," Ryx said, leaning back with a smirk. "My family's rich, my ship's a monster, and I've got clean socks. Feels pretty damn good, actually." All three of them laughed.

Kaelen squinted at the screen. "You're looking thin, boy. They feed you in there?"

"Barely," Ryx snorted. "Food was trash. Work was brutal. Can't wait to get some noodles in me."

Kaelen smiled. "Good. Get jumping. I'll have takeout here by the time you hit the dock. Your treat."

"You got it, Pops," Ryx said warmly. "See you tomorrow."

Kaelen gave a small wave. "It's gonna be good to have you home, kid."

The comms cut.

Tess looked over at Ryx, her voice softer now. "He really missed you, Ryx. We both did."

Ryx held out a fist, and Tess bumped it gently.

"I missed you both too," he said, voice thick with quiet emotion. Then he threw back his head dramatically. "But you two didn't have to eat prison food! Let's go home!"

He engaged the Wraithburn's warp drive. The stars around them stretched into white streaks and then vanished into the silence of faster-than-light.

Ryx and Tess moved to the Wraithburn's compact living area. She tossed him a paper-wrapped sandwich from the fridge, which he tore into with savage delight, crumbs scattering like confetti.

"STARS I MISSED REAL FOOD!" Ryx groaned, half-choking on his first bite, his voice muffled by a mouthful of sandwich.

Tess smirked. "It's just a sandwich, you maniac."

But to Ryx, it wasn't just a sandwich. It was warmth. It was home. It wasn't the gray, nutrient-dense bricks he'd eaten in the prison mess. It had flavor, spice, salt, texture. Humanity.

They talked for hours. Ryx told her everything, his time on Varrix Delta, the beatings, the work, his strange, wordless friendship with Shandar Kress. He told her about the assassinations, the investigation, the night in the showers. And finally, he told her about his research into the bracelet.

"Nothing?" Tess asked, incredulous, eyes flicking to where she knew the band on his wrist was.

"Nothing," Ryx repeated flatly, his voice hollow with frustration. "Rexa's been digging too, BSD's xenoarcheology division, anything connected to Vess' expedition. Not a damn trace."

Tess leaned forward, staring at his wrist where it rested against the table. "How the hell did you even keep it in there? With all their scanners and shakedowns?"

Ryx smirked and pulled back his sleeve. "It got creative. I passed it off as a war wound with a cybernetic correction. Check this out." He showed her its current state, fused with his wrist like an implant.

With a thought, and a ripple of cool blue light, the implant shimmered and shifted, folding, stretching, transforming, until the full golden bracelet sat around his wrist once more, gleaming faintly in the ship's low lights. Then as if in reverse it was back to the implant.

"It did this on its own once," Ryx said softly. "Like it knew I was in danger. Like it was trying to save me."

Tess's brow furrowed, her eyes narrow and cautious. "You're saying it can think?"

"I'm saying I don't know what else to call it." Ryx's voice dropped. "It seems to sense danger, protect me, warn me. I can almost hear it deep in my thoughts asking me to call for it. And when I do… it listens back."

The silence that followed was uneasy.

"That's spooky as hell, bro," Tess muttered. "That thing is alive?"

"I don't know," Ryx said, slowly turning the bracelet back into its disguised form. "But it's not just a tool. I can feel it in my thoughts, like… like an echo that's always one step behind me."

Tess said nothing, but her expression told Ryx everything. She was worried, and maybe a little afraid.

They stayed up late, catching up. Tess talked about the shop, her designs, the rotating chaos of engineers and suppliers and shady station mechanics. They fantasized about their own private fleet, about owning a real design lab and hangar. Kaelen would run the place from a raised catwalk, barking orders like an admiral. Tess would moonlight as a mad genius inventor. Ryx would do what he did best, fly, fight, survive.

They laughed about Ryx calling the place "King's Fleet," complete with a cheesy logo and an over-the-top slogan. Ryx claimed Kaelen could wear a crown. Tess threatened to pass out from laughing so hard.

Eventually, they both called it a night. Ryx stepped into his cabin for the first time in nearly a year.

No ceremony. No words. Just the overwhelming pull of something familiar, something his.

He flopped onto the mattress and melted into the soft bedding with a groan of relief. It felt like being swallowed whole in the best way. He kicked off his boots, peeled out of his clothes, and pulled on his favorite shorts. With a content sigh, he wrapped himself tightly in his plush blankets, and let the exhaustion pull him under.

Ryx awoke to a smell he hadn't realized he missed so badly it would haunt his dreams: a Quick&Ez Breakfast Burrito™.

He bolted out of bed, still half-asleep, and stumbled into the galley. Tess stood with a smirk, waving the burrito through the air like a hypnotic pendulum.

"Fresh outta the reheater," she grinned. "Stuffed the fridge before I left. Figured you'd appreciate it."

Ryx made a low, desperate groan of joy. "I owe you so much, Tess."

He caught the tossed burrito mid-air like a starved animal and unwrapped it with reverence. The first bite nearly made him weep.

"Calm down," Tess said, amused. "It's just a reheated burrito."

"No," Ryx mumbled, eyes closed in rapture. "This is nirvana."

They spent the rest of the day in light conversation, running final system diagnostics, inventorying gear, and checking new modules. Ryx was delighted to find his armor safely stowed in the hidden locker, refurbished, pristine. His TalonX-5 was missing, of course. That left a dull ache in his chest. But the rest… it felt like him again.

The cockpit of the Wraithburn was silent as Ryx and Tess sat side by-side, watching the stars stretch and shimmer around them. The final minute of warp felt unbearably slow.

Then,

A soft chime, a flicker of warning light.

And with a shuddering flick, the stars snapped back into sharp points of starlight, revealing a familiar shape ahead.

Vorrthani Station.

It loomed in the void like a rust-colored steel colossus. Half-lit docking arms arced from its central body like broken fingers. Antennas blinked their silent warnings, and the glow of navigation lights sparkled across its battered hull. It was ugly. Industrial. Cluttered with years of expansions, repair scaffolds, and ad-hoc cargo modules. All built into a huge asteroid like it was some kind of high-tech ant hill.

But to Ryx, it was home.

His chest tightened at the sight of it. A strange cocktail of relief and dread swirled in his gut.

A comms request came through.

"Vorrthani Station traffic control," a bright, unfamiliar woman's voice crackled through the speakers. "Please state your business."

Ryx leaned forward. "This is the Wraithburn, requesting permission to dock at Rhoen's Maintenance."

There was a pause on the other end. Longer than it should've been. Tess glanced sideways at him.

The woman's voice returned, more hesitant this time. "We're... currently experiencing issues with our dock assignment systems. We can't confirm whether Rhoen's bay is in use."

Another pause. A faint background murmur like she was being fed instructions.

"You're listed as a permanent tenant. Proceed with caution and visually confirm the bay is clear before attempting to land. Please have the shop owner contact us to resolve the registry issue." Ryx frowned and exchanged a look with Tess.

"Copy that, Vorrthani Control," he replied tightly. "Proceeding with visual confirmation." The comm cut out.

Almost immediately, Tess started punching commands into the terminal, opening a direct channel to the garage's private line.

Ryx maneuvered the Wraithburn around the station's outer shell, tension building with every second they crawled closer to the other side.

"No answer," Tess said flatly. Her voice was calm, but there was an edge to it.

"He's probably running errands," Ryx muttered, trying to dismiss the knot forming in his chest. But he could already feel it, that old itch between his shoulder blades. Something was wrong. Every instinct he'd sharpened over a decade in the field screamed at him.

"Just hurry," Tess said. "Pull us around."

The Wraith curved smoothly around the station's belly. The familiar curve of Deck Nine came into view. The garage bay was just beyond it.

Silence pressed down on them like gravity.

Then, there it was.

Rhoen's Maintenance.

At first glance, it looked like it always had closed bay doors, a few ships parked nearby, flickering perimeter lights. Ryx felt a flicker of hope.

Until the Wraithburn's trajectory shifted slightly, and the internal view from the exterior cameras adjusted for angle.

That's when they saw it.

The doors were blown inward.

The interior, their shop, the beating heart of their makeshift family, was in ruin. The metal deck plating had been scorched and twisted by multiple blast points. Panels were torn from the walls like ripped skin, and acrid black smoke poured upward in slow coils, leaking into the vacuum above through torn roof vents.

Sparks flickered from exposed wiring. Flames licked at oil-slick machinery. At least one of the hydraulic lifts lay in a crumpled heap. The hangar's overhead gantry had partially collapsed across a wrecked hoverbike. The damage was surgical, efficient.

A breach and clear. Mercenary work.

In the dim light, Ryx could just make out them, figures in matte black tactical armor, helmets glinting with embedded visors. They moved like predators, rifles slung casually but always ready. Two of them were dragging a crate across the garage floor. Another knelt at a data terminal, hands dancing across its interface.

BSD. Or worse.

Tess gasped, hand flying to her mouth. "Dad..." Ryx's heart stopped.

He couldn't breathe.

Then, without thought, his fingers began to move, slamming the cockpit into manual override and rerouting auxiliary power to the Wraithburn's shield array.

He didn't even remember making the decision. His world had narrowed to a pinpoint of fury and dread.

"They hit the shop," Tess whispered, her voice cracking.

Ryx stared at the devastation. His mouth was dry. His fingers tightened around the controls until his knuckles went white.

"Not just hit it," he growled. "They knew exactly what they were doing."

He blinked, forcing himself to think, to focus.

"I need you to take the helm and park nearby," he said finally, voice strained. "We can't land there. Not yet. We don't know what we're walking into."

"But Dad," Tess began.

"I know," Ryx said, cutting her off gently. "I'm going in to get him."

His eyes never left the screen. "But first, we're going to find out exactly who the hell is in our garage."

CHAPTER 10

HAMMER OF GOD

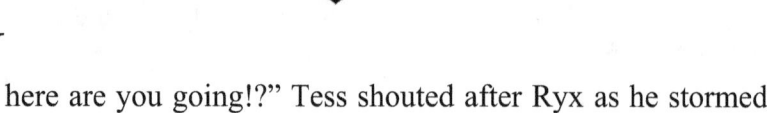

W here are you going!?" Tess shouted after Ryx as he stormed out of the cockpit with deadly purpose.

"Turn the Wraith so the main hatch faces the garage!" he barked over his shoulder.

Tess scrambled into the pilot's seat and complied, swiveling the ship slowly as Ryx disappeared down the corridor. The urgency in his voice sent ice through her veins.

He moved like a man possessed, like a storm in human skin. Ryx marched with dark purpose directly into his closet, and the armory hatch hissed open with a low, serpentine whisper. Deftly, he strapped on every piece of his white neoplate armor, tightening clasps, locking joints, feeling the familiar pressure form around his body like an old second skin. Each click of metal was a promise. The mask snapped into place with a hydraulic hiss. His heart thundered like a war drum. He loaded the Iron Howl, stuffed his belt full of grenades, extra ammo cells. Angrily, efficiently.

When he returned to the cockpit, he stood just outside the doorway. "I'm air-sealing the rest of the ship from the door," he said flatly.

"What the fuck are you going to do?" Tess demanded.

Without answering, Ryx pressed a series of commands into the wall panel. Environmental seals shimmered over every internal bulkhead, casting a blue hue down the corridor. He reached for his emergency air system switch, fitted his mask tighter, and took a steadying breath.

"I'm going to get the old man," he said.

Tess screamed after him. "You're gonna fucking jump across open space into the garage!? Are you FUCKING crazy!?"

"No," he said, hand resting on the hatch release. "I'm in a rush."

He hit the panel. The exterior hatch cracked open with a rising whine, and then a howl of escaping pressure as the last of the internal air vented into the vacuum. He held tight to the doorframe until the rush settled and only the stars stared back.

The garage loomed across the short void, maybe thirty meters, no more. But it might as well have been a battlefield.

He could see them. Five heat signatures on his HUD. Masks. Armor. Moving with purpose through the garage.

The bracelet on his right wrist stirred. Ryx felt it, not just physically but in his mind, a low thrum like a beast waking from slumber. A whisper through the back of his thoughts. Ready. He willed it free. The gauntlet enveloped his right arm.

He gritted his teeth, bent his knees, and launched.

The micro-thrusters on his back and boots flared with sharp bursts, pushing him out of the Wraith and into the vacuum. His body cut through the void like a missile, arms tucked, velocity increasing.

Wind didn't exist out here. There was no resistance. Just cold silence.

But in his helmet, everything pulsed, heartbeat, vitals, the glow of the enemy silhouettes. The gauntlet pulsed brighter as he neared the field, and for a moment he thought he saw circuits of ancient light flowing across the metal like veins. It was almost... eager.

The garage's environmental shield shimmered like a translucent curtain, and he crashed through it like a bullet.

The moment he passed through, Ryx disengaged the thrusters and dropped fast. The artificial gravity of the station took him, pulling him downward like the judgment of a god.

At the last second, the gauntlet responded.

Blue light flared across his entire arm, the shield springing into full power as if summoned by instinct, not his own, but the artifact's. It flared wide and concave, transforming into a full-force kinetic barrier that caught the brunt of the impact as he slammed down onto the crouching merc at the terminal.

The shield hit the man like a warhammer. Bones shattered. Blood sprayed against the wall. The terminal cracked. Ryx hit the floor in a rolling crouch, the gauntlet steaming from the sheer force of the transfer.

He didn't pause.

He flowed to his feet, the Ironhowl already drawn from his back with practiced speed. The rifle locked into his shoulder with a satisfying mechanical snap.

Target highlighted. Chest shot. Another down.

Helmet alarms flared in his ears as the other enemies whirled in surprise, completely disoriented by the human missile that just destroyed their teammate.

Ryx's hands moved with lightning precision. His gauntlet pulsed again, feeding into the rifle's energy systems, overcharging the next shot. Headshot. The merc dropped like a sack of stone.

He moved like a ghost, eyes locked, rage coiled beneath his calm.

Another flare from the gauntlet, not a command, but a response. It projected micro-barrier pulses, catching stray rounds fired in panic, letting him close the distance untouched.

This was no ordinary armor. No ordinary weapon.

The gauntlet was awake now.

And Ryx wasn't alone in this fight.

The remaining two mercenaries dove for cover, shouts echoing through the garage as the sharp, electric scent of gunfire filled the air. Ryx didn't flinch. He advanced, slow, deliberate, unstoppable.

Blue light shimmered across his gauntlet as another kinetic shield expanded with a low hum, forming a gleaming oval that moved with his steps, deflecting incoming fire with bursts of crackling energy. The shield didn't just block, it absorbed and flexed, almost like it anticipated the next shot before Ryx did.

Rounds slammed into it and ricocheted off into the walls. Sparks burst against the shield's edge. The two remaining mercs panicked, shouting into their comms.

"He's got a, what the fuck is that thing!?"

"Fall back, regroup,!"

Ryx wasn't listening. He was already moving.

One of the mercs popped up from behind a flipped hovercart, gun raised to lay down suppressive fire. But before he could get a shot off, Ryx was there.

The gauntlet's blade flared to life, a searing, blue-edged construct, curved like a predator's fang and radiating heat in the visible spectrum. He brought it up in a savage arc that sheared through the man's helmet and cleanly removed his head. The body collapsed in a twitching heap.

Ryx barely spared it a glance. The second merc turned to run.

Coward.

Ryx leveled the Ironhowl and fired. A clean, center-mass shot. The man folded mid-stride and hit the floor hard.

He scanned the room, breathing hard, muscles tense, ears ringing. Nothing moved. Not yet.

Then came the hiss of the inner door, leading from the garage into the machine shop.

Ryx spun toward it, already moving. He dove for cover behind a scorched tool locker just as two more voices shouted into the space.

"WHAT THE FUCK HAPPENED!?"

Ryx peeked around the corner.

Two more. Their movements weren't coordinated, they were scattered, confused. No formation, no discipline. *Poorly trained*, he thought with disgust.

Ryx didn't hesitate.

He surged forward, silent on his boots, and closed the distance like a shadow cutting across the light. The gauntlet's blade sang to life again, and in a fluid lunge, Ryx drove it through the spine of the nearest merc, lifting him off the ground for half a second before dropping him like trash.

The other merc turned, eyes wide in horror, trying to raise his weapon, but the Ironhowl was already in Ryx's off hand, and the shot punched through the man's chest plate like paper. He dropped instantly.

Ryx paused. Listened. The garage was silent now, only the hum of repair machinery in standby behind him, the crackle of distant sparks from damaged terminals.

"Tess," he said through the transponder. "I've secured the,"

Her voice cut in, frantic. "Ryx, I've docked in the market. I'm heading to you."

"No! Stay on the ship!" he snapped.

But the connection crackled, already muted. She was ignoring him.

Of course she was.

Ryx clenched his jaw, scanned once more to ensure there were no other hostiles, then turned toward the shop door. It was scorched, dented, half hanging from its mount.

He breached it fast and low, Ironhowl raised, heart pounding.

The shop was wrecked, tools flung across the room like thrown bones, heavy workbenches overturned, scorch marks peppered across the floor and ceiling. Debris littered every corner. Something had gone off in here, likely a grenade.

Too messy, Ryx thought. They didn't just search this place; they tried to erase it.

Then, he heard it.

A low, broken sound, half groan, half breath, issuing from beneath a scorched, overturned workbench in the far corner of the shop. Ryx's breath caught in his throat.

It couldn't be.

He moved on instinct. The Ironhowl slipped from his fingers and hit the floor with a dull metallic clatter, forgotten. His boots pounded over scorched metal. Smoke curled through the air like the remnants of a nightmare.

Just an arm was visible, sticking out from beneath the workbench. The skin was a familiar tan, dusted with soot, streaked with dried blood. A lattice of white scars stretched across the knuckles, faint lines Ryx knew as intimately as his own hands.

No.

No no no no no.

His pulse went supersonic. His stomach lurched like the gravity had tripled.

That hand had once taught him to hold a welding torch, to gut an engine, to reset a dislocated shoulder with grit and a half-empty bottle of Station No. 9. That hand had ruffled his hair the first time he brought in a bounty. That hand had gripped his shoulder the night he'd come home bloodied and half-alive and said, "You're still here, kid. That's what matters." And now it was just… limp.

Crushed. Motionless.

"Kaelen," Ryx whispered, his voice cracking like glass under pressure. "Kaelen…"

He dropped to his knees beside the bench, armor clanking against the warped flooring. The gauntlet pulsed with concern, responding to his elevated vitals, the glow around his arm flickering erratically like it sensed the pain surging through him.

"Kaelen, hold on," Ryx breathed, a frantic edge in his voice.

He gripped the edge of the overturned workbench with both hands, fingers digging into the twisted steel like claws. The gauntlet responded with a surge of strength, feeding power into his frame. Ryx's muscles coiled, back arched, breath held,

And with a scream of pain and fury, he ripped the massive table off the ground and hurled it across the shop.

It crashed into the far wall with an earsplitting metallic shriek, embedding into the plating with a thunderous clang.

There he was.

Kaelen Rhoen.

His father.

Half-buried in blood and debris, clothes charred and torn. His right side was blackened; skin blistered from an explosion. His chest barely moved. One leg was bent at an unnatural angle. His once proud face was slack, smeared with soot and streaked with red.

Ryx couldn't breathe.

He couldn't speak.

He stared.

And the world shattered.

He fell beside the man, hands trembling violently. His vision blurred with tears that spilled unchecked down his cheeks, soaking into the padding of his mask. He tore it off with shaking fingers and dropped it aside, eyes locked on Kaelen's broken form.

"No," he whispered. "No, no, no, please, please, stars, not like this,"

He reached out and touched Kaelen's shoulder, afraid it would crumble under his fingers. It was warm. Still warm.

That made it worse.

That meant he'd only just missed him.

That meant he wasn't there.

That he'd failed.

A choking sound broke from Ryx's throat, raw and ragged. He doubled over, pressing his forehead against Kaelen's chest, shaking from the storm tearing him apart inside.

"You didn't deserve this," he rasped, voice hoarse and hollow. "You... you were good. You were too good. You kept us together when everything else fell apart, and" He couldn't finish.

He just screamed.

The grief ripped through him like a nova, loud and brutal and uncontainable. It echoed through the ruined shop, bouncing off twisted steel and cracked walls and broken dreams.

He screamed until his voice gave out.

Until his lungs seized.

Until there was nothing left in him but shaking.

The gauntlet dimmed. The power in it curled tight, almost like it was trying to comfort him, like it knew. But there was no comfort. No answer. Only silence.

Ryx knelt beside Kaelen's body for what could've been minutes or an hour. Time had no meaning anymore.

He stared at the man who had taken him in, fixed his broken bones and broken spirit, taught him how to survive, how to fight, how to hope. The man who treated him like a son without ever saying it, because he didn't need to.

Ryx didn't realize until much later that he'd stopped crying. That he'd gone completely still.

His hand drifted to his right. Found the Ironhowl on the floor. Lifted it.

He turned it over slowly, like it was some artifact from a dead civilization.

The barrel was still hot. The safety glowed amber. All he had to do was aim it, just like before. Just like then.

Just like after he defected.

Easy way out, that part of his mind whispered.

But the moment shattered when he heard the scream.

Tess.

Ryx blinked.

Then he was moving.

The Ironhowl dropped to the floor with a clatter. He was already out the door, the mask snapping back onto his face, the gauntlet reigniting like a wrathful star. A pulse of electric light ran down his arm like it was bracing for war.

He didn't feel his legs.

Didn't feel anything.

Only the heat. Only the rage. Only the red haze blurring the edge of his vision.

Eryx Thorne, broken and hollow, stormed into the fire again.

And the stars trembled at what was coming next.

Ryx barreled through the garage entrance and into the house like a thunderclap. His boots hit scorched flooring, metal-plated and marred with soot, blood, and impact burns. The air smelled like fire, like carbonized plastic, like a place that had been turned inside out.

And then he saw her.

Tessa.

His sister. His anchor.

She was in the open space between the entryway and the kitchen, swinging a heavy spanner with both hands, desperation carved into every motion. The tool whistled through the air as she fended off two mercs, both wielding humming hardlight blades, their flickering edges leaving burning streaks in the air.

Ryx's heart stopped.

"TESS!" he shouted, but too late.

One of the mercs, taller, faster, slid inside her guard and cut.

A flash of blue-white light as the hardlight blade arced under her left elbow. And then, Blood. Spraying like a jet from a broken hose. Her forearm hit the floor with a dull, wet sound. Tessa screamed. The wrench clattered away.

The second merc stepped forward and kicked her square in the chest with the flat of his armored boot. She flew back, smashing into the wall with a crack and crumpled to the floor, twitching, her remaining hand clutching at her shoulder, red pouring from between her fingers.

The second the blade severed Tessa's arm, something inside Ryx snapped.

He didn't feel the scream leave his throat. Didn't register the hot splash of her blood across his boots. His vision tunneled, turned red, as every cell in his body screamed to move, to kill, to end.

And the gauntlet answered.

With a roar of energy, the blue light shimmered and enveloped him fully, flaring outward like a barrier, but alive, moving, breathing with his fury.

Three more mercenaries surged from the back hallway, rifles already firing.

Too slow.

He was gone.

The first two men, blades still raised, barely had time to register the blur that passed between them before Ryx materialized behind them. He lifted both of his arms. Both of his now *gauntleted* arms. He grabbed both men by their helmets, the gauntlet's grip searing hot with energy, and crushed.

Skulls caved in like soft fruit. Blood sprayed the walls. Their bodies dropped like sacks of meat.

The first man in the hallway screamed and fired,

Ryx blinked forward again, appearing just inches from him. He punched the man's rifle aside and drove his fist through his chest. The blue blade of the gauntlet ignited mid-strike, piercing through armor, bone, and spine. The man didn't even have time to scream.

Two left.

The last two mercs in the hallway turned tail, trying to flee,

"You don't get to run," Ryx growled, voice metallic and warped through the mask.

He extended his hand and fired a pulse of concussive energy from the gauntlet. The nearest man slammed into the wall hard enough to shatter it, ribs crushed, spine fractured.

The final merc ducked through a doorway, scrambling into Kaelen's bedroom, trying to barricade the door.

Too slow.

Ryx blinked again, through the wall, reappearing inside the room behind him.

He grabbed the man by the back of his armor and threw him across the room like a rag doll. The merc slammed into Kaelen's workshop bench and dropped hard. Ryx stalked toward him slowly, methodically, gauntlet glowing like a living storm.

"Please," the man rasped, holding up a shaking hand. "Wait, wait"

Crack.

The armored boot came down on his neck. One brutal stomp. Silence.

Ryx stood over the last body, chest heaving.

Blood steamed on the gauntlet. His hands trembled.

And then,

"TESS."

The rage faded like smoke from a dying fire.

He turned and ran, the memory of her body hitting the wall playing over and over in his head.

ΔΔΔ

Ryx ran like hell had broken loose behind him.

Tessa's body was limp in his arms, blood still hot against his chest plate. The cauterized stump of her arm bounced gently with

186

every stride, too gently. Her face was pale, lips parted, breath shallow. His own heart thundered, a deafening beat that drowned out everything else, the clamor of crowds, the sound of his boots pounding the station floor, the voices shouting as he shoved past them.

"MOVE!" he barked, voice distorted through the helmet. "SHE NEEDS HELP, NOW!"

People scrambled aside, some too stunned to speak. Others called for security or medical, but Ryx didn't wait for help. He couldn't. He had one thought, Rexa. Only Rexa Vorn had the knowledge, the equipment, the nerve to help right now.

The market stretched ahead, a kaleidoscope of neon signs and steel stalls blurring past as he sprinted. A vendor dropped a crate of fruit. Another screamed at the blood trailing behind him. Ryx barely noticed.

Her pulse was slipping.

It was so light. Too light. He tried not to see the blood dripping from her fingers. Tried not to hear the faint, ragged sound of her breath faltering against his collarbone.

"Hold on, Tess."

The door to Rexa Vorn's shop slammed open as Ryx hit it with his shoulder. The steel creaked and bent around his armored form.

Rexa spun from her workbench, her rifle half-raised on instinct. She froze when she saw his face, his mask, drenched in blood. Then her eyes fell to the broken girl in his arms.

"ERYX! What the hell,"

He dropped to his knees.

"Tessa," he gasped. His voice cracked. "Help her."

Everything hit him at once, the blood, the pain, the loss, the relief, and the world tilted. He didn't even feel himself fall. He just saw Rexa leap over the counter, screaming for her assistant, her gloves already on, a medical scanner in her hand. He felt the moment her hands touched Tess, the panic in her voice as she barked vitals and cursed. And then,

187

Black.

CHAPTER 11

OIL AND STEEL

Ryx sat slumped against the wall outside Rexa Vorn's back room, his breath shallow, the sting of smoke and dried blood clinging to him like guilt. Tessa was inside, alive, Rexa had said, but just barely. The cauterized stump where her arm used to be had needed emergency reinforcement, and they weren't out of the woods yet. Every time he closed his eyes, he saw it: the severed limb, the blood, the scream that didn't stop ringing in his ears.

His armor was still partially on, crusted with carbon scoring and someone else's blood. His mask lay discarded near the door, cracked at the edge. The bracelet was dormant now, silent, dim, but still warm against his wrist. He had no memory of what exactly it did back there. Only the aftermath.

"Ryx." Rexa's voice pulled him from the haze.

He stood too fast, staggered, caught himself.

"She's stable." Rexa's face was hard to read, relief edged with fatigue. "She'll need surgery, stim-recovery, maybe prosthetics down the line. But she's alive."

Ryx nearly collapsed again, all the tension in his body threatening to snap his spine. He nodded, swallowed hard. "Can I see her?"

"Not yet," Rexa said. "She needs rest. And so do you."

He looked past her toward the closed door, jaw clenched. "I'll wait."

Rexa didn't argue. She just pulled a chair over beside him and dropped a thermal blanket over his shoulders. "You smell like death," she muttered, sitting next to him.

"I think part of me died back there."

She didn't offer platitudes. Just sat in silence, keeping vigil beside him as the weight of everything, Kaelen, Tess, the garage, the mercs, the gauntlet, settled into the cracks of his exhausted soul.

The walls of Rexa's shop felt too narrow, too quiet. Each tick of the wall-mounted chrono was another crack in Ryx's mental dam. He sat motionless in the chair beside the med-room door, the thermal blanket slipping off his shoulders. He didn't notice. He didn't notice Rexa leave his side. His hands were clenched into fists against his knees, nails biting into his palms until the bracelet on his wrist quivered, reminding him it was still part of him, still awake even when he wasn't.

Kaelen's hand looked so small under that work bench.

That was the first thought that broke through. Not the blood. Not the burn. Not the stillness of the body. Just the hand, scarred, calloused, worn by years of labor and age and love. Still stretched out, like maybe he'd been trying to reach for something. Or someone.

Ryx buried his face in his hands, trying to blot out the memory. But the images came anyway.

Tess's scream, sharp, animal, and suddenly silenced. The sickening thud of her body hitting the wall. Her arm, severed just below the elbow, still twitching where it landed. Blood spraying like her body was trying to fight the loss with everything it had.

He had failed them both.

You are the reason he was under that workbench.

You were the reason she had to go in alone.

You were the one they wanted.

You brought this to their door.

The thoughts weren't just intrusive. They were consuming. His chest constricted as if the walls themselves were collapsing. He could barely breathe, but he couldn't move, either. He wanted to stand, scream, punch something until his knuckles shattered. But he sat frozen. Guilt. Shame. Grief. It was all just... too much.

I should've been faster.

He could still feel the gauntlet burning in his blood when he had crushed those helmets, split that mercenary in half with light and fury. But it hadn't been enough. Not nearly enough. The weapon had awoken, turned him into something... else. But even that power hadn't saved Kaelen. It hadn't saved Tess in time.

He clenched his jaw so hard it clicked.

"I should've died back there," he whispered aloud, his voice raw and cracked.

A memory drifted up uninvited, Kaelen laughing in the shop, holding a half-finished stabilizer unit. "You try that reckless nonsense again, I'll weld your boots to the floor, kid." He let out a broken breath. He'd give anything to hear that voice again. Even just one more time.

The med-room door hissed softly. Ryx's head snapped up, pulse thundering in his ears. Rexa stepped out, her expression unreadable.

"She's asking for you."

Ryx stood. The motion was stiff, like it took more than just muscle to get his legs moving. He left the blanket behind, like a shed skin. One more piece of useless armor that couldn't protect him from what came next.

Ryx stepped into the med-room like he was crossing the threshold of a tomb. Tessa lay on the padded med-slab, her body pale against the sterile fabric, her left arm heavily wrapped in synth-fiber bandages, an IV line snaking into her good one. The stump of her right arm was hidden under fresh biofoam gauze, but Ryx's eyes went there anyway. He hated himself for it.

Her eyes were open, but unfocused, staring through the wall. She didn't acknowledge him at first. Just blinked slowly, as if it took effort.

He stepped closer. Quiet. Careful. Like he might shatter her if he made a sound.

"I'm here, Tess..." he whispered. Her eyes shifted, found him. She didn't cry. She didn't flinch.

"Hey," she said, voice dry and rough as gravel. "Took you long enough."

Ryx cracked a broken smile, barely able to hold it together. He knelt beside her bed, brushing a blood-matted lock of hair away from her face.

"Stars," he breathed. "I thought I lost you."

She huffed, something between a scoff and a sigh. "You almost did."

Her face was hard. Not cruel. Just worn down to its core. Like she had no strength left for shields or sarcasm. Her eyes were red rimmed, but dry. She wasn't letting herself cry. Not yet.

"I'm sorry," Ryx said.

She turned away slightly.

"I should've been faster. Should've seen it coming. Should've,"

"Stop." she said, sharp despite the rasp in her voice. "Don't you dare." He shook his head, trembling now. "Tess, I... I got him killed. I let you walk into that house. I,"

"Stop!" she repeated, louder. He did. But his breath caught in his throat. And then, he couldn't hold it.

"I should've died there. It should've been me." His voice cracked like splintering glass. "You lost your arm. Kaelen's... Kaelen's gone. And I , I lived. I lived, and I'm still standing here, and I can't fucking breathe because of it."

Tessa turned to face him then. Her expression broke just a little. And when she reached out, only one arm now, gods, he leaned into it like a child. Her hand trembled as it cradled the back of his head, and he buried his face against her shoulder and wept. Silently, violently. Like everything inside him had been torn loose and set on fire.

She held him there, saying nothing, just breathing. Just letting him break. Letting the weight fall.

After a long while, when the sobs turned to gasps and then to silence, she said quietly: "Get what you can from the garage." Ryx lifted his head, confused, blinking through the haze. "What?"

Tess's jaw tightened. Her eyes stared past him again, like she was already somewhere else. Somewhere far. "Anything you can salvage. Tools, equipment, whatever Kaelen didn't lock up. I want it out. Gone. Rexa can sell the rest."

"But... Tess,"

"No." Her voice was flat. Final. "It's over, Ryx."

Silence hung between them, heavy and dense.

"I'm not building anymore. Not fixing. Not inventing. Not here. Not in that place." Ryx felt something cold seep into his spine.

Tess swallowed hard, looking down at her bandaged stump. "I'm not who I was. And I'm done pretending I can be." He opened his mouth. Closed it.

She looked at him again. There was no anger in her face, not for him. Just grief. And something deeper.

"I'm going back to the Orellin system. To stay with Aunt Marla. She has space. And quiet. And I can heal there... whatever that means now."

Ryx didn't try to argue. He saw it in her eyes. The conviction. The heartbreak. The ghost of Kaelen Rhoen standing between them, watching, silent.

She reached out again and took his hand. Her grip was firmer than he expected. "You're not to blame for this, Ryx."

"I don't believe that" he whispered.

"Then believe I don't blame you," she said. "Because I don't. And Kaelen wouldn't have either." That name. Spoken aloud. Ryx looked away, blinking hard. His throat ached.

"I'll get everything we can from the shop," he said finally. "You don't have to go back." Tess nodded, and for the first time since the attack, her lips trembled.

"He loved you too, Ryx."

"I know," he said. "I know."

The med-room fell into silence again, but this time it was different. Not peace, but something close.

Ryx found Rexa in her back room, cross-legged on the floor with three data slates laid out in front of her and a half-empty cup of stim-tea steaming to her left. She looked up as he entered, and for once, didn't meet him with her usual dry wit.

She just nodded, her voice soft. "She's awake?"

"Yeah," Ryx said quietly, leaning against the wall. "She's... holding together."

Rexa nodded again, then tilted her head. "And you?" Ryx hesitated, eyes flicking down to the floor. "No idea."

A beat passed.

"Rexa," he started again, shifting his weight as if the words were heavy, "we're done with the garage. Tess asked me to clean it out, anything worth salvaging. She wants you to handle the sale."

Rexa's face didn't change, but her shoulders tensed slightly. "She's serious, then."

"Deadly."

Rexa nodded solemnly. "I'll get in touch with a couple buyers. Discreet ones. We'll keep Kaelen's name clean."

"Thanks." Ryx started to turn, then paused. "One more thing." Rexa raised a brow. "You still have that blueprint?" he asked. "The one for the shield battery Kaelen built?"

She leaned back slightly, as if surprised. "Of course. It's already logged and time-stamped. Protected too. I was going to tell Kaelen after... everything." She trailed off, then continued more softly. "It's revolutionary tech, Ryx. What he made, I've never seen anything like it in my career. "The patent should go to Tess. He built it for her. For you both."

Ryx nodded. "I agree."

"Then I'll,"

"No," Ryx said, holding up a hand. "Not yet."

Rexa frowned. "Why?"

"She's not ready. She'd never accept it right now. She's leaving.

She's bleeding inside and trying to breathe. If she finds out about the patent now, she'll see it as charity, or worse, as Kaelen's last burden."

He let out a slow breath. "When she's healing, when she's herself again… tell her then."

Rexa studied him for a long moment. Then nodded.

"You hold it until she's ready."

She got up, moved to her bench and pulled out a small data stick and handed it to Ryx.

"Thanks, Rexa."

Ryx turned and left before the knot in his throat could grow any tighter.

ΔΔΔ

Back at the garage, silence reigned.

He stood outside the wrecked bay, hands still for a moment, eyes roaming over the shattered place that had once been home. The lights still flickered in places, half the floor blackened by fire. The air smelled like char and coolant.

He walked inside slowly, footsteps echoing in the dead quiet. He started with Tess's room. The walls still bore faint scorch marks where the explosion had rocked the structure. The door was hanging askew, the hinges half-melted.

Inside, it was mostly intact. He moved gently, reverently.

Her bed sheets messy but untouched. Her old flight jacket hung on a hook behind the door, faded patches stitched carefully into its sleeves. He touched it with one gloved hand, thumb grazing the frayed edges.

He folded it gently, laying it into the bottom of the bag he'd brought.

On the small bedside table sat a holo-frame, the projection half flickering but still functioning. Kaelen stood in the middle, younger than Ryx remembered him, one hand on Tess's shoulder. She was maybe ten in the photo, gap-toothed and smiling, her other hand held by a woman Ryx had never met but recognized immediately.

Tess's mother.

He stared at it for a long time, then deactivated the projection and packed it with care.

From the shelves above her workbench, he gathered small boxes of tools, half-built circuit boards, a few half-finished projects she'd been tinkering with for fun. The small things that made her... her. One caught his eye, some kind of emitter or lens he didn't understand.

He took them all.

Once Tess's things were packed, Ryx lingered outside Kaelen's room. The door was still closed. It felt wrong to enter.

The last time he'd opened this door, Kaelen had been inside, half shouting at him to come grab his tools or fix a damn coolant line. Now the silence behind it felt... sacred. Like breaking it would shatter something that couldn't be put back together. His mind flashed back to the previous night, how he appeared in the room. The way he killed the mercenary.

He rested his hand on the metal handle. It was still warm. He pushed the door open slowly.

Kaelen's room was exactly as it had always been. Neat. Functional. A pair of worn work boots by the corner. A folded flannel shirt over the back of his chair. Except for the workbench across the room. It was dented, bloodstained. A remnant of the battle last night.

Tools scattered around the worktable and floor. But, the bed was made, as always, tightly, precisely. The blanket stretched smooth across it like a soldier's bunk.

Ryx stepped inside.

The door whispered shut behind him, and the noise of the rest of the garage fell away.

He crossed to the edge of the bed and sat down slowly, his body heavy. The springs groaned beneath him, Kaelen's weight had trained them to expect someone stronger, older.

He sat there in stillness for a long time.

His fingers brushed the worn quilt Kaelen had always used, the one Tessa's mother had sewn from scraps decades ago. A faded patch in one corner still had an old pilot insignia stitched in uneven thread.

He picked up Kaelen's flight jacket from his dresser. Dark synth leather, stylish in an old-fashioned way. Worn in all the right places. His name tag stitched inside the coat. Rhoen.

Ryx's chest tightened.

Memories crowded in, thick and loud and unstoppable.

Kaelen laughing while welding something with the face shield lifted, daring the sparks to hit him. Kaelen slapping a spanner into Ryx's hand and growling, "No, you hold it like this, kid, or you'll shear the threads clean off." Kaelen falling asleep in this very bed after pulling a thirty-hour refit shift. Kaelen with a grease-smeared face and that crooked smile, proud as hell when Ryx brought home his first bounty.

Kaelen, broken on the floor of the shop, burned and crushed and dying alone. Ryx pressed his hands against his eyes and tried to hold back the rising tide. It didn't work. Tears slipped through his fingers as he hunched over, elbows on his knees.

"I should've been faster," he whispered. His voice didn't echo. Kaelen's room had always been quiet. Now it felt like a tomb.

Ryx stepped out of Kaelen's room, numb, and made his way back to the front entryway. He dropped the packed bags by the door, then crossed the ruined garage to one of the overturned hovercarts they used for hauling gear. With a touch to the panel, the unit hummed to life, righting itself and floating obediently beside him. He guided it back into the house.

One by one, he stacked the cases and bags into the hovercart waiting in the foyer.

Then he turned back to the garage.

Time passed in a haze as he moved methodically through the space. Every undamaged tool he could find, every spanner, diagnostic unit, multi-calibrator, he collected into worn-out tool bags and hard cases. When he finished, he added them to the hovercart. It was nearly full now, weighed down by what little remained.

The only place left to check was the machine shop.

He stopped at the door. The jagged blast marks on its frame made his chest tighten. The edges were still charred from the grenade that had torn through the space, and Kaelen.

Ryx stared at the doorway for a long time, fists clenching and unclenching at his sides. He knew the body was gone. He'd seen Rexa's people move it. And yet... it felt like Kaelen was still in there, waiting. Still laying broken beneath that bench. Still gasping for breath, still dying.

His legs resisted. His breath came shallow. But he forced himself to move. The door slid open with a reluctant hiss. Inside, nothing had changed.

The floor was littered with scorched tools and blackened debris. Tables overturned. Scorch marks painted like shadows on the walls. The air still carried the acrid tang of plasma discharge and blood.

His eyes went, inevitably, to the far corner. Where Kaelen had been. Where he'd found him.

The memory hit like a hammer. Kaelen's burned side. His crushed frame. His stillness.

Ryx's throat closed. His breath caught. The edges of his vision blurred, and his heart thundered like a war drum in his chest.

Breathe, he told himself. But no air came.

He staggered a step forward, then dropped to one knee as the pressure in his chest grew unbearable. Images bombarded him: Kaelen's calloused hands handing him a tool. His rough voice barking orders. That bellowing laugh echoing from the shop. That last, shattered moment, the blood, the silence, the death.

The grief strangled him. He clawed for air that wouldn't come. His vision swam. The world tilted. He tried to cry out, but nothing escaped his throat.

And then, light.

From his wrist. The gauntlet. It had activated, shifting seamlessly from the dormant bracelet form. The soft blue glow pulsed in slow, steady waves, out of sync with his racing heart.

Too slow. Too calm.

He stared at the light through the haze of panic. Each pulse seemed to reach inside him, settle in his lungs, his mind. Like it was whispering: Steady.

He focused on it.

Thum…

Thum…

His heart began to slow.

Then, with a ragged gasp, Ryx sucked in a lungful of air and collapsed forward, sprawling across the scorched floor, cheek pressed to the cold metal.

The panic receded like a tide. Sweat dripped down his back. His chest still heaved, but he was breathing again.

He lay there for a long time, staring at the pulsing artifact wrapped around his forearm. The glow was back in sync with his heartbeat now. Warm. Present. Anchoring.

"Thank you," he rasped, voice cracking.

The gauntlet pulsed once, bright and firm, before receding back into its bracelet form with a faint hiss of metal and energy. Ryx pushed himself slowly to his feet. His limbs ached, but his mind was clear again.

There was still one last thing to do.

He crossed the shop carefully, stepping over mangled tools and shattered plating. In the far corner, opposite the one that had nearly destroyed him, he knelt beside a heavy cabinet that had been toppled in the blast.

Underneath it, half-hidden by a bent wall panel, was a loose tile in the floor. He pried it up and reached inside. A small lockbox greeted him, scuffed but intact. His emergency cache.

He opened it.

Stacks of credit chips. Secure. Undetected. Untouched. Ryx ran a thumb over the top chip. It was dusty. "Forty thousand credits," he muttered. "I always tried not to spend it unless it mattered." Well. It mattered now.

He pocketed the chips into pouches along his belt, then turned and looked back at the ruined room one last time.

No part of him wanted to stay.

He activated the hovercart, which hummed to life and began to follow him. Ryx left the machine shop behind. He didn't look back.

The streets of Vorrthani Station felt too quiet. The hovercart floated behind him, heavy with salvaged tools, personal keepsakes, and the only tangible remnants of a home that no longer existed. Ryx didn't rush. His boots echoed on the metal walkway as he moved through the market district, head low, shoulders stiff.

The weight wasn't just the gear. Every step away from the garage felt like betrayal. Like abandonment.

The Wraithburn came into view ahead, parked where Tess had landed her during the chaos. Ryx paused, hand on the back rail of the hovercart, just staring at the ship. Its silhouette had always stirred something in him, freedom, fire, a future. Now it looked more like a shelter against a storm he couldn't stop.

He climbed the ramp slowly, the cart gliding up behind him with a low mechanical hum.

Inside, the familiar air of the ship embraced him. Sterile. Still. Comforting, in a way that made his chest ache. He guided the cart into the cargo hold and parked it near the workbench, deactivating the field latch and stepping back.

Everything felt surreal.

There was no victory in returning here.

He looked down at the gear. Tessa's bags. Kaelen's jacket. The tools they'd used for a hundred jobs. A thousand repairs. He traced one finger along the edge of the closest case and then turned wordlessly away.

He knew the cockpit lights blinked quietly in standby down the hall. The hum of the engines reminded him the Wraith was waiting for him. Ready. But right now, he wasn't ready for her.

Not yet. Ryx exited down the ramp and locked the ship behind him.

The walk back to Rexa Vorn's shop felt longer this time. Slower. He passed vendors reopening stalls, a few citizens cleaning up debris. Some of them glanced at him, recognizing him, maybe, or just wondering why a man in battered armor was wandering the market alone with haunted eyes. He saw Lyn out of the corner of his eye.

He didn't stop. Didn't speak. Didn't feel much of anything until the familiar shape of Rexa's heavy metal storefront came into view. The door slid open at his approach.

He stepped inside, the scent of hot circuitry and solvent welcoming him like an old friend.

Ryx stood in silence near the counter of Rexa's shop, eyes fixed on nothing, hands still faintly shaking. The metallic tang of gun oil and solder filled the air, but it was the quiet that pressed hardest, too quiet. Not like the garage. Not like home.

Tess emerged from the back room, her left arm still tightly bandaged, her face pale but resolute. She leaned her good shoulder against the counter and studied him for a long moment.

"You cleaned it out?" she asked softly.

He nodded. "Yeah. Took what I could. It's on the Wraith."

She didn't say anything right away, just let that linger between them. Her eyes were red from earlier, crying, pain, maybe both, but now they were steady. Determined.

"Thank you," she said. Ryx just nodded again.

Tessa watched him, saw how his shoulders hadn't dropped since the attack. How his jaw was locked. How his eyes refused to meet hers.

"You're not done, Ryx."

His head tilted slightly, not quite a shake, not quite an acknowledgment.

"You think hauling tools out of the garage is enough?" Her voice wasn't harsh, it was tired. But there was something ironclad in it now. "That Kaelen's death is just something you pack into a bag and leave behind?"

He winced at his name. "Tess…"

"I'm not blaming you," she said quickly, crossing the floor and stopping in front of him. "You saved my life. You tried to save his too. You did everything you could." Ryx looked away.

"I know you did," she said, voice firm now. "But he didn't die because of some random merc squad. You know that."

His hands clenched into fists at his sides. He closed his eyes. Tessa leaned in. "You said it yourself. BSD wanted something. They tore our home apart for it. You think it ends there?" He said nothing.

"You've been trying to figure out that thing on your wrist since before they even locked you up," she continued. "You researched. You reached out to Rexa. You obsessed over it. Because deep down, you already knew it was dangerous. Valuable. Important."

202

She took a breath. Her voice cracked slightly. "And now my dad is dead. Because of it." That landed like a hammer.

Ryx's face crumpled as he staggered back, hitting the wall behind him with a dull thud. "I should've known. I should've done more. Kept it hidden. Or destroyed it. Or left before they ever came looking,"

"You couldn't have known," she said fiercely. "None of us could. But we do now." She took a step forward. "So, what are you going to do? Keep blaming yourself? Sit here until they come back for you? For me?"

Ryx looked up at her finally, really looked at her. Saw the exhaustion in her eyes. The rage beneath it. The loss. But he also saw something else.

Hope.

"You're the one who found that thing," she said, quieter now. "You're the one it listens to. Whatever it is… whatever it means… it killed to protect you. It hid itself to save you. That thing isn't just some relic. It's tied to something big. And I think you're tied to it."

Ryx swallowed hard. "Tess, I,"

"You're not done, Ryx," she said again. "And I don't want to be either. But I can't chase this thing. Not like this. Not without an arm. Not without…" her voice faltered, but she steadied it. "Not without you."

He looked at the golden band around his wrist. Faint blue light pulsed within the grooves. It was like staring at a locked door. And he was the only one with a key.

Tessa's voice softened. "Do this. For him. For me. For yourself." Silence hung heavy again. Then Ryx nodded, slowly. "Okay."

"You're going to find out what it is," she said. "And you're going to find out why they want it." "And then?" he asked. Tessa's eyes narrowed. "Then we burn BSD to the ground."

203

Ryx sat in the corner of Rexa's shop long after Tess had gone to rest. The overhead lights hummed, casting long shadows across the scattered gear and crates. Outside, the Vorrthani market had quieted to a late-evening lull, distant voices, the low hum of transports, and the ever-present murmur of the station's artificial atmosphere.

He stared at the band on his wrist, watching it pulse faintly, almost like a heartbeat. Tess's words echoed through him, cutting deeper than any blade.

"You're not done."

She was right. Every fiber of him knew it. The garage was gone. Kaelen was gone. But what they stood for, their life, their family, it wasn't. Not yet.

He still had the Wraithburn.

He still had Tess.

And he still had the artifact.

A relic that moved on its own, defended him, reached into his very mind to keep him from drowning. Whatever it was, ancient weapon, living machine, curse or blessing, it was tied to all of this. To Kaelen's death. To the mercs. To BSD.

That made it his responsibility.

He pushed up from the crate he'd been sitting on and walked through the shop until he found Rexa, hunched over a disassembled targeting array. She looked up, frowning.

"You look like shit," she said.

"I feel worse," Ryx replied, voice hoarse but steady.

Rexa tilted her head, eyes narrowing. "Something's changed."

"Tess reminded me who I am," he said. "And why I can't stay buried." Rexa studied him a moment longer, then went back to fiddling with the targeting array. "Good. Because sulking doesn't look good on you."

"I need something," Ryx said, stepping closer. "A weapon."

Rexa didn't look up. "Didn't you have a fancy hand cannon before BSD wrecked your shop?"

204

"It was a TalonX-5," he said quietly. "It was issued to me by the VPM years ago."

Rexa nodded. "I remember."

Ryx hesitated for a beat, then said it: "I want the Fury-RZ7." That made her pause. She looked up slowly. "The Fury?" Her eyebrows rose. "The same one you said was too big, too loud, and 'like strapping a fusion core to a recoil spring?' That Fury?"

Ryx gave a tired smile. "I think I said it was overcompensating."

"You did," she said dryly. "Multiple times."

"I need it now."

Rexa leaned back on her stool, arms crossed. "Ryx, that gun's a goddamn tank. You didn't like the weight, the draw speed, or the recharge cycles. You said it didn't fit your style."

He nodded. "Yeah. Because back then, my style was precise. Controlled. In and out. Quiet." A long breath. "That style got our father killed. That style didn't save Tess's arm. Or the garage. Or anyone I ever failed when I thought I could outsmart a fight instead of outlasting one." He met her gaze.

"I don't want quiet anymore, Rexa. I want loud. I want brutal. I want the kind of firepower that makes people think twice before even lifting a weapon in my direction."

Rexa didn't speak right away. Her eyes softened slightly.

"This isn't just about a gun, is it?" she asked.

"No," Ryx said. "It's about surviving. It's about protecting what's left of my family. And it's about hitting back hard enough that BSD never forgets my name."

She exhaled slowly and stood, walking over to a heavy metal case tucked beneath a bench. She crouched and popped the seals with a hiss. Inside, resting in custom foam, was the Fury-RZ7.

It was massive. Matte black with brushed steel plating, reinforced rails, and a deep-barrel compensator that hissed faintly even when idle. Rexa lifted it like it weighed nothing and held it out to him.

Ryx took it in both hands. The grip was heavier than his old Talon, the frame broader. But it settled into his arms like it had been waiting for him all along.

"You sure?" she asked one last time.

He looked down at the weapon, then at the band on his wrist.

"No more holding back," he said quietly.

CHAPTER 12

WASTED STARLIGHT

The Fury-RZ7 felt heavier in Ryx's hand than he remembered, not because of its weight, but because of everything it meant now. It wasn't just a weapon anymore. It was a vow. A line in the sand.

He turned it over once more in his grip, inspecting the matte-black finish, the thick barrel, the faint hum of its capacitor core. Rexa watched him from her bench, arms crossed, expression unreadable.

"Take it," she said. "It's yours."

Ryx blinked. "What?"

"The Fury," she said, more firmly this time. "No price tag. No IOUs. Just take it."

He shook his head. "Rexa, no. That thing's worth,"

"Thirty-five grand on most markets," she interrupted. "Forty with your mods. And right now, I'd give it to you for a hot cup of caff and the promise you don't die using it."

He gave her a long look. "It doesn't feel right. Especially not after everything else."

Rexa stepped forward, arms falling to her sides. "Ryx, you just buried the closest thing you've had to a father. You dragged your half-dead sister into my shop and passed out from exhaustion and grief, and the moment you got your breath back, you started packing up what was left of your lives so you could make sure Tess had something to hold onto."

She softened. "You don't owe me a damn thing." He stared at her, jaw clenched , not from anger, but the weight of everything pressing inward.

"You said it yourself," he said quietly. "This isn't just about a gun."

She opened her mouth, but Ryx reached for his belt and pulled out two thick stacks of U-credits, placing them firmly on the counter.

"Twenty thousand," he said. "That's final."

Rexa frowned. "You're underpaying, and I'm still overcharging."

"Good," he said with a thin smile. "Then we're both unhappy, which means it's a fair deal."

For a long moment, she stared at the credits. Then she huffed and rolled her eyes, dragging the stack off the counter and tossing it into her lockbox.

"You're impossible, Thorne."

"Been told."

She narrowed her eyes at him as if considering something. "Give me the Fury and your holster."

Ryx blinked. "Why?"

"I'm going to retrofit the holster, so it doesn't ride like a brick under your coat," she said casually, already pulling a tool kit from the shelf. "And... I've got something I want to add."

He hesitated, sensing something deeper behind her tone.

"What kind of something?" She met his gaze.

"Kaelen deserves to ride with you." The words hit him in the chest.

Rexa held out her hand. "Give it over."

Ryx slowly unsnapped the magnetic holster from his belt, then handed her the Fury.

She turned, moving to her workbench. "I'll give it back before you leave. It'll be yours, same as before." She glanced at him over her shoulder.

"But next time you draw it, you'll be drawing it for all three of you." Ryx nodded once, silent, and let her work.

He didn't ask what she was going to add.

He had a feeling it would say everything he couldn't.

"Rexa I need one more favor" He sat another credit chip on the counter and Rexa gave him a cautious look. Ryx smiled as best he could. "This one a little happier" Rexa sighed visibly relieved. "What do you need Eryx?" She asked exasperated "I need you and your network to find me a Vlexari Doctor named Lanara Kress."

△△△

Back aboard the Wraithburn, Ryx sat hunched over the console in the dim light of the cockpit. The glow of the Hunter Net login screen bathed his tired face in orange. He hadn't touched this terminal since before his arrest. His fingers hovered over the keys for a long moment before he finally exhaled and keyed in his credentials.

GUILD STATUS: INACTIVE

LICENSE: SUSPENDED: (AUTO-FLAGGED: INCARCERATION)

LAST ACTIVITY: 322 STANDARD DAYS AGO

He chewed the inside of his cheek and clicked through the prompts. Every warning felt like a judgment, unfit for field duty, reduced clearance, temporary reinstatement under review.

STATUS: REACTIVATED

LICENSE: D-RUNG (PROBATIONARY)

LIMITED ACCESS GRANTED

A short, clinical chime acknowledged the update. No welcome back. No apology. Just bureaucracy. He closed the terminal and leaned back, letting the hum of the Wraith's engines settle into his bones like a lullaby.

But sleep wouldn't come, not yet.

ΔΔΔ

Later, in the cargo bay, he helped Tess load her salvaged belongings into storage bins. She moved slowly, her one arm cradling a padded case while he secured the rest.

"You sure we got everything?" he asked, tightening a strap. Tess gave him a tired nod. "Everything worth taking."

She paused, eyes distant. "I told Rexa to handle the rest, sale, clean-up, all of it. I don't want to see that place again."

Ryx gave her a glance, careful and measured. "You really doing this?"

She looked at him, jaw clenched. "I can't stay here, Ryx. Not after what happened. Not after what they did to Dad." Her voice cracked on the last word, and she quickly looked away. "Who's all in the Orellin system?"

"My aunt," she said after a moment. "Aunt Marla. On Corvellis. She's quiet, private. Used to be a medical engineer before she retired. She lives off-grid now, on the southern continent's ridge line. It's peaceful there."

Ryx nodded slowly. "You'll be safe."

She scoffed. "Safe. Sure." Her eyes darkened. "Doesn't mean I won't be pissed."

"Pissed?"

"Not at you," she said firmly. "At them. At BSD. At whoever thought they could take what Dad built and burn it to the ground. And at myself for not stopping them."

Ryx's jaw worked, but no words came. Then, quietly, he said, "I should've seen it coming. I should've,"

"Stop."

210

She stepped forward and pressed her good hand against his chest, forcing him to meet her gaze.

"Ryx, don't do this to yourself. Don't turn his death into a weight you drag forever."

"I left you both behind. I let this happen."

"No," she said, voice trembling. "They did this. Not you." He broke then. Shoulders trembling. A quiet sound escaped his throat, something between a breath and a sob, and he lowered his head. She didn't speak again. She just stood there with him, hand still pressed to his chest, until the storm passed.

When Ryx finally looked up, eyes red, voice rough, he said, "I don't know what to do anymore."

Tess swallowed hard. "Then do what you do best. Hunt. Track. Dig. You said you still don't know what this artifact is or why BSD wanted it... then find out." He blinked.

She stepped back and looked him in the eye.

"You owe it to him. To us. To yourself. Dad died because they wanted something from you. So, make sure they never get it."

Ryx nodded slowly, the fire reigniting in his chest. Quiet at first, but steady. Familiar.

"I'll make them regret coming near us," he said. Tess gave him a tired smile. "Good. Now help me finish packing. I could use the extra hand" Ryx groaned at her macabre joke.

The Wraithburn's engines were on standby. Tess's things were stowed. She sat strapped into one of the passenger seats in the hold, one arm resting across her lap, the other, what remained of it, wrapped in a med-sleeve and layered under a fresh coat. She looked out through the bulkhead window at the market lane beyond, quiet now in the early hours.

Ryx stood nearby, his posture stiff with everything he wasn't saying. Tess noticed. "You okay?" she asked gently. He nodded once, then shook his head. "Just need to square something with Rexa."

Tess looked back at him, understanding flickering in her tired eyes. "Take your time. I'll be here." He gave her a long look, then stepped out into the station.

The walk to Rexa Vorn's shop was short, but every step carried weight. The overhead lights flickered dimly as the station cycled power, casting long, thin shadows across the corridor. It reminded him of how much had changed in so little time.

Ryx stepped through the threshold of Rexa Vorn's shop, the familiar buzz of her security grid flickering as it recognized his ID. The air smelled of solder and grease, same as always, but today it was different. He was different.

Rexa didn't look up from the bench right away. She was finishing a careful weld on a small device, and only when it hissed with cooling vapor did she glance at him.

"Right on time," she said, and there was a gentleness to her voice that felt rare. Ryx approached, his steps slow, deliberate. His eyes drifted to the long black case sitting closed on the workbench beside her.

"You said you wanted to borrow it," he said quietly. "I assume that's it?" Rexa gave a subtle nod. "Go on. Open it."

He lifted the latches and eased the case open. Inside, the Fury-RZ7 gleamed like forged vengeance. Its frame had been meticulously polished, the plating matte black and sleek, its grip a composite of reinforced metal and carved ironwood.

What caught his breath was the engraving.

On the inside curve of the grip, small but sharp, etched in old Vorn script beneath the clear lacquered finish, were the words: "Wasted Starlight."

Ryx's chest constricted.

It wasn't just the gun; it was the weight of the saying. The one Kaelen always tossed at him when Ryx would linger too long in thought or stare at a sunrise like it meant something. "Daylight is just wasted starlight." Kaelen would mutter. A reminder that the universe didn't wait, and that beauty could burn out before you ever saw it.

Ryx's fingers hovered above the grip.

"You remembered," he said, voice ragged.

"I never forgot," Rexa replied softly. "Neither did he. He'd been planning it. He wanted to put it on the Wraith's engine cowling when you two got around to rebuilding it after the last job. Said you needed to see it every day."

Ryx closed his eyes for a beat, swallowed hard, then picked up the weapon. The Fury was heavy, confident. No longer just a gun, now it was something else entirely.

He drew it from the case and turned it in his palm. "It feels right," he murmured. "It should," Rexa said. "You already paid me for it. But I figured... this made it yours."

Ryx holstered the Fury and adjusted the strap of the new rig. It fit perfectly. "You didn't have to do this."

"I know," she said. "But you needed something to carry him with you. And you're going to need more than firepower where you're headed."

There was a pause. A silence that felt like memory. Then Ryx looked her in the eye. "Thank you." Rexa leaned on the bench again, arms crossed. "Don't make me regret it, Thorne." He chuckled, low and tired. "I'll try not to."

Rexa stepped forward and gave him a look, one part goodbye, one part challenge. "This isn't over. You know that, right?"

"I know." Ryx's voice was quiet steel. "And when I find out who gave the order... who sent those bastards to our door, I'll make sure the stars themselves remember."

Rexa nodded once, her jaw tight with the same fire that smoldered behind Ryx's eyes.

They didn't need more words. Not now.

Ryx turned toward the door.

As he stepped out into the corridor, the Fury-RZ7 Wasted Starlight , rested heavy on his hip, a part of him now.

Kaelen might be gone. But his legacy had just found a new trigger.

ΔΔΔ

The Wraithburn hummed softly, her engines warmed and calibrated, flight systems green across the board. In the cockpit, Ryx sat in the pilot's chair with his fingers resting lightly on the throttle. Tess was beside him in the co-pilot's seat, her single hand clasped tightly around a steaming cup of bitter caff. She hadn't said much since they boarded, neither had he.

The station loomed before them through the forward viewport: Vorrthani Station, home for so long. A patchwork of steel and ancient gravity plating. A scarred and sputtering relic that had, somehow, sheltered them. Betrayed them. Held memories too deep to bear.

Below them, the hangar that once held the garage was dark. Gutted. Smoke-charred metal and broken lights, no longer a place, just a shell.

Ryx let out a slow breath.

"Can't believe we're leaving it behind," he murmured, barely louder than the Wraith's idle rumble. Tess didn't answer at first. She stared straight ahead, jaw set, eyes reflecting the distant glint of the station's outer hull. Then, almost to herself, she said, "Part of me thought we'd always live here."

Ryx looked over. Her face was pale, shadowed in the glow of the nav lights, but there was something fierce behind her silence. The kind of silence that holds grief like a blade. He reached over and gave her shoulder a gentle squeeze.

She didn't flinch. "We'll find who did this," he said. Tess nodded once. Another quiet stretch passed between them. Outside, the last docking clamps released with a clunk and hiss, and the Wraithburn drifted slowly away from the station. Ryx input coordinates for the Orellin system, the next step.

The moment hung heavy. The stars beyond were vast, open, waiting.

Ryx took one last look at Vorrthani Station. At the place that took him in. Gave him his family. And broke him all over again.

He raised a hand in a small, private farewell. Tess followed suit with her cup, her fingers trembling just slightly.

"Ready?" he asked.

Tess took one last sip of caff, then nodded. "Punch it." Ryx pulled the lever.

The stars stretched, then vanished, swallowed by streaks of light as the Wraithburn tore across space.

Vorrthani disappeared behind them, and the past with it.

They didn't look back.

ΔΔΔ

A soft chime stirred Ryx from a light doze in the galley, warp exit alert. He stretched, the low thrum of the Wraithburn's core fading into silence as the drive began to spool down. Footsteps echoed down the corridor as Tess emerged from the living quarters, tying her jacket with one hand and tossing her empty caff mug into the recycler.

Without a word, the two of them slid into their seats in the cockpit. A practiced rhythm. Ryx brought up the display and eased his fingers across the control panel. The stars began to snap back into focus, stretched streaks slowing until the real space starscape of the Orellin system blossomed before them.

Ryx whistled low.

Orellin was stunning.

Six planets hung like jewels in the black. Two gas giants swirled with vivid blues and deep emeralds, their rings casting long shadows across nearby moons. One world shimmered with a pinkish haze of atmosphere, while another gleamed gold, its surface like polished brass under the light of a soft white sun. And then there was the fourth planet, green and blue, with sprawling oceans and scattered continents draped in vibrant cloud cover. It spun gently below them, peaceful, alive.

"That one?" Ryx asked, eyes fixed on the lush world.

Tess nodded. "That's Corvellis. Aunt Marla's there. Middle of nowhere. She owns a greenhouse research estate outside one of the smaller coastal settlements." She offered a soft smile, one that didn't quite reach her eyes. "Good people. Quiet life."

Ryx took a moment to appreciate it. The vastness. The contrast. After Vorrthani's scars and blood and ash, it felt like standing on the edge of a dream. He didn't realize how much weight he'd carried until this quiet splendor met him like fresh air after suffocation.

The ship's console pinged.

Incoming message: Encrypted channel - Origin: Teraxis Relays | Sender: MAEL-423 (Freelance Contact)

Ryx blinked, confused for half a second, then a flicker of recognition passed over his face. Mael. A contact from his pre-imprisonment network. A scout, intel broker, and sometimes star system drifter with a reputation for wandering off-grid.

Tess raised an eyebrow. "Old job lead?"

Ryx tapped the message and skimmed the contents. His brow furrowed.

"Not exactly. Mael says he heard from Rexa I was back on the grid. He figured I might be interested in a xenoarcheology gig."

"That's fast," Tess said, leaning over. "What's the job?"

Ryx frowned deeper. "It's not a job, it's a rescue." He tapped open the full message:

Contact: Dr. Yessari Quarn– Xenohistory Division. Atraxan Archive

Location: Surface of Myrrh IV, system edge. Vessel: Private Research Shuttle TND-91 - Disabled.

Situation: Distress signal received. Grounded due to nav thruster malfunction. Surrounded by aggressive native fauna. Requesting immediate evac. Minimal supplies remain.

Urgency: High – Threat of exposure/fatality within 48 hours.

Ryx through a quick response to Mael:

Acknowledged,

Job Accepted. Should arrive within 24 hours.

-Eryx Throne

I could use the extra credits, or a contact with Xenoarcheology background.

He thought to himself as he looked down at the bracelet lying dormant against his wrist.

The Wraithburn descended smoothly through Corvellis's cloud cover, soft rays of amber sunlight cutting through the mist-drenched atmosphere. Below, the terrain bloomed in deep greens and rich golds, massive, rolling meadows interrupted only by thickly forested hills and winding rivers. It was quiet country. Clean. Open. The kind of place that felt like it had never heard of war or loss.

Tess leaned forward in her seat, gazing through the cockpit glass as Ryx brought the ship around a low ridge. A narrow road cut through the tree line below, leading to a modest estate nestled in the clearing: A long, single-story house of dusky green stone and timber siding, wrapped in sprawling greenhouses and suncatchers that shimmered like stained glass. A garden path split the flower beds and led up to the front porch, where two small gardening droids paused in their weeding as the Wraithburn cast its shadow overhead.

"That's it," Tess murmured.

Ryx nodded. "Nice place."

He brought the ship down gently, landing her on a flat patch of soft grass just outside the estate's perimeter fence. The ship hissed quietly as her systems wound down.

Together, they stepped into the hold where the hovercart of luggage and packed salvage waited. Ryx keyed the ramp and helped guide the cart down onto the soft dirt path.

The air was warm and damp, tinged with the scent of distant flowers. A wind stirred the grass. The front door opened. A woman stepped out.

She was older than Tess by two decades at least, but the resemblance was clear: sharp green eyes, prominent cheekbones, the same stubborn set of the jaw. Her dark auburn hair was tied back with a worn kerchief, and her apron was streaked with fresh soil. She looked like she'd just come from pruning a hedge or pulling up roots, and maybe she had.

The moment she saw Tess, the gardening gloves fell from her hands.

"Tessa?"

Tess moved like a ghost across the lawn, her pace steady until it wasn't. She broke into a run, one arm swinging awkwardly at her side, the other reaching. Marla ran too, voice caught on a sob, and they met in the middle of the garden in a crushing embrace. Tess's face pressed against her aunt's shoulder, and though Ryx couldn't hear what was said, he saw it all: the tremble in Tess's knees, the way Marla rocked her like she was five years old again, and not a grown woman bearing a thousand-yard stare and a missing limb.

Ryx stepped back. Gave them space. When Tess finally pulled away, her eyes were glassy but dry. Marla looked to Ryx as they returned, her gaze keen and assessing.

"You're Ryx," she said.

"I am."

"They wrote about you. Often."

Ryx glanced at Tess with a smile. "Hopefully the good parts." Ryx shifted, the air suddenly heavier. "I'm... sorry for how it ended. Kaelen was, he was everything to both of us." Marla nodded gently. "I know. I'm glad he had the two of you."

Ryx cleared his throat and helped them guide the hovercart up the path to the house. Once inside, he helped carry Tess's suitcases to the guest room. He set them down beside the bed and took one last look around. The room was simple but cozy, sunlight poured in from an arched window overlooking the wildflower fields beyond.

Back in the front room, Tess stood near the door with her aunt, her gaze fixed on the distant treeline.

Ryx approached slowly. "You all set?" he asked. Tess nodded. "Yeah." A long silence passed between them. Finally, she turned to him, expression pulled tight with emotion, but no tears now.

"I hate this," she whispered. "Letting you go."

"You're not," Ryx said. "This isn't goodbye. It's just... a pause."

"I don't want to pause. I want it to go back to the way it was."

"I know." Her lip quivered, and she sucked in a shaky breath. "You'll message?" she asked. "Every day," he promised. "You'll be sick of hearing from me."

Tess cracked a tiny smile. "Not possible." They stood for a moment longer, just breathing the same air. Ryx reached out, gently touched his forehead to hers.

"I'll figure it out," he whispered. "The gauntlet. Why they came for us. What we lost him for."

"I know you will," Tess said, her voice stronger now. "Just... don't forget that we're still here. I'll be here." Ryx stepped back and looked to Marla. "Take care of her?"

"With everything I have."

He gave them both a final nod, then turned and headed back down the garden path toward the waiting Wraithburn, the hovercart long since emptied.

At the edge of the field, he paused and looked back.

Tess stood at the top of the path with Marla beside her. The wind caught her short hair and the hem of her coat. She raised her one good arm and waved.

Ryx waved back, and then boarded his ship, sealing the hatch behind him.

It was time to go to Myrrh IV.

CHAPTER 13

SHADOWS BENEATH A RED SUN

The Wraithburn dropped out of warp with a flicker of blue distortion and a low shudder, stabilizing instantly as her hull adjusted to the new gravimetric pull of the system. Ryx sat forward in the pilot seat, eyes scanning the data now flooding his screen. Ahead, the system's red dwarf star burned low and steady, casting a blood-colored hue over the planets and gas clouds in its orbit.

He tapped the console. "System designation...Ravanos 6," he muttered, reading aloud. "Six planets. one gas giant. Four uninhabitable. One terrestrial... there you are." Myrrh IV rotated slowly on the outer fringe of the habitable zone, barely within the green band. A small, dark world with high magnetic readings, volatile storms, and a thin but breathable atmosphere. It was home to almost nothing. No cities. No stations. No settlements worth naming.

Ryx keyed in a closer scan. A dense forest biome covered nearly half the planet. Jagged cliffs and craters formed the rest. And on the far side of the equator, a single, weak distress signal.

There you are, Doctor.

The coordinates matched what Mael had forwarded to him: an old research shuttle, grounded on a ridge near the edge of a collapsed basin. No guild-affiliated beacon. No automatic defenses. Just one scientist stranded with nothing but a weak distress ping and the sound of his own breathing. Ryx ran a systems check, fingers dancing over the controls.

Shields: full.

Cloak: stable.

Comms: encrypted.

Engines: clean.

The Wraithburn purred like a living thing, Kaelen's upgrades humming beneath every surface. The shield battery he'd gifted Ryx thrummed faintly behind the walls like a second heartbeat, strong and ready.

"Alright," Ryx muttered. "Let's go fetch ourselves a doctor."

He brought the ship around and angled toward Myrrh IV's surface, cutting speed as he entered atmosphere. The clouds over the basin churned with heavy static, flashes of white heat streaking through rust-colored haze. The wind buffeted the ship as Ryx dipped beneath the storm's edge, riding low toward the beacon's coordinates.

Visibility was shit. The planet's electrical storms weren't just for show, they scrambled sensors, made flying a nightmare, and blocked short-range scanning. But Ryx had dealt with worse. He gripped the controls tight, fingers flexing automatically with every jolt of turbulence.

He could feel it again, Kaelen's voice in the back of his head, barking flight instructions in that gravelly growl after he installed new flight sensors on the Wraith and wanted to watch Ryx test them out.

"Angle off the downdraft! Get your nose up! You're fighting the storm, not flying through it!" A ghost of a smile passed over Ryx's lips.

"I know, old man. I've got it."

The Wraithburn dipped beneath the lowest cloud shelf, and the ridge came into view. At the edge of a split canyon stood the doctor's shuttle, angled on its landing struts, scorched from multiple impacts and half-collapsed on one side. The beacon was clearly jury-rigged to the hull, sparking with every other pulse.

Ryx narrowed his eyes. And surrounding the shuttle, in the thick brush at the treeline… movement. He tapped the console and zoomed the external cam.

Slinking, hulking forms, low to the ground, four-legged, with glinting red eyes and spines that shimmered when lightning cracked overhead. Pack hunters. Six of them. Maybe more hidden in the trees. Circling the downed shuttle like carrion, waiting for something to move. Waiting to strike.

"Guess the doc wasn't exaggerating."

Ryx stood, grabbed his mask off the co-pilot seat, and slid it on with practiced ease. His voice was a low whisper over the transponder.

"Let's go make an entrance."

Ryx moved fast through the corridor of the Wraithburn, the thunder from outside echoing faintly through her hull. He ducked into his small quarters, flipping open the concealed panel his closet with a palm press and quiet click. Inside, neatly nestled in its magnetic cradle, lay his Ironhowl. The matte-black rifle gleamed faintly under the low light, its power cell indicators blinking green. He slung it across his shoulder with care, then grabbed his holster. Resting in it, lovingly retooled and cradled in fresh leather and reinforced polymer, was the Fury-RZ7. Its brushed metal grip still bore faint smell of fresh carbon, the elegant etching on the grip catching the light: Wasted Starlight.

The name brought a weight to his chest. Not sadness this time, resolve. Kaelen's last gift.

"Alright," Ryx muttered, stepping into the airlock. "Let's see what this thing can do."

The loading ramp hissed open, revealing a shelf of rock and brush sloping down to the shuttle site. The storm churned overhead, hot wind and static lightning dancing across the distant basin. Below, the shuttle sat like a wounded animal, and the creatures were closing in.

He dropped to prone on the outcropping, unslung the Ironhowl, and toggled the scope.

"Let's thin the crowd."

One of the beasts, a sinewy, scaled quadruped with translucent bone ridges down its back, lurched into the open. It sniffed the air. Ryx's scope pinged off its hide: strong heat signature, dense muscle, armored plating around the shoulders. Eyes on either side of the head. *Good.*

He let out a breath, slowed his heartbeat, and squeezed the trigger. The Ironhowl barked, and the round streaked through the air like a lance of burning blue. It struck true, just behind the eye, and the creature crumpled mid-step. The others flinched, hissed, scattered.

Ryx stayed calm. Adjust. Lead. Fire. Another fell. Then a third. But they were adapting. Moving fast.

He was just lining up a fourth when the forest exploded with motion. More of them, half a dozen at least, burst from the underbrush with terrifying speed, leaping low and fast across the ravine, flanking wide toward the Wraithburn's position.

"Shit,"

He was already moving, swinging the Ironhowl back across his back and drawing the Fury as the first beast cleared the ridge.

The Fury-RZ7 roared in his hand with a sound like righteous thunder, louder than anything he'd ever fired before. The kick jolted up his arm, and the shot cracked through the creature's chest, pulping flesh and bone in a geyser of red mist.

Ryx didn't pause.

Another shot, and the second creature's foreleg exploded mid-lunge. It hit the rock screaming and rolled.

A third was on him, too close, too fast.

Ryx ducked to the side, rolling under the snapping jaws and bringing the Fury up under its chin. He fired point-blank. The shot vaporized half its head.

Blood sprayed his mask, hot and coppery. His heart was a thunderclap in his chest, but his mind was calm, clearer than it had been in weeks.

Another beast charged from the left, he spun, fired once, missed high, then adjusted and fired again, catching it square in the side. It spun out and fell hard, twitching.

He lowered the weapon slowly, breathing heavy.

The Fury pulsed in his hand, warm, alive, brutal.

"Hells," Ryx muttered, staring down at the weapon. "You were worth every damn credit."

He holstered the sidearm with a smooth twist and surveyed the ridge. The remaining beasts were gone, either dead or driven back into the trees. Below, the shuttle still stood quiet. The distress beacon flickered its rhythm, a heartbeat in the dark.

Ryx clicked on his helmet mic, hoping the doctor was scanning local signals. "Landing zone secure. Moving in."

He started down the rocks, bootsteps crunching over cracked stone, Wasted Starlight heavy on his hip.

Ryx reached the basin floor with caution, his boots crunching over dry roots and sand baked into brittle crust. The air smelled metallic, like scorched copper and ozone. The shuttle was listing slightly to one side, hull pocked with blast marks and smeared with grime from the dense foliage.

He circled toward the main hatch, rifle raised, sensors scanning.

Nothing on radar. The predators were either dead, hiding… or waiting.

The hatch was scorched and warped, its seams blackened and fused at the edges, maybe from a close-range detonation. Ryx knelt beside the locking mechanism and pried at the manual override panel. Stuck.

He tried again, this time with more force. The handle groaned but held fast.

Then his comms chirped, a weak signal, just barely patched through the shuttle's outer array.

"...ello? Can anyone hear me? This is Dr. Yessari Quarn. Please respond."

Ryx pressed a finger to his ear. "Dr. Quarn, this is Eryx Thorne. I'm with the Wraithburn. I received your distress signal. I've secured the landing site, but your main hatch is fused. You alright in there?"

There was a pause. Then a breath of relief came through the line.

"Thank the stars. Yes. I'm alive, though barely. Life support is damaged but holding. I sealed the cockpit after the crash and rerouted emergency power. The blast sealed me in and destroyed the external access. I've tried every method short of a charge detonation to open it."

Ryx rose and stepped back from the hatch, inspecting the structural damage with a practiced eye. He could blow it open, but if life support was already compromised,

"Hang tight," Ryx muttered. "I'll find another way." There was another pause on the line.

"I owe you my life, Mr. Thorne. I'll explain everything, but please, get me out of here first. I was shot down. This wasn't an accident."

Ryx's eyes narrowed. "Copy that."

He stepped closer and tapped the outer hull. "Internal layout standard?"

"Yes. Class IV surveyor model, modified for planetary research. Emergency maintenance hatch should be near the rear venting manifold, lower port side. You'll need to cut through a heat-shield panel."

"Got it."

Ryx moved fast, circling to the shuttle's rear. As he went, he scanned for any signs of tampering, blaster scoring on the hull, shrapnel patterns, anything that might tell him who hit this poor bastard. But the jungle had already begun claiming the wreck.

The heat shielding was intact but badly scraped, just as Quarn described. Ryx willed the gauntlet into being and extended the energy blade from it with a flick and began cutting through the scorched plating, careful not to breach too deep.

225

Sparks hissed in the wind as he worked.

"While I've got you, Doc," Ryx muttered over comms, "mind telling me who exactly you pissed off enough to shoot down a research shuttle?"

There was a dry chuckle, laced with weariness.

"I work for the Xarithan Assembly, civilian arm of our government. I'm an archivist. My focus is ancient cultural histories, particularly in systems with lost empires or Xeno civilizations. Someone clearly didn't want me recovering what I was sent here for." Ryx arched a brow.

"And what species do I owe this mystery to?"

"Ah. Right. Forgive me. I'm Tayveri."

Tayveri.

He'd heard of them, maybe only once or twice in passing. Elusive, reclusive, and mostly aligned with science and diplomacy. Not a species known for making enemies.

The panel clattered free.

Inside was a tight, smoke-filled corridor. Dim emergency lights flickered red along the floor plates. Ryx climbed in, crawling sideways through the narrow conduit until he reached the sealed bulkhead behind the cockpit.

Another voice echoed faintly through his comms.

"I'm on the other side. Releasing the interior lock."

A metallic thunk sounded, and the panel slid open.

Inside the cramped cockpit, Dr. Yessari Quarn stood, tall and slight, with thin limbs, long fingers, and deep orange skin patterned in pale, branchlike fractals. His head was elongated slightly in the back, tapering smooth into the neck, and his large, glistening black eyes held almost no visible whites, just deep pupils that shimmered like liquid ink.

He wore a tight-weave utility suit marked with field insignia, one shoulder scorched, and his left arm in a makeshift sling. The air inside reeked of scorched plastic and antiseptic.

"I'd shake your hand," the Tayveri said, bowing slightly. "But I'm afraid I'm not quite in the shape for protocol." Ryx just stared for a moment.

"Damn, Doc," he muttered. "You weren't kidding."

Ryx ducked back through the crawlspace and extended a hand into the smoke and flickering light of the ruined cockpit.

"Come on, Doc. Let's get you outta this flying coffin."

Dr. Yessari Quarn hesitated for a breath, then clasped Ryx's gloved hand with surprising strength. His skin was smooth but faintly scaled, like polished orange obsidian. Ryx braced as he helped the tall, thin Tayveri out of the cockpit and through the open maintenance panel, steadying him when the alien wobbled on unsteady feet in the dense jungle air.

"I'm not as young as I once was," Quarn muttered, wincing as his injured arm jostled.

"Let me guess," Ryx said, guiding him down the sloped hull to the jungle floor, "this was your first planetary crash?"

"Fourth, actually," Yessari grumbled. "But the others were controlled descents. This one... not so much."

"Right. Let's just hope there isn't a fifth."

They stepped out into the reddish-orange sunlight filtering through the dense canopy above. The shuttle crackled behind them, the cooling hull ticking like a dying engine block.

Ryx led the way up the slope, back toward the clearing where the Wraithburn waited. As they walked, he glanced side long at the alien.

"So, you're an archivist. This seems like a dangerous job for a librarian."

Dr. Quarn gave a short laugh. "Yes, well, I'm more of a polymath, really. Most Tayveri are. We tend to change vocations every few decades, keeps the mind from rusting."

"Huh. So, you just woke up one day and said, 'I think I'll trade brain surgery for ancient ruins?'"

"Something like that," Quarn said with a faint smirk. "I spent nearly forty standard years as a neuroscientist, published quite a bit, actually. But I grew tired of the peer review process. Xenoarchaeology seemed... liberating by comparison."

Ryx's brow arched. "Neuroscience, huh?"

"Yes?"

Ryx gave a low whistle. "Well, now I definitely gotta introduce you to my sister."

That earned him a look.

"Oh?"

"She's a genius mechanic, bit of a madwoman when it comes to designing tech. She's been trying to track down a good neuro specialist to talk about Hard light projection medical applications or something." He said continuing to step over wreckage.

Dr. Quarn tilted his elongated head curiously. "I'd be happy to speak with her. Assuming she doesn't mind long-winded lectures and unsolicited diagrams."

Ryx grinned. "Oh, you two are going to be unbearable."

They crested the ridge, and the Wraithburn came into view, sleek, black and grey, crouched like a hunting bird among the wind scoured rocks. Quarn paused and took it in with a whistle of appreciation.

"Impressive craft. Yours?"

"Mine. Built with the blood, sweat, and borderline masochism of my family."

"I'm beginning to understand your attachment to it."

As they neared the ship, Ryx's posture stiffened. His boots slowed. One hand reached instinctively toward the Ironhowl slung across his back.

Yessari noticed. "What is it?"

Ryx didn't answer at first, his eyes were locked skyward, jaw tightening. Through the red-tinged canopy, a dark silhouette cut

228

through the atmosphere like a dagger falling from orbit. Sleek. Angular. Matte-black hull panels that swallowed the sunlight.

As the sleek black fighter broke through the clouds, Ryx tensed. It wasn't a ship he recognized, no visible insignia, no transponder signal, and built like a predator: all sharp angles and matte plating. It cut through the atmosphere with a silent grace, banking low over the valley where the shuttle had crashed.

Yessari, limping slightly but upright, spotted it too. The pale orange of his skin looked suddenly a few shades duller in the dusty light.

"That's the one," he said, voice tight. "That's the ship that shot me down."

Ryx's jaw clenched. His eyes tracked the fighter as it looped around, scouting the crash site before banking toward a plateau a few klicks west and touching down with a low hiss of retro-thrusters.

"You sure?" Ryx asked, already checking the ammo count on Wasted Starlight.

Yessari nodded. "Positive. I saw its silhouette through the smoke. It didn't hail me, didn't warn me. Just... fired. They wanted me out of the sky."

Ryx exhaled through his nose, trying to contain the quiet fire simmering in his chest. "Then they probably didn't expect you to survive."

"Or to be rescued," Yessari added grimly.

Ryx pointed toward the Wraithburn, which waited silently on the rocky outcrop behind them, its hull gleaming like a sleeping beast.

"Medical supplies are in the galley wall compartment behind the emergency rations. There's a derm regen patch there for your arm, too. Get inside, lock the ship behind you, and don't open it for anyone but me."

Yessari hesitated. "You're going to them?"

"I'm going to ask a few questions," Ryx said, already moving.

Yessari called after him, "You might not like the answers."

Ryx didn't turn back. "I usually don't."

The wind picked up behind him as he started down the ridge, Wasted Starlight at his side and his fingers flexing inside the gauntlet's grip. He didn't know who was in that fighter or why they wanted a xenoarchaeologist dead. But he intended to find out.

The plateau waited ahead like a graveyard. And Ryx was done running and hiding.

The fighter's hatch hissed open with a slow exhale of steam. A single figure stepped out.

Dark grey armor clung to him like a second skin, every edge matte and deliberate. The helmet was smooth, featureless, save for a blacked-out visor that swallowed the light around it. He moved with sharp purpose, calculated, calm.

Ryx stayed crouched behind a patch of rust grass and shale, Ironhowl locked and trained. He didn't know this ship. Didn't like it either.

He stood slowly, keeping the rifle level.

"You lost?" Ryx called out, voice hard but casual.

The armored figure turned his head toward him, no sudden movements, just that slow, unsettling focus.

A moment passed. Then the modulated voice came through Ryx's comms.

"Not today."

Ryx narrowed his eyes. "Then what's your business here?" Another beat of silence. Then:

"I'm looking for someone."

Ryx shifted his stance. "That someone wouldn't happen to be a Tayveri xenoarchaeologist with a busted shuttle, would it?"

The figure gave a small tilt of the head. "You've met him." It wasn't a question.

Ryx frowned. "He's my client."

A pause. "Shame."

Ryx's grip tightened on the Ironhowl. "Name."

The figure hesitated just long enough to make it a power play. Then: "Nyl Strade."

"Guild?"

A longer pause this time. The air between them thickened.

"I don't work Guild," Nyl said at last, almost like the words were beneath him. "I take corporate contracts. Private business." Ryx's stomach turned. *Black Sable?*.

"And who exactly hired you to bag a government-licensed xenoarchaeologist?" Ryx asked, voice dropping into a darker register. "I like to know who's shooting down scientists these days."

Nyl's visor gave away nothing. But Ryx felt it, the twitch of tension in the air. The storm brewing beneath the stillness.

"That information," Nyl said coolly, "isn't for sale."

Ryx sighed. "Didn't think so." Then he fired.

Ryx's first shot echoed like thunder through the brittle air of Myrrh IV's dry basin.

The charged round from the Ironhowl streaked toward Nyl's chest, dead center. But the bounty hunter was already moving, body tilting unnaturally to the side with speed that didn't belong in that much armor. The blast missed by inches, melting a crater into the rock behind him.

Ryx moved, fast and low, diving for a stack of broken shuttle plating half-buried in the dust. A burst of white-hot fire chewed through the spot where he'd just stood. Nyl's weapon sang in a deep, concussive rhythm, suppressor dampened, but brutal.

That's not standard issue, Ryx thought as he slammed into cover.

They traded bursts, Nyl's fire disciplined, two shots per squeeze, always low-to-high, trying to flush Ryx up. Ryx returned fire in sweeping arcs, using the Ironhowl's charge capacity to light up the field.

The first thing Ryx learned: Nyl didn't panic.

Even pinned, even flanked, Nyl didn't shout, didn't scramble. He repositioned without noise, disappearing behind a jagged outcrop, leaving behind only the hiss of scorched dirt.

Ryx's HUD lost visual contact.

"Shit."

He swapped out a depleted ammo cell and peeked, slow and careful. Nothing.

The valley had gone still, unnervingly so. Even the local fauna seemed to sense that death had walked onto the field.

Then, **CRACK.**

The round impacted the shuttle scrap next to Ryx's head, splintering it into shrapnel. He ducked, rolled to the left, and fired twice at the ridge line, blind shots, more to make Nyl move than to hit.

"Slippery bastard," Ryx muttered.

"Likewise," Nyl's voice said, somehow now behind him.

Ryx spun on instinct, pulled the trigger, Nyl was gone again.

He's flanking. Fast.

Ryx activated his visor's motion tracker, but whatever Nyl was wearing was jamming most passive scans. Still, a blip, far right, moving toward his ship.

No way in hell, pal.

Ryx bolted across the basin, using the gauntlet to trigger a low energy barrier, blue arcs crackling to life as he sprinted, rounds bouncing off with bone-jarring force. His armor took a few hits along the left pauldron, the ceramic plating spider-webbing.

He leapt behind another boulder and hissed into comms.

"Yessari, stay locked in the Wraith. We've got a live one out here."

"I-I will comply," the alien's voice came back, shaken. "Please, try not to let him kill you."

"Working on it."

Nyl advanced steadily through the smoke and dust, his gun high, his aim tracking every breath Ryx took behind cover.

Ryx knew he was better than this in a one-on-one. But something about this guy,

He moved like he'd studied Ryx. Knew his rhythm. Wasn't just some merc. He was surgical. Trained.

Corporate black ops. Has to be.

Ryx ducked out, fired again. Nyl dodged like a shadow and returned fire, but this time, Ryx was ready. He punched the ground with his right hand, gauntlet glowing hot, and the shockwave launched a cloud of dust and debris into the air.

He used the cover to sprint, closing the gap in seconds.

CLANG.

Their shoulders collided. The force sent both men sprawling backwards. Nyl rolled to his feet like a cat, his rifle snapping back up.

Too slow.

Ryx was already there.

He surged forward, gauntlet flaring. His strange energy blade sprang from his forearm, blue and humming with lethal intent. He slashed, Nyl blocked with his rifle, but the energy blade carved into the weapon, shearing part of the barrel clean off.

Nyl dropped it instantly and pulled a short plasma knife from his belt.

They circled each other, breath heavy, dirt swirling at their feet like ghosts.

"This your idea of negotiation?" Ryx spat.

"I don't negotiate with interference." Nyl replied coldly.

"Wrong day, asshole."

They clashed again, blade against blade, plasma edge sizzling against The gauntlets energy. Ryx landed a brutal punch to Nyl's ribs with his opposite hand, sending sparks off the armor. Nyl ducked a follow-up strike and drove his knee into Ryx's side, nearly knocking the wind from him.

But Ryx twisted with the impact, opened his gauntleted palm with a flash of blue light,

BOOM.

A localized concussive pulse launched Nyl backward. He slammed into a boulder with enough force to leave a dent. His helmet cracked along one side. He didn't move.

Ryx staggered forward, panting, smoke rising from the gauntlet's seams.

"You're done."

He stepped toward the downed figure, reaching for a stun restraint on his belt.

Then, **Pop**.

Flash bomb.

Ryx's visor dimmed instantly, but it wasn't enough. Light exploded in his vision, and then, **Pain.**

A hard boot to the chest sent him sprawling. By the time Ryx regained focus, the fighter's engines were roaring to life.

"Son of a.."

Nyl was back in the pilot seat, visor glinting in the light of the systems red sun.

Ryx sprinted for the ship, but the fighter kicked up dust and fire, lifting off in a screaming arc and vanishing into the clouds.

Ryx stopped at the edge of the smoke, heart hammering, fists clenched.

Someone had sent Nyl Strade to kill Dr. Quarn.

And now?

Now someone out there knew what Ryx and his bracelet could really do and had lived to tell the tale.

The wind had finally stilled by the time Ryx reached the last ridge near the Wraithburn. Dust clung to the plates of his armor, his muscles ached, and the Fury still hummed faintly in its holster like it wanted to be used again.

He was halfway to the ramp when something zipped out from behind a boulder, small, metallic, round. A drone.

Ryx froze. His fingers twitched toward the Fury. The drone hovered perfectly still, its burnished surface catching the light. Then a familiar, crisp voice issued from a speaker on the underside:

"Please don't shoot. That drone was rather expensive."

Ryx relaxed a fraction. "Yessari?"

"Indeed. You're very quick on the draw, by the way. From a neural response standpoint, it's impressive."

The drone spun in a slow orbit around him, its single lens focusing and narrowing. Ryx narrowed his own eyes.

"You sent this thing after me?"

"I launched it to observe the man trying to kill me," Yessari said plainly. "Instead, I caught you fighting like a star-cursed storm front. It was... enlightening."

Ryx kept walking. "Glad I could entertain."

"No need for modesty," the Tayveri said through the speaker, his tone tinged with barely restrained excitement. "I saw it. That thing on your arm. It projected a full energy shield, then an energy blade, and finally, some sort of kinetic emission. Like a directed shockwave."

Ryx didn't respond.

"I've never seen tech like that before," Yessari pressed. "Not from this cycle of civilizations. Tayveri weapons tech doesn't come close. Neither does yours."

Ryx finally stopped just outside the Wraithburn's open hatch. He turned, voice cautious.

"You don't recognize it?"

"No," Yessari replied. "And that's what makes it so intriguing. It doesn't behave like normal augmented tech. No external triggers.

No power readouts. It responds to your will... as if it's bonded to your neural impulses."

Ryx glanced down at the gold-brushed bracelet on his wrist. It looked dormant now. Silent. Sleeping.

Yessari's drone tilted slightly in the air.

"Where did you get it?" Ryx hesitated.

"Was it manufactured?" the Tayveri pressed. "Or did you find it, salvage, inheritance, inheritance-from-a-salvage, a cursed tomb somewhere?"

Ryx smirked faintly. He was starting to like the scatterbrained doctor.

"I'll let you know when I figure that out myself."

Yessari made an amused noise. "So, a mystery to both of us."

"It saved my life," Ryx said. "More than once."

"And possibly made you a walking target," Yessari added brightly. "But an incredibly interesting one."

The drone hovered closer. "Have you tried separating it from your body? Running diagnostics?"

"It doesn't come off," Ryx said flatly.

"Even more fascinating." A pause. "And slightly alarming."

Ryx stepped into the ship. Before the hatch closed, the drone floated just inside the threshold.

"Do you mind if I... study it? Noninvasively. Visual scans. Magnetic resonance. Just baseline readings?" Ryx stared at the small orb.

"You're a weapons expert now, huh?" Ryx rubbed the back of his head "I thought you were a nuero scientist turned Xenoarcheologist"

Yessari chuckled. "Career number four, actually. But this might be the one that sticks."

Ryx raised a brow. "How many degrees do you have?"

"Six and a half," Yessari said, completely deadpan. "But who's counting?"

Ryx exhaled. He looked down at the gauntlet again. Its edges pulsed once, slowly, like it was breathing.

He looked back at the drone.

"You can look. But you don't touch." The orb buzzed, pleased. "That's all I ask." Ryx turned toward the cockpit.

"And if you figure out what this thing is..." he added without looking back, "let me know before it kills me."

Yessari's voice followed him down the corridor, almost cheerfully.

"I'll do my best to catalog the warning signs."

CHAPTER 14
STRANGE COMPANIONS AND STRANGER QUESTIONS

Ryx stepped into the Wraithburn's common corridor with a low sigh, pausing just inside the hatch to listen. Nothing but the soft hum of the ship's systems and the faint static whine of the atmosphere shields cycling down.

A moment later, the small orb-like drone zipped in after him, whirring with curious energy.

"Eryx Thorne," came Dr. Yessari Quarn's crisp voice from behind. "Now that the immediate threat of death has passed, may I resume analyzing the object bonded to your arm?"

Ryx grunted. "Didn't even get a chance to sit down."

He walked into the main compartment and peeled off his gloves. The bracelet, gold and smooth with faint seams, sat inert on his wrist like a dormant beast. No glow, no hum. Just presence. Always presence.

Yessari followed, good arm folded behind his back, his long orange features composed in what Ryx was starting to recognize as barely contained scientific glee. His large, almost entirely pupil-black eyes flicked toward the gauntlet and back.

"I'd like to run some passive spectral imaging," he said, already moving toward the sensor rig built into one of the utility consoles. "I won't touch it. I swear on my third doctorate."

Ryx raised a brow. "Third?"

"Neuro-cybernetics," Yessari said, loading the scan modules.

"Followed by galactic ethics, which was boring, and then I changed careers. I'm Tayveri, remember? We collect careers like humans collect bad tattoos."

Ryx smirked. "You really do talk like a university grant proposal."

Yessari turned with a flick of his long fingers. "You're one to talk, You just use your firearm and a mysterious bracelet to do it."

Ryx chuckled and collapsed into the pilot's chair. "Fair." He was getting used to Yessari Quran's odd mix of literal talk and humor.

He leaned forward and brought the Wraithburn's engines online. "We're lifting off. Whatever that fighter was, I don't want to be here when his friends decide to check in."

"You mean there might be more of them?" Yessari asked, not sounding particularly concerned. "Good. Perhaps they've seen that device before. You can beat the answers out of them."

The Wraithburn rose from the surface with a low rumble, dust trailing in her wake. Ryx keyed in coordinates to enter orbit above the planet. Safer up there. Easier to run if things got dicey again.

As the ship breached atmosphere, Ryx opened his encrypted comms and shot a quick message to Tess.

TO: Tess

Picked up something weird. Doctor I rescued is a Tayveri xenoarchaeologist , used to be a neuroscientist. Smart, strange, probably gonna try to scan my brain eventually.

You still looking for someone for your hardlight neural interface project?

A few minutes passed.

Then her response came through with characteristic fire:

FROM: Tess

239

I KNEW IT.

I told you the universe would send me the weird brain I needed. Yes. A thousand times yes. Bring him here. I want to pick that oversized alien brain apart. And also thank him for putting up with your dumb ass.

PS: Tell him I have questions. Lots of them.

Ryx grinned. He swiveled in the chair to face Yessari, who was finishing the first passive scan and humming to himself in a tone that sounded vaguely like a pleased violin.

"She wants to meet you," Ryx said.

Yessari looked up, blinking. "Who does?"

"My sister," Ryx replied. "The one with the hardlight project I told you about. She said she needs someone with a neural science background. And she's very excited to meet the Tayveri who is researching her idiot brother."

Yessari tilted his head. "Eryx Thorne, I would be honored. I owe you my life, after all. A proper Tayveri cannot let such things go unpaid. And…" he trailed off, eyes flicking back to the gauntlet. "This artifact of yours, and your sister's neural tech ambitions, well… it may prove to be a collision of curiosities too tempting to ignore."

"You'll like her," Ryx said. "She's smarter than me."

Yessari raised a hand. "That's not a high bar."

Ryx chuckled. "No. But she's also the reason I'm still walking around after the last six months."

He keyed in a message to Tess with their heading and estimated arrival time.

A few seconds later, another ping lit up on the console.

A different sender.

Encrypted Message , Source Unknown Subject: BSD , Trail Found.

Ryx,

Two things:

240

1. Lanara Kress has been found sending her contact info attached.

2.Got a tail on someone connected to BSD's Planetary operations in the region Kolen Vess was last in.

I'll let you know where it leads.

Details to follow. Stay sharp.

-Vorn

Ryx's stomach dropped.

He leaned back in the chair and rubbed the bridge of his nose. His mind flicked back to the garage. To Kaelen. To Tess's screams. To the blood on his hands.

A trail.

He looked back at Yessari, who was scanning the gauntlet with a precise sensor array and muttering under his breath.

"Tess said we're cleared to visit," Ryx said, trying to steady his voice. "Her aunt's place isn't far from our current orbit. We'll drop in tomorrow."

"Excellent," Yessari said, eyes still fixed on the readings. "Hopefully she has good tea. I always think better with tea."

Ryx leaned back, hand resting loosely on the armrest, over the golden brace of the artifact, pulsing faintly beneath his fingertips.

It wasn't over.

ΔΔΔ

The Wraithburn glided through the atmosphere of Marla Rhoen's green-and-gold home world, cutting smooth arcs between lazy weather fronts and sunlight-drenched oceans. Ryx sat in the pilot's chair, one boot braced on the console as the auto-nav guided them toward the familiar estate.

Yessari Quarn hovered behind him, utterly transfixed, not by the approaching landscape, but by Ryx's wrist.

"Well?" Ryx asked, half amused, half exhausted.

"I have never seen biosympathetic conductivity in any known material like this," Yessari murmured. He turned the floating drone he used for mobile interaction in slow, deliberate circles around the golden band. "Whatever it's made of, it's… listening. Reacting at the neural level. This isn't just interfacing with your nervous system, it's harmonizing."

Ryx tilted his head back. "Is that Tayveri science talk for 'weird'?" Yessari smirked. "Yes. 'Weird'… and beautiful."

Ryx huffed a dry laugh. "You're lucky I like you, doc. Anyone else orbiting my arm like a nosy moon would've been drop-kicked out the airlock by now."

Yessari's wide-pupiled eyes gleamed with amusement. "I will note the privilege, Eryx Thorne."

"Stars help me," Ryx muttered, shaking his head. "You're worse than my sister."

At the mention of Tess, Ryx opened the encrypted comms line and tapped out a quick message.

TO: Tessa Rhoen

We're here.

Got a delivery for you.

You sure you want this weirdo? (he's kind of growing on me) P.S. he's obsessed with my wrist.

The reply came quickly.

FROM: Tess

YES.

YES.

BRING HIM NOW.

DO NOT LET HIM DIE.

TELL HIM I MAKE LASERS.

—Tess

Ryx rolled his eyes but couldn't stop the grin. "Hope you're ready for the full Tessa Rhoen experience, Doc."

Yessari blinked. "She sounds... invigorating."

"You'll either love her or run screaming," Ryx said, easing the Wraithburn into its descent pattern. "But she's family. If you're even half as curious about this gauntlet as you act, you two'll be closer than hardlight particle colliders by breakfast."

ΔΔΔ

Marla Rhoen's estate shimmered in the afternoon sun, low, elegant structures nestled against a cliffside grove, surrounded by lazy flocks of flying mammals and drifting mist. Ryx guided the Wraithburn into a soft landing on the far pad. Tessa was already waiting, her slinged arm held close, her grin wide.

She met them halfway. Ryx barely got through introductions before she pulled Yessari into a hug that left the Tayveri stiff with confusion.

"I need to make tech that talks to the brain through the nerves," she said by way of greeting, eyes gleaming. "You study brains. We're going to be best friends."

Yessari, utterly bewildered, glanced at Ryx. "She's delightful."

"Told you," Ryx muttered. "You're doomed."

The three of them chatted for a few minutes, but Ryx kept checking the horizon, heart already pulling toward the stars. He didn't want to admit it, but standing still felt like death now. Tessa saw it before he said anything.

"You have to go."

Ryx nodded. "Rexa sent another message."

He tapped his wrist, pulling up the new encrypted file.

FROM: Vorn

Found your lead.

BSD execs, mid-tier, not just field agents. Meeting at a relay station just outside the Jaro Fold in two days. It's deep in the system Vess was last seen working in.

Small team. Quiet. My agent keeps hearing the term "Echofall".

If you're going to shake the cage, this is the time.

-Rexa

Tess read the message over his shoulder, then looked up at him. "You going?"

"You know I am."

Tessa stepped back, letting her hand trail across his armored forearm. "You be careful, Eryx. If you die before I get to finish my prototype.."

"I won't," he said softly.

Then, to Yessari: "You watch out for her, doc."

"I owe you my life, Eryx Thorne. I will guard hers with mine."

Ryx gave one last look to the estate, the wind in the trees, the peace on his sister's face, and then turned back to the Wraithburn.

As Ryx walked back toward the Wraithburn, the hum of the ship's systems rising in his ears, he paused near the edge of the landing pad. The wind rustled through the tall, sun-drenched trees beyond the estate, but his attention lingered on the voices behind him.

He turned slightly, catching sight of Tessa and Yessari standing under the archway to the courtyard garden.

She was animated, her good arm gesturing wildly as she talked about neural-resonant hardlight feedback loops and prototype signal scaffolding. Ryx could hear the excitement in her voice, and it struck him how alive she looked, more so than she had since Kaelen's death.

Yessari was transfixed, his wide dark eyes following every word like she was unraveling the mysteries of the cosmos. He leaned in when she spoke, nodded eagerly when she explained something with rapid enthusiasm, and when she laughed, he laughed too, not out of politeness, but with real, growing delight.

Ryx tilted his head, watching for another moment. The two of them, so completely wrapped in their shared curiosity and endless drive to understand, looked like they were standing in their own universe.

He smiled, just a little.

Whatever else had happened, whatever darkness still waited ahead, Ryx knew he was leaving his sister in good company. Not just someone capable, but someone who saw her brilliance like he did.

He stepped onto the Wraithburn's ramp, took one last look back, and muttered under his breath, "Try not to blow anything up, you two." The hatch hissed closed behind him.

It was time to hunt shadows.

The Wraithburn's hatch sealed with a hiss behind him, the soft rumble of its reactor thrumming under Ryx's boots like a heartbeat. He stepped into the cockpit, sat in the pilot's chair, and stared at the empty co-pilot seat for a breath too long. Tess would've already had the nav route plotted. She was only co-pilot a few days here or there recently, but he missed her already.

He keyed in a secure comms request to Rexa Vorn. No delay, no bouncing through relays, he wanted her voice, not another message.

She answered on the second ping.

"About time you called me directly, scrapper," she said, leaning back in a folding chair, feet on a counter littered with tools and databoards. "Was starting to think you were afraid to hear my voice."

"Not afraid," Ryx said, managing a dry half-smile. "Just tired of your charming sarcasm."

"Well, tough shit. I've got plenty of it, and a lead."

Ryx straightened. "Go on."

Rexa's face shifted, still sharp, but more focused now. She tapped something offscreen, and a small rotating star chart lit up beside her.

"System's called the Jaro Fold. Backwater, mining-heavy sector, mostly corporate-owned space. But it's quiet, so perfect for meetings nobody wants to get tracked."

Ryx leaned in. "BSD?"

She nodded. "Three mid-to-high tier execs from different divisions: cybernetics, interstellar development, and... xenoarcheology. Guess which one I'm interested in."

Ryx's pulse ticked higher. "You're sure?"

"Sure enough. One of my sources caught a burst-encoded flight path from BSD's own comms net. Meeting's listed under some bullshit designation: 'Project Echofall.' But that's the same tag that came up in briefly in the Dossier BSD gave you about Kolen Vess's expedition before he dropped off the grid."

"You think these people are Involved?"

Rexa nodded. "Strong possibility. These execs either funded it, lost track of it, or covered it up. Maybe all three."

Ryx gritted his teeth. "You think one of them sent Darna Kent after Kolen?"

"I think someone's scrambling to make sure no one else learns what Vess found," she said, her voice cooling. "That's why they're meeting off-grid, no digital footprint. And if they learn you're sniffing after them,"

"They won't," Ryx said flatly.

Rexa didn't smile. "If you're going in, Eryx, be smart. I won't have eyes inside that meeting. It could be a dozen guards. Could be none. But if you get close enough, record everything. Faces, names, what they're saying. If they spill anything about Vess, we'll finally have a thread to pull."

"Copy that," Ryx said. "One more thing."

"Yeah?"

"Thanks. For keeping this alive."

Rexa tilted her head. "I figured Kaelen would haunt me if I didn't."

That hit him harder than he expected. He gave a small nod and cut the feed before his throat locked up. He exhaled, steadying himself.

Jaro Fold. Three suits, maybe the exact ones who sent Kolen Vess to find his last expedition.

Ryx tapped the nav console, locked in the jump coordinates, and leaned back as the warp engines began to hum.

Let's find out what you were chasing, Kolen.

Stars bent and bled into streaks as the Wraithburn vanished into the dark.

ΔΔΔ

Ryx dropped out of warp with the Wraithburn just outside sensor range of the Jaro Fold a day later. The system was as empty as the rumors said, just a few scattered asteroid fields, a pale gas giant, an unnamed terrestrial planet, and one lonely blinking dot on the nav grid.

The station.

He leaned forward, narrowing his eyes as it came into view.

The outpost was small. Unmarked. Floating between the folds of gravity wells like some forgotten roadside diner from a dead route. From the distance, it looked like a squat industrial hive grafted onto a half-finished freighter. No corporate branding. No callsign beacons. Just cold steel and blacked-out windows.

But the ships told a different story.

Three BSD Luxray shuttles, sleek and angular, were docked along the curved spine of the station like predators crouched on a carcass. Their hulls gleamed even in the dim light of the fold, clearly top-of-the-line transports built for comfort, not cargo.

Ryx felt his jaw tighten.

So, they were here. Rexa was right. Executives didn't travel in Luxrays unless something was important. Hell, even regional directors barely rated that kind of ride. Whoever was aboard this station, they were the real deal, people with clearance, power, and blood on their hands.

He knew what Rexa wanted. Stealth. Patience. Listening devices, long-range recording, drone surveillance. She wanted a ghost to haunt their meeting, not a blade to shatter it.

But Ryx wasn't feeling ghostly.

Not today.

Kaelen's face, pale and bloodied beneath a fallen workbench, burned behind his eyes.

No defensive satellites. No security fighters. No visible patrols.

Ryx almost laughed & moved to suit up.

The neoplate clicked into place with muscle memory efficiency. The

Ironhowl was magnet-locked to his back, and the Fury-RZ7, Wasted Starlight, was holstered at his hip with a quiet promise of vengeance. He donned a long dark coat with a hood. A good way to obfuscate his armor and face from a quick glance.

This wasn't a raid. Not yet.

But if these BSD bastards knew anything about Kolen Vess, or worse, if they had anything to do with the ambush on Vorrthani Station, Ryx wasn't leaving without answers. Or blood.

He tapped into the station's public landing queue and sent a docking request under an old alias. The kind a bounty hunter might use when they didn't want to make noise.

A beat passed.

Then the station pinged back with an acceptance code. A specific docking ring lit up on the station's underbelly, like an invitation to a dinner party hosted by killers.

Ryx narrowed his eyes and leaned into the comm.

"Alright," he whispered. "Let's talk, gentlemen."

The Wraithburn adjusted trajectory silently, gliding toward the ring like a knife sliding back into its sheath.

The airlock cycled with a hollow hiss as Ryx stepped into the outpost.

Dim overhead fluorescents flickered to life above dull gray walls, casting a sickly hue across the interior corridor. It smelled like recycled air, cheap coolant, and old grease. Half the lights in the corridor buzzed inconsistently, casting soft shadows that seemed to shift every few seconds.

Two station security officers stood just beyond the bulkhead, relaxed but attentive. Both wore mismatched armor sets and sidearms slung low in worn holsters. Contractors, Ryx guessed. Likely local hires, cheap, expendable muscle. The kind BSD liked using for deniability.

One of them, a woman with tired eyes and a data slate in hand, looked him up and down as he approached.

"Docking under the alias 'Korrin Vale'," she read aloud. "Ship: Ardent Shroud. Weapons declared: personal sidearm and rifle. Purpose of visit?"

Ryx exhaled like he hadn't spoken in days. He lowered his hood, scratched the stubble on his jaw, and gave a weary half-smile.

"Been in warp for three days straight," he said, voice hoarse. "Chasing a contract that turned into a ghost trail. Burned my last stim pack and ration bar yesterday. Figured I'd grab a bite and see what news I missed before heading back out."

The woman scanned his face, then glanced at her partner. The other guard gave a small shrug. Nothing in his file pinged red.

She nodded and waved him through. "Main promenade's straight ahead. Caf-bar's to your left. Try not to start any fights, you won't like the way we break them up."

Ryx smirked. "Don't plan to make any noise."

He stepped past them, boot falls echoing down the steel hallway as he moved deeper into the station.

ΔΔΔ

The promenade was sparsely populated. A handful of travelers drifted between vendor stalls, mostly tired freight haulers, system hoppers, and one nervous-looking gambler being chewed out by a blue-skinned pit boss. The entire place felt like a liminal space caught between nowhere and nothing. A perfect hiding spot.

Ryx's eyes swept the area.

At the far end of the corridor, past the cracked-glass window of a rundown bar, sat a polished, oddly pristine entryway. The metal frame gleamed like it had been recently replaced. Dark glass obscured the room beyond, but two men in identical charcoal-gray suits stood silently in front of the doors, each one with a visible sidearm and a subtle neural comm node behind the ear.

BSD.

Ryx didn't need to see the logo, he knew that posture, that cold-eyed presence. Company muscle, suited and sterilized, guarding something, or someone, inside.

The VIP lounge.

He took a seat at the nearest food stall, a dinged-up synth-café with a sputtering neon sign that read "Outpost Roast". The barista bot didn't even look up as Ryx ordered a stim coffee and a plate of whatever protein was labeled as "spiced." He barely touched it.

Instead, he watched the lounge from behind the rim of his cup.

One of the guards turned his head slightly every so often, scanning the room with a slow, patient rhythm. The other stood perfectly still, a statue of corporate silence.

Whoever was inside that lounge mattered.

Time to find out how much.

Ryx considered his options. He could wait, track their movements, maybe follow them when they left. Or he could force the issue, pick a crack in their armor and wedge himself in.

He sipped his caff slowly.

His next steps would depend on whether he wanted to be a shadow...

...or a storm.

The hum of background conversation faded under the roar in his skull.

He wasn't just here because of a lead. He was here because of what happened to Kaelen, What happened to Tess, and what happened on Tarrin Station.

Ryx's jaw clenched.

Ryx rubbed the heel of his palm against his temple. He could still see the look on Kolen's face. Could still hear the way his voice had cracked when he said Ryx's name. Could still feel the weight of the weapon in his hand when the shot went off.

And now here he was again. BSD in front of him. Tied to the artifact. Tied to Kolen's death. Tied to Kaelen's murder. Tied to Tessa's missing arm.

He looked down at the fused bracelet, sleek, golden, deceptively beautiful. It shimmered faintly as if responding to his heartbeat.

Ryx thought of Tess, her pale face in that medbed.

Of Kaelen, crushed beneath a bench in the place he called home.

Of Kolen, bleeding out on the cold floor of Tarrin Station, betrayed by the last person he trusted.

The storm rose again.

Quiet. Inevitable. Ryx stood.

He left the coffee on the table. Let it go cold without him. The two BSD guards flanked the lounge doors as he approached. Professional posture. Glassy visors. They clocked him immediately.

"Restricted area," one said. "Keep moving."

Ryx didn't stop walking. He slowed, just slightly, letting them get a good look at his armor. At the rifle on his back. The pistol at his hip. The shimmer of something strange around his right arm.

He stopped three steps short.

"Inside that room," he said quietly, "are people who cost me more than they'll ever understand."

The guards straightened, uncertain now.

"Sir, if you don't leave,"

Wasted Starlight slid into his hands like an old friend shaking his hand.

Kolen. Kaelen. Tess.

He squeezed the trigger.

The bark of Wasted Starlight was thunder in the narrow corridor.

The first BSD guard didn't even get his hand to his weapon. A precision shot punched straight through his hidden body armor, armor-piercing, ion-charged. His body dropped like a marionette with its strings cut.

The second staggered back and fumbled for cover.

Ryx was already moving.

He advanced low and fast, a perfect weave of motion born from hundreds of hunts. Another shot cracked out of the Fury, center mass. The second guard slammed against the lounge doors and crumpled with a smoking hole in his chest plate.

Ryx didn't pause.

The security panel blinked red. Locked.

He holstered the Fury just long enough to engage the gauntlet. Blue light rippled up his arm. A kinetic pulse slammed into the reinforced door, blowing it open with a screech of shredded servos.

The VIP lounge was plush. Dim lighting. Velvet booths. Expensive bottles. Three BSD executives looked up in surprise, mid-conversation, mid-drink. One of them was raising a datapad. Another was already scrambling for a weapon.

Ryx strode through the smoke and doorframe like death in white armor.

They all saw it: the burning blue glow of the artifact curling across his right arm. The weapon in his hand, still smoking.

"Who?"

Ryx didn't wait for the question to finish.

He shot the man reaching for his gun.

The man hit the back of the booth they were in with a dull thud, hole still smoking in his chest. The second man froze in place, hands raised and shaking.

The last, a woman in a sleek BSD-blazer with silver tech-lenses over her eyes, snatched up her pad and yelled, "We're compromised, dump the logs!"

Ryx aimed at her legs and fired. The round blew through the table and into her thigh. She collapsed with a cry, screaming and cursing as she bled into the lounge carpet.

He moved quickly. Secured her pad. Smashed the transmitter embedded in her jacket.

"You're not deleting shit." he said.

The one exec who'd frozen was still standing, eyes wide and breath ragged. Ryx pointed the barrel of Wasted Starlight at his chest.

"You," he growled. "Sit down." The man obeyed instantly.

The bleeding woman groaned, half-conscious.

Ryx turned his attention to the suit still sitting, visibly trembling. "You've got one shot," Ryx said. "You tell me what you know about Kolen Vess. About his expedition. About why BSD wanted him dead."

"I, I was never told,"

Ryx stepped closer, raising the gauntlet. It glowed in quiet threat. The suit swallowed hard.

"He was part of Project Echofall," the man said. "Top-tier xeno division work. Artifacts. Recovery from dead systems. Whatever he found... he stopped reporting in."

Ryx's eyes narrowed. "So, you sent me to clean it up."

The suit blinked. "You were the one who..?"

Ryx backhanded him across the face with the gauntlet. Not enough to kill. Enough to remember.

"Kolen Vess was my friend," Ryx said. "You're going to tell me where his data went. Who was on the team. And where the rest of them are."

The man whimpered. "I, I have a name. A scientist. Oversaw the operation after Vess died. Took over his field data." The woman spat from the ground. "Traitor!" Ryx ignored her.

"Name."

"Dr. Arwell Marn. He's in the Lazax Drift, BSD keeps a research post out there."

Ryx memorized it instantly.

The woman on the floor spat at Ryx.

"You'll never get there. We've seen your face; we'll mark your ship" Ryx smirked. *This woman is delirious from the pain*. Ryx thought to himself. She gave her whole hand away without thinking of one glaring mistake.

The thunderclap of Wasted Starlight sang, and she was still.

The final suit screamed " I won't talk I won't tell anyone anything!" Another retort from his pistol was Ryx's only reply.

He secured the datapad and locked it down. Tapped his comm to send encrypted logs back to Rexa.

Then, finally, he looked around.

The Fury cooled in his hand. The blue light of the gauntlet flashed as it returned to its dormant state.

Five dead.

Security on the way.

Cameras all over the station.

A whisper of Kaelen's voice echoed in his mind: *Daylight is just wasted starlight, kid.*

Ryx reloaded the weapon with reverence.

"No more wasted time." he muttered.

He turned and strode out of the lounge.

CHAPTER 15
ECHOES IN THE DRIFT

T he stars outside the viewport stretched into long ribbons of white fire as the Wraithburn coasted through the void. Warp was always quiet, too quiet. Just him, the hum of the ship, and the endless beat of thoughts he couldn't shake.

Ryx sat alone in the cockpit, one boot up on the dash, eyes unfocused. He wasn't looking at anything. Not really.

The Jaro Fold was behind him, but it hadn't left him.

The station had gone into full alert the second he'd exited the VIP lounge. Klaxons screamed in his ears as he moved through the corridors. Emergency lights pulsed red. Civilians ran, scrambling to get off the station or hide wherever they could. He hadn't needed to fire another shot.

The two security guards at Dock 9 stood ready when he arrived, weapons in hand, fear in their eyes. But Ryx just walked up, slow, steady, gauntlet glowing faintly under his cloak, and they backed down. One stepped aside without a word. The other keyed the door open for him.

They saw his face. The cameras saw his face.

Good.

Let Black Sable Dynamics run the footage through every database they owned. Let them know who walked into their den and burned their secrets to ash.

He wanted them to know. To see him coming. To feel the cold edge of the war they'd started.

He sat there for a while, stewing in it. Staring at nothing. Thinking of Kolen Vess, of Kaelen, of Tess's bloodied body slumped against the wall.

No more hiding.

Eventually, the tension became too much.

Ryx stood, peeled off his jacket, and made his way down the corridor to his room and to the shower unit.

The hiss of steam filled the small chamber, fogging up the mirror as he stripped out of his clothes and armor and stepped under the hot stream. He let it pour over him like a ritual, scrubbing away smoke, sweat, and someone else's blood. For a few minutes, he let the noise of the water be louder than his thoughts.

He stepped out twenty minutes later, wrapped in a towel, steam curling off his shoulders as he padded barefoot to the living area.

The fridge unit hissed open with a soft click.

Inside, lined neatly among ration trays and synth-food packs, something familiar caught his eye.

His heart actually stuttered.

A cardboard box faded yellow and red branding. He reached in slowly, almost reverently, and pulled out the Prexan Fire Noodles, his favorite instant heat-pack meal since his military days when he was sent on missions in the Prexan system. He hadn't seen these in years. They were impossible to find outside Prexan space. And yet... here they were.

Tessa.

He smiled in spite of himself, jaw tight with emotion. She must've smuggled them in during her stocking spree before leaving the Wraithburn. Typical.

He popped the meal into the auto-heater, and as it whirred to life, he leaned on the kitchen counter, watching steam rise and feeling, for just a moment, human again.

Thank you, Tess. He thought.

The bracelet, still in its dormant, cuff-like state, rested snug on his wrist, quiet but present. Like it was listening. Always.

He pulled the noodles out, cracked the seal, and took a bite. *Still spicy as hell.*

Ryx slid into the chair at his small workstation back in his room, a warm container of Prexan Fire Noodles balanced in one hand, and the familiar hum of the Wraithburn's systems vibrating softly underfoot. He set the food down beside the console and tapped a few keys to bring up the secure comms relay.

The cursor blinked at him, waiting.

He stared at it a long time, chewing slowly.

What was he supposed to say? He paused, Better now than forgetting he thought to himself.

He flexed his hand, eyes dropping to the golden band still fused to his wrist. It glinted faintly in the dim light. Not glowing. Not pulsing. Just… watching.

He cracked his neck, sighed through his nose, and started typing.

To: Tessa Rhoen

Hey,

Just checking in. Things got a little hot at that last stop, nothing I couldn't handle. Don't worry, no injuries on my end and no need to run the sirens.

Got a new lead, and it's promising. On my way to follow up now. I think I'm getting closer. I'll let you know what I find.

How are things planet-side? I imagine Yessari is talking your ear off by now. Try not to let him break any furniture.

Talk soon.

-Ryx

Ryx exhaled slowly, eyes drifting back to the stars streaming by outside the viewport. The next system was close. With any luck, this Dr. Arwell Marn would give him what he needed: a lead on Project Echofall, on Kolen's last expedition, and on BSD's true intentions.

But luck rarely had anything to do with it anymore.

After finishing his meal, Ryx didn't head straight to his bunk. Sleep could wait. Instead, he drifted down the corridor, boots echoing softly as he passed the holding cells, the galley, the cramped lounge.

His hand slid along the bulkhead, a familiar motion, more muscle memory than anything else. His fingers brushed across the panels, rough in places, smooth in others, every scorch mark, dent, and welded seam telling a story he could recite without thinking.

The Wraithburn had saved his life more times than he could count.

She wasn't just a ship. She was armor. She was escape. She was his last chance and his oldest ally. When every other fallback burned to ash , when the war ended, when Kaelen patched him up, when BSD put a target on his back , the Wraithburn was always there, humming, waiting, flying.

In the engine room, Ryx ran diagnostics again. Not because they were needed, Tess and Kaelen had tuned her up to near perfection, but because it gave him something to do with his hands. Something quiet. Methodical. A ritual.

Every sound in here was comfort. The gentle whirr of the cooling systems. The low throb of the hypercore. The faint buzz of sensors aligning and recalibrating themselves. It was like being inside a heartbeat. Like the ship was alive in her own way.

He remembered the time a Vlexari gunship had chewed through his dorsal stabilizers and the Wraithburn had still limped them into a black zone for emergency repairs. He remembered outrunning a Penta-class cruiser by jamming the manual override on the warp coils and waking up half-fried but alive.

259

He remembered Tess passed out in the co-pilot chair, when she had pulled an all nighter to retrofit the extra crew rooms into holding cells.

He remembered every tune up Kaelen ever walked him threw.

Ryx walked over to the cockpit and lowered himself into the pilot's seat. His fingers danced across the console with reverence. The seat creaked the same way it always had. The panels blinked, waiting for him like an old friend, patient and unshaken.

He could still hear Tessa's voice in the back of his mind, teasing him for the way he always treated the Wraithburn like a sentient partner.

"Damn fool talks to his ship like it's his girlfriend." Maybe he was a damn fool.

But maybe the ship had listened.

Ryx finally turned in late, long after the Wraithburn's systems went into passive night cycle. The ship dimmed around him, her low pulse humming like a lullaby through the deck plating. He lay in his bed for a while, one arm draped over his eyes, mind flickering between too many things: BSD, Kolen, Kaelen's laugh, the new doctor, Tessa's voice.

Sleep didn't come easily, but eventually exhaustion pinned him down.

When he woke, it was still dark. That false dark, the kind unique to deep warp, where time lost its meaning and the stars outside were warped into unknowable streaks.

He sat up slowly, rubbing the back of his neck and blinking sleep from his eyes. No alarms. No messages yet. Just the low whisper of engines and the faint, rhythmic click of his old wall chrono ticking.

Ryx swung his legs over the side of the bed and got to work.

He started with his armor. Pulled each piece from the rack beside his closet, set them out on the bench like sacred relics. The white neoplate plating was scuffed in places, still singed near the knee where the fire had licked through the garage. But it had held. It had kept him alive.

He wiped each panel down with care. Repaired a cracked wrist clamp. Re-tuned the magnetic seals on the chest plate. Reinforced the thigh harness straps. The bracelet, he polished with a soft cloth, watching as the pale blue lines flickered faintly in response to his touch.

Then came the gun belt.

Ryx reloaded his ammo cells , three full packs, two charges left in the one already loaded. Two stun grenades. One flash. One old neo plate knife Kaelen had given him with a smirk and a warning. He slid Wasted Starlight into the custom holster Rexa had made, the grip familiar and cool against his fingers.

He stood in the mirror and gave himself a long look. He was starting to recover he knew. The food, The sleep. He was mentally exhausted still. But ready.

Always ready.

The console in the cockpit chimed.

[WARP EXIT IN T-MINUS 6 MINUTES.]

Ryx nodded to himself. He moved down the corridor, each step precise and silent, like muscle memory from a past life. He dropped into the pilot's seat, leaned back, eyes fixed on the slow countdown.

A new system waited on the other side.

And with it, more questions, more ghosts, and maybe... some answers.

The stars snapped into place as the Wraithburn exited warp with a subtle tremor. Ryx exhaled and leaned forward in the pilot's seat, watching as the new system unfolded before him, a slow swirl of amber light from the system's sun, planets spinning like marbles across the distant void.

The soft ping of incoming messages broke the silence, drawing his attention to the console. Two messages. He scanned the headers and immediately recognized the senders.

[Message Received – From: Tessa Rhoen]

So...

I know you said it was "a new lead," but you always say that when it's something dangerous and you don't want me to worry.

Yessari agrees.

(Yes, we're gossiping about you behind your back. Deal with it.)

Things here are actually nice. Quiet. Yess is... weirdly great. I swear, the man fixed Aunt Marla's entire solar grid while explaining quantum temporal drift with zero effort. He asked her if she wanted a built-in tea warmer in the process. Anyway. Be careful. And message us when you land.

-Tess

Ryx smirked at the screen. She knew him too well. His thumb lingered over the reply, but before he could type, the second message lit up.

[Message Received – From: Dr. Yessari Quarn]

Eryx Thorne,

Your sister is brilliant and dangerous. I mean this in the highest scientific regard.

I am currently building a prototype based on our breakfast conversation. Your aunt nearly wept when I repurposed her burnt-out kettle into a geothermal battery.

I am considering making this my long-term field post. Please advise.

P.S. I still want to discuss your gauntlet.

Warm regards,

-Dr. Y. Quarn

Tayveri Council of Interdisciplinary Sciences

(Currently Retired)

Ryx snorted. *Yeah, they're gonna get along just fine. I may need to save Aunt Marla and her house from those two though..*

He leaned back, staring out at the pale-blue crescent of a nearby moon. That brief wave of comfort began to ebb... replaced by something heavier.

A name returned to him. A promise.

Lanara Kress.

Shandar's daughter.

He hadn't reached out yet. He wanted to kick himself.

He should have done it sooner.

Ryx opened a new comm draft and began to type, each word weighed with deliberate care:

To: Lanara Kress

My name is Eryx Thorne.

I believe you and I have something very important in common.

I would like to speak with you directly; there's something I need to tell you.

If you're willing, I can call I'd prefer to do this as close to in person as possible while ensuring your comfort.

- Eryx

He stared at the message for a long beat. Then hit send. The console dimmed again, leaving him with only the hum of the ship and the slow rotation of a foreign world out the viewport.

Ryx stared at the screen a little longer, watching the "Message Sent" indicator flicker for a moment before it faded. No reply yet, not that he expected one instantly. He had no idea what time it was in Lanara Kress's system, or even if she still checked her messages regularly. For all he knew, she could be in surgery halfway across the galaxy.

He leaned back in his seat, exhaled, and rubbed the bridge of his nose. The fact that she was alive, that she existed at all, still sat in his mind like a fragile miracle. He hoped the message didn't come off as too vague; important personal news always sounded ominous. But what else could he say? Your father, the Vlexari war general, is alive and serving out a reduced sentence in a prison moon where I also did time after deserting the military that assaulted your home world. Probably not the kind of thing you drop in a text.

He let out a quiet chuckle at the absurdity of it.

But he couldn't wait around. Not now. Not with another lead pulling him forward. The station he'd left behind was probably still on high alert, Black Sable Dynamics scrambling to control the damage from the mess he just kicked into motion. He'd shown them his face. Let them know he was alive. That he remembered everything, and that he was coming.

He stood from the console and stretched his arms overhead with a groan. "Alright, Wraith," he muttered, patting the wall beside him. "Let's go see what kind of trouble's waiting this time."

The mission wasn't going to wait. Lanara would respond when she could, and when she did, he'd be ready with a truth that might finally bring something good into someone's life again.

∆∆∆

As the Wraithburn crested low orbit above the unnamed, gray-green planet, Ryx keyed in the coordinates he was given by the BSD executive back in the Jaro Fold. The planet had no registered colonies, no trade routes, no designation beyond a coded identifier in BSD's own records. Perfect for the kind of secret they wanted buried.

On approach, the outpost wasn't hard to spot, a metallic scar carved into the side of a rocky cliff, flanked by two automated gun towers. Ryx muttered a curse and dropped the Wraith into evasive maneuvers the moment the towers lit up with target locks.

"Let's see what your new shields can do, Kaelen." Ryx whispered to himself, flipping the shield modulation panel into combat sync. The upgraded shield battery roared to life, glowing a golden hue as the twin towers opened fire. Plasma lances struck the

Wraithburn's hull and dissipated harmlessly across the reinforced energy field.

Ryx whooped, spun the ship hard, and swept in close. The first tower never got a second shot, he clipped it with a precision volley from his nose cannon, and it exploded in a plume of shattered alloy. The second tried to track him, but he was already in a lateral spin, dropping a pair of torpedoes that blasted it clean off its platform.

Smoke still curled from the burning wreckage as Ryx landed the Wraith just outside the facility perimeter. His scanners picked up only a handful of life signs, too few for a military post. Mostly scientists. No distress calls. No evacuation. Just fear.

He disembarked cautiously, Wasted Starlight holstered but ready, Ironhowl strapped across his back. As he approached the outpost's reinforced door, it hissed open without resistance. A handful of guards stood there, young, poorly armed, and clearly terrified.

"I'm here for a conversation," Ryx said calmly. "Nobody has to get hurt."

The guards exchanged nervous looks. One of them, barely older than a cadet, nodded and turned without a word, motioning for Ryx to follow.

The guards led Ryx down a low, dim hallway, exposed conduits buzzed overhead, the metal walls scuffed and unpolished. This wasn't a high profile BSD facility; it was something put together in a hurry and meant to be forgotten. Everything about the outpost reeked of secrecy.

The door at the end of the hallway opened with a lazy hiss, revealing a compact office lit by flickering fluorescents. Inside, behind a desk cluttered with datapads and half-drained stim packs, sat a gaunt man with a receding hairline and a tremor in his hands.

"Dr. Arwell Marn," Ryx said flatly as he entered.

The man flinched. "I, uh… yes. Yes, that's me."

Ryx shut the door behind him with a click, slow and deliberate. The guards didn't follow. It was just the two of them now.

"You know who I am?" Ryx asked, his voice calm, too calm.

Marn's eyes darted. "I… no. Should I?"

Ryx stepped closer, his silhouette blocking most of the dim light.

"No," he said. "But you know the name Kolen Vess, don't you?"

That got him. The man paled visibly, and his shoulders stiffened like a mouse caught mid-scamper. He didn't answer right away.

"Doctor," Ryx continued, pacing slowly in front of the desk, "you took over his research. You continued Project Echofall. So, tell me what it is. What he found."

Marn fumbled to stand, knocking over one of the datapads. "I, I'm not cleared for field classifications. I only processed the recovery files. Just logs, data packets, signal echoes. I never saw the site."

"Don't bullshit me." Ryx turned sharp. "I've bled for this. For him. So, if you've got something to say, say it before I decide BSD doesn't need your services anymore."

Marn's jaw opened and closed twice. Then, reluctantly, he reached down and opened a drawer beneath the desk. A small metallic case emerged, coated in dust, sealed with both biometric and passcode locks.

"This is everything I have. Kolen's final reports, sensor logs, encrypted transmission fragments. I don't even know what half of it means. Some of it's in a format our systems couldn't decipher."

Ryx took the case and tucked it into his belt pouch without comment.

"BSD didn't give you access?" he asked, skeptical.

"They were compartmentalizing everything," Marn said quickly. "I was just supposed to catalog it. Run neural simulations. They didn't want interpretations, just confirmation."

"Confirmation of what?" Ryx growled, stepping closer again.

Marn hesitated. His voice dropped, eyes flicking toward the door as if it might bite him.

"That what he found… wasn't from known space."

266

Ryx froze. His heart skipped. "Say that again."

Marn swallowed. "Some of the signal artifacts. The materials referenced in Kolen's geo scans. The energy patterns, none of it matched any known spectrum in BSD's archives. None. It was… like someone else left it behind. Someone we've never seen before." Ryx said nothing. But his hand clenched slowly at his side.

Marn looked down. "Whatever Vess found… they buried it. They buried him. They made sure we only got half the story. And even that half terrified us."

A long pause settled over the office. Ryx watched Marn like a hunter appraising a wounded animal. Then, "Thank you, Doctor," he said coldly.

Marn nodded, nervously hopeful. "So… we're done?"

Ryx paused at the door. "Yeah. we're done." And he left the man in silence, the sealed data case heavier than its weight should have been.

The moment Ryx stepped onto the loading ramp of the Wraithburn, the hair on the back of his neck rose.

The sky was wrong.

Clouds had thickened unnaturally fast, streaking black across the copper horizon. A strange hum vibrated in the air , low, barely audible, but felt in his chest. He moved faster, storming up the ramp and sealing the hatch behind him just as the ship's proximity alerts began to scream.

He bolted back to the Wraithburn. External cams lit up with flashing red indicators.

Three ships had dropped from low orbit, BSD cruisers, sleek, angular, and far too heavily armed for "containment."

Ryx dropped into the pilot seat. His fingers danced over the controls, and the Wraithburn rumbled to life.

"Time to see if you still bite, girl," he muttered.

He punched vertical thrusters and launched the ship straight into the clouds.

The sky erupted.

Laser fire lanced through the haze like lightning , red and blue bolts stitching through the atmosphere as the cruisers opened up. Ryx yanked the controls hard, the Wraith veering into a steep corkscrew as a plasma bolt sizzled past the hull, close enough to rattle the dampers.

"They were waiting," he muttered. "Guessed I'd be here…"

He angled toward the lead cruiser, twin barrels of the ventral guns tracking targets already. With a pull of the trigger, the Wraithburn spat a storm of fire, plasma bolts splashing against the enemy's forward shields, then scoring one of the forward fins.

A satisfying explosion belched smoke from the cruiser's side.

But the other two were circling. Faster than expected.

Ryx slammed the throttle and boosted into a tight climb, skimming the edge of the atmosphere. The Wraith bucked, but the upgraded inertial dampeners held. He banked hard, twisted the ship backward in a reversing drift, and let loose a stream of guided micro-missiles.

Tess's targeting suite locked on before Ryx even confirmed. The missiles screamed toward the closest cruiser, hammering its rear thrusters and sending it reeling sideways with a spray of flaming debris.

"Hell yeah," Ryx whispered.

His comms chirped. The ship's AI, basic but loyal, flashed red across the nav display:

"SHIELD BATTERY AT 87% , REDISTRIBUTING POWER"

Kaelen's custom work was singing now. Even with hits landing, the Wraithburn was absorbing fire like a brawler in a bar fight. The cruiser ahead tried to pin him with a forward cannon, but the Wraith's new shields bloomed gold-white with a pulse of energy and absorbed the brunt of it like a slap on the wrist. These cruisers weren't expecting a scout ship like the Wraith to be able to take this kind of damage.

"Come on," Ryx growled, flipping the ship mid-drift again and diving straight down through the atmosphere, trying to lose one of the damaged cruisers in the low clouds.

But they followed.

As Ryx dove, he opened a panel near the throttle and flipped a switch Tess had labeled with a sticker: "Panic Juice."

The rear thrusters overloaded with a burst of emergency speed, another Kaelen-Rhoen special, launching the Wraithburn forward like a shot.

Below, the jungle blurred.

Above, the cruiser tried to bank and follow but couldn't handle the maneuver.

Ryx pulled up hard, the ship's wings clipping treetops. He spun behind the cruiser, locked missiles, and sent them screaming.

BOOM.

The enemy exploded mid-air, fragments raining into the forest.

One left.

The last BSD cruiser climbed fast behind him. The Wraithburn shuddered under a full blast of concentrated laser fire.

SHIELD BATTERY AT 42%

"Don't give out now…" Ryx muttered.

He spun into orbit, clawing his way through the last few kilometers of atmosphere. The cruiser followed , too close.

Then Ryx saw his move.

He cut the main engines.

The Wraithburn suddenly dropped in velocity, the enemy overshooting him in an instant, and Ryx hit the thrusters again full force.

He came up behind the cruiser, aimed his primary cannon, and fired.

The bolt drilled into the rear housing of the cruiser, and then,

BOOM.

A chain reaction sent fire spiraling into the vacuum.

Ryx exhaled hard.

The ship drifted in silence, stars around him, smoke trailing off the Wraithburn's damaged left wing.

"Yesss!," he said into the open comms, his voice hoarse.

He slumped back in the seat, heart racing, shield levels slowly climbing.

But he had the files.

And Black Sable Dynamics had just lost three cruisers.

He hoped they were watching.

The Wraithburn coasted silently in orbit, the stars blinking steady now after the chaos. Smoke still curled off the forward plating. Alarms were silent, damage reports mostly green. Kaelen's masterpiece was holding together, barely, but gloriously.

Ryx leaned back in the pilot's chair, the adrenaline seeping out of his body like steam. His arms ached. His ribs felt bruised. The adrenaline comedown hit harder than usual.

But he couldn't do this next part alone.

Ryx turned to the side console, fingers flying as he opened the comms system. The little notification icon blinked red, a reminder of all the unread chatter he hadn't had time to look at yet.

He ignored it for now and began to write a new message.

To: Tessa Rhoen, Dr. Yessari Quarn

Hey, you two, hope you're not terrorizing Marla too badly. I just walked through something ugly, and I've got a data cache. A big one. It's Kolen's work. Something called Project Echofall, maybe more. I won't understand half of it, and frankly I'm not in the headspace to do it alone.

Would it be alright if I headed back your way? I could really use both of you right now. Let me know. I'll sit tight in orbit for a bit, get the ship patched while I wait.

Also, Yess? Please don't reconfigure anymore of Marla's cookware. I have a suspicion you and Tess might talk me into modifying this ship into a flying lab by the time this is all over.

-Ryx

He hit Send and leaned back again, eyes unfocused now, staring out into the black.

Kolen's memory still clung to him. Not the way he died. The way he lived. His watery laugh. The late night talks in the bunks in the academy. His conviction to protect the artifact.

Ryx's eyes once again fell to the bracelet. Where it hummed, quiet but aware.

He hoped this data wasn't just another dead end.

He hoped the next steps were worth it.

Ryx exhaled and leaned forward, fingers tapping out a new set of commands on the nav console.

"Let's not get boxed in twice."

He pulled up the star maps and plotted a backup course , a clean warp route to the outer edge of the system. A quiet one. Remote.

Somewhere the Wraithburn could vanish if BSD sent more hunters.

He didn't plan to run.

But he wasn't going to die for stubbornness, either.

The nav systems accepted the input and hummed to life, holding the course in standby. The ship's warp drive idled with a low growl, ready to punch them into the void the moment he gave the word.

With that safety net in place, Ryx turned and slid his hand across the control panel. "Maintenance mode," he muttered.

The Wraithburn responded with a soft chime and began her automatic diagnostic sweep. Hull sensors flickered. Power conduits hissed and clicked as they cooled. The low background hum of her reactors dimmed slightly, a ship-wide exhale. She'd taken a beating, but she was still running. Still loyal. Still his.

While systems scanned and stabilized, Ryx set to work. He cleaned scorched plating along the corridor with practiced efficiency, recalibrated the shield capacitors, and ran a full check on the fusion core's containment field. His fingers moved on instinct, routines he hadn't forgotten. Every valve tightened, every readout logged brought a flicker of clarity back to his mind.

Hours passed like this, physical tasks giving his brain something else to focus on. Something that wasn't the weight in his chest.

By the time the final diagnostics ticked green, the artificial light of ship-night had fallen across the Wraithburn. Ryx headed to the shower.

The water hit him like a confession. Heat and pressure and steam working to scrub the last few hours from his skin, but not his mind.

He stood under the spray until it went cold.

Back in the galley, he rummaged through the cooling unit until he found another of his favorites, smoked Viari slices wrapped around salt sticks. He took a bite and shook his head, lips twitching in the closest thing to a smile he'd managed all day.

"Damn it, Tess."

He ate slowly, sitting alone in the dimly lit galley. The hum of the ship around him was the only company. When the last crumbs were gone, he stood, stretched, and padded barefoot back toward the cockpit.

A single message notification blinked on the comms screen.

His breath caught in his chest when he saw the name.

Lanara Kress.

She had replied.

He sat slowly, jaw tightening as he clicked the message open, unsure what would be waiting on the other side.

Ryx stared at the message for a long beat, then let out a slow breath.

Lanara Kress:

I'll accept a call. But only briefly. I don't know what a human wants from me, but if it concerns my work or my past, I suggest you tread carefully.

He leaned back in the pilot's chair, running a hand through his hair. "Yeah. Figured this wasn't gonna be easy."

Still, his fingers tapped out the call with quiet determination. He requested a live comm. As the system began to dial her line, a soft pulse lit the cockpit. The sound of a connecting call echoed in his ears , slow, rising tones, each beat giving him just enough time to second-guess everything.

What do I say first? How do you tell someone their father's alive after a decade of thinking otherwise?

Then the screen lit up.

A Vlexari woman filled the frame, tall, elegant, with luminous golden eyes set in a sharp, intelligent face. Her gem-like scales shimmered in muted violet and deep obsidian across her forehead and cheekbones. She was unmistakably Shandar's daughter; the resemblance struck Ryx like a wave. The same silent weight in her gaze. The same quiet strength.

But where Shandar had carried the stoic gravity of a fallen general, Lanara was something different, a flame tempered in stillness, sharp with intellect.

Her brow furrowed. "What does a human bounty hunter want with a Vlexari doctor?"

Ryx's throat tightened, but he managed a smile. Warm. Honest.

"Hi, Dr. Kress. My name's Eryx Thorne. I'm calling to talk about your father."

Her expression didn't shift at first. Her voice was cool, measured. "I don't have a father. He died in a war nearly a decade

273

ago. The reports were clear." Ryx took a deep breath, steadying himself.

"That's just it," he said softly. "He didn't." Silence. Her expression faltered.

"What... did you say?"

Ryx leaned forward, voice gentle. "Shandar Kress is alive. He's on Varrix Delta, a high-security prison moon. He's been there for the last ten years."

Lanara froze. Her jaw tightened, eyes darting slightly as if searching her screen for signs this was some elaborate cruelty. "That's not funny," she whispered. "That's not,"

"It's not a joke," Ryx interrupted, quietly but firmly. "I met him there. Served time in the same block. We've been working the mines together, eating meals together. We're... friends, actually."

Stillness again. But not cold, shocked, this time. Her posture loosened a fraction. She blinked rapidly, one hand rising to cover her mouth as if to hold something inside.

"He's alive..." she murmured.

Ryx nodded, his smile fading into something quieter, more reverent. "He talks about you. Not often, but... when he does, it's with so much pride it nearly floors you. Said you were already a doctor before the war. Said you left to help people, to teach. He never knew how to find you."

Lanara's eyes shimmered. Her voice cracked. "I thought... I never even looked. I assumed,"

"No one told you the truth," Ryx said, softly. "But now you know. And you can talk to him. Reach out. He only has two years left on his sentence."

She nodded slowly, the emotion finally catching up to her composed features. She wiped the corner of her eye, clearly fighting to keep it together.

"Thank you," she said, voice quiet. "Eryx Thorne. I don't know who you are... but thank you."

Ryx smiled again, something raw and sincere behind his eyes. "He saved my life once. I owed him more than I could pay. Figured helping you find each other was a start."

"I want to talk to him," Lanara said, breath shaky. "I want to... reconnect. After everything."

"I think he'd like that. A lot." Ryx nodded. "I can get you the comm protocols for Varrix Delta's system. The Warden's fair. He'll make it happen."

She looked at him again, more closely this time. "You're a good man, Eryx Thorne."

"Don't say that too loud," Ryx chuckled, wiping subtly at his own eye. "Might ruin my whole brand."

She smiled softly. The first real one.

"Please keep in touch."

"You got it."

The screen went dark a moment later, but the feeling lingered, a warmth, a weight lifted. For Shandar. For Lanara. For himself.

Ryx leaned back in the chair, staring out at the stars, and whispered,

"Two years, old man. And she'll be waiting."

CHAPTER 16
SIGNAL PATH

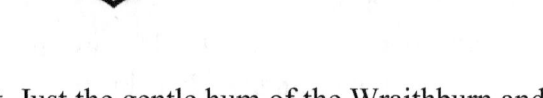

The cockpit was quiet. Just the gentle hum of the Wraithburn and the faint crackle of comms static, comforting in its own way. Ryx sat motionless for a few long moments after the conversation with Lanara, fingers still curled over the console edge in a state of peace, grateful to have something happy to do for once.

Then came the replies:

New Message – From: Tessa Rhoen

You're a dumbass.

You know you don't have to ask, right? of course we'll help.

We're part of this whether you like it or not. me and Yessari already started going over the fragments you forwarded. his eyes nearly popped out of his skull. I think he said, "reality adjacency drift" and then forgot to eat for five hours.

Also? We built something. It's awesome. You're gonna lose your shit.

Get back here soon. I want your feedback. And to see your stupid face when you see it for the first time.

-Tess

Ryx let out a low exhale, a smile tugging unbidden at the edge of his mouth. He didn't realize how much tension he was still holding until that moment.The second reply followed immediately.

New Message – From: Dr. Yessari Quarn

Eryx Thorne,

I've reviewed the data you sent. It's incomplete, dangerous, and utterly fascinating.

Tessa and I have begun preliminary hypotheses. They are wildly speculative and very fun.

Your "Project Echofall" appears to interface with non-linear sensory harmonics. We'll need more, obviously. But for now, I've requisitioned the back parlor. It's now a lab. Your aunt may not approve.

Also: I've taken your suggestion about retrofitting the Wraithburn into a mobile analysis hub under advisement. I have sketched out three configurations. One involves gutting the cargo hold. Another requires a modest rewrite of local physics.

You were joking, I'm aware. I am not.

Please return soon, with more samples, your artifact telemetry, and any emotional breakthroughs you've had regarding the gauntlet.

P.S. The tea warmer works beautifully.

-Dr. Y. Quarn

Tayveri Council of Interdisciplinary Sciences (Still Retired)

Ryx snorted mid-read, nearly choking on the last line of Yessari's message.

He skimmed back through both replies, a crooked smile tugging at his lips. Tess's chaotic enthusiasm, Yessari's deadpan brilliance… stars, they made an odd pair. But somehow, it worked. Like a plasma torch and a philosopher. Loud, sharp, and probably dangerous, but better together than apart.

He tapped out a quick response to Yessari before he could talk himself out of it.

Yess,

Do not retrofit anything in Marla's house. I'm serious. you cannot have the full cargo hold. that is where the goods and explosives live.

However,

If you and Tess are feeling inspired, you can retrofit one of the holding cells on the Wraithburn into a compact lab. just promise me you'll leave Marla's beautiful home exactly as it is: untouched, unmodified, and preferably still standing when I arrive.

-Ryx

He hit send, still shaking his head, and leaned back in the chair with a soft exhale.

Odd, he thought. But damn if it didn't feel good to have them in his corner.

Outside the viewport, the stars drifted, silent, waiting.

Time to get moving.

Ryx tapped a fresh nav route into the console, double-checking the coordinates against the last ping from Marla's estate.

Destination: Corvellis , Orellin System

The Wraithburn's thrusters flared to life. He eased the throttle forward and aligned the ship and engaged the jump. The stars stretched, shimmered, and vanished.

Warp engaged.

Twenty-four hours until arrival.

Ryx settled into the cockpit's half-dark, stretching his arms above his head until his joints popped. There'd be no chasing ghosts for a day. No gunfights. No cryptic messages. Just drift. Quiet. The kind of isolation that used to comfort him, lately it started to feel like a cage.

He spent the first hour going over the decrypted files again. Parsing Echofall logs, cross-referencing BSD personnel, and marking anomalies for Yessari to review later. Most of it looked like science fiction, even to him. He wasn't a scientist, but he did find the personnel logs and tactical files useful. He was a Hunter, these things he could learn. Use later to hurt BSD in ways only he could.

Then came maintenance. Cleaning out the ventilation system. Recalibrating the targeting sensors. Re-soldering a cracked stabilizer bracket in the forward comms panel. Little things to keep his hands busy while the clock ticked.

Later, he tried sleeping. He got five hours before the dreams chased him out of it.

The rest of the jump, he sat in the dim galley with a cup of caff, watching old training vids from his military days. Tactical breakdowns. Counter-ambush routines. Stuff that now felt more like memories than lessons.

At one point, he pulled up a still image of Kaelen and Tess, some long-forgotten moment, captured in the garage when they were both laughing, her hair still long, Kaelen wiping oil from her cheek.

He let it stay on-screen for a while. Just… breathing in the silence.

Then the nav console pinged.

Warp exit in five minutes.

Ryx stood slowly, rolled out the tension in his shoulders, and headed back to the cockpit.

Corvellis awaited.

ΔΔΔ

The sky over Corvellis was streaked with amber and cloud-swept blue as the Wraithburn broke atmosphere, gliding over the vast stretch of green that surrounded Marla's estate. The ship settled with a low hum on a gravel pad just outside the orchard rows, engines cycling down to a purr.

Ryx powered down the nav console and exhaled slowly. He didn't realize how tight his chest had been until now.

The landing ramp hissed open.

The sun was warm. The air smelled like soil, flowers, and something faintly citrus. Ryx stepped out, squinting into the daylight, and saw them waiting.

Tess and Yessari stood a few meters off, near the edge of the orchard path. Tess wore her usual beat-up mechanics vest and a crooked smile that looked like it hadn't left her face in days. Yessari stood tall and cool beside her, hands tucked behind his back, his blue-gray robes spotless despite the trees around them.

"Hey, dumbass," Tess called, voice already teasing.

"Dumb, but alive," Ryx shot back, grinning as he stepped off the ramp.

They met halfway. A quick, familiar clasp of hands with Yessari, professional, firm, with a shared nod of mutual exhaustion. Then he turned to Tess and pulled her into a one-armed hug.

"Good to see you too, storm cloud," she murmured into his shoulder.

But as he pulled back, something caught his eye. Something small, metal, fastened to the end of her left elbow.

His breath caught in his throat.

"Tess…" he said, eyes locked on the object. "Is that?" She followed his gaze and slowly lifted the limb.

At the end of her sleeve, right at the severed joint, was a compact, oval-shaped lens. Sleek. Familiar. The emitter lens. The one he'd found dusty and forgotten on the workbench of her room back on Vorrthani Station.

A slow, proud smile spread across her face, and her eyes shimmered with unshed tears.

"I told you," she said softly, voice cracking just a little, "that I was working on a hardlight project. This," she held it out, "this is it."

Ryx's eyes widened. "You finished it?"

She nodded, glancing sideways at Yessari. "Not alone. Yess filled in the neuro gaps, turns out having a former Tayveri brain specialist in the house is good for more than deciphering alien relics."

Yessari inclined his head modestly. "I merely translated her genius into neuroactive language."

Tess huffed a laugh and turned back to Ryx. "It doesn't connect to the brainstem like the old biotic implants. No risky spinal threading. No dead zones. It links directly to the nerve endings in the residual limb."

Ryx blinked. "Wait, you mean it reads the normal nerve signals?"

She nodded. "Yeah. The brain sends the same commands it always did, open hand, close fist, move arm. The emitter interprets them and builds a hardlight limb in real-time. Seamless."

She pressed a button on a slim wrist controller tucked into her vest.

The device flared to life.

A green hardlight arm materialized from her elbow, sleek, translucent, perfectly proportioned. The fingers flexed fluidly. Light shimmered through the edges, humming faintly like a living thing.

Tess grinned through watery eyes and held up her hand.

Ryx stared in awe for half a second, then lifted his own and slapped her a perfect high five.

The impact gave off a satisfying snap and a faint electrical thrum.

"You absolute genius," he whispered. "Tess, this is, this is, holy shit."

She laughed, wiping her eyes. "I can't really feel pressure like you can, not in detail. But it gives me haptic feedback. I can tell when I'm grabbing something, lifting something. I just don't get the texture. Or temperature."

"But it works?" Ryx asked. "Like it really works?" She nodded.

"It moves like a real arm. I don't have to concentrate on it. It's just... there. Part of me. And it doesn't hurt." Ryx's face lit up with joy, pure, unfiltered.

He whooped, arms thrown wide. "You two mad geniuses! I am losing my mind right now. I... I had no idea the emitter was important!"

"I know," Tess said, laughing now, glowing. "You dragged it out of the ruins on accident. I was planning on this for a while, just not for myself. My original plan was to create Hardlight landing gear but had the crazy idea for prosthetics" She grew quiet. "Just never thought it'd be for me…"

Ryx tried to turn the subject.

"Look at this!" Ryx spun, gesturing wildly to Yessari. "Do you understand how many people could use this? This changes everything."

Yessari raised a brow. "We've discussed that possibility. One step at a time."

Ryx turned back to Tess, visibly choked up now. "I'm so damn proud of you."

She looked away, wiping her cheek again. "Don't make me cry in front of the neuro-goblin."

Yessari cleared his throat. "Technically I'm a bioarchivist, Neuro Scientist, Xenoarcheologist… But I accept the title."

Ryx pulled both of them into a rough, impulsive hug.

"This," he said quietly, "is the best thing I've seen in a long time."

And for a moment, there were no corporations, no mercenaries, no alien relics or fading ghosts of war.

Just three survivors. A sunlit orchard. And a glowing green arm that shouldn't exist but did.

The orchard breeze softened as the laughter faded. The glowing green shimmer of Tess's hardlight arm slowly receded as she showed it off one more time.

For a moment, everything was still.

Then Tess sighed and glanced back toward the distant greenhouse roofline of Marla's estate.

"I've been thinking," she said, voice quieter now. "It's time we left."

Ryx frowned. "Already?"

She nodded. "We've been here long enough. Marla's trying to be supportive, but we're stressing her out. Between the tech experiments, the strange visitors, and Yess nearly blowing out a window with that neural field generator,"

"That was an unintended side effect," Yessari interrupted mildly. "She deserves her peace." Tess finished.

Ryx looked between them. "I mean… yeah, okay. That's fair. But where would you even go?"

Tess looked him dead in the eye. "With you." Ryx blinked.

"Tess,"

"I'm serious. I've got the arm now. I'm back. I need to work again. And we still don't know what that bracelet of yours is really capable of."

Yessari stepped up beside her, hands clasped neatly. "I would also like to accompany you. Temporarily. To study the artifact under varied conditions. And perhaps to ensure you don't accidentally obliterate a city block."

Ryx scoffed. "You two make it sound like I'm flying a science fair project."

"You are," Tess said. "A hostile, sentient, interdimensional science fair project."

Ryx sighed, rubbing his face. "It's too dangerous. You've both seen what BSD is willing to throw at this thing. Gunships. Mercs. Full black site raids."

"We're not saying we'll stay forever," Tess said. "Just… long enough to do something that matters."

283

"Besides," Yessari added, "you did promise a mobile lab conversion. I believe your exact words were, 'Sure, retrofit one of the holding cells if it'll shut you up.'"

Tess grinned. "We're calling that written consent."

Ryx stared at them both. "So, what, you want to turn my prison cell into a research bay?"

"Yes," they said in unison.

Tess stepped closer. "Give us a few weeks here. I'll handle the retrofit. Strip out the second cell, convert it into a lab space for Yess and me. You two will dig into the data you recovered from BSD, and I'll upgrade the bunk compartments, make them co-pilot friendly."

"We'll be useful," she added. "Not just dead weight."

"We can monitor the artifact while you're in the field," Yessari said. "Provide real-time data assessments. Manage ship systems midflight. Patch you up between fights."

"Hell," Tess smirked, "you might even sleep better knowing someone else is watching the sensors while you fly."

Ryx hesitated. The practical part of him, the part that had survived too much, buried too many, screamed no. Keep them safe. Keep them far away.

But the truth was… he missed them. Missed the noise. The bickering. The brilliance. The feeling that maybe, just maybe, he wasn't facing the galaxy alone.

He let out a groan.

"Fine," he muttered. "But it's temporary. Just until you get that prosthetic patent pushed through. Once you two start rolling in credits, I expect you to open a proper garage or a fancy lab or something."

Tess opened her mouth to retort, but Yessari beat her to it.

"That sounds entirely reasonable," he said smoothly. "A joint laboratory, perhaps. For neural prosthetics and experimental field tech, A star garage attached. I'd be honored."

Tess blinked. "Wait… really?"

Yessari looked at her, something unreadable, almost shy, flickering in his expression.

"You're brilliant. Focused. And when you're not setting things on fire, surprisingly competent. I think we'd make an excellent team."

Tess flushed. Her smirk faltered into something softer. "Well… I mean… I wasn't actually serious about a joint lab. But now that you said it out loud…"

Ryx tilted his head, watching the exchange with a raised brow.

He'd seen that look before on soldiers, mostly. The kind of silent math two people do when they start realizing the space between them isn't just professional anymore.

He crossed his arms slowly. "So. This is happening." "What?" Tess snapped, cheeks still pink.

"You two. You've been working out of the same greenhouse for two weeks and you haven't killed each other? That's practically marriage."

Yessari tilted his head. "Unlikely. But not…."

Tess groaned, threw her hands up, one flesh, one hardlight. "We are not talking about this."

Ryx grinned, wide and unrepentant. "I'm just saying, if I end up third-wheeling my own ship, I expect hazard pay."

Yessari glanced thoughtfully at Tess. "Actually… I might have a form for that."

Tess slapped him lightly in the chest with her new arm. It flickered faintly at the point of contact, warm and precise.

And Ryx laughed, deep, real, and unguarded.

For the first time in weeks, the future didn't feel like a weight.

It felt like a team.

ΔΔΔ

The night air over Corvellis was quiet, still, and cool with the kind of breeze that carried the scent of trees and damp earth.

Every night of the first week had been the same.

Tess was tucked inside the Wraithburn, deep in the belly of the ship, sleeves rolled to her elbows and a micro torch balanced between her teeth. The faint sound of welding and metal tools echoed from the aft corridor as she methodically stripped out the bunk brackets and rebuilt the hold's side alcoves into personal compartments, one for her, one for Yessari. Comfort wasn't a luxury anymore. It was necessity.

Outside, under the stars, Ryx and Yessari sat across from each other at a collapsible field table, bathed in soft lamplight. Each had a data pad in hand, surrounded by loose cables, partially decrypted files, and a half-eaten meal tray Tess had left them out of guilt.

Yessari, ever composed, scrolled silently with one hand while sipping tea with the other.

Ryx, by contrast, looked like he was ready to throttle the tablet.

"This all reads like science fiction ran face-first into a war report," Ryx muttered, tapping the screen with growing irritation. "Dimensional harmonic spikes, resonance bleed, photonic intelligence layering. I don't even know what language this is."

Yessari didn't look up. "It's pre-application theory. A lot of this was conjecture before they started testing. Still useful. Just... half formed."

Ryx let the pad clatter gently to the tabletop. "You get any closer to figuring out what the hell this thing is?"

"I'm nearly ready to form a working hypothesis," Yessari said calmly. "Just missing a few key data points."

Ryx leaned forward, eyes narrowing. "What kind of points?"

Yessari finally looked up, eyes catching the reflection of starlight. "There's no mention of a bracelet. Not in any of the files we've recovered so far. Only references to an artifact referred to as "The Box". Descriptions are vague but consistent: it reacts to light patterns, thought commands, and physical proximity."

Ryx sat back, gears turning in his head. "That's how I found it," he said slowly. "It was a box at first. Black. Smooth. Reacted when I touched it, light patterns, humming, the works. Then it just... came

286

apart. Like it was unfolding. Next thing I knew, I had the bracelet locked to my arm and the box was gone."

Yessari's eyes lit with sudden understanding. "That changes everything. If BSD only ever encountered it in box form, they may not even be aware it can change shape. Let alone that it's become symbiotic."

"Which means," Ryx added, voice low, "they have no idea what it's really capable of."

Yessari's posture shifted with quiet urgency. "That would explain the fragmentation in the research logs. The team at the dig site wasn't just studying the artifact, they were arguing over its origin. Half believed it was pre-scociety tech from an advanced, uncontacted civilization. The other half believed it wasn't from our dimension at all."

Ryx blinked. "Another dimension?"

"Or a region of space so far beyond our reach that its technology might as well be magic. The planet where they found the artifact, according to the data, was badly damaged. Soil destabilized. Cities obliterated. But the terrain itself remained mostly intact. No tectonic shift. No impact craters."

Ryx's brow furrowed. "What happened to the people?"

Yessari's voice dipped, suddenly solemn. "Gone. Every living thing, vanished or dead. Total biosphere collapse. No known pathogen. No radiation signature. Just… an empty world."

He tapped a section of his pad, bringing up a fragment of a decoded field log.

"No signs of weaponized infrastructure. Orbital scans show no conventional blast damage. But the atmospheric composition is warped, like the planet was... sifted. As if something scrubbed it clean."

Ryx swallowed hard.

"What were they trying to prove?" he asked. "What do they think this thing can do?"

Yessari paused. Then answered quietly.

"They believe the artifact can interact with thought and intention. That it may respond to neural input patterns. In theory, it could be a weapon, a tool, a processor, or all of those things at once. They suspect it has the ability to rewrite or displace biological matter on a planetary scale. If their assumptions are correct…" He looked Ryx in the eye.

"…BSD wants to harness it for military deployment. A precision extinction device. Cleanse a planet of all inhabitants, without harming the infrastructure or resources. An efficient colonization solution. A god weapon."

The words hit like a railgun to the gut.

Ryx's vision swam.

He wasn't looking at the orchard anymore.

He was on Eleos V.

Dark corridors. Heavy breathing. Gunfire behind him. Running through an oxygen processing plant toward the main air scrubber in the heart of the facility. Orders barked over his earpiece. His boots slamming metal grates.

"Thorne, this is Rendyll. Proceed to the scrubber core and arm the device. Then mask up and evacuate. Immediately." He'd stopped cold.

"Why the air scrubber, General?"

"You have your orders."

His hands had been shaking. He thought he was here to plant an EMP device. To destabilize this facility, to destabilize the region, to end the war. A bargaining chip.

He stopped and pulled out the device in question. Why would they want an EMP in an air scrubber? His brain fought hard against the logic of the order.

Then it hit him, they don't want an EMP in the air scrubber, they want a Bio weapon. Ryx activated his comms again in a panic.

"No. This is wrong. We've still got boots on the ground. We've got civilians on this planet."

288

A long silence before the unflinching voice of Kennedy Rendyll came over the comms again.

"They'll be casualties of war. Just get it done."

Ryx's heart was pounding now. He couldn't do this; He couldn't kill an entire planet.

"You're insane! This isn't a strike, this is genocide!"

He remembered the politician, the orbital strike, the child's picture.

"Thorne, if you disobey this order,"

He cut communications and put the device away. *If I escape this place alive, Rendyll's getting a taste of my gun.* Hot fury pouring out of every inch of Ryx as he turned down another corridor looking to escape. "Ryx."

A voice.

"Ryx."

His eyes snapped back into focus.

Yessari was standing beside him, one hand gently pressing down on his shoulder.

"You're safe. You're here," Yessari said quietly.

Ryx's mouth was dry. His heart thundered. He realized his hands were clenched so tightly around the data pad his knuckles had gone pale.

He swallowed. Nodded. "Sorry. Just... memory hit me sideways."

Yessari didn't pry. Just stayed silent for a beat longer, then quietly sat back down.

The stars wheeled overhead in silence.

Somewhere inside the Wraithburn, Tess's micro torch flared back to life.

Ryx rubbed a hand down his face, trying to shake off the lingering ghosts of Eleos V. The silence between them stretched, companionable now, not awkward. Yessari had returned to his seat, but his eyes never left Ryx.

"You said they want it as a weapon," Ryx muttered, voice rough. "A clean wipe. No fire, no rubble. Just... people gone."

"Yes."

Ryx leaned forward, arms braced on the table. "That's why Kolen Vess ran with it."

Yessari's brow twitched. "That seems plausible."

Ryx nodded. "He found it first, right? With his dig team. Something must've scared the hell out of him. He knew what BSD would do with it or try to. That's why he went dark. That's why they came after him like a pack of rabid wraith hounds."

Yessari tapped his fingers on the datapad. "Which would explain why BSD is executing full black site purges. No traces. No witnesses. They're not just protecting a secret. They're protecting a potential market."

Ryx looked at him. "Market?"

Yessari's expression flattened into something grim.

"They don't want to keep the artifact, Eryx. They want to understand it. Replicate it. Manufacture it. And then sell it." Ryx's stomach twisted.

"Think about it," Yessari continued. "Every major planetary power with interstellar conflict potential, every empire, every syndicate, would pay untold billions for a weapon that can depopulate a planet in one night without touching infrastructure. No nukes. No orbital fire. Just one device, and the planet's ready to be resettled the next day."

Ryx swore under his breath. "Colonize by force."

Yessari nodded. "Efficient. Clinical. Profitable."

"Stars," Ryx muttered. "No wonder they're going scorched earth. It's not just about hiding what it is, it's about controlling who gets to make it."

"And ensuring no one else figures it out first," Yessari said.

The orchard wind passed through again, rustling the tall grass. Somewhere distant, a nightbird called. The table lamp hummed softly.

Ryx stared down at his hand, the bracelet glinting faintly under the light.

"I've been carrying this thing," he said quietly. "Fighting with it.

Getting people killed over it. And I didn't even know what it was."

"You're still here," Yessari said, just as softly. "Which means maybe you're meant to do something with it besides deliver it to another monster."

Ryx glanced up.

Yessari didn't look away.

And for once, Ryx didn't argue.

A breeze stirred the datapads slightly, rustling the edge of a decrypted report like a whisper.

Yessari shifted, folding his hands neatly in front of him as his gaze returned to the bracelet wrapped around Ryx's wrist. The subtle glow within its seams pulsed faintly, steady, alive.

"You know," Yessari said after a pause, "for all the power they think this thing holds... I'm not convinced that destruction is its primary function."

Ryx blinked. "Come again?"

"The logs show evidence that the artifact is capable of planetary scale interaction. That much I believe. But the assumption that it was built to destroy life?" He shook his head. "That feels reductive. Almost... human."

Ryx raised an eyebrow. "You're saying it's not a weapon?"

"I'm saying it might not be just a weapon," Yessari replied. "We're looking at a piece of technology potentially millions of years ahead of us. And BSD's first instinct is to point it at someone's head and pull the trigger."

He leaned forward, voice soft but steady.

291

"But I've been studying it since you saved me. Watching how it responds to you. It's reactive. Intuitive. It doesn't lash out on its own. It protects. It integrates. It adapts. That doesn't sound like a mass extinction engine to me."

Ryx tilted his head, eyes narrowing slightly. "Then what is it?"

"I don't know yet," Yessari admitted. "But I think Kolen Vess believed the same thing. That it had a greater purpose. Something older. Misunderstood. And BSD just… hijacked that mystery. They looked at a thing they couldn't define and immediately asked, 'How do we sell this?'"

He looked at Ryx again, a rare intensity in his expression.

"Destruction might only be a side effect. A misuse. Like using a surgical laser to start a fire. Technically possible. But wrong."

Ryx let that hang in the air for a long moment. Then he exhaled and sat back.

"That's almost worse," he said quietly.

"How so?"

"Because if you're right… it means this thing wasn't built to kill anyone." He looked down at the bracelet again, eyes shadowed. "Which means all the people who've died because of it? That's on us."

Yessari didn't answer right away.

Eventually, he said, "Maybe. Or maybe this is just the part where we figure out how to stop it from happening again."

Ryx looked away, jaw tight, shoulders rigid. But he didn't argue this time either.

The wind moved through the orchard again, cool and calm beneath the starlight.

Inside the Wraithburn, Tess hummed along to a tinny audio track while she rewired her new bunk wall. Somewhere nearby, a power drill buzzed to life.

Ryx stared out at the treetops.

△△△

The days passed in slow, deliberate rhythm. For the first time in years, Ryx wasn't waking up to alarms, battlefield comms, or the stench of plasma discharge. Just sunlight through orchard trees. The quiet clink of tools. Tess's off-key humming. Yessari's voice dictating notes into his recorder.

Ryx split his time between trying to help with the ship retrofits, mostly by holding things and getting yelled at by Tess for putting the plasma cutter on the wrong voltage or working in Marla's sprawling gardens. The woman was intimidating, but fair. She appreciated hard work and didn't ask questions when Ryx didn't feel like talking. Yessari, meanwhile, became a machine.

The lab retrofit inside the old holding cell had quickly outpaced Tess's initial design thanks to an unexpected revelation: Yessari was independently wealthy. Very.

Apparently, his early neural mapping research and private practice on the Tayveri homeworld of Atraxan, had raked in a fortune in licensing fees and silent partner investments. Ryx had no idea how someone that elegant-looking could be rich and still get excited about haptic transducers, but there he was, ordering rare alloy panels and microfilament stabilizers like it was grocery shopping.

The small lab blossomed overnight: compact, sleek, and intimidatingly efficient. A full spectrum sensor array. Hardlight mapping rig. Neural wave isolator. It looked more advanced than half the med bays Ryx had served in during the war.

But what really caught his attention over time wasn't the tech, it was them.

Tess and Yessari.

He caught them in stolen moments. Working side by side with their heads bent over a tablet, Yess's hand lingering just a second too long on her back when he leaned past. Tess, normally prickly and sarcastic, didn't flinch from it. She even smiled, genuine, crooked, and soft in a way Ryx had rarely seen.

He noticed the way she looked at him when he was speaking. Not just listening. Hearing.

And Yessari, in turn, paid attention to her in the way a scientist pays attention to a miracle he doesn't want to scare off.

Ryx never brought it up. Just observed, quietly. Filed it away.

At night, after Tess went to bed and the orchard sank into silence, Ryx and Yessari resumed their studies.

They'd work late into the night, hunched over glowing data pads in the lab or out at the field table beneath the stars. Reviewing decrypted BSD reports. Running theory tests on Ryx and the artifact. Analyzing gauntlet reactions under different emotional stimuli.

And one night, things shifted.

The lab was quiet but for the soft chime of a sensor readout. Ryx sat on the reinforced floor of the cargo hold, sleeves rolled, boots off, breathing slow.

Yessari monitored from behind a shielded observation panel, eyes fixed on the gauntlet strapped to Ryx's right arm.

"It's been stable tonight," Yess said. "No spontaneous charge buildup. Heart rate normal. No unusual cortical spikes. Perfect time to test expansion."

Ryx tilted his head. "You mean… try and make it do something new."

Yessari nodded. "Push it. See if it responds. Think of how it reacted when Tess lost her arm."

Ryx's jaw tightened at the memory.

"I didn't tell you," he said quietly. "What really happened that day." Yessari looked up from the panel.

Ryx flexed his right fingers, the gauntlet responding with a low pulse of light. "I wasn't fast enough. That's what I thought at first. But when Tess… the gauntlet didn't just get stronger. It split. Covered both arms. I didn't even realize it until later. It was like… it evolved."

Yessari straightened. "Both arms?"

Ryx nodded. "And then, during the fight, I found out I could," he paused, thinking back, ".. Pulse. Project energy. Force. I don't know what to call it. It was like I could knock a man back ten feet just by thinking."

Yessari's eyes lit up. "You're describing the kinetic discharge you use. Consecutive energy translation. That would explain the strain patterns I've seen in your muscle tissue and gauntlet energy curves."

He stood quickly. "Ryx, I need you to try again. Try to summon both gauntlets. Think back to that moment. Not the panic. The need. The instinct."

Ryx hesitated. His left arm lay bare under the cold white lab lights, nothing but scar tissue and memory. It felt wrong, empty, like a missing piece he had carried so long he had almost stopped noticing. Almost.

He drew a slow breath and closed his eyes.

Come on. The thought burned through his mind. *I know what you can do. I've felt it, the way you answer me, the way you burn when I call. You've felt me too. So if you're in there; if you can hear me, then show me.*

The silence stretched, taut as wire. For a heartbeat, nothing happened. He almost laughed at himself.

Then the right gauntlet stirred.

Its sapphire glow pulsed once, faint but steady. A ripple of heat ran up his arm, across his chest, into the scarred muscle of his left. Ryx hissed, fingers twitching. Then..

A flicker. A shimmer of blue light lanced along his bare forearm, quick as lightning.

He gasped, staring. Another flicker followed, stronger, crawling like veins of fire beneath his skin. The air crackled.

The artifact's hum deepened, reverberating in his bones, and the light surged. Blue fire erupted across his left hand, wrapping fingers, wrist, forearm, each pulse layering plates of energy that hardened into shape. The sound was sharp, electric, like thunder breaking inside the lab.

With a final snap of charged air, the gauntlet *locked* into place.

Ryx staggered, staring at it. Sleek, angular, alive. A perfect mirror twin to the right, yet not identical, its lines sharper, the glow running deeper, veins of energy tracing patterns like alien script. It thrummed with power, not as a borrowed tool, but as if it had always been meant to be there, waiting for him to claim it.

His breath shook.

For the first time since it chose him, the artifact hadn't just answered. It had *grown*.

Yessari gasped. "Oh, stars. It worked."

He scrambled for the console. "I'm getting readings across all three resonance bands. Neural sync is still stable. No rejection markers. Ryx, this is incredible."

Ryx stood slowly. The weight of the second gauntlet was heavier than he remembered, but it felt right. Balanced.

"Let's take this outside," he said, voice low.

They stood beneath the stars again. The orchard rustled in the wind.

Ryx flexed both fists. Twin pulses of energy danced up his forearms. He shifted his stance, took a few steps forward, then launched into a test roll, low, smooth, controlled.

He felt the weight, the balance, but not the warp. Not the flicker of momentum he'd had before.

"It's not the same," he said. "I don't feel faster."

"Warp might only trigger under adrenaline," Yessari replied. "Or danger. The gauntlets may adapt to combat states."

Ryx crouched, then lunged forward, firing a low kinetic burst from both palms. The ground rippled with concussive force, dust and leaves scattering in a radial bloom.

He grinned.

"But I've got way more control."

Yessari was scribbling notes furiously, nodding. "This doubles your close-combat potential. Shielding, striking power, kinetic bursts. Tactical versatility just tripled."

Ryx stood in the center of the clearing, both arms glowing.

For once, the weapon didn't feel like a burden.

It felt like something else.

A choice.

The twin gauntlets shimmered in the darkness, blue light flickering along Ryx's forearms like living circuitry. The orchard was still around them, moonlight washing through the trees, shadows shifting with every movement.

Ryx flexed both fists again, feeling the weight, the balance.

"Alright," he muttered. "Let's see if the left one can do more than just look pretty."

He turned his body, lifted his left hand, and concentrated, not on pulsing, but on the blade. The one his right gauntlet had formed before in a tight, seamless sweep of blue energy.

"C'mon," he said under his breath. "Just mirror it."

The gauntlet whined, a mechanical sound beneath the hum of power. Then a small cylinder popped out of the top of the left gauntlet, just above the wrist joint.

Before Ryx could say a word, it fired.

A tight burst of concentrated sapphire energy lanced out and obliterated a nearby orchard tree. The blast sheared clean through the trunk with a high-pitched crack and sent leaves, branches, and bark shrapnel spiraling into the air. The tree groaned, smoldered, and collapsed in a hiss of flame and splintered wood.

"OH SHIT!" Ryx shouted, stumbling back.

"OH STARS," Yessari yelped, grabbing a nearby bucket.

The fire spread fast, licking up the dry bark toward the nearby hedges.

Ryx slapped the gauntlet into his side, cut the energy flow, and sprinted forward. "Get water!"

"I'm getting water!" Yessari yelled, already dragging over a portable extinguisher from the garden cart.

Together, they worked quickly, smothering the flames, kicking dirt, slapping embers with old thermal blankets. The fire died in spurts of smoke and hiss, leaving the once-proud tree charred and toppled in a halo of blackened earth.

Ryx stood, panting, smoke in his hair and sleeves covered in soot.

He looked at the smoking stump.

"…Tess is gonna kill me."

Yessari, brushing ash from his sleeve, let out a strangled laugh. "Assuming Marla doesn't first."

They both stood in silence a moment, then turned toward each other at the same time.

"That wasn't a blade," Yessari said.

"Nope," Ryx agreed.

"That was a compressed energy discharge cannon."

Ryx looked down at the left gauntlet, now inert and slightly warm. The cylinder had retracted back into the housing, leaving only a soft glow behind the metal seams.

"So… you're saying my left arm is a gun now?"

Yessari's expression was part wonder, part wild enthusiasm. "A high density, localized plasma launcher, based on the discharge signature. It's not a mirror of the right gauntlet, it's a variant."

Ryx raised an eyebrow. "You're telling me I've got a sword on one arm and a cannon on the other?"

Yessari gave a reverent nod. "Tactical asymmetry. Brilliant." "Unintentional," Ryx muttered.

"Still brilliant."

Ryx flexed his left hand slowly. "I didn't even think about it firing. I just wanted the blade."

"The artifact might be evolving its capabilities based on contextual needs. You already have melee options. It probably identified ranged combat as the next priority."

Ryx looked back at the charred stump. "Yeah. It sure identified something."

Yessari was already pacing, datapad in hand, muttering to himself. "This changes everything. If the gauntlets can differentiate based on neural intent, we could be looking at a branching capability system. Modular. Adaptive."

"You're gonna need a new notebook," Ryx said dryly.

"I'll start with a new orchard map. So, we don't accidentally deforest the place."

Ryx chuckled, despite the ringing in his ears.

Still staring at the twin gauntlets, he flexed his fingers, and for the first time, felt like he was only scratching the surface of something much, much bigger.

The next morning, Tess stood at the foot of the Wraithburn's newly retrofitted corridor with a smirk so smug it could power a reactor core.

"Alright, gentlemen," she said, arms crossed, and chin tilted up. "Prepare to be impressed."

Ryx glanced at Yessari, who raised a single, mildly curious brow.

Tess spun on her heel and led them down the corridor. The once cold overly cramped four person bunk room was gone, completely restructured with warm lighting, composite wall paneling, and a

299

folding privacy divider that actually looked like it had been designed by someone with a soul.

"First stop: the bunk rooms."

"Modest, but cozy. Built-in storage under the beds, integrated climate panels, ambient sound control, and soft dimmable lighting overhead." Ryx stepped in and blinked.

"…Is that a tea station?"

Tess beamed. "Programmable. One pot at a time. You're welcome."

He laughed, genuine and warm. "Damn, Tess. This is better than half the outposts I've slept in."

She gestured toward the walls. "Noise-canceling panels. Fold-down desks for mission briefs. And an actual door you can close so you don't have to listen to Yess talking to himself while he calibrates an emitter array."

"I prefer 'conversing with brilliance,'" Yessari said mildly from the hall.

They moved on.

Tess keyed open the lab with a flourish. "And now… behold the crown jewel."

Yessari stepped past her, hands already clasped behind his back, eyes bright.

"The workstation integrates six-axis hardlight stabilization, full spectrum sensor arrays, and a quantum-linked analysis hub that allows us to remotely ping data across encrypted relays. All biological scans are sandboxed. And the neurolink calibration platform includes,"

"Yess," Tess cut in gently, "Ryx doesn't speak High Science. Remember?"

Yessari blinked. "Ah. Right." He turned to Ryx. "It does cool things. Fast."

"That I can understand," Ryx said, chuckling.

The lab was sleek. Clean. Compact. Blue ambient lighting wrapped around a curved bench of instruments Ryx didn't dare touch.

Tess had mounted the original prototype emitter lens casing in a recessed shelf, almost like a trophy.

Ryx gave a low whistle. "This doesn't feel like a retrofitted prison cell."

"That's because it isn't," Tess said. "It's home. For now."

Later in the day a goodbye was waiting for them on the front path. Marla, in her ever-pristine garden robe and tall boots, arms folded, lips pressed thin.

"I've lost a tree," she said as Ryx approached.

Ryx winced. "That... may have been me."

She looked him up and down. "Mmm. Yes. I assumed. Blue blast crater was a giveaway."

He nodded solemnly. "In my defense, the tree started it."

Marla rolled her eyes but smiled faintly. "Take care of my niece."

"I will."

Yessari stepped forward, holding out a wrapped basket. "For your hospitality. Organic Tayveri tea leaves. Rare. Very calming. Also, mildly hallucinogenic in high doses."

Marla blinked. "...Noted."

He bowed slightly. "It was an honor sharing your greenhouse. Even the parts you said were off-limits."

Her eyes narrowed. "Which parts did you touch?"

"I'll leave that a mystery," Yessari said, and Ryx physically had to hold in a laugh.

Tess stepped in for the real goodbye, longer, tighter. Ryx didn't listen in. That was between them.

When they finally boarded the Wraithburn, the ramp lifted slowly, sealing the orchard, the warmth, the quiet behind them. Their last bastion of peace and quiet.

ΔΔΔ

The stars swirled below as the ship entered a steady drift. Their first meal as a crew was simple, nutrient bowls, local bread, and an indulgent bottle of off-world cider Tess had stashed in Ryx's emergency locker "for morale."

The common space was tight but surprisingly comfortable with present company. They sat at the collapsible table, shoulders relaxed, a quiet energy between them.

"To not dying," Tess toasted, raising her mug.

"To unexplained alien tech," Yess added.

Ryx clinked mugs with them both. "And to hoping this ship holds together."

They laughed.

It felt good.

"So," Tess said after a while, pushing aside her empty plate, "what's the plan?"

Ryx leaned back, gaze on the stars beyond the viewport. "Honestly? I don't think we can take down BSD. Not directly. They're too big. Too buried."

Yessari tapped a finger to his lips. "Maybe we don't have to destroy them. Just... scare them." Ryx arched a brow.

"Scare them bad enough that they bury Project Echofall and never dig it back up. All it would take is making the wrong people nervous. Risk outweighs reward. They have no leads on where the relic actually is."

Ryx considered that. "I don't know who all's involved in Echofall. It's compartmentalized. Shadowy. But I know one person who does." He met their eyes.

"Darna Kent."

Tess leaned forward. "The woman who hired you to track Kolen Vess."

Ryx nodded. "She's the thread that ties me, Kolen, and BSD together. And if anyone knows who's really behind Project Echofall, it's her."

Yessari's eyes sharpened. "Then we find her." Ryx exhaled. And nodded.

"Darna Kent resides on Delva Minor as the head executive of personnel." Yess said looking down at a datapad.

"At least according to BSD's public records." Ryx Stood up.

"That tracks she was in BSD HQ both times, private office, terrified assistant."

Tess sighed from where she sat.

"How do we kidnap a high level mega corp exec directly under the nose of the very beast itself?"

A smile crept onto Ryx's face slowly as a plan formed in his head.

Tess wasn't going to like it; Yess would love to run tests during it.

"We don't kidnap her; we give her a house call." Tess groaned audibly from her seat.

"Urban operation, high stakes, high reward." Yessari paced behind the couch in thought.

Ryx knew they'd agree once they heard the whole plan. Even if Tess didn't like it fully.

He was close, one more step, one more lead, one more hunt.

Target acquired.

CHAPTER 17

THE CHROME GHOST

Delva Minor buzzed with heat and wealth, steel spires scraped the sky, neon danced off mirrored walkways, and the air stank of secrets and credits. Ryx walked with purpose through the heart of the city, boots steady on polished neoplate, coat collar high, eyes always moving.

BSD's corporate HQ loomed somewhere overhead, part fortress, part temple, guarded by layers of bureaucracy and blood contracts. Tess's voice came through his transponder, clipped and calm.

"Okay, you're close. Kent's tag just pinged near Sector 12. Designer district."

Ryx glanced up at the skyline, catching the glint of a floating retail wing ahead. High-end logos shimmered above street-level storefronts. The kind of places where everything smelled like money and security clearance.

"She's in a store called Vellaris Atelier," Yessari added, his voice precise as always. "Looks like a private fitting. You'll want to wait. Drawing attention in that sector will get you flagged."

"I know," Ryx muttered. "Ghost mode."

He slipped into the pedestrian flow, just another shadow with a comm bead and nowhere to be. He stood near a corner flower vendor, half in a holographic ad wash, pretending to look at his wrist link.

A few minutes later, she emerged.

Darna Kent.

Elegant, composed, power wrapped in silks and credits. She moved like someone used to being obeyed.

Ryx's pulse slowed. His fingers twitched reflexively, but he didn't move yet.

"There she is," Tess murmured. "Still looks like someone who drinks red wine and yells at waiters."

Ryx allowed a small, grim smile. "Yeah. That's her."

He followed.

Not close. Not fast. Just steady.

She moved through the crowd, flanked by no guards, just her confidence and a high-end facial ID system scanning everyone around her. Ryx kept to tactical angles. Crossed behind kiosks. Used reflective glass to track her path like a veteran scout.

She reached a luxury hovercar waiting curbside, sleek, black, and barely humming. The driver seat was empty. No guard detail. Just her and her overconfidence.

She opened the rear door and slid in, muttering, "Home." The vehicle's AI chimed in acknowledgment and began to rise, Until the other back door opened.

Darna turned, startled, then froze.

Ryx stepped inside and pulled the door shut behind him. Smooth. Slow. His eyes never left hers.

She opened her mouth, panic flashing across her face. "Wh," He drew Wasted Starlight.

The gun sang softly as it cleared its holster and settled across his lap, angled casually, threat thinly veiled in quiet steel.

Ryx's voice was low. Calm. Final.

"We need to talk."

The moment the hovercar lifted off, Darna shifted, too quick, hand darting toward her clutch.

Ryx moved faster.

Wasted Starlight came up like a thunderclap, the barrel pressed hard against her ribs as he pinned her sideways into the door with a sudden, brutal push. Not enough to injure, yet, but enough to let her know how thin the ice was.

"Don't," he growled.

Darna froze, lips parted. Her breath trembled.

"You don't get to play victim now," Ryx muttered, eyes burning into her. "You want to know how we got here? Let me remind you."

The anger leaked through, controlled, coiled like a knife under the skin.

"You hired me to hunt Kolen Vess, a man who found something you didn't understand and refused to let your monster of a company have. You lied to me. Told me he'd gone rogue. You left out the part where he was trying to stop you from building a genocide weapon." She opened her mouth, but Ryx wasn't finished.

"You sold me out. Threw me to the Varrix Prime military like trash. Signed off on a 'no retrieval' clause so I'd rot in a frozen prison until someone put a bolt through my skull." He leaned closer, voice razor-thin.

"You sent BSD cleaners to Vorrthani Station. Destroyed my home. Kaelen's shop. Tried to kill my family." Darna flinched.

"And now..." His voice dropped to a deadly calm. "Now you want to mass-produce something that can wipe out a world without damaging its resources. Clean genocide. Sanctioned extinction." A long silence.

Darna's voice cracked when she finally spoke. "How much do you know?"

Ryx didn't answer. The thick silence did.

The hovercar banked slightly and slowed as it approached a landing pad on the upper floors of a glittering spire, her penthouse suite, set high above the chaos of the city.

306

She shifted, preparing to get out.

Ryx didn't move the gun.

"You're not going anywhere."

"What do you want?" she spat.

"I want reporting structure," he said, voice low. "Everyone tied to Project Echofall. Their names. Faces. Schedules. Locations."

Her eyes narrowed. "I won't betray Black Sable Dynamics."

Ryx tilted his head, smiling cold and humorless. "Why not? You already betrayed the rest of the galaxy to protect them."

"I'm loyal."

He chuckled. It wasn't friendly.

"You're the reason Kolen is dead. Kaelen's dead. Tessa lost her arm. And you want to make a product line out of planetary extinction?" She tried to hold his gaze. Failed.

"You have two choices, Darna," Ryx said. "Cooperate, give me what I want, and maybe you'll land in a white-collar prison with decent wine and legal counsel. Or…"

His voice dipped, dark and low.

"…I could take my time. I learned a lot of ways to inflict pain in Special Ops. How to make people scream without breaking the skin. You'd be amazed what I could teach you." Her throat bobbed.

Ryx leaned in. "This isn't justice. This is personal."

Darna's voice came out as a whisper. "The files are inside."

He watched her for a beat longer, the fire in his chest not quite dimmed. "Ryx," Tess's voice crackled over the transponder. "She's stalling. Her penthouse will have layered security protocols, facial ID, biometric traps. It's a bad idea."

"I know," Ryx murmured.

"Then don't do it."

But he was already opening the door.

"I've got this."

He motioned with the barrel of Wasted Starlight. "Out. Slowly."

Darna stepped out onto the private landing pad, her heels clicking faintly on the polished floor. Her face was pale, composed, but barely.

Ryx followed, weapon low but steady. The city lights glittered behind them like a sea of lies.

He didn't trust her.

He didn't trust BSD.

But he needed those names.

And no matter what security measures waited behind that door, he was going in.

The door's biometric reader blinked twice as Darna stepped up to it, palms open, gaze cold but restrained.

"Deactivate everything," Ryx said behind her. Wasted Starlight stayed level at the small of her back. "Or I paint the entryway with your brain matter."

She hesitated, just a flicker of rebellion behind her polished expression, then pressed her hand flat to the wall panel.

A brief hiss. The cameras above the door slumped with a soft whir. A light in the threshold turned from red to amber.

Security deactivated.

Ryx watched the shift closely.

"Good," he muttered. With his free hand, he reached down and pulled his neoplate mask from his belt, pressed it into place until the seal clicked. His HUD lit up in soft blue arcs, cycling scans for electromagnetic activity, hidden traps, turret signatures, or security nodes.

"No motion signatures in the hallway," Tess said in his ear. "Thermals are clear. Proceed."

Ryx gave Darna a tap with the muzzle of his pistol. "Inside. And keep it slow."

She stepped into the penthouse. He followed.

The space was absurd, soaked in wealth, with full-wall glass overlooking the entire city, pale marble floors, minimalist art fixtures, and soft synth-music whispering from recessed speakers. A faint citrus scent lingered in the air.

Ryx's eyes moved constantly, HUD highlighting possible threat zones:

drone bay above the fireplace, hardpoint turret concealed in the crown molding, a weapons cache under a false wall in the lounge.

He memorized them all.

"Computer's this way," Darna murmured.

She led him to a recessed command terminal, elegant and matte black, embedded into a steel-sculpted desk. A projection display hummed to life.

She hesitated.

Ryx pressed Wasted Starlight to the back of her head, steady and cold.

"Don't even think about it," he growled. "I've got a computer genius in my ear watching your every keystroke. If you try anything that isn't transferring the full Echofall data, your brains will redecorate this overpriced shithole."

Darna's fingers trembled slightly as she typed.

A minute later, she pulled a small data fob from a side drawer and passed it back to Ryx. He didn't even glance at her, just slotted it into his encrypted transfer module.

"Team, transmitting now. Confirm when you've got it."

He stood over Darna, unmoving. She dared a glance over her shoulder.

"You're really going to let me go?" Ryx didn't answer right away.

His eyes never left the skyline.

Finally, he spoke quietly. Tired. Icy.

"You destroyed my life. Multiple times. Kolen's dead because of you. Kaelen's dead. Tess lost her arm. All while you sat behind corporate glass, building a weapon to erase entire populations like they're names on a spreadsheet."

He looked at her now. No rage. Just a flat, empty steel. "I would love nothing more than to erase you from the galaxy." Her breath hitched.

"But I'm not you," he said. "You cooperate, you get the cushy trial, the white collar cell with a view. Not a hole in the ground. That's my word."

"We've got it," Yessari chimed in. "The full archive. Project Echofall files, chain of custody logs, and even internal memos. This is everything."

Ryx nodded and took a step back, finally lowering the pistol.

Then,

"Wait," Darna said, eyes flicking toward the desk again.

"Ryx," Yessari snapped. "She activated something. An outbound signal burst. Frequency spike on a BSD emergency relay, she's called for help."

Ryx's blood turned to ice.

He raised the gun again. "I know you called for help, Darna."

She smiled now, dark and bitter. "You won't make it out of here. BSD will retrieve what you stole. Kill your little helpers. Reclaim the data."

Ryx's lips curled into a cold grin. "You really don't get it, do you?" He took a slow step forward, gaze narrowing.

"The artifact? It was right in front of you..."

He raised Wasted Starlight to fire.

Then, the skylight shattered above then. Glass exploded inward, shards spraying like shrapnel as a black-armored figure crashed through the penthouse window like a missile.

Nyl Strade.

He hit Ryx like a freight train, shoulder-first, knocking him off his feet and slamming them both to the marble floor. The room cracked with the force of the impact. Wasted Starlight pinned to his chest.

Ryx barely had time to raise his arms before Nyl's armored fist came down like a piston. The first blow crunched against Ryx's forearm with bone-rattling force, his HUD flaring red with impact warnings.

"Damn," Ryx growled, twisting beneath him. Nyl was fast, faster than last time. No hesitation. No banter.

Just violence.

Ryx bucked his hips and drove his knee into Nyl's ribs. A grunt. A shift in weight. He rolled with it, getting half a second of separation, just enough to hurl them both into the glass table behind them. The table shattered on impact, splinters of chromasteel slicing skin and armor alike.

They scrambled to their feet.

Nyl advanced again. Heavy combat armor. Fists like mallets. Energy dampening plating glinting with embedded null-weave, smart design. His helmet was sealed, visor black as space.

He wasn't here to talk.

Ryx ducked a swing, threw a hook. Blocked. Counter. Spinning elbow. Miss. Nyl lunged, and they crashed through the divider wall, slamming into the modern art sculpture Darna Kent probably paid a fortune for. It exploded into useless geometry.

Fists. Knees. Forearms.

Too close for guns. Too fast for finesse.

Nyl moved like a machine, targeting Ryx's right side again and again. Every feint to use Wasted Starlight met with instant reaction, his arm pinned, his movements countered. *He's tracking the gauntlet too*, Ryx realized. That wasn't instinct. That was training.

That was intel.

They staggered into the open air of the landing pad, boots skidding across synthcrete, fists flying. The early evening wind howled around them.

"You've adapted," Ryx rasped between breaths, blood in his mouth.

Nyl said nothing. No pause. No gloating. Just methodical murder.

Professional.

Ryx gritted his teeth. He feinted with his right hand, bringing it up to fire. Predictably, Nyl lunged to intercept, pivoting his entire stance to block it, locking Ryx's dominant side.

Big mistake.

With a sudden shift, Ryx dropped low, twisting his torso. His left arm flashed blue, light surging from the newly acquired left gauntlet.

Nyl hesitated, just a second.

Too long.

"I've adapted too."

The gauntlet's mini energy cannon discharged point-blank, a compact blast of kinetic light hammering into Nyl's side. His armor ruptured, molten edges flaring as the force lifted him from the ground and slammed him to the concrete.

He hit hard. Rolled once. Blood and smoke.

Breathing ragged. Armor hissing with venting coolant.

Ryx stepped forward, slow, deliberate, sparks still flickering across his gauntlet.

Nyl struggled to rise, dragging himself back. "What the fuck are you!?"

Ryx opened his mouth to answer, something cold, maybe clever.

Then he heard it.

Whirrrrrr.

Repulsors.

Too close.

His HUD pinged too late. He turned,

Darna Kent's hovercar roared forward, pilotless, its onboard AI overridden, slamming toward him like a hammer from hell. "Shit!"

WHAM.

It hit Ryx full-force. Metal crushed into his chest like a battering ram. The wind tore from his lungs. His body launched backward, boots leaving the ground, and then he was falling.

Off the edge of the landing pad.

Into open air..

"NOOOOO!"

Tess's scream ripped through the comms channel as Ryx vanished off the edge of the landing pad.

Yessari surged to the console, scanning telemetry readouts and

trajectory patterns. "We'll never reach him in time. His descent speed, there's no way,"

"Shut up, shut up, shut up," Tess's hands flew over the control board. "Come on, Ryx…"

Wind roared in Ryx's ears. The skyline blurred into a kaleidoscope of lights and noise as he spun downward, pressure folding in around his chest like a vice.

He stashed Wasted Starlight in its back holster with a practiced flick and activated the HUD. Target overlays flared across the visor.

There.

Unoccupied hovercar. Civilian model. Four lanes down.

"Alright," he muttered through gritted teeth, "stupid plan it is."

He slammed his thumb on the armor's micro-thruster pad. Jets on his hips and shoulders sputtered to life but barely nudged him.

The suit wasn't built for this. The thrusters were built to move his body through weightless space not a full grav freefall.

"Dammit, come on,"

Another idea struck.

He flared both gauntlets, blue energy pulsing in his hands.

"Let's try this."

He fired a concussive blast from his left gauntlet, angled downward and to the right. The counterforce shifted him mid-air. Another blast from the right. Then the left again. Slowly, he adjusted his fall angle.

He was burning altitude fast. Seconds left.

The hovercar passed below, silver-blue, sleek, autopiloted, unaware.

"NOW."

He flared both gauntlets one last time, using twin bursts of concussive force to hurl himself down like a missile. Just before impact, he ignited both gauntlet shields and brought his arms up to brace,

CRASHHHHH!

Ryx tore through the hovercar's rear canopy in a shower of glass and blue light, slamming into the passenger seats and crumpling the interior. The car lurched violently off course, warning klaxons blaring as the AI initiated emergency landing mode.

Ryx groaned, chest heaving, shoulders aching from the impact.

"Tess," he rasped through the transponder, "I'm alive."

"WHAT THE HELL," Tess's voice cracked with relief and fury. "You absolute, you insane metal-brained space roach,"

"Confirmed," Yessari cut in, voice tight with awe. "Vital signs stable. You actually did it."

Ryx pushed himself upright from the ruined seat, glass raining off his armor. He stood shakily, gaze drifting to the glowing gauntlets at his sides.

He stared.

"Okay," he whispered. "I love you both a little right now."

314

The moment shattered as his HUD blinked red, incoming targets.

Hostile vehicles detected. BSD signature. Four black hovers in pursuit. ETA: 28 seconds.

Ryx cursed and vaulted from the ruined hovercar before it touched down.

Ryx hit the ground hard outside the crashed hovercar, boots skidding on smooth neoplate. Pain lanced up his ribs, bruised, but not broken. No time to think.

His HUD screamed red.

Inbound Hostiles – BSD Tactical Vehicles (x4)

Altitude: Variable – Speed: Rapid Approach ETA: 24 seconds

The first shriek of engines roared overhead.

"Tess, I've got company, heavy."

"We see you!" she yelled. "Yess is pulling orbital override, stay alive!"

Easier said than done.

Ryx sprinted into a narrow alley, ducking under neon signs and between open-air cafes. Civilians screamed and scattered. A child cried out. He banked left, straight into an outdoor market.

Blaster fire erupted behind him.

Plasma bolts tore through hanging banners and ceramic fruit stands. Ryx spun, lifting a gauntlet, and fired a concussive pulse that blasted a market stall into shrapnel, flipping one of the BSD foot pursuit drones into a concrete pillar.

Screams rose.

Shit. He couldn't risk open conflict in the crowd.

Ryx dropped low, rolling behind a delivery truck. One of the hovercars dove, its undercarriage opening, minigun drone deploying.

He didn't hesitate.

Ryx fired a full-power disruption burst into the ground, launching himself upward in a corkscrew of blue force. He slammed into the hovering vehicle, grabbed the drone mid-deploy, and ripped it free.

The hovercar spiraled, careening into a service tower with a fiery impact.

The heat wave slapped Ryx mid-air. He fell three stories, caught himself with a pulse-burst from the gauntlet, and landed hard on the side of a moving tram. He rode it five blocks, crouched and waiting, until they found him again.

Two more BSD hovers cut in low, closing from above.

He had seconds.

Ryx spotted a courier biker dismounting at a restaurant delivery zone, a sleek mono-repulsor hoverbike still idling at full power.

"Sorry!" Ryx shouted, diving forward and kicking off the edge of the tram.

He landed hard on the bike's seat, turned the handlebars with a growl, and blasted off into the vertical skyline.

The bike howled like a wounded animal, its repulsors climbing into overdrive as Ryx gunned the throttle.

"I'm heading vertical, open that bay, Tess!"

"We're already moving, get up here, fast!" The BSD pursuit kicked into high gear.

Three hovercars behind. One above.

One cut in sideways, ramming his bike mid-air. Ryx nearly lost control, spinning wildly toward a holo-billboard. He fired both gauntlets, left to stabilize, right to blow a hole through the ad tower.

CRASH. He burst through the other side, trailing smoke.

His HUD was blinking target lock warnings in all quadrants.

"Ryx, 2 kilometers, north by vertical arc, Wraithburn's in position." Yessari's logical recap was too calm.

"I see it!"

The Wraithburn was descending from the atmosphere like a phantom. Rear cargo bay yawning open. Lights inside strobing with landing beacons.

The BSD cars converged.

Ryx's mask warned him of a missile lock.

"Come on, come on,"

He saw the red glow behind him, felt the burn in his lungs. The bike was rattling apart beneath him.

A missile streaked forward, Ryx twisted just as it exploded behind him. Shrapnel tore through his coat, hot metal slashing his shoulder.

"Gah, damn it,!"

He hit the last throttle burst, blazing through the sky.

The Wraithburn loomed ahead, cargo bay roaring.

"NOW, YESS!"

"I'm clear! HIT IT!"

Ryx gunned the bike forward, straight into the open hold.

He leapt off at the last second, letting the hoverbike careen into the bulkhead as he rolled across the deck.

The ship's interior alarms were screaming, hull rattling from an impact outside. The rear hatch slammed shut with a deafening hiss.

Tess was already grabbing him, dragging him up, blood on her fingers.

"Are you, Ryx, are you hit?!"

"Shoulder. Just a scratch."

Yessari was strapping into the nav seat, eyes wide. "Missiles inbound, initiating slip drive now!"

WRAITHBURN – JUMP ENGAGED

Outside the hull, space folded and twisted.

The skyline of Delva Minor disappeared in a streak of light.

And they were gone.

△△△

Ryx sat shirtless on the edge of a reinforced table in the lab, muscles tight, a sheen of sweat still clinging to his skin from the chaos on Delva Minor. His shoulder was singed, clean through the dermal layer, raw and angry, but manageable.

Dr. Yessari Quarn worked in silence, hands smooth and efficient as he applied the dermal sealant. A soft hiss filled the room as the gel bound synthskin began fusing over the injury.

"You know," Ryx muttered, voice a little hoarse, "it's kinda nice having a doctor onboard. Almost makes getting shot worth it."

Yessari didn't look up. "You'll forgive me if I don't encourage repeat performances."

Ryx chuckled lightly, then winced as the adhesive tightened.

His eyes drifted down to the nearby bench, where his old coat lay.

Scorched. Torn. The shoulder blown out. The left sleeve ripped from elbow to cuff. Stained with soot and streaked with shrapnel burns.

He stared at it for a long moment, something heavy settling in his chest.

"Damn," he murmured. "That was my favorite one."

Yessari paused in his work. "Ah. The grim black long coat of haunted mystery. A tragedy."

"It was weathered," Ryx corrected. "Had character. Worn in all the right ways. I've had it since, hell, since before I met Kaelen."

He rubbed his good shoulder and let out a sigh. "Too broke to replace it with anything decent now, anyway."

A soft shuffle behind them cut through the quiet.

Tess stood in the doorway, arms full, holding something wrapped in deep charcoal cloth.

"Yess," she said quietly. "Can I have a moment with Ryx?"

Yessari glanced between them, wiped his hands, and nodded once.

"Don't reopen that wound," he said to Ryx as he left. "Tessa will yell. I don't need that energy in my lab." He closed the door behind him.

Tess crossed the lab in silence. Her movements were calm, but her face was pulled tight at the edges, like she was holding something back.

She didn't say anything at first.

Just stood there, staring at the bundle in her arms.

"I've been holding onto this for a while," she said finally, her voice low. "Couldn't bring myself to look at it for the first few weeks. It smelled like him."

Ryx's throat tightened.

Tess lifted it to her nose and inhaled, deeply, shakily.

"I miss him, Ryx."

"I know," Ryx said softly. "Me too."

Silence stretched for a moment. The hum of the ship barely audible.

Ryx reached for his ruined coat again, fingers brushing the frayed collar.

"I should've gotten there faster," he muttered. "If I'd just,"

Tess's head snapped up. "Don't." He looked at her.

"Don't do that thing where you spiral," she snapped. "Where you take every bad thing and chain it to your own throat like it's your fault."

Ryx lowered his gaze.

Tess stepped forward and dropped the bundle into his lap. He unwrapped it carefully.

It was a coat. Kaelen's coat.

319

Heavy. Dark Nanoleather. Familiar. Faintly smelling of oil and solder and something warm beneath it, Kaelen's old Pilots patch "Rhoen", home.

"You know what that is," she said quietly. "You grabbed it from the wreckage the day after the shop burned. Couldn't let it go." Ryx stared at it.

"Tess…"

"I've already fitted it with an inner lining," she said, cutting him off. "Composite weave, laser resistant. Nothing that'll stop a plasma bolt point blank, but better than what you've been running around in." He still didn't speak.

She exhaled hard. "And before you say anything about not deserving it, or Kaelen would've wanted you to have it only if you weren't an idiot, you'd know this."

She stepped closer, eyes fierce.

"He would've wanted you to wear it. You were family. You are family. Take the damn coat."

Ryx's hands closed around the sleeves, slowly pulling the fabric toward him.

"It's his," he said, voice barely audible.

"It was," Tess corrected. "Now it's yours. And if you could please take it off before getting blown to hell on every mission, I'd appreciate it."

Ryx barked a laugh, tight and raw.

"No promises."

He slipped the coat over his shoulders, and for a second, something inside him settled. Like a weight he hadn't realized he was carrying had shifted just enough to breathe again.

It was a little too big in the arms.

A little too Kaelen.

But it felt right.

Ryx stood slowly, Kaelen's coat settling across his shoulders like a memory made manifest. The scent, the weight, the feel of it, it wrapped around him like a second skin. His throat tightened again, but this time it wasn't guilt. It was something gentler. Something quieter.

Tess stepped forward.

They didn't speak.

They didn't need to.

She pulled him into a hug.

Ryx hesitated just half a heartbeat before wrapping his arms around her, careful, but firm. She pressed her forehead into his chest, her hardlight arm hummed against him, and he held her like something fragile that had finally stopped falling.

"I've got you," he whispered.

"Yeah," she murmured. "I know."

A few seconds passed before she pulled back and cleared her throat with a sniff. "Alright. Go clean yourself up. You smell like burned shuttle parts and ego."

Ryx smirked. "Both of which are extremely hard to scrub out."

Tess rolled her eyes and turned toward the door. "I'll grab Yess. Meet us in the common room when you're presentable."

Steam rolled off the shower walls as Ryx stood beneath the hot stream, letting the water run down his face, across the bruises blooming over his ribs, and over the sealed wound on his shoulder. The adrenaline was fading.

All that was left was the weight of what they'd been through, and what was coming.

He stepped out, toweling his hair dry, and stared at himself in the small mirror over the sink.

Scars. Tired eyes. Faint lines of worry etched around his mouth. But something in his expression had changed. Hardened. Focused.

He pulled on a simple black shirt and dark cargo pants, tugged on his boots, and finally, reverently, picked up Kaelen's coat from where he'd hung it.

The inner lining caught faint light from the room's glow panel, new, reinforced, but the rest of it was unmistakably the old man's. Ryx slipped it on with care, his fingers tightening briefly on the lapels.

"Let's see what you left me, Darna," he muttered, and stepped out.

Tess and Yessari were already waiting at the table, datapads and projection modules laid out in a neat cluster. A pot of stim tea sat untouched between them.

Tess looked up as Ryx entered.

Her gaze swept the coat. She gave a faint nod. Approval, and something like peace.

"Alright," Ryx said as he sat, voice firm and calm. "Let's dig into what we pulled out of BSD."

Yessari activated the main display.

The ghost of Kaelen's memory still warmed Ryx's shoulders. But the fire in his chest was all his.

The ship's common room was dim, lit only by the shifting blue glow of the holo-projector. Ryx sat still, elbows on his knees, Kaelen's coat draped over his frame like armor made of memory. He didn't speak. Didn't move. He just watched the files cycle past, lines of redacted names, technical blueprints, death logs dressed up as statistics.

Tess leaned forward, one hand gripping a mug of cold stim tea she hadn't touched. Her jaw was set hard.

Yessari stood behind her, arms folded, but tension radiated off him like heat. His eyes were locked on the display, flipping through the latest decrypted files.

And then the next document bloomed into the air.

PROJECT: ECHOFALL – PHASE 2

322

The air in the room seemed to snap tight.

Ryx didn't blink. He just stared.

Tess turned toward him slowly, voice quiet. "Ryx…?"

But he didn't respond. His eyes were fixed on the name glowing in the center of the screen.

Rendyll.

The man who ordered the strike on Eleos V. The man who tried to make him a murderer. The man whose voice still haunted his sleep.

"How is the Varrix Prime Military involved with Black Sable Dynamics?" Tess asked Ryx's mind floated back to seeing Kennedy Rendyll in Darna Kents office. It was all starting to make sense.

"They've been involved the whole time…" Ryx said coldly.

"What…?" Tess asked and even Yessari looked intrigued.

"Rendyll was on Delva Minor when they sold me out." Ryx breathed out. "I thought he came as a personal slight to me, but no. This makes more sense."

Tessa picked up the thread. "They don't send Admirals to recover deserters.." she said quietly.

Ryx nodded still staring at the screen. "If BSD is looking for a buyer or partner in a genocide machine, then Rendyll would be first in line."

Ryx let out a breath. "It's possible that Kolen wasn't working exclusively for BSD, that he was the bridge between the VPM and Black Sable. It's possible that Rendyll had the idea to send me after him.."

There was a long pause. The weight of realization in the air.

Yessari read on, his voice cool but shaken.

"According to this file, they stopped active artifact work shortly after you were imprisoned, never gave up looking. But shifted their focus. This is plan B for Echofall. They're building a weapon, but not like yours, Ryx. This one's sonic. Same purpose. A resonance-based extinction device."

He brought up a rotating schematic. A bulbous core structure, surrounded by harmonic rings, with long satellite arms extending in every direction.

"It uses subharmonic frequencies to destabilize biological matter. Renders a biosphere uninhabitable in minutes. Everything dies. Cells rupture. Nerves disintegrate. But the buildings? The infrastructure? All untouched."

Tess's mouth moved, but no sound came out.

"They must have been working on this for years." Ryx said a confused look on his face.

"This was Plan A before they found the artifact." Tess said reading deeper into the files.

Yessari finished the slide. "It's a ghost-maker. Efficient. Reusable.

And from what I'm seeing... they're preparing a live test."

Ryx's voice came out low, guttural. "Where."

TEST SITE: AEXIS-9

CLASS: DECOMMISSIONED MINING WORLD – NO MAJOR LIFESIGNS

CURRENT STATUS: RESTRICTED. OBSERVATION ONLY.

ORBITAL COMMAND: ECHOFALL STATION 02

"Of course it's Rendyll," Ryx whispered. "He would love another shot at genocide."

Then, without warning, something inside him shifted. A cold pressure bloomed in his wrist. Not pain, but presence. A slow, persistent thrum beneath his skin. Faint at first, then growing.

He looked down. The bracelet was pulsing.

Not glowing. Not flaring. Just... beating. A soft, sapphire rhythm in time with nothing but itself.

Ryx flexed his hand.

Nothing changed. Tess noticed. "Is that?..."

"Yeah," Ryx murmured. "It's never done this before. Not like this."

Yessari stepped forward. "Artifact-based tech reacts to input, environmental factors, sometimes emotional states. But this, this looks intentional."

He reached out, touched the projection with his fingers.

The bracelet pulsed again.

Faster.

"Ryx," Tess said, her voice tight now, "you think it's... warning you?"

"I don't know," he admitted. "But it feels like it is."

The next pulse wasn't just brighter. It was sharper. Like a jolt sent through his arm. Ryx hissed and grabbed his forearm.

"Okay," he muttered. "That one hurt."

Tess was already on her feet, eyes wide.

"Ryx, stop touching it."

"I didn't touch anything!"

The bracelet dimmed again, pulsing softly now. Steady.

Waiting.

Almost like it was alive.

Almost like it was afraid.

Yessari lowered his voice. "There may be a link. Between the artifact's origin and this weapon. They may resonate on similar frequencies, or worse, interfere."

Ryx turned his eyes back to the station schematic. "Or something else" The structure looked so clean. So clinical.

But something was wrong. Something beneath the obvious. He felt it deep in his chest, a pressure that didn't belong to him.

Tess finally broke the silence.

"We have to stop them."

Yessari nodded. "We'll never get close through official channels. Rendyll will have the place buried under black-site security protocols."

Ryx stepped forward, eyes never leaving the projection. "Then we go in quiet." Tess looked at him. "You serious?"

"Yeah."

He flexed his hand, feeling the pressure echo up his arm.

"I've faced Rendyll before."

"And?"

"He tried to bury a planet under a lie. This time, he doesn't get the chance."

The gauntlet pulsed once more.

And didn't stop.

The projection flickered and faded to black, leaving only the low hum of the Wraithburn and the shallow breathing of three people who had just seen too much.

No one spoke for several seconds.

Tess stared at her clenched hands like she was trying not to throw them into something. Yessari sat back, running his fingers along the edge of his datapad, brow furrowed in thought.

And Ryx just stood there, coat half-draped across his shoulders, eyes on the cold darkness beyond the viewport.

"I know his plan," he finally said, voice rough as broken glass. "Rendyll's MO hasn't changed. Cold, precise, efficient. No risk unless there's reward. Which means, if he's there in person, he thinks he can control this thing."

Yessari's voice was carefully measured. "And if he can't?"

"Then he wipes the site and walks away clean," Ryx said.

Tess shook her head. "We can't let this get off the ground."

Ryx turned slowly to face them, the storm behind his eyes fully awake now.

"We don't just stop it. We dismantle it. We ruin it so thoroughly they never build anything like it again. I want the tech gone. The data gone. I want Rendyll's name buried with the ashes."

Tess swallowed. "That's a suicide run."

"Then we don't run." The room went still.

Yessari leaned forward. "We can't brute-force this. BSD's smart, but the Varrix Prime military? They're disciplined. That station'll have layered access gates, thermal and magnetic tracking, armed response AI, and a dozen black site protocols."

"Good," Ryx said, voice low. "Let them bring everything. I'm not afraid of Rendyll anymore." He paused. "But we're not going in loud. Not at first."

He crossed to the tactical console and opened a systems map. The Wraithburn spun slowly in space, a soft blue shape amidst a starfield.

"Echofall Station sits in low orbit above Aexis-9. Shielded. No open dock for standard vessels."

Tess stepped in, pulling up a schematic overlay of the station's superstructure.

"Ventilation shafts, maintenance tunnels, rear fusion coil bypass. Looks like it still uses old GenTen docking arms for transport haulers."

"They're automated," Yessari said. "But with the right signal and timing... we could slip in a boarding drone."

Ryx nodded. "Not a drone."

He tapped the interface and brought up a small file labeled Gorgon Pod: Wraith Variant.

Tess's eyes widened. "You still have that thing?"

"Had it buried under Kaelen's cargo crates for five years. He Stripped it down, re-armed it with a recon shell and point-jump magnetics. Built it for station insertion. Stealth deployment only."

Yessari folded his arms and frowned. "Let me guess. You fly it manually."

Ryx just smirked.

Tess stared at the plan, then looked at Ryx.

"Alright. You get in. Then what?"

"You both help me find the weapon. We find the core and sabotage it. Yess, you tell me how to get whatever data we can on the prototype. Rip their files, scrub the backups." "And Rendyll?" Tess asked quietly.

Ryx met her eyes.

"I'll handle him."

No hesitation.

No fear.

Just the cold promise of reckoning.

Yessari broke the silence. "I'll prep the boarding pod. Rig a secondary pulse disruptor just in case. Tess?"

She straightened. "I'll get the Wraithburn into ghost-mode. Low emissions, silent orbit. But I want a det cord rig on the hull. If BSD tags us, I'm making a hard burn for the sun." Ryx smiled, faint, but real.

"Let's burn a super-weapon."

He turned back to the viewport, the weight of Kaelen's coat heavy over his shoulders. The bracelet on his wrist pulsed once more, slower now. Calmer.

Like it was ready.

ΔΔΔ

A couple hours later the Wraithburn's belly was dark, quiet, save for the faint hum of the boarding pod's internal systems warming up. The Gorgon Pod sat nestled against the far wall, reassembled from Ryx's days in the VPM. Sleek and scarred, waiting like a blade about to be drawn. Gorgon Pods were meant for orbital drops, Ryx retrofitted this pod years ago with Kaelen's help. Now the slender wedge shaped pod was meant to quietly breach stations, or large ships.

Ryx stood alone in the glow of a single overhead light, shadows stretching across the deck like cracks in memory.

His armor reattached, damaged still, from his fight on Delva Minor. His coat lay across a bench, Kaelen's patch still sewn inside the lining. Wasted Starlight sat beside it, cleaned, checked, reloaded.

He hadn't spoken in nearly an hour. Tessa and Yessari were prepping the ship and mapping the layout for the mission.

Ryx Just paced.

Checked his gear.

Then sat with his thoughts.

The bracelet on his right wrist pulsed faintly, like it was breathing.

"You feel it too, don't you?" Ryx muttered, his voice barely audible. "Somethings wrong with that place."

It pulsed again, twice. Uneven. Like a heartbeat stumbling.

Ryx leaned forward on the crate in front of him, bracing his forearms against his knees.

"Rendyll was in command at Eleos, I was following orders. Good soldier. Loyal to command."

He exhaled slowly, jaw clenching.

"I didn't know I was the one arming a planet-wide grave."

The memory of Eleos V hit sharp. The air scrubbers. The panic in his lungs. The way his hand had trembled holding that device, realizing what they'd tried to order him to do.

The way Rendyll's voice had sounded in his ear: Clean deployment. Get it done, Thorne.

"I told him I was coming back to expose him." He looked up, eyes hard now.

"But I ran from him instead."

He stood slowly, bones cracking from the tension in his shoulders.

"I ran from him, from the VPM, from my past, for years."

He grabbed the coat and slid into it. The weight grounded him.

He holstered Wasted Starlight, willed the bracelet to shift to its implant form, and finally pulled his mask from its case, holding it in both hands.

There was no turning back from this. No running. No hiding.

Just the quiet hum of his ship. His friends waiting in the wings. The ghosts of Eleos. And the reckoning he'd owed for far too long.

He slid the mask on. The HUD blinked awake. A targeting sweep. Vital signs. Atmospheric readout. One line stood out, glowing faint in the corner of his vision:

MISSION OBJECTIVE: INSERTION – ECHOFALL

Ryx stared at the Gorgon pod.

"No more running."

CHAPTER 18

SURVIVOR

The stars didn't move. From here, the station looked like a spiderweb strung across the void, thin limbs extending from a central ring, all of it black and sharp against the ghostly blue of Aexis-9 below. Silent. Patient. A predator waiting to pounce.

Tess stood at the forward view plate, arms folded tight, breath held too long. Her eyes were locked on the distant glint of BSD steel in orbit.

No chatter. No signals. No threats detected.

It was too quiet.

Behind her, Yessari worked at the sensor console, one hand tapping steadily on the edge of the screen, his posture deceptively calm. But his jaw kept clenching.

"Telemetry locked," he said. "The pod's heat signature is buried. No scans pinging from the station so far."

Tess nodded once. "Still moving?"

"Seventeen minutes to magnetic sync. No course correction needed." A beat of silence.

Then Yessari added, "His vitals are steady. Elevated cortisol. But nothing abnormal."

Tess's voice was low. "That man doesn't know what normal is anymore."

She turned back to the viewport.

"Be careful down there, Ryx," she whispered.

ΔΔΔ

[Gorgon Boarding Pod – 17 Minutes to Dock]

Inside the pod, the world was blue-lit and humming.

Ryx sat motionless in the crash couch, fully sealed into his armor. The restraints bit into his shoulders. The artifact on his wrist glowed softly, each pulse lining up with his heart. Wasted Starlight rested at his hip, magnetically clipped.

The Gorgon pod spun slowly, its trajectory aligned with one of the outer docking arms on Echofall Station. Just a sliver of drift. Just enough to be a ghost in their blind spot.

His HUD scrolled data in tight arcs around his vision.

DISTANCE TO TARGET: 21.3 km

EMISSION PROFILE: CLEAN

STEALTH SIGNATURE: WITHIN THRESHOLD

Another readout flickered:

PULSE ANOMALY – RIGHT WRIST: SYNC UNSTABLE

He looked down. The artifact was pulsing again, but slower now. Uneven.

Like it didn't want to get closer.

Ryx exhaled through his teeth, trying to center his breath.

"Not now," he whispered. "Not when I'm this close."

He thought of Kaelen. Of Tess. Of the garage. Of the fire. Of Kolen.

Of Rendyll's voice, calmly ordering the extermination of everyone on Eleos V, civilians and soldiers alike.

And of the lies that had buried it all.

TARGET: ECHOFALL STATION 02

The name burned on the HUD like a brand.

Ryx's thoughts and emotions pleaded with the artifact. *We need to do this.*

As Ryx had come to realize, it understood.

The implant form of the artifact around his wrist calmed and the readings on the HUD returned to nominal.

The pod vibrated slightly as its thrusters whispered, making the final micro-corrections to align.

INSERTION VECTOR LOCKED. IMPACT IN: 07:58... 07:57...

In the distance, the station loomed larger.

Lights glimmered across its hull. A pair of slow-moving patrol drones circled, but not near the docking shaft Ryx was aiming for. His insertion corridor was invisible to standard scans. No alarms. No chatter.

Perfect silence.

Too perfect.

The pressure in the artifact built again, spiking along the inside of his forearm.

Warning.

It was trying to warn him again.

But about what?

He clenched his jaw.

"No time," he muttered.

Outside, the stars began to spin faster as the pod adjusted angle for soft impact.

HARDLOCK IN: 01:45...

In the Wraithburn's orbit, Tess and Yessari watched in tense silence, the timer mirrored on their screens. Yessari whispered, "Come on..."

333

Tess didn't blink.

01:12... 00:44... 00:19...

Inside the pod, Ryx gripped the handrail. His knuckles white inside the gloves.

00:03... 00:02...

IMPACT

The pod slammed into the docking ring with a quiet hiss and a magnetic snap.

Ryx's harness disengaged.

He stood and reached for the manual release. Quick. Efficient. Lethal.

The Gorgon pod's release bolts hissed in a muffled sequence. Ryx braced himself, artifact pulsing faintly as the hatch yawned open to reveal a narrow maintenance shaft bathed in sterile white light.

He stepped forward, low, quiet, every movement controlled.

The station was too clean. Too polished. Even the vents had a surgical stillness to them.

"You're in," Tess's voice crackled softly in his comms. "No visual pings. Keep it that way."

"Telemetry's still holding," Yessari added. "Internal thermals show minimal crew presence in your ring. They've automated more than I expected."

"Less crew, less witnesses."

Ryx's boots made no sound on the grated floor as he crept forward, bypassing a sealed hatch to reroute through a vent run. The bracelet pulsed again, irregular, jittery. Like it was resisting something.

He whispered, "Still don't like it in here, huh?"

"Who doesn't?" Tess asked.

"The artifact. It's twitchy. More than usual."

"We're picking up some odd harmonics," Yessari replied. "Subsonic pulses. You wouldn't hear them. But the artifact might."

"Ryx," Tess again, sharper this time. "Something about that place is wrong. Just get what we need and get out." He didn't respond.

He was already moving again, lower, quieter, as the corridor turned into a curved spinal walkway of flickering lights and recessed sensor nodes. He could feel the hum beneath the plating now. Not through his boots, through his bones.

The deeper he went, the more the pressure built.

ΔΔΔ

A quiet hum filled the command chamber of Echofall Station, broken only by the precise tap of Rendyll's silver spoon against ceramic. The Admiral's medals caught the blue refracted glow of Aexis-9 through the reinforced view plate, a perfect planetary silhouette, luminous and indifferent.

Then: a whisper of motion. Soft boots on polished flooring. A young technician stepped in, datapad gripped so tightly his knuckles had gone white.

"Admiral..."

Rendyll didn't look up. "Speak."

"Sir, there's been... a reading. Possibly an incursion. Brief. The signal was fragmented. But we logged a power fluctuation in Ring C-4. Unauthorized."

Rendyll's spoon stopped mid-stir.

A silence hung in the air like frozen breath.

Finally, he looked up, his obsidian-black eyes locking onto the young officer. Cold. Calculating. Impassive.

"Define breach, Lieutenant."

The technician swallowed audibly. "No physical signature. But... interference. Something passed through the sensor net. Only for a second, but"

The Admiral set his cup down on the console with a delicate click. He stood.

"Saturate the grid with EM pinging. And send a drone."

"Sir, with respect, our drones aren't rated for hostile retrieval. If this is an infiltration op,"

"I didn't say retrieve." Rendyll's voice sliced the air. "Send. A. Drone." A pause.

"And if you detect another spike?"

The Admiral stepped close. His voice dropped to silk, quiet, intimate.

"Scrub the deck."

The technician paled, his breath hitched. "Y-Yes, sir."

ΔΔΔ

Ryx held his breath as he slipped deeper into the conduit shaft. The smell of ozone and old coolant filled his nose, sharp, metallic, almost chemical. The bracelet pulsed faintly under his sleeve, its glow a rhythmic heartbeat against his wrist.

He was thirty feet above the deck now, wedged between two coolant lines with just enough space to move his head.

His chest pressed against the steel wall. Every movement felt like it might betray him. One elbow nudged a rivet. He froze.

"Ryx," Yessari's voice crackled faintly over the secure channel in his earpiece, "we've got ping. Drone inbound. Twenty seconds."

"I see it," Ryx whispered, eyes locked onto the shaft's access vent. And then, movement.

A sleek, disc-shaped drone crawled along the corridor ceiling like a black crab. Its motion was jerky, artificial, yet precise. Multi-limbed. One optic sensor panned left, right, red glow pulsing softly. He watched as it skittered across the floor below him.

His fingers twitched toward Wasted Starlight, but he stopped.

No shots. Not yet.

The drone's sensor lingered. Ryx held still, trying not to breathe. Sweat beaded on his forehead and ran down his cheek. The bracelet chose that exact moment to throb once, sharp and electric.

Not now, not now… The drone halted.

A low click emitted from its hull. Its eye turned directly upward, at him.

It saw.

"Ryx," Yessari again, louder this time. "Field's rising, they're launching a thermal sweep."

Shit.

The eye began to glow.

Ryx moved.

CRACK,

A pulse shot erupted from Wasted Starlight, striking the drone midframe. The blast was surgical, clean, but the explosion wasn't. Shards of the drone tore through the air like razors, some pinging off the conduit around him as alarms erupted overhead.

Klaxons screamed. Red emergency lighting bathed the corridor in blood hues.

ALERT: DECK C-4 BREACH

UNAUTHORIZED PRESENCE DETECTED

LEVEL 1 RESPONSE INITIATED

"Damn it," Ryx spat. He dropped from the shaft, hitting the floor in a crouch and sprinting before his boots fully landed.

"Tess?" he snapped.

"You're burned," her voice came through, all sharp edges and urgency. "Go loud. Go fast."

"I've got your route," Yessari said, already uploading. "Secondary core access, vectoring to Sector B. Sending exit path to your HUD now."

337

The bracelet flared with full power now. Sapphire circuits rippled across both arms, energy lighting up like ancient sigils awakened.

It wasn't hiding anymore.

And neither was he.

Ryx rounded a corner and came face-to-face with BSD operatives. Four shock troopers in full armor.

He didn't slow down. He didnt hesitate.

He let the storm loose.

They saw him just before he hit.

"CONTACT..."

Too late.

Ryx was a thunderbolt.

He slammed into the nearest BSD trooper like a kinetic missile, shoulder-first, his left gauntlet flaring as it discharged a concussive pulse at point-blank. The soldier flew backward, armor cracked, body limp before it hit the ground.

The others opened fire.

Red bolts screamed through the corridor.

Ryx twisted, the sapphire shield erupting from his left arm in a curve of brilliant light. Plasma rounds struck it with violent sizzle-screams, ricocheting in every direction. Sparks burst from the walls. Heat washed over his face.

He dropped low, slid under one trooper's aim, and came up with Wasted Starlight already barking.

Two shots. One to the gut, charged mag rounds doing what they did best. The next to the throat, fatal.

A third trooper raised his rifle. Ryx saw it coming.

He shifted his stance, braced, and punched forward with the gauntlet cannon.

BOOM.

A searing bolt of blue energy blew a crater in the man's chest plate, sending him crashing into the opposite wall.

The final BSD soldier tried to flee. Ryx didn't let him.

He moved like liquid fury, closed the gap in three steps and drove his knee into the man's gut, then drove an elbow into the base of the helmet. The soldier dropped.

Smoke filled the corridor. The air stank of scorched armor, and blood.

"Yessari, report." Ryx snapped, panting.

"You're closing in on the inner corridor junction. But I've got at least two more teams moving to intercept. Rendyll just locked down every exit past Core B. You're gonna have to punch through."

"Copy. Reroute me. Fast."

ΔΔΔ

The control room buzzed with frantic voices and blinking alerts.

Holographic displays glitched under stress, flickering like dying stars. The schematic of Deck C-4 now showed a swath of red, static where live feeds had been lost.

Admiral Kennedy Rendyll stood at the center of it all, arms folded, unmoved.

"Deck C-4 is compromised," said the security chief, sweat beading at his brow. "Fireteam Delta is down. Target's... unconfirmed, but their movement pattern suggests ex-military."

Rendyll's mouth quirked upward, just barely.

"Correction," he murmured. "Not just ex-military."

He tapped a nearby console. A classified personnel file appeared.

THORNE, ERYX

STATUS: UNKNOWN

VARIX PRM PRISON RECORD – SEALED CLEARANCE: REDACTED

Rendyll's eyes glittered. "Special Recon. Level Eight." His voice was calm. Icy.

"Deploy Archon Protocol. Intercept and erase."

ΔΔΔ

Ryx slammed into cover, the sapphire energy shield erupting from his left gauntlet as BSD shock troops advanced in formation. Wasted Starlight roared from his right, every time he broke cover, precise bursts punching through armor plating and blowing the lead soldiers off their feet.

He was thunder and lightning.

Another guard opened fire as he broke cover to advance. Ryx rolled low, the gauntlet shield flaring blue as it absorbed the worst of the impact. He popped up behind a support strut and unleashed a double burst from the left gauntlet, one concussive, one lethal.

Every time Wasted Starlight roared. Every time Sapphire energy bloomed in the corridors.

Bodies dropped.

Smoke filled the hallway.

"You've cleared the bulkhead junction," Yess said calmly. "You're thirty seconds from the fusion spine. Once you're inside, Rendyll won't be able to ignore you."

The lights flickered overhead. The entire station groaned.

Power was being rerouted.

"Ryx," Tess cut in, sharper now. "Something's charging. The core is going live."

He moved faster..

ΔΔΔ

Ryx didn't run, he launched himself down the final corridor.

Steel grated beneath his boots, each step hammering the deck like war drums. The gauntlets on his arms thrummed with power now, no longer tools, but extensions of his will.

Pipes overhead hissed steam. Vertical reactors blinked past on both sides, lining the tunnel like a cathedral of industry. The heat was suffocating, the air crackling with energy. Lightning crawled along the edges of the conduits, flickering violently.

The artifact buzzed, urgent. Alive.

Ahead, the security bulkhead slammed down.

"Yessari!"

"Already on it," Tayveri Dr said cooly. "I'm burning every override. Punch the panel, now."

Ryx didn't hesitate. He raised his left gauntlet and slammed it into the locking panel. The sapphire energy flared, and the door detonated inward.

BOOM.

Smoke and sparks washed over him. The steel bulkhead lay in twisted pieces at his feet.

"Holy shit.." Ryx took a moment to stare in wonder at the bracelet. "Didn't know you could do that..."

Ryx looked up.

Beyond him was the Core Chamber.

A colossal, domed space, humming with unnatural energy. The air vibrated with the resonance of something old and waking. In the center: a raised platform with a massive control array.

And above it… It hung.

Like a bell carved from obsidian and suspended in midair.

The weapon.

Its surface pulsed with violet-black circuitry, ringed with floating glyphs. Veins of crimson light throbbed from its apex to its core, cycling energy into the suspended crystalline containment field below.

Ryx's boots hit the metal walkway hard as he stepped into the light.

Standing before the console, calm as ice… was Admiral Kennedy Rendyll.

Flanked by two more VPM elite. Their armor bore no insignia. No names. Just matte black plating and crackling shock-spears.

Rendyll turned, slowly. His coat hung perfectly from his shoulders.

The blue-white light of the core reflected in his medals like fire in frozen glass.

"Thorne."

His voice was almost amused.

"I wondered when you'd crawl out of your hole." Ryx said nothing.

He stepped forward, coat billowing, face dark beneath his mask. The gauntlets gleamed with a rising light, both arms vibrating faintly now, awake, sensing something deeper in the chamber.

He stared into the eyes of the man who caused him so much pain. Every injury, every comrade he lost on mission, Every nightmare.

Images flashed before his eyes. Kolen, Kaelen, Tessa, Shandar.

A voice echoed in Ryx's memory.

What are you standing around for, kid? Daylight..

Ryx let out all the tension, all the anger, all of the nightmares of the last ten years in a single breath.

"...is just wasted starlight." Ryx finished his fathers words out loud.

Ryx didn't answer Rendyll's jab verbally. His reply came in velocity.

All of this pain, all of this madness. It ended now.

Wasted Starlight roared from his right hand.

CRACK.

A round took the first guard in the throat, the impact knocking him off the platform. Blood sprayed in a red arc.

342

The second guard lunged.

Ryx pivoted, firing the gauntlet cannon from his left arm, a pulse of blue energy slammed into the VPM trooper's chest, launching him backward into a control pillar with bone-crunching force.

Sparks burst from shattered glass and conduits.

Ryx stood and stared down the only remaining obstacle.

The source of all of his pain. Every horrible memory. Every nightmare.

"You murdered good people." Ryx growled, stepping forward.

Rendyll's eyes narrowed slightly. "No. I removed liabilities."

The words cracked something loose in Ryx. He surged forward again. Anger knocking loose any sense he had left.

They collided in a flash of light and motion.

Rendyll moved with deadly grace, a shock-pike snapping out from a concealed holster. It sparked as it arced toward Ryx's chest, but the gauntlet caught it, throwing off shards of blue light. Ryx grunted, shoving back hard, both arms alive with energy.

Rendyll twisted, swept at Ryx's legs, and jabbed the pike into his side. Static burst through his body like lightning. Ryx roared in pain but didn't fall. He grabbed the weapon's shaft and tore it free, snapping it in two with a surge of augmented strength.

"Still a soldier," Rendyll spat, retreating half a step, pulling a compact sidearm. "Still predictable."

"You have no idea what I've become," Ryx snarled.

Rendyll fired, twice. One bolt grazed Ryx's shoulder, the second he deflected with a burst from the gauntlet shield. He dove to the side, tumbled into a crouch, and snapped Wasted Starlight up, firing two return shots that punched holes in the far console.

"You will answer for this Rendyll, all of this!" Ryx shouted.

Rendyll didn't flinch.

Ryx screamed and charged again.

This fight was personal.

Their fists collided, elbows slammed into ribs, gauntlets cracked against reinforced plating under Rendyll's uniform. Blood sprayed from Ryx's lip, Rendyll's jaw split open. They locked together and crashed into a support beam, sparks raining down. Ryx broke free and slammed a knee into Rendyll's side, feeling something crack.

But the Admiral was still fast. Too fast.

Augmented. Ryx thought to himself.

Rendyll pivoted with military precision, slamming his elbow into Ryx's throat, then followed with a brutal headbutt that sent Ryx staggering.

"You orchestrated all of this!" Ryx coughed out. "You sent me after Kolen." He dodged another round from Rendyll's gun. "You killed Kaelen!" Wasted Starlight returned fire.

"You tried to kill my sister," Ryx said, wiping blood from his mask.

"You should've let BSD finish the job. Now little Tessa can't build you any new toys. Not with one arm." Rendyll said with a cold smile.

Time stopped.

Tessa's scream invaded his mind, the sick wet thud of her body hitting the wall, her broken body laying in Rexa Vorn's shop.

Rendyll was trying to hurt him. Trying to throw him off. Ryx knew it. He didnt care, and neither did the artifact.

Ryx's vision blurred red. The artifiact heated his arms. Alive. Like it shared his fury, like he was fueling it.

Rendyll took advantage of Ryx's pause, his anger. He lined up a shot right for his heart. Already smiling at his victory.

But Ryx wasn't there anymore.

Rendyll's mind couldnt catch up, as a gauntleted hand entered his line of site from his left. The had closed around the gun, and it crumpled like paper.

344

He turned to see Ryx standing next to him. And for the first time in years, felt fear. "Impossible" Rendyll breathed.

He locked eyes with Eryx Thorne. But not the Eryx Thorne he remembered. The eyes behind the white mask were glowing. This wasn't his former subordinate. This wasn't some rouge scout. This was a monster.

The gauntlet's blade roared to life, carving through Rendyll's shoulder plate with a shriek of metal. The Admiral screamed, dropping his destroyed weapon. But Ryx didn't stop. He slammed Rendyll into the console, sparks exploding around them, systems flickering wildly.

"You don't get to speak her name!" Ryx howled, fist hammering down, again, and again, each strike fueled by ten years of silence, of rage, of helplessness.

Rendyll's face was a wreck. He choked, groped for a hidden blade, but Ryx caught his arm, twisted it, and drove a gauntlet punch into his sternum that sent him sprawling.

"You took Kaelen from me!" Ryx was roaring now, chest heaving. "You took Kolen. You took everything!"

"I gave you purpose!" Rendyll spat back, blood running down his chin. "I gave you the fire!"

"You made me a killer." Ryx said quietly, raising his left gauntlet, its wrist cannon whirring to life meanacingly. "The man you had killed in that garage, gave me purpose."

The cannon flared.

Point blank. Sapphire light tore into Rendyll's abdomen and threw him back like a ragdoll. He hit the floor with a thud, smoking, twitching.

Still breathing. Barely.

The gauntlets power faded back into the bracelet.

Ryx limped forward, gaze locked.

"You're just another rabid dog." Rendyll coughed out with a mouth full of blood. How he was still alive, Ryx couldnt fathom. But part of him, a very cold part of him. Was greatful.

He raised Wasted Starlight and pressed it to Kennedy Rendyll's temple.

"It doesn't matter what I am prick." Ryx said with venom, before dropping his voice.

"I'm alive."

Ryx pulled the trigger.

CRACK.

The shot echoed like a final heartbeat.

Rendyll's body went limp. The light from the core dimmed. And in that moment… the silence returned.

But this time, it didn't feel hollow.

Ryx stood over the corpse, hands trembling, body failing, but soul finally unchained. The energy in the chamber shifted. His mask retracted into its frame.

The console, now smeared with blood and crackling from damaged circuits, pulsed weakly beneath Ryx's shaking hands. Every part of him burned. His leg was nearly numb, his ribs throbbed with each breath, and the bracelet flickered, unstable.

He staggered back, still staring at Rendyll's ruined body. The bastard was finally dead.

But it wasn't over. Far from it.

A low hum filled the chamber, different from before. Not mechanical. Not man-made. It resonated deeper, like a sound in the bones rather than the ears. The core, the weapon housing, began to shift.

A ring of blue light spiraled around the platform as vents hissed open, releasing plumes of vapor. The bell-shaped weapon structure began to rise. Metal plates retracted with hydraulic groans, exposing something hidden beneath it.

A containment chamber. Fluid-filled.

Suspended within, something alive.

Ryx took a cautious step forward, hand drifting to Wasted Starlight on instinct.

"What the hell…" he breathed.

The being inside the stasis chamber was humanoid, but elongated, alien and ancient. It stood upright, limbs graceful, yet unnaturally long. Its skin shimmered in deep violet hues, like oil beneath glass.

Its head fanned out in the back, tapering into a narrow, regal shape. No nose. Just two closed, slitted eyes and a thin mouth.

Still. Breathing.

The artifact on Ryx's arm flared.

Not in alarm, but recognition.

"Yessari," he said hoarsely, activating his comm. "I've found something. There's… something in the core."

His voice crackled through. "You need to scrub the system now, Ryx. Rendyll's files were tied to an encrypted deployment routine, if the station finishes the boot process, it could initiate, wait… what do you mean you found something?"

"Stasis tank," he said still dazed. "I dont know what it is but. It's alive." There was a long pause.

Then frantic tapping over the line. "I'm in the backfiles. Cross-referencing what I just pulled from the uplink. Hold on, hold on, Ryx, the files say it's classified Xenosapien Class Alpha. Precursor tier."

"What does that mean?"

"It means," he said, voice trembling, "no one alive has ever seen one. They're older than recorded galactic history. This isn't just some alien. It's part of whatever the artifact responds to. Maybe even where it came from."

The bracelet on his arm surged again, hotter now, as if… its anger resonated in proximity to the thing.

The being inside stirred. Only slightly, but unmistakably.

347

And then Tess's voice hit the channel. Urgent. Breathless.

"Ryx, something just warped in system-side. I don't.." Tess's voice was quiet. "This thing is huge.. No ID, no registry, no signal pings."

Ryx turned toward the thin viewport slit above the chamber.

Outside, against the stars, a shape began to blot out the system light. It wasn't a ship.

It was a cathedral of metal, vast and fluid, covered in glowing runes of alien design.

Not sleek. Not BSD.

This was ancient.

"This isn't good." Tess said, panic rising in her tone. "It's not VPM or BSD. I've never seen anything like it, Yessari?"

"I, I don't know," Yessari said, typing furiously. "I'm trying to trace anything similar. Ryx, this may not just be here for the weapon. It might be here for that thing."

Ryx looked back at the tank. The being's eyes were still shut.

But the bracelet pulsed again.

Harder now. Urgent. Warning.

Yessari's voice sliced in:

"Scrub the system now! They can't get this data!"

Ryx spun back to the console, fingers flying over the cracked surface.

TRANSFERING: ALL RESEARCH FILES

PURGING: ECHOFALL DEPLOYMENT PROTOCOLS

LOCKING: TACTICAL ACCESS RELAYS TRANSFER COMPLETE.

SCRUBBING...

Sparks burst from the core interface. Lights dimmed. The stasis tank began to descend, the alien being slowly lowered back into the depths. A final hiss of air vented around it.

And then,

The station shook.

Not from engines. Not from weapons.

From proximity. Something massive was drawing close.

"Ryx, that thing is charging something," Tess snapped. "Get out. NOW."

Alarms blared again, this time from the external defense grid. Ryx grabbed the side of the console to stay upright.

"I'm heading to the pod," he barked, turning and sprinting back into the corridor.

His body screamed. But his fear of what was coming was stronger than the pain..

ΔΔΔ

Tess slammed her palm into the nav console. "He's moving. I've got a signal. Dock with the pod the second he breaks the ring."

Yessari's eyes were wide, pale in the glow of the approaching ship on screen.

It was impossible, a black and crimson cathedral of smooth plates and glowing runes. Technology centuries beyond what they knew. No visible weapons. No markings.

And yet the dread it cast was palpable.

"Ryx, you've got sixty seconds," Tess called into the comm.

ΔΔΔ

Doors exploded open as Ryx bolted down the corridor. His lungs burned. His leg throbbed.

The bracelet flickered erratically now, unstable.

Behind him, the station shuddered.

"Thirty seconds!" Yessari barked.

Ryx skidded into the Gorgon launch bay, jammed the hatch, dived into the pod. The locks sealed.

"Tess, I'm in, get me the hell out of here!"

The pod shot from the ring with a violent hiss of decompression. The Wraithburn moved to intercept, magnetized grapplers extending.

Ryx's pod slammed into the hold.

"Go!" he roared.

Tess didn't need to be told twice.

The Wraithburn pivoted in space, its drives igniting.

Behind them, the massive alien ship unfolded a single red aperture.

A soft glow.

Then, A beam

It wasn't a cannon.

It wasn't a laser.

It was… a void..

A ripple tore through space, silent and deadly, as if existence itself had been peeled open. Echofall Station cracked.

Not exploded. Not vaporized.

Cracked.

Like ice under pressure.

Then it shattered.

Aexis-9 fractured as the beam struck its orbit. The sky split open. Energy, impossible, devouring, unmade the station from the inside out.

And in the silence between stars, the cathedral ship remained.

Watching.

Waiting.

A final message flashed on Yessari's screen as she punched the jump coordinates:

Unregistered vessel ID: UNKNOWN

"Hold tight," Tess warned.

Ryx's knuckles were white on the harness.

They were already moving, already escaping.

But behind them?

A war had just begun.

And something ancient had just fired the first shot.

CHAPTER 19
DESTROY/REBUILD

The ship's engines were silent now, the hum of jump-space fading into the normal quiet of drifting through the void. The overhead lights buzzed faintly in the Wraithburn's med bay, sterile and steady.

Ryx sat on the edge of the table, armor stripped down to the waist, his ribs wrapped, shoulder bleeding through a hastily patched dermal seal. His hands hung loose between his knees, still trembling.

Tess sat across from him, a stim can untouched on the tray beside her. Yessari stood near the med console, fingers white on the railing, eyes staring through data that wasn't there.

No one had spoken in a full minute.

Then finally, Ryx broke the silence.

"What the fuck... was that ship?"

His voice cracked in the middle, like it hadn't figured out how to breathe yet.

Yessari blinked, finally looking up. "I don't know."

Ryx laughed once, sharp and humorless. "Great."

Tess shook her head slowly. "It didn't have a transponder. No active signal. No ID. Nothing. Just... appeared."

"It didn't fire a weapon," Yessari added. "Not like we understand. That wasn't heat or radiation or kinetics."

Ryx looked up at him. "It unmade that station. And the planet. Just... blinked them out."

"Matter didn't even collapse," Tess said, voice low. "It just broke. Like glass."

Ryx leaned forward, running his hands down his face. "We weren't supposed to see that."

Yessari exhaled, slow and hollow. "We weren't supposed to survive that."

He moved to the console, pulled up the few seconds of visual telemetry they had before the jump. Froze it.

The ship.

Black, organic-seeming. Its hull shaped like it had grown, not been built. Covered in patterns and grooves that defied standard engineering.

"And the person," Ryx muttered. "The one in the core."

Tess looked at him. "What happened in there?"

Ryx met her eyes, voice flat. "It wasn't powering the weapon. It was the weapon. Or part of it."

Yessari's brow furrowed. "A biological key? A reactor conduit? Some kind of cognitive interface,?"

"No idea," Ryx cut in. "It was like a component." He leaned back, eyes haunted.

"It was a prisoner." Yessari blinked.

Tess's voice went cold. "You're saying BSD and Varrix Prime found something ancient, locked it up, and tried to use it to power their genocide machine?"

Ryx didn't answer right away.

Then, finally, "I think they found something they didn't understand. Tried to reverse-engineer it. And I think the alien ship... we just saw its answer."

Yessari went pale.

"Not just an answer," he said softly. "A message." Ryx nodded.

"Don't touch what you don't understand." The silence came back, heavy as lead.

Then Tess pushed her stim can across the tray toward Ryx and broke the spell.

"So," she said softly. "What the hell do we do now?"

Ryx stared at the frozen image of the impossible ship, still lingering on the console.

And didn't have an answer.

Not yet.

The emergency lighting had faded, replaced by the ship's soft ambient glow. The storm had passed, for now.

The Wraithburn drifted in quiet space, far from where Aexis-9 used to be. Far from BSD, from Rendyll, from the ashes.

The galley was dimly lit, just a few soft wall-strips casting amber light across the table where the three of them sat. No one touched the mugs in front of them. The silence between them was heavy, but not oppressive. Just… waiting.

Finally, Ryx leaned forward, resting his forearms on the table, fingers steepled beneath his chin.

"We're done with BSD."

His voice was low. Final.

Tess looked up at him. Her eyes were rimmed with red, but steady.

"You sure?"

He nodded, slowly.

"They'll recover. Cut deals. Scapegoat whoever's left. But Project Echofall's dead. The weapon's gone. The people who built it are either dust or about to burn each other to the ground trying to cover it up."

Yessari spoke next, voice quieter than usual.

"We can't stop the machine. But we can expose it."

354

He reached out and tapped the edge of his datapad, illuminating the sealed folder of stolen BSD files.

"We put together a packet. Schematics, logs, memos, everything. Wrap it tight, anonymized, and drop it on the desk of someone who can't ignore it."

Tess's brow furrowed. "Delva Minor's government?"

Yessari nodded. "They're corrupt, but image-conscious. You hand them the right political grenade; they'll throw it at BSD just to score points."

"And BSD will do what they do best," Ryx muttered. "Sell each other out. Burn files. Buy their way into amnesty."

Tess frowned. "So, they walk?"

Ryx looked at her, eyes steady.

"No. Project Echofall burns. That's the win."

Silence again. Then Tess exhaled slowly and leaned back, her shoulders finally sagging.

"Okay. So, we go quiet. Compile the evidence. Plan our next move."

Yessari nodded. "We'll need somewhere safe. Remote. Low scan profile."

Tess sighed dramatically. "If only we had that lab we joked about." Then she let out a light laugh.

Yessari blinked. "Why don't we buy one?"

She turned to him. "Wait, what?"

Ryx looked just as confused.

Yessari tapped a different file on his pad. "The hardlight prosthetics patent cleared approval six hours ago. I've already received three buyer offers from major manufacturers, military and civilian both." He said it like he was talking about the weather.

Tess blinked. "You're serious."

Yessari nodded. "Fully. We could purchase a small orbital platform within a week. Retrofit it. Garage on the lower deck. Lab up top. Somewhere quiet. Ours."

Ryx blinked once. Then leaned back, hand over his eyes. Kicking himself internally

"Shit," he muttered. "Tess, I forgot to tell you." She turned toward him slowly, brow furrowed.

"What?"

He went back into his cabin and returned with a small drive, thin, silvery, engraved with Kaelen's personal mark.

"Kaelen's shield battery design. It's patented. Rexa saved the documents and transferred ownership to you before I left Vorrthani." He set the drive down in front of her with quiet reverence.

"You're gonna be richer than you can imagine." Tess stared at the drive like it was alive.

Her fingers hovered just above it. Trembling.

And then she broke.

She didn't cry hard, no sobbing or wailing. Just quiet, steady tears that streamed down her cheeks. Her mouth opened, then closed. Her breath shuddered.

Ryx reached over gently, placing a hand on her shoulder.

"Hey," he said, softly. "You earned this. Kaelen wanted this for you." Across the table, Yessari's eyes widened in alarm. "Tess, I'm sorry. Did I say something wrong? If my suggestion offended you,"

She stood up suddenly, wiped at her cheeks with the back of her sleeve, took a deep breath, And kissed him.

Not tentative. Not careful.

Just real.

Yessari froze. The kiss lingered for a moment. Tess pulled back just slightly, eyes red but smiling.

He blinked.

Then cleared his throat. "My pulse just spiked by forty-seven percent. Fascinating."

Tess gave a watery laugh and kissed him again.

Ryx leaned back, a quiet smile breaking across his face for the first time in hours. His chest ached in ways that had nothing to do with wounds.

But for once, it wasn't grief.

It was the slow, unfamiliar ache of something starting to heal.

ΔΔΔ

The scent of plasma-burnt metal and old coolant hit Ryx the moment he stepped through the door.

Rexa Vorn's workshop hadn't changed much, still cluttered, still humming, still half-lit by lazy overhead strips that buzzed like cranky bees. Tools hung from racks above aging benches. Two small loader bots buzzed around in the corner, stacking crates in the exact wrong order.

Ryx smiled faintly and stepped through the haze.

He wasn't in armor this time.

Just dark civilian boots, work pants, a fitted black shirt, And Kaelen's coat.

The weight of it rested differently here. Like it remembered the place.

Rexa looked up from under the hood of an old survey shuttle and froze.

Her eyes landed on the coat first.

Then she stepped forward slowly, wiping her hands on an oil smeared rag.

"Well," she said softly. "That's a familiar thing."

Ryx offered a small smile. "Hope you don't mind."

Her voice gentled. "Would've been real damn sad if it just sat in a closet somewhere."

She looked like she was trying not to get emotional. Ryx didn't push it.

He pulled a thin credstick from his jacket and slid it across the table, followed by his scuffed armor case, dented from recent chaos.

"Didn't know where else to go."

Rexa arched a brow, smirking. "You always come here when you're halfway broken."

"Yeah," Ryx muttered. "I've got a habit of getting shot."

She chuckled, grabbing the armor case with a grunt and setting it on her workbench. "Maybe you just like my patch jobs."

"You do good work."

"Damn right I do."

She popped the case open and frowned at the damage. "Looks like you wrestled a reactor core and lost." "That's... not entirely inaccurate."

Rexa snorted, hands already moving over the cracked shoulder plate.

"So," she said casually, "where's Tessa?"

Ryx leaned against the nearby worktable, arms folded. "Off scouting property with her equally wealthy boyfriend. They took a shuttle out this morning to look at a small station."

Rexa blinked, then grinned. "Seriously? Good for her."

"Yeah," Ryx said, softer now. "She deserves it."

Rexa grew quiet for a moment, her hands pausing. Her voice dropped when she finally spoke again.

"Kaelen would've loved to see this. Her. All of this." Ryx didn't answer.

He just stood there in the coat.

Letting the moment hold him.

The quiet that followed wasn't heavy. Just real.

After a while, Rexa cleared her throat and slid a few components aside.

"Oh, speaking of news. Got word from the Hunter's Guild." Ryx looked up.

"They're ready to fully reinstate you," she said. "You just have to show up for an in-person review."

He exhaled through his nose. "Because of Kolen Vess."

Rexa nodded. "There've been people asking questions about that last job. Digging through old logs. Enough buzz to wake the Guild's compliance board." "VPM?" he asked.

"Maybe. Delva Minor too. Could be both, trying to spin a narrative before your files get public."

"Of course they are."

Ryx stood upright, his posture tight but steady now.

"I'll go. I owe them that much."

"You don't owe them a thing, Ryx." Rexa said.

"I owe me."

She met his eyes. Nodded once.

"I'll have your armor ready before you leave."

Ryx turned to go, the coat brushing behind him like a memory following close.

"Thanks, Rex," he said.

"Anytime, Thorne. Try not to get shot on the way out."

ΔΔΔ

The neon sign still flickered the same way it had ten years ago, one of the kanji characters half-burned out, as though no one could be bothered to fix it. The shop was tucked into a crooked bend off the main thoroughfare, wedged between a secondhand comms store and a vape vendor with four health code violations.

Ryx stepped through the beaded entry curtain and into the steam heavy scent of broth, ginger, charred protein, and nostalgia.

A deep voice called from behind the counter before Ryx even made it to a booth.

"Back from the dead again, Thorne?"

Haren Ilyo, Lyn's father, leaned over the service station, wiping his hands on a grease-stained apron. His face was round, weathered from heat and smoke, and perpetually amused.

Ryx gave a lopsided smirk. "You know me. I like to keep my cardiac rhythm optional."

Haren barked a laugh and gestured to Ryx's usual corner booth. "Sit. I'll get your bowl started. Spicy as hell, yeah?"

"You know it."

Ryx slid into the booth, the faux-leather seat creaking beneath him, and let himself lean back for the first time all day. The warmth. The smell. The familiarity, it all landed like a blanket over old scars.

Haren shuffled over, a steaming mug of house tea in hand, and slid it across the table before leaning on his elbows.

"So," he said. "You got that far-off, freshly-survived look. How's life?" Ryx took the tea and sipped it, buying a moment.

"Oh, you know," he said casually. "Things are… quieter. Had a few jobs go sideways. Got caught in a systems dispute. Lost a coat. Got a new one."

Haren's eyes flicked down to the coat, Kaelen's coat. The older man nodded slowly. "Yeah. I know that one." His tone was softer now. He didn't press.

Ryx offered a small shrug, grateful for the shift in subject. "Tessa's doing well."

Haren smiled at that. "Good girl. She used to sneak extra spice packets out of my daughter's pockets when they were kids."

Right on cue, the curtain behind the counter fluttered, and Lyn stepped out, balancing a large bowl in both hands.

She froze when she saw Ryx. Nearly tripped over herself.

"Oh, I, I didn't know you were, hi."

Ryx gave her an easy smile. "Hey, Lyn."

She swallowed, cheeks flushed instantly pink. "Extra spice, just how you like it."

"Appreciate it."

She slid the bowl onto the table and nearly dropped the chopsticks before catching them with a flustered laugh.

"I, uh, I'm glad you're back. You look…" She glanced at his coat, then away again. "You look different. Good. I mean, healthy. I mean, not shot."

Ryx chuckled. "I'll take it."

She lingered half a second longer before scurrying back behind the curtain.

Haren watched her go and gave Ryx a long look. "She still gets nervous every time you come in."

Ryx cleared his throat and focused on his noodles. "She's a good kid."

Haren gave a knowing grunt and shuffled away.

Ryx ate in peace.

When he finished, he left double what the bowl cost, nodded his thanks, and slipped out through the curtain into the station's cool air.

△△△

The street was quiet this time of day.

Across from Ryx stood what remained of the old garage.

Scaffolding framed its skeleton, support beams stripped bare, fresh plating being welded over charred metal. A new sign was being hoisted overhead. Bright, corporate. Sanitized.

Kaelen's sign had been taken down that morning.

Ryx didn't cross the street.

He just stood there, hands in his coat pockets, watching.

361

Silence was heavy in the air.

And then, without meaning to, Ryx was back in that first memory.

ΔΔΔ

He remembered the pain first.

A low, grinding throb behind his eyes, the copper sting of blood on his tongue. Every part of his body felt like it had been dragged through atmosphere without shielding.

The ship, a barely flyable hunk of carbon-scored scrap, groaned as it was towed into the bay, sparks still trickling from the exposed engine housing. Smoke curled from the vents. A wing was half missing.

Ryx could barely keep his head up in the pilot seat.

Through the main entryway, walked figure, broad, gruff, arms crossed over a sleeveless mechanic's vest blackened with grease and time. His jaw was square, half-hidden beneath a gray-streaked beard, and his face was fixed in a frown so deep it could cut stone.

Kaelen.

He didn't speak right away. Just stood there, taking in the wreckage like it had personally offended him.

Then he spat into a can and said, flat as a broken plasma line:

"Your ship smells like someone welded it together with spit and last rites."

Ryx coughed blood into his elbow. "Not far off."

Kaelen raised a brow. "You leaking anything I can't mop up?"

"Just pride."

Kaelen snorted. "You got any credits?"

Ryx blinked slowly. "Not… currently." Kaelen didn't move.

Didn't sigh.

Didn't scowl.

He just stared at him for a long second, then jerked a thumb toward the inner bay.

"Fine. I'd rather deal with a broke bastard than clean out a corpse." The hauler pulled the ship the rest of the way in.

Ryx passed out before the airlock cycled shut.

It had been almost a month.

Ryx had stitches in three places and couldn't yet lift his left arm without something popping, but he was walking. He was working. Sweating with tools in his hands again.

Kaelen never asked him what happened.

Never pushed.

He just barked orders, shoved tools at him, taught him the quirks of Vorrthani voltage regulators and fusion coil diagnostics. Like Ryx had always belonged there.

Ryx kept expecting it to end.

Kept expecting a bill, or a speech, or an eviction.

But Kaelen never gave him one.

One night, Ryx came back from grabbing takeout and found Kaelen standing in the corner of the main bay, a tarp draped over something tall.

"Pulled a few pieces from the scrapyard," Kaelen said without turning. "Couldn't stand looking at your drift core. Rebuilt it. Tweaked the stabilizers." He pulled the tarp away.

Ryx's ship gleamed beneath the bay lights.

The burnt plating had been stripped, replaced with matte gray and cool black accent lines. The thruster casing had been swapped for a tighter, leaner unit. He could already hear the new hum it would make when it lifted off.

There was a stillness in his chest that tightened unexpectedly.

"You did this?" he asked.

Kaelen gave a noncommittal grunt and cracked a beer. "She'll fly cleaner now. Still needs a name."

Ryx blinked. "You're giving her back?"

Kaelen glanced at him sideways. "What else am I gonna do, sell her? She's been in my garage long enough to grow mold." He tossed Ryx a beer.

It was dented and half-warm. Ryx caught it like it was sacred.

He turned to the ship. The way the bay lights hit her. The way his reflection looked steadier than he remembered.

"Wraithburn," he said.

Kaelen grunted again. "Pretentious."

Ryx shrugged, cracking the can open. "Sounds fast."

"Better be."

They drank in silence after that.

And for the first time in years, Ryx felt like he wasn't just passing through.

ΔΔΔ

The Wraith welcomed him back like a familiar rhythm a few hours later.

The quiet thrum of systems on standby. The muted hum of atmospheric recyclers. The faint creak of aged steel cooling under station gravity. It was home. Not the walls, or the wiring. The weight of memory.

Ryx stripped down in the shower, scrubbing away hours of smoke, station dust, and the residue of old wounds that hadn't quite healed. It was ritual now, his nightly absolution.

Rinse the blood. Clean the skin. Pretend, just for a few minutes, that there wasn't another war around the corner.

When he stepped out, Kaelen's coat waited neatly draped over a chair in the corner. He didn't put it on. Not yet.

He towel-dried his hair, tugged on loose black pants, then moved barefoot across the ship, entering the nav alcove.

He keyed in new coordinates for tomorrow.

DESTINATION: HUNTER'S GUILD HQ – AUREN VI SYSTEM STATUS: LOCKED. LAUNCH DELAYED – LOCAL TIME HOLD.

Ryx confirmed the entry, then leaned back, running diagnostics on the Wraithburn's drive systems.

The ship purred under his fingers. Thrusters: optimal. Nav sensors: clean. Weapon calibration: recent, thanks to Tess.

He smiled faintly.

And without warning, another memory pulled him back.

ΔΔΔ

They were deep in the edge systems, just past a repair run.

Kaelen's sleeves were rolled up, a burn mark streaked across one wrist, and a half-dismantled filter unit lay in pieces on the galley floor.

Tess was nineteen, grease on her cheek, holding a diagnostic wand like it was a sword. She was arguing with Kaelen about power coupling logic.

Ryx had no idea what she was talking about.

"Just let me rewire it!" Tess insisted, waving the wand. "You're using a Series-B coupler on an A-line housing."

Kaelen grumbled, "If it ain't melting, it's fine."

Ryx, seated on the countertop, said, "You're both wrong. That filter housing's been squealing in FTL. Sounds like a dying loth cat." They all paused.

Then, Tess burst out laughing.

Kaelen threw a bolt at Ryx, missed, then grunted, "Fine. Fix it, smartass. But if you burn out the inverter, you're fixing everything."

They worked side by side after that. Wires in hand, tools passed between them, arguments turning into teamwork. The Wraithburn was still mainly stock then, not yet a war machine, not yet a memory vault. Just a home being made.

Later that night, the three of them ate steaming stew from plastic bowls around the nav table.

Tess had her boots up on the bench.

Kaelen pretended to scold her.

And Ryx remembered thinking, this is what family felt like.

ΔΔΔ

Ryx sat in that same chair, alone now.

He let the ship settle around him like a blanket. Ran his hand over the tabletop.

Still scratched from Tess's first, of many, soldering accidents.

He stood, finally, and headed to his bunk.

Sleep came slow, but steady.

ΔΔΔ

"Looking sharp," Rexa said as Ryx stepped inside.

She stood behind the counter, already elbow-deep in a weapons overall, but she wiped her hands and reached for a tall, sealed case.

His armor. Polished. Reinforced.

"Got the chest plate rebalanced, adjusted your right arms plate sync, and patched the plating on your lower back. Again." "Seems like a weak spot," Ryx muttered.

"You keep getting shot there, yeah," she said with a grin.

She pushed the case toward him. "You're ready."

He took it, slinging it over his shoulder like old baggage.

"Come back if you need anything," Rexa added, softer now.

"You'll never get rid of me," Ryx said.

They didn't hug. They didn't need to.

Ryx made his way through the morning bustle, spice vendors, scrap peddlers, holotoy stalls, all packed into the narrow corridors of the market level. Music played somewhere in the distance. A trio of kids sprinted by, laughing.

It wasn't peace.

But it was alive.

And that was enough.

He strapped into the pilot's seat, set the jump protocols, and keyed the drive for launch.

The station's lights faded in the viewport as he pulled away.

He sat back, letting Kaelen's coat settle around his shoulders.

"Let's see what ghosts the Guild wants to dig up." The stars stretched, and the Wraithburn jumped.

ΔΔΔ

The Wraithburn dropped out of warp with a smooth lurch, sublight engines purring as Ryx angled toward the pale green gas giant hanging at the heart of the system. The Hunter's Guild HQ spun lazily in high orbit above one of its moons, a gleaming metal ring installation, bristling with antennas, docks, and gun platforms.

It looked the same as always: professional, neutral, and ready for violence.

But before Ryx could even hail the station, his comms pinged.

Incoming Video Message: Tess & Yessari

He tapped it, and the holoscreen lit up with two familiar faces, Tess half-sitting on a desk, grinning like a kid who'd found a lost treasure, Yessari standing beside her with a datapad in one hand and his other arm slung awkwardly around her shoulders like he didn't know if he was allowed to relax yet.

"Hey, Ryx!" Tess said brightly. "We did it. We bought the station."

"It's small," Yessari added, "but structurally sound. High-value orbit, mostly private traffic, minimal surveillance."

Tess rolled her eyes. "It's perfect."

The feed shifted to show a rotating 3D schematic of their new purchase, a three-deck orbital outpost, tucked into a quiet Lagrange point. It looked old, but solid, with ample docking space, expandable interior bays, and a rugged charm Ryx immediately recognized as them.

"We're already drawing up plans," Tess continued. "Lab on the upper level, garage underneath, and" she glanced back at Yessari.

"We want to build you your own dock," he said, smiling slightly. "And maybe… a personal apartment. For when you stay longer than ten minutes."

Tess smirked. "So don't be a stranger. Coordinates attached."

Ryx exhaled as the message ended. For a second, the stillness of the cockpit wrapped around him like a second skin.

He opened a reply.

If you two build me a dock and a place to live, I'm going to have to take bounty contracts until I'm a hundred to pay you back.

He paused, then added:

But I'll still never catch up. You're the best thing I've got.

He hit send.

And sat there a moment longer, smiling quietly.

But as he turned the Wraithburn into docking position near the Hunter's Guild HQ, his breath caught.

One ship stood out on the dock ring: sleek, sharp, with dark crimson paneling and hull lines that bent the light just enough to feel... wrong. It looked too smooth. Too quiet. Too perfect.

A fighter-class, no visible registration.

And it looked almost exactly like the one that had appeared and erased Echofall Station just smaller.

Ryx's pulse slammed into overdrive. The Bracelet went on alert again.

"No," he whispered. "No way."

He sat frozen for several seconds, hand hovering near the comms, unsure if he should run, or fire up the Wraithburn's guns.

But nothing moved.

No energy flares. No weapons locks. No anomaly warnings from the ship's sensors.

Just that thing sitting in Dock 7 like it belonged there.

Ryx clenched his jaw.

He cut the engines and descended toward his assigned bay.

Whatever that ship was, it hadn't attacked the station.

Not yet.

But Ryx had questions.

And he was going to find whoever was piloting it.

△△△

The air inside the Guild HQ was sterile and cold, intentionally clinical. Wide floors of matte white tile reflected the overhead light in a dull haze. Every sound was softened, every voice hushed. A place of neutrality. Authority.

Ryx stepped through the main entry arch, eyes scanning every corner like he was back in a blacksite.

The memory of the fighter in Dock 7 still sat like a rock in his chest.

He adjusted Kaelen's coat, reminded himself to breathe, and approached the tall reception desk near the atrium.

The receptionist, a sharp-featured Draenari woman in a gray Guild uniform, looked up at him with a smile that felt just a little too polite.

"Hunter Thorne. Your timing is excellent. The arbiter for your review case just wrapped a meeting, not five minutes ago. An inquiry related to your last contract." Ryx stiffened.

He masked it with a nod. "Convenient." Inside, his mind screamed.

Another inquiry? My case? Right before I walk in?

The image of that ship came back again, sleek, dark, and impossible.

He forced a thank-you through clenched teeth, took the access badge she handed him, and walked toward the inner offices.

Each hallway felt too long. Too bright.

Every shadow stretched the wrong way.

And then,

He turned a final corner.

And froze.

Two figures stepped out of the hallway ahead.

Both were tall, perhaps half a head above Ryx. Their armor was black and crimson, sleek with faint light-thread seams along the plating. The design wasn't BSD. Or Guild. Or anything Ryx had ever seen in the known systems.

Their movements were fluid. Too fluid.

Their skin, deep violet.

Their faces, the same species as the one he'd seen in stasis on Echofall Station.

But awake.

Eyes open.

Those eyes burned red, with narrow, vertical pupils that locked forward like predators tracking motion.

They didn't look at him.

But they saw him.

Ryx stood completely still.

He could hear the faint click of their boots as they passed.

No words. No nods. No acknowledgment.

Just two alien figures walking through a human's space like they didn't care who knew they were there.

They moved with purpose, down the corridor, through the glass airlock tunnel, Toward Dock 7.

Ryx swallowed hard and bolted into the Guild office behind them.

The door hissed shut behind him.

"Thorne," the arbiter said, rising with a calm, disarming smile. He was a dark-skinned man in late middle age, dressed in the charcoal robes of Guild legal staff. His desk was clean, datapads stacked with obsessive order.

Ryx didn't sit.

"Who were they?" he demanded, eyes still wide. "The ones who just walked out."

The arbiter blinked, then gestured slowly to the chair. "You're alright Thorne. Sit. Breathe." He sat down.

"I don't know what they call themselves," he admitted. "Their language isn't in any public lexicon. All we've learned is that they come from far beyond the mapped borders, deep space, uncolonized sectors. They call it their 'sacred frontier.'"

Ryx finally dropped into the chair, heart still hammering.

"They looked like they belonged in a war."

"They looked like they didn't need one," the arbiter replied.

Ryx scoffed. "So, what'd they want with my case?"

The arbiter tapped his fingers against a slim datapad.

"They didn't ask about you directly. More about BSD. Where they were housed. What they were building. And your mission log, specifically the part where you reported the item was never recovered."

Ryx blinked. "They read my mission file?"

"They requested the Guild's internal archives. I don't know how they were authorized, but... someone signed off. High-level clearance."

"And they weren't angry?"

The arbiter shook his head. "No. Disappointed, maybe. But not hostile. They said something about 'correcting mistakes made by others.' And then they left."

Ryx sat in silence for several seconds. Then leaned back slowly, dread pooling in his stomach.

They knew about the weapon.

They were watching.

And now they're here.

He glanced down at his right arm, where the bracelet lay hidden under the coat sleeve. As if summoned by thought, a pulse rippled through it.

Not a glow. A signal. Soft. A tone behind the bones.

Ryx swallowed.

Are they connected to you? he whispered inside his mind.

The bracelet pulsed again, stronger.

Not fear. Not threat.

Recognition.

Like the memory of someone long gone stepping into the room.

Ryx looked up, throat dry.

Something ancient had stepped back into the galaxy.

The rest of the interview passed in a blur. The arbiter asked his required questions, about Ryx's time in prison, the Vess contract, his handling of Black Sable Dynamics, and how he avoided escalating the situation on Delva Minor the first time. Ryx answered mechanically, keeping his tone even, his posture polite.

Every time he tried to focus, the image of those red eyes flickered behind his own.

He remembered what Yessari had called them when they'd examined the logs from Echofall.

"Xenosapien Class Alpha. Thought extinct. Myths." They weren't extinct. They were here.

And the bracelet on his wrist wasn't humming with energy anymore.

It was listening.

"...Mr. Thorne?" the arbiter prompted gently.

Ryx blinked back into focus.

"Sorry. Long few months."

The arbiter gave a patient smile and slid a slim brass-colored chip across the desk.

"Then you'll be happy to hear this. You're reinstated. Officially. Full access to Guild contracts, benefits, and intel resources." He extended his hand.

Ryx took it, firm and brief.

"Thank you."

But his mind was already halfway out the door.

△△△

The moment the hatch sealed behind him, Ryx exhaled like he hadn't in hours.

The engines hummed beneath his boots. The old deck creaked like always.

He was home again.

Slipping into the pilot's chair, he let himself sag back, eyes tracing the swirling clouds of Auren VI below.

But peace didn't last long.

His comms chimed.

Encrypted Message – YESSARI QUARN

Packet's complete. Every file. Cross-referenced. Anonymized. Attached with a data tree BSD's lawyers couldn't unravel in a thousand years.

If we deliver this to the right office on Delva Minor, Project Echofall dies permanently.

Do you want me to come with you?

Ryx stared at the words a long moment.

His fingers hovered over the interface.

Thanks, Yess. But I need to do this part alone.

I just want to get it over with.

He hesitated. Then added:

Make sure Tess doesn't tear the station apart until I get a tour.

He hit send.

The reply came back almost instantly.

Yessari:

No promises. She found an arc welder this morning.

Ryx smirked faintly despite himself.

He set the course for Delva Minor.

And as the stars began to stretch again outside his viewport, he rested his hand on the console near the gauntlet, silent, cold, unmoving.

But still there.

Still waiting.

CHAPTER 20
ASHES OF JUDGMENT

The hum of the ship was the only sound. It filled the Wraithburn like breath in a chest, steady, low, alive. Ryx moved through its narrow corridors barefoot, sweat drying against his skin as he toweled off from a brutal workout. Every motion was precise. Deliberate. Run. Push. Breathe. Repeat.

No room for thinking. Not yet.

He passed the galley, grabbed a ration bar, didn't taste it, and downed a bottle of synthwater before finally circling back to the cockpit.

The timer on the nav console ticked forward in soft blue light.

WARP EXIT – T MINUS 00:44:18

He sat in the pilot's seat and let the Wraithburn cradle him.

His hand rested near the console, fingers flexing, one knuckle still swollen from a sparring program gone too hard earlier.

He didn't mind the pain.

It kept him anchored.

Because today, if everything held, justice would finally land.

He closed his eyes and exhaled slowly through his nose.

He thought of Kaelen. Not just the gruff words or the engineering lessons or the occasional shoulder squeeze when he didn't have anything better to offer. No, he thought of how that man had chosen him. Given him shelter. A second chance.

He thought of Kolen, too. Nervous. Kind. Smart enough to realize he was in over his head and brave enough to run anyway.

Both gone.

Burned away by the machine they tried to expose.

And now Ryx had the evidence. The full body of it. BSD memos, test logs, deployment drafts, the entire blueprint of Project Echofall locked up in his databanks.

He imagined handing it over to the Delva Minor Council. Watching it hit the public records like a shockwave.

He imagined someone, anyone, in the BSD boardroom finally getting dragged down with it.

For a second, he smiled.

Bitterness and satisfaction twined together.

A short time later he was cleaned up and dressed, back in the cockpit for arrival.

WARP EXIT INITIATED

He leaned forward, pulled Kaelen's coat tighter around his shoulders, and whispered:

"Time to bury the bastards." The stars elongated.

Then snapped back.

And what Ryx saw made his blood turn to ice.

He didn't breathe.

Didn't blink.

Didn't move.

Because where Delva Minor should've been, was nothing.

Not a planet. Not a station. Not a shadow.

Just... a field of glass and ruin.

Chunks of fractured world floated in a slow, spiraling drift. Jagged black stone sliced into crystalline slivers, catching the starlight like broken mirrors. The orbit was smeared with planetary guts, mantle, ocean crust, cities reduced to atoms.

It was quiet.

Ryx gripped the edges of the console as if he might fall into the void just by looking at it.

"No..."

He whispered it, but there was no one to hear him.

His HUD kept feeding him data, as if it hadn't realized it was looking at the impossible.

GRAVITY SIGNATURE: FAILED COLLAPSE

DEBRIS FIELD: PLANETARY CORE VERIFIED

TEMPORAL ECHO MATCH: 94.2% ,

ENERGY SOURCE: UNKNOWN – RESIDUAL NON-LOCAL DISCHARGE

He stared for a long time before his hand finally moved.

Automatically.

Shaking.

He tapped the recording function, pulled clips from every viewport, every sensor. Started a deep scan. Fragment composition. Energy residuals. All of it. His hands moved.

His mind didn't.

There was nothing left. Not the council. Not the city. Not the chance to deliver justice.

Just silence.

Just glass.

Billions of lives. Erased.

He encrypted the packet and opened comms. His voice was flat.

Distant.

Encrypted Message – Tess & Yessari

Delva Minor is gone. Same as Aexis-9.

Something erased it. Same energy signature. Same pattern.

No survivors. No trace.

Sending everything I have. Lock it down. Don't trust anyone. We're not done.

Stay safe. I mean it.

He sent it.

And sat there.

The planet's corpse kept drifting.

Somewhere deep in his wrist, beneath the skin, the bracelet pulsed.

Not warm. Not angry.

But something else.

Something like mourning.

Ryx didn't know if it was reacting to what had been lost, Or who had destroyed it.

But for the first time in weeks, he wasn't sure he wanted to know the truth.

The last scan finished with a cold chime.

Ryx's fingers hovered over the console, already keying in the jump coordinates to Tess and Yessari's new station. He needed to debrief them. He needed to get this information into the hands of the only two people he trusted.

He needed to feel real ground beneath him, to hear Tess ramble about infrastructure, to see Yessari lost in schematics and logic again. He needed something human to cling to. His hand hovered over the jump command,

When the comms crackled.

Incoming Transmission – ENCRYPTED – ORIGIN: UNKNOWN

Ryx frowned.

The source didn't match anything known.

But the encryption signature? He knew it. He knew it too well.

He opened the message.

Warden Vance.

The voice that came through was strained. A little rougher than he remembered. Like it had been dragged through fire and dust.

"Ryx. If this message reached you, then I'm alive. Barely."

"Varrix Prime is gone." Ryx went still.

Vance's voice continued, low and fast.

"It came from nowhere. A ship, black and crimson, larger than anything we've ever seen. It warped into the system like it had done it a hundred times before. The Varrix fleet was already in orbit, full formation, didn't matter."

"The big ship opened fire first. It tore through half the fleet before they could even form a line. And then... then other ships appeared."

"Not BSD. Not Varrix. Not anything I've ever seen."

"Angled. Dark silver. Like folded knives in motion."

"They started fighting the big one. Full engagement. Whoever they were... they weren't on our side, but they weren't with the destroyer either."

"Then came the message. No origin. No ID. Just a single command: Evacuate."

Ryx's heart dropped into his stomach.

"We barely got the prison transports launched. Some of the inmates lost their minds, screaming, fighting. But one of them helped us."

"Shandar Kress."

"Kept them calm. Got them aboard. Didn't ask for anything."

"When the last transport lifted, I saw it. A red beam."

"It hit the planet."

"And Varrix Prime shattered. Im not sure about Delta, but I doubt it survived."

Ryx slumped forward, hands gripping the edge of the console as Vance's voice cracked for the first time.

"We weren't followed. I took the remaining prisoners and staff to a remote system; coordinates embedded in this message."

"Ryx… there's nothing left. The government. The fleet. The records. Everything." "And… Shandar." A pause.

"He's been with us a decade. No violence. No attempts to escape. Helped us in the darkest moment."

"He asked if you'd come for him."

"And I've decided… I'm going to let him go."

"It's done, Thorne. All of it."

"Come get your friend." The message ended.

Ryx didn't move for nearly a minute.

His face was stone.

But his eyes glistened.

Varrix Prime. Gone.

An entire world. Billions of people. Burned out of existence.

Not because they fought back against anything.

Not because they resisted anyone.

Because they were connected.

Echofall. BSD. The artifact. Anyone who had touched it, even by proximity, was being erased.

One by one.

Delva Minor.

Now Varrix Prime.

And still the galaxy had no idea.

Ryx didn't speak.

He just reached forward and changed his destination.

He activated the jump. The stars blurred. And the Wraithburn vanished.

End Of Book 1.

AUTHORS NOTE

Writing this book has been a journey, one filled with late nights, second guesses, and more emotional moments than I ever expected. Worn By Power began as a story about a broken bounty hunter and turned into something larger: about grief, purpose, found family, and what it means to choose your path even when you're carrying scars.

Thank you for taking this journey with Ryx, Tess, Rexa, and the rest. Book Two is already in the works.

See you in the stars.

– Zach

ACKNOWLEDGEMENT

I owe a tremendous thanks to the people who helped make this possible:

To my early readers and beta readers, your feedback shaped this book in invaluable ways. You know who you are.

To my editors, for challenging me to dig deeper, punch harder, and cut what didn't serve the story.

To every friend who let me ramble about space station politics and gauntlet tech at 1 a.m.

To my family, your patience and encouragement meant everything.

And to every reader who saw a piece of themselves in Ryx:

Thank you.

You're not alone.

SPECIAL THANKS:

HUNTER'S GUILD

This book could not have come to life without the incredible support of the Hunter's Guild backers from our Kickstarter campaign. Your belief in this story, and your willingness to help bring it into the world, means more than words can capture.

To each of you who stood by this project from the very beginning, thank you for hunting alongside us, for your generosity, and for making this dream a reality.

This book is dedicated in part to you, the Guild, whose names are etched here as a lasting reminder that stories are never told alone;

Hunters Guild IDs:
ID-001 // Adam Goetz
ID-002 // Morgan Wesley
ID-003 // Kevin Sproul
ID-005 // Brandin Watson
ID-006 // Sunita Austin
ID-007 // Frank Minniti
ID-008 // Lara Stewart
ID-009 // Dustyn Simpson
ID-010 // Alexey Goldberg
ID-011 // Lydia Jensen
ID-012 // Alan Olasin
ID-013 // Zack Misner
ID-014 // Rachel

ID-016 // Jon J Lohman
ID-017 // Justin Hand
ID-018 // Forrest Hamrick
ID-019 // Micah
ID-020 // Harrison Cook
ID-021 // Shaunna Mantooth
ID-022 // Sarah Rogers
ID-023 // Luna Addison
ID-024 // Jordan Vance
ID-025 // Fire Wolf
ID-026 // Dan Johnson
ID-027 // Overlord Kain